W9-BEQ-106

THE QUEEN'S PROPHET

The QUEEN'S PROPHET

DAWN PATITUCCI

TURNER

Turner Publishing Company
Nashville, Tennessee
New York, New York

www.turnerpublishing.com

The Queen's Prophet

This is a work of fiction. All the characters and events portrayed in this book are either products of the author's imagination or are used fictitiously.

Cover design: Maddie Cothren
Book design: Tim Holtz

Library of Congress Cataloging-in-Publication Data

Names: Patitucci, Dawn, author.
Title: The queen's prophet / Dawn Patitucci.
Description: Nashville : Turner, [2017]
Identifiers: LCCN 2 017008977 | I SBN 9 781683366829 (softcover :
acid-free
  paper)
Subjects: LCSH: Dwarfs--Fiction. | Queens--Spain--Fiction. |
  Nobility--Spain--Fiction.
Classification: LCC PS3616.A8669 Q44 2017 | DDC 813/.6--dc23
LC record available at https://lccn.loc.gov/2017008977

9781683366836

Printed in the United States of America

16 17 18 19 20 9 8 7 6 5 4 3 2 1

For my parents

THE QUEEN'S PROPHET

Chapter 1

THE STOAT'S CHOICE

he Countess of Walther died in fresh bedclothes, in the warmth of a lively hearth fire, her curtains open to the night, and the moon, a waxing crescent, in plain sight. Mari had just sat bedside for a night of distracted reading and futile prayer when silence fell, as sudden and commanding as a man entering the room. After days of gasping and twitching, the Countess lay dead, her mouth still gaping from her last breath, hands curled against her wasted breast.

Spurred by panic and an overwhelming sense of officiality, Mari recorded the time for the deacon: eight o'clock p.m., 25 Oktober. Under the rule of Mars, in quadrature with Mercury, she also noted, as the Countess would have pleased.

She lay down her pen and braced for grief, though she didn't weep—tears were rarer than diamonds in this household—nor was her heart heavier than it had been these past weeks as she watched her lady's flesh wither and her dispassionate, analytical mind run mad with fever. If anything Mari felt hoodwinked, Death having sneaked in while her eyes were averted and hands fiddling with a bookmark, cheating her of any poignant last moment with her lady. She had imagined at least a hand squeeze, or one last lucid look from her delirious mistress, a locking of gazes through which decades of fondness and easy companionship would be acknowledged and cherished though unspoken to the end. If tears were rarer than diamonds in this house, *I love you*s were like winged horses.

Mari had also hoped for some cogent last words to replace the now-official last words the Countess had uttered a few days ago—maudlin, brainsick words—which would have mortified their speaker, the very woman who had once cheerily sliced into small animal corpses to diagram their insides and tried to melt her anniversary ring to observe the properties of gold. "Let no one unacquainted with sorrow enter here," she had said as her last, and left fingernail marks in Mari's wrist.

There seemed less cause for sorrow now. The lady lay in peace, at the impressive age of six-and-fifty, in a warm, flickering bedchamber larger than Mari's childhood home, surrounded by her dearest possessions: stacks of ledgers filled with decades of data, columns upon columns of celestial coordinates, lunar phases, and orbital velocities; her optic tube, which Mari had mounted by the window two weeks ago with the vain hope of tempting the Countess from her bed to track the stars; Leviticus, the albino stoat, asleep in a plump white curl on the hearthrug; and Mari herself—Maria-Barbara, Dwarfess of Walther—in her bedside chair with its sawed-off legs, wondering what would come of her now that her owner was dead.

తిన

Days later, the Countess's absence loomed thickly in the too-quiet manor. By now Mari was appropriately aggrieved and wondered how a person's absence could register like an anvil on her chest, how nothingness could exert such weight. Still, she hadn't wept. Their mistress-dwarfess relationship hadn't been one of tears, certainly not *I love you*s. It had been love, but a peculiar kind, simple and passionless—not unlike the bond between man and dog, or woman and cat, though nobles never spoke in such indelicate terms, not to Mari's face anyway. It had been Mari sitting bedside when the mistress died, Mari whose company she had favored, even when the Count had been alive. But the lady had been a thinking sort, unemotional, her love as quiet and frosty as Alpine snow. Maybe that was what this weight was. Love with no receptacle, no target, nowhere to go. A mountain on Mari's chest.

Mari sat in the library, writing "Let no one unacquainted with sorrow enter here" in a diary, when footfalls sounded in the corridor. Brigitta, one of the maidservants, sailed through the doors in a miff. "There you are," she said. She wore her coat and gloves, and her usually merry face looked grave. "We've been dismissed."

"What? Who?" Mari asked.

"Ursula, Eva, Otto, myself. Only Karl is being kept on, for now."

"So soon?" The Countess had only just been laid to rest.

"The kin in Saxony won't be bothered for two hundred acres. They're selling the estate, sight unseen. The sheriff's coming tomorrow to secure the property. They want us out today. We were fools to think we'd be allowed to stay through the winter, even as tenants."

Dread stirred in Mari's heart. She and the maidservants had been speculating about the new master and mistress, whether they'd be warmhearted or cold, young or old, if there'd be any children. No one had considered the estate being shut down and them being turned out to the winter. "Did they say anything about me?"

"No, but Herr Schneider wants to speak with you. He's waiting in the Count's study."

"Good God," Mari whispered.

"Don't worry yet. He could have put you out with the rest of us just now, but he didn't. And I'm told the kin have sent for some of the furnishings, the paintings mostly, and the younger horses. They may collect you as well."

But Mari was already overcome with worry, already on the worst case scenario, mapping her trajectory of homelessness to suffering to untimely death by way of this very moment.

Brigitta knelt before her and squeezed her hands. "Listen. It would be cruel to turn you out with no place to go. They know that."

Mari's thoughts raced. Cruel indeed, but far from impossible.

Brigitta glanced at the window. "I have to go. Karl's taking us to the ferry."

"Where are you going?"

"Upriver. See if I can find work in Mannheim or Ludwigshafen." She gave Mari a quick, firm hug and laid her gloved hand on her cheek. "God be with you, little Mari."

Mari squeezed the girl's wrist. "And you also."

"Go now. Herr Schneider's waiting."

ঙ্গ

Herr Schneider looked up from his ledger. "Ah, Mari. Please sit." He politely looked elsewhere as she hoisted and rocked herself into a chair. "I'm sure you're curious about your fate," he said, parking his pen. "You'll be pleased to know it rests in your hands."

Mari had no idea what this could mean. She waited.

"As property of the estate, you've been bequeathed to the kin with the rest of the lady's effects. Your new owners, however, are offering you emancipation." He peered at her over his spectacles. "You may walk free if you wish."

Mari's heart lurched. They were really going to do it. They were turning her out. "And if I don't wish?"

"In that case, I'd have to find you a new home."

"The kin won't have me?"

12

"I'm afraid they're not the sort to keep a dwarf," he said with a wistful smile. "They can scarcely be troubled to collect the silver service."

"Have you another home in mind?"

"Not yet, but I would certainly try to place you in noble company. But remember your other option. You're free to go if you will."

Mari's gaze drifted out the window. Free to go. A sick feeling crept into her gut: the dread of uncertainty, the terror of homelessness, anger at the Countess for not having foreseen this—she with her endless scientific contingencies and permutations and calculations, she who had forecasted every lunar event of the past decade with frightening accuracy. Then there was the shame of being rejected by the faceless kin, the humiliation of being helpless and powerless and at the utter mercy of this man across the desk, of being reduced to an administrative nuisance.

"Have you kin of your own?" he asked.

She had a nephew, Georg, whom she'd last seen as a boy. He was now a man of two-and-twenty, living in Vienna last she'd heard, feeding a family of five on a toll collector's salary. Mari wouldn't dream of taxing him with her company, taking bread from the mouths of his children. Besides, winter was nigh. Soon the Alps would be impassable.

"Think it over for a couple of days," he said, slapping his ledger shut. "For now the manor is being secured. You can shelter in the longhouse with Karl until we figure out what to do with you."

He walked her out to the corridor. "You were a loyal companion to the lady for, what, twenty years or more?"

"Indeed, nearly thirty." Mari had been a maiden of twelve when she came here. Now an old woman of one-and-forty, she was being wrenched from her home once again.

"She only ever spoke fondly of you. Heavens, I'd take you myself if we weren't so crowded at home. I'm sure the children would be delighted with the likes of you."

"And I with them," Mari said, but he didn't seem to hear. Her words were always getting lost in the billowing folds of women's skirts, or slipping through men's legs.

ɷɷ

She took the Countess's optic tube. The lady would have wanted her to have it. Mari packed in a stupor, shocked, humiliated, intensely worried, and heavy with hurt over the Countess's negligence. She wondered if the lady had really cared about her at all, or if that love, like Alpine snow, had really been just frost—not suppressed affection but the complete absence thereof. Hadn't the lady herself always insisted, while poring over her data, that that which was not observable did not exist?

The longhouse was a horse stable with a groom's apartment attached, situated uproad from the manor. The apartment was thinly furnished and smelled like horse. The truckle bed had been ravaged by mice, so Karl, the stable hand, fashioned a small mattress for Mari with a couple of feed sacks.

It was November now, and night came early. They supped outdoors, fireside, on roasted beets and salted fish. With Karl absorbed in a bottle of spirits, Mari stargazed through her optic tube, seeing little but for the constellation of worries fixed in her mind.

She lowered the tube to see Leviticus, the stoat, scavenging from Karl's supper tin on the ground. "Don't let him eat from your plate," she said. "He has to learn to go forth and hunt." Soon there'd be no one on site to feed him.

"He'll never leave," Karl said, his speech already sluiced with drink. "A stoat would sooner die captive than run free and get his coat dirty. It's why they trim kings' robes with stoat. Most pristine furs of all God's creatures." He stroked Leviticus's silky white coat with his grubby hand, oblivious to the irony. He was an old man, nearly fifty, with a slack body and silvering beard. He had never been a favorite of the Countess. *Kasperl* she had called him behind his back—fool—or sometimes just *der Clown*.

"He'll have no choice tomorrow." They were going to market and would be gone all day. With days or, God forbid, weeks of rough living ahead, Mari needed warm gloves, toilet objects, and candles that didn't smell like rancid pig fat.

This got them talking about the market. Mari hadn't been since the spring, but Karl went weekly. With firelight tickling his face, now shiny and rosy from the spirits, he relished telling Mari his foulest market stories, tales of squirming maggots and infernal stenches, rats swinging from sausage chains while women shrieked in terror. Then there were the many strange people: African merchants over six feet tall, slender as spoons; a woman so fat she had to be wheeled around in a barrow; and every now and then someone ugly enough to put one's hair on end. "So don't worry, you'll blend right in," he said.

It had been a long day, and tomorrow would be another. Mari needed rest. "Are you coming?" she asked from the longhouse stoop, fearing he might not leave his bed tomorrow.

"In a minute," he said, uncorking the bottle.

She lay awake for hours, steeped in horse stink and worry. The feed sacks had lain too near the hearth and were baking hot, and her hips and knees ached from the move. Outside, Karl made merry alone, talking, laughing, drifting in and out of song. He stumbled in after midnight and was soon snoring loudly, with Leviticus rising and falling in a white loaf on his chest. Mari wondered how quickly she could get in touch with Herr Schneider to tell him to start looking for her new owner. She was unfit to live like this, quartering with drunks and animals, nary a soul caring if she were alive or dead. Her life in the manor with her lady already seemed a lifetime ago, a world away. The crudity of her new living conditions threw into sharp relief the enormity of what she had lost—and what she must get back: comfort, cleanliness, privacy, and most importantly, a noble lady to keep her, protect her, *need* her, because the world at large certainly had no use for the likes of her.

A tear slid down her temple and plopped on the rim of her ear. The mountain on her chest was back. The lady hadn't meant to neglect her, Mari knew in her heart. She'd be horrified to see Mari now, lying in the stable, on feed sacks, with Karl the Clown as her surrogate protector.

It *had* been love. It had been care, comfort, safety, respect, company, conversation, laughter, trust, loyalty. It had been observable, unmistakable, *it had existed*, and now it was gone. Her lady really was gone.

༺༻

Mari woke to birdsong and washed in the stable, taking no care to be quiet for Karl, who managed to wake shortly after. He was in a prickly mood but otherwise willing to go to market. They breakfasted on bread and beer and soon left, with Mari resting on her feed sacks in the wagon, her optic tube scanning the autumn hillsides.

She hailed from Graz. The Count of Walther had purchased her as a companion for his wife, who'd been newly childless a second time and hadn't the will to court grief again. A traveling rector had arranged the sale having persuaded Mari's mother that dwarfs were coveted by persons of exalted rank. The rich were different, he had explained. They had strange ideas and proclivities, homes filled with exotic wares, pictures and trinkets, rare dogs, black servant boys dressed up in silks and jewels—the curiouser the better, and there is none so curious as the dwarf. It'd be a soft job in a decent house, he had said—all she'd have to do is be a merry and gentle creature, devoted to her mistress. What other options had she? Certainly not marriage.

There were no other options. Sickness had ravaged their town and claimed Mari's little brother, a dwarf like she. Her proper-sized sister escaped with a husband and lived long enough to birth Georg, the toll collector in Vienna. After a fortnight in transit, twelve-year-old Mari was delivered to the Walther estate on 8 August 1626, under the sign of Leo and rule of Sun, the Countess always told her. She never told Mari the sale price. She, with her reams of data, claimed not to know the exact number.

Mari had never seen a house so big, nor a woman so blessedly idle. The lady had her own study, her *laboratory* she called it, a place of books and measures and strange devices. She put Mari to sorting dead butterflies, happily, within hours of her arrival. The Count showed his affection for her by cutting off furniture legs. In winter a letter came: Mari's mother had died. By then she only lived in Mari's mind anyway, in flashes of memory decreasing in frequency and intensity, like the lightning of a receding storm. Mari scarcely even remembered her own existence before that renaissance moment, when she'd first spied Saturn through an optic tube.

She woke to shouting men and bleating sheep and Karl banging on the wagon with a stick. "Wake up," he said. "We're here."

Karl helped her off the wagon to snatches of laughter from idling farmhands. They'd never seen her before, and the younger ones might never have seen a dwarf but for drawings in books. Karl came to the Tübingen market because it was closer and his brother's widow kept an onion stall there. The Countess had always gone to the Stuttgart market, where a shop called Mercury sold optic tubes and tiny mixing chambers. Many there knew Mari, so the laughter and curiosity had long abated.

"Finally got yourself a woman, Karl?" one of the workers shouted as she and Karl walked off the wagon lot in taut silence. Mari walked quickly, hoping to outpace the laughter and cruel remarks that were sure to follow.

"That's a woman?"

"It's dressed like a woman."

"What's under that skirt, Karl?" Raucous male laughter. "Get back here, dwarf! We need to check something."

Mari tried to walk faster but felt like she was in chest-deep water. The panicked, sluggish movement of nightmares.

"Uh oh, Uebel's up to no good!"

"Get her, Uebel!"

Quick, predatory footsteps pounded the dirt behind her. Mari heard herself scream, shrill and clear like a child. Something slapped her violently between the shoulder blades, knocking her breath out—a bursting bladder of liquid, probably beer or piss, already soaking through her coat. She ran toward the market square, breathless, terrorized, warm and heavy with humiliation, and hating herself for being grateful to her tormentors for not having lifted her skirt.

"Look at her go."

"Now that is a waddle."

She reached the cobbled market plaza, where she paused to catch her breath and to try to collect her dignity. Karl ambled forth and handed her his unclean handkerchief. She'd been foolish to come here, expecting an ordinary day at the market. There were no ordinary days for her kind, not in public at least. Now all she could do was keep walking, hobbling behind Karl, who seemed keen on walking ahead. She focused on the fruits and breads and hanging meats, the scent of cooked sausages and mulled wine, the cakes and cheeses and tin-glazed honey jars. She tried to ignore the people staring, people stopping cold and gaping, people asking, "What is it?"—the whispers, the laughter, the mother saying, "Look, a little witch!" to her children, or these boys following her now, laughing and clowning behind her wet back. She kept her face down, hoping it didn't look like it felt—hot and glowing with shame—and tried to convince herself that a small child's horrific wailing had nothing to do with her.

ᔕᔕ

By noon Mari had finished shopping and was waiting for Karl by the fountain, squatting on the steps in hopes of looking less conspicuous, breaking in the children's gloves she had bought from a glover who had seemed afraid to touch her; he'd even seemed loath to touch her money. She could only imagine how she must look and smell in this beer-soaked coat, with her ruddy, wind-nipped cheeks. If she had fared this badly after only one day of emancipation, God only knew what prolonged vagrancy would do to her. Shorten her days, is what.

She would return to the manor house first thing in the morning. If Herr Schneider wasn't there, she'd leave him a letter imploring him to start looking for her new owner. How she hated being so desperately dependent on him, so powerless over her fate. Such was a dwarf's life, a life lived entirely at the mercy of others. Mari looked around at the hordes of people—blessedly unremarkable people who were blithely unaware of their privilege in being unremarkable, in being anonymous, able-bodied, employable, marriageable. Even the poorest among them had a chance at scraping by unaided. Even the homeliest was vastly more fortunate than the loveliest dwarf. Because the loveliest dwarf would never be permitted to walk through a crowd without trails of laughter or loathing in his or her wake, and an unspoken apology always perched on his or her tongue: sorry for shocking you, for unnerving you; sorry for waddling, for offending, baffling, frightening, saddening; sorry for *existing*. And the unspoken plea always on the tongue: please, please be merciful and just look away.

Mari hadn't been this downhearted in years, a testament to the Countess's ability to safeguard her from cruelty. Now the thought of going forth in the world without her lady, without the protection and dignity afforded by noble company, was terrifying. She had forgotten how vicious baser folk could be, but it was all coming back to her now—those long-buried childhood memories of ridicule and humiliation. And lest she forget those stories she'd once heard from that loquacious drunk in a tavern in Stuttgart. The man had been uncommonly knowledgeable about dwarfs and chock-full of tales of sterilization, extermination, breeding, drowning, exorcisms, mechanical stretching, erotic games, glass display cases, birdcages …

"I believe you dropped this?"

Mari snapped out of her trance. A man knelt before her, holding a pfennig. "Oh. *Danke.*" No sooner had she reached for the coin than it had vanished.

A magician. She should have known by the foolish hat. She was a magnet for these types.

He closed his hand and waved the other over it. Mari smiled tepidly, hoping for a swift conclusion. When he unfurled his fingers, a silver groschen lay in his palm. "Just as I thought," he said, "a lucky dwarf." He nodded at the coin. "Take it. It's yours."

Mari hesitated. He grinned but kept his hand still. She took the silver. "*Danke.*"

He tipped his hat. "*Bitte schön.*"

She studied the coin. It was real. When she looked up again, the magician was gone.

තය

Karl left her at his sister-in-law's stall while he shopped for horse goods. After an hour of sitting on a crate, agonizing about her future and ruminating on the humiliations of the past day, Mari asked Heike if she could help weigh onions and count silver. Having spent decades in the Countess's lab, she was clever at the balance scale and arithmetic as well. Heike hesitated, but when business slowed, she lowered the scale for Mari. In a quarter hour they moved a hundred pounds of bulbs together, while Heike boasted to customers about her keen little helper and jested about hiring Mari on a permanent basis.

Mari welcomed the diversion, losing her worries in the rolling onions and jangling brass weights. She was considering asking Heike how exactly one would go about becoming a market stall attendant when a thin, crusty voice intruded on her thoughts. "I won't have the cursed one handling my onions," it said.

Mari looked up and was met with a dozen stares, and the evil eye from an old lady in front. Heike shuffled Mari aside and filled the order herself.

"She looked like she knew a thing or two about curses," Heike said after the hag had hobbled off with her onion sack. They tried to carry on, but the remark had plunged Mari back into despair. She kept fumbling onions and weights, dropping them in the scale pans with thunderous clangs that set everyone in the vicinity on edge, and making embarrassing mathematical errors. Heike finally sat her back on her crate with a cup of hot wine.

Another hour passed. Karl still hadn't shown. They would have to leave before nightfall. Bored now, and emboldened from the wine, Mari decided to brave the crowd and seek out the magician to see what other tricks he could do.

She found him on the edge of the plaza with the other novelty merchants—the bookseller, the toymaker, the sweetmeat maker—chasing a ball around his tabletop with three tinplate cups for a group of boys. In the stall next to his, a bawdy marionette show played before a thin audience.

The trick ended with one of the boys finding the ball in his pocket. Baffled and delighted, they paid the magician and left him to count his coins. Mari stepped forth.

"The lucky dwarf finds me again," he said, without looking up. His tabletop was worn bare and strewn with implements: balls and cups, bodkins and knives, handkerchiefs, a candlestick, a spool of thread.

"I'm not feeling so lucky. In fact, an old woman just charged me with hexing her onions."

He slipped his coins into his pocket. "Ah, yes, the maleficent onion hex. I've heard of it before, but I've never had the pleasure of meeting someone who could do it, until now." He tipped his hat. Mari had never seen such an odd hat—a flaccid red cone, like a giant red pepper, fringed by his black snarls of hair.

"Pleased to meet you. Maria-Barbara of Walther. Or just Mari."

"Similarly pleased. Udo." Mari's gaze drifted to the stagecoach behind him, with its two dingy white horses and flaking black paint.

The sign above the hatch read *Udo, die Harzlegende*—Legend of the Harz, the mountains of the north.

"Are you heading home to the Harz?"

"I am home." He nodded to his coach. "I'm headed south, to France, for the winter. Land of rich wines, rich cakes, and rich travelers."

"Sounds wonderful."

"Where do you call home?"

"Rottenburg."

He cocked an eyebrow. "Wasting her talents in Rottenburg."

"I haven't any talents."

"Neither have I." With this he conjured a cork ball out of nowhere and rolled it through his knuckles with astounding grace. "Don't tell them that." Two women were approaching his table.

"Have you a trick for us?" one of them asked, rather lewdly.

"Have you a groschen, young lady?" he said. The women were not young, although they behaved like silly maidens, and Mari suspected they were tiddly with wine.

While the woman fished in her purse, Udo cut a foot-long piece of thread and held it taut. "My confederate will accept your money," he said, nodding to Mari to take the woman's coin. "Very well." He had the woman cut the thread into a bunch of short threads, which he balled up and set on the flat of a knife. "My confederate will light the threads," he said, nodding at the candle.

Mari obeyed. While the threads burned, she looked around. Passersby were slowing down, keeping a respectful distance, watching Udo with an air of cautious curiosity. Mari felt safe standing at the hip of this spellbinder, this sneak, and wondered if ignoble company might afford even better protection than noble company.

Udo tapped the ashes into his palm and kneaded them in his fist. A thread wriggled out from the tunnel of his fingers. He let the woman pull out the foot-long thread while Mari and the other woman applauded.

"Teach us how to do that!" one of them said.

"Have you twenty years to learn?" the Legend asked. He took the groschen from Mari. "Well done, confederate."

"Is she a seer?" the woman asked.

Everyone looked down at Mari.

"What, me, a seer? No. Definitely not."

"I thought all of your kind were seers," the woman said.

The Countess had always bristled at this sort of inanity, but Mari welcomed inanity over cruelty. "Indeed, not all," she said.

Udo tipped his hat and sent them off. "Why didn't you tell them you were a seer? We could have sold them a prophecy."

"I'm not a seer."

"You should tell people you are. Otherwise you're just an unlucky dwarf in their eyes."

"I don't care to fib."

"What fib? Everyone sees."

"Not the future."

"The future is just a dream. Only fools try to look." Another woman was coming toward them.

"Welcome, fine lady," Udo said to the coarse-looking woman. He did the thread trick again. This time Mari took the money and lit the threads without cue. When it was over, the woman tucked the thread into her purse, whereupon the Legend said, "The lady dwarf brings luck to those who touch her." Mari shot him a mortified look. He winked.

The woman looked down at Mari, her rough face softening with delight. She reached forth. Udo halted her. "Two groschen, if you please."

The woman plunged into her purse, paid Udo, and laid a brawny hand upon Mari's shoulder.

"Luck be with you," Udo said, tipping his hat. The woman went away looking pleased. He passed the coins to Mari. "Wasn't that easy?"

"Too easy."

"People believe what they will. It's not for you to try to change feeble minds." He wiped the soot from his knife. "Besides, did you see how happy you made her? And luck will find her, because now she's looking."

It was late; Mari had to find Karl. She bade Udo happy travels. "Farewell, lucky dwarf," he said, tipping the hat.

Karl was waiting for her at Heike's stall. She thought he'd be angry over her disappearing, but he couldn't have been merrier—nor rosier. Apparently he had found the distiller. Getting home before dark was no longer possible. They would have to lie in Tübingen for the night.

∽∾∽

The *Gasthaus* on the edge of town was comelier than it appeared from outside, with a richly woodworked lobby, roaring hearth fire, and the scent of sausages and sauerkraut wafting from the dining room. The innkeeper stood behind the counter in the amber glow of a lantern. His eyes quickly found Mari and lingered on her, calculating her smallness, her incorrectness. With today's humiliations fresh in her mind, she tensed at the thought of being turned away and having to lie in the wagon all night.

The man nodded. Mari slackened with relief, her heart strung with gratitude. A life lived entirely at the mercy of others.

"Have you vacancy?" Karl asked, swaying under the feed sacks. He had brought them in.

"How many beds?" the man asked.

"One," Karl said. The man sifted through a tinkling ring of keys. "The dwarf will sleep on her feed sacks," Karl saw fit to add, probably so as not to be mistaken for Mari's husband or a man of strange appetites.

Their room was small and tidy with crisp white linens. The innkeeper built a fire and left. Karl plunked on the bed and pulled a bottle from his coat while Mari rummaged through the pans and kettles near the hearth.

They supped in silence, with Karl glass-eyed and listless and eating little, and Mari heartsick for the Countess. If the lady were here, they'd be downstairs dining on sausages and sauerkraut and warm buttered rolls, probably talking about Kepler's *Astronomia nova*, or Galilei's *Starry Messenger*. They'd get tiddly on beer, and the Countess would educate Mari on the brewing process. Then they'd retire upstairs, where Mari would have her own bed, her own crisp linens, and a night of blissful sleep.

"We should rise early and leave at first light," Mari said. She feared Herr Schneider would come early tomorrow and she would miss him. Karl nodded and undid his belt. Exhausted, sore, and unsated by her bread-and-onion supper, Mari lay on her feed sacks and fell into a shallow sleep almost instantly.

She woke to the sound of Karl's feet hitting the floor and a grunt as he hoisted himself from the bed. The fire still burned, but feebly. He dragged the chamber pot noisily over the floorboards, and Mari had to listen to his shameless, happy piss and the pot careening across the floor as he kicked it on his way back.

The huge distorted shadow of his head bobbed on the wall as he climbed into bed. Mari waited for it to slide away as he lay, but it loomed queerly. She turned. He was sitting up in bed, staring at her. "What's wrong?" she asked. "Are you sick?"

"Come lie with me."

Mari's heart quickened, pumping warm, heavy dread into her limbs. "I'll stay here." She turned to the wall.

"There's plenty of room for both of us." The sheets whispered as he threw them back. "You'd be more comfortable up here." Mari remembered the pokers by the hearth, the friendly enough innkeeper downstairs. "You must wonder what it's like to lie with a man. I can show you."

She pretended to sleep, wondering how long to wait before commencing a fake snore.

His purse tinkled in the dark. "I'll pay you. A full groschen."

Mari's self-preservation dissolved in acid indignation. "I'm not a whore."

"Are you not for sale?"

"I'm an asset of the estate," she said calmly, though her voice quivered with rage, "and even then I should walk free if I please, or be placed in a new home."

"You mean sold to the highest bidder."

"I mean *acquired* by a noble family, to live among them as their own. We are extremely valuable, my kind. Many live with kings."

"If you're so valuable, why haven't your owners sent for you? Why did the executor put you out with the horses until he can figure out what to do with you? You may have been valuable once, but you're old now. Who's going to buy a little old dwarf, waddling to her grave?" He belched quietly, slid beneath his sheets. "God only knows where you'll end up. Your new master could be a right pauper who'll have you begging for pfennigs in the streets, or a nasty person who likes to beat you, or a twisted sort who'd love nothing more than to lie in bed with the likes of you."

Mari pulled her coat over her ear and listened to her blood raging. She watched the firelight caress the wall like silent, sneaky magician hands, and thought of Udo.

"You're like the stoat," Karl said. Despite herself, Mari uncovered her ear. What in God's name was the fool talking about? "You'd sooner die in custody than go out in the world and get dirty. If you're as clever as everyone says you are, you'd walk free and sell yourself, keep the money. People do it every day; it's called work. If you don't want to lie with sick men, you can get a job cleaning floors, or picking turnips or some other low crop, or clearing horseshit from the roads. There's plenty someone like you could do for work. I say get out there, dwarf. Go out and get dirty."

He snorted and choked his way back to sleep, leaving Mari wide awake and crackling with anger. She cursed the Countess for her negligence. She who had always admonished against things like *faith* and *assumptions*—"enemies of logic"—had apparently just *assumed* her kin would be perfectly pleased to inherit a dwarf. Mari also cursed Herr Schneider for selling her to some sick, nasty sort who would have her any way he pleased, which, thanks to Karl, she was now certain would happen. And she cursed herself for needing a drunk fool to tell her what she'd already known but hadn't wanted to admit. She was indeed far less valuable than she once was. What noble family would invest their money and affection in an elderly dwarf, only to see her die in a few years? Even her rightful owners wouldn't have her, yet they had wasted no time collecting the two young stallions.

Her thoughts roiled throughout the night. The *Gasthaus* fell silent but for Karl's snoring. The candles died, the fire died, chill seeped into the room. Returning to the longhouse with him was unthinkable now, impossible. After what felt like an eternity, Mari heard birdsong. It was time to go.

She collected her knapsack and shoes and Karl's purse from the night table. It was deliciously heavy; he must have at least fifty groschen in there. If she lived leanly, it would last her for months, even if she couldn't find work right away.

She crept out the door and down the stairs. The innkeeper wasn't at his counter, but the lobby hearth was ablaze. A sparse chime of dishware trickled from the dining room. Mari walked out into the cold, dark morning.

A few men and horses were already on the move. Within minutes she found a seamy looking wagoner who, for two groschen, agreed to drive her to the market—in addition to unbridling Karl's horse and spooking it away.

They reached the market under a chilly autumn sunrise. Mari should have been exhausted, but her body hummed with a strange mix of excitement and dread. Avoiding Heike's stall, she bought a bottle of beer and a bread knot and set forth for the novelty merchants.

She found Udo's shabby coach and knocked on the hatch. There was rustling within. The hatch swung open revealing the Legend, hatless and wild-haired, his eyes glazed with slumber. His befuddled gaze swept the empty space above Mari's head before finding her down below. "Mari. What brings you here at this hour?"

"I'd like to travel with you to France. And you could use a confederate." She stole a swig of beer before handing it to him with a shaky hand.

He looked confused, then slightly amused, then slightly annoyed. He rubbed his eyes, shaking his head and letting out a bitter little snort. He noticed the beer bottle in his hand and took a long pull, draining half of it.

After conjuring a handkerchief from nowhere and wiping his mouth, he leveled his dark gaze at her. "Are you a seer?"

She was indeed, she told him.

❦

Chapter 2

THE MAGICIAN

Mari loved the way the fog seeped into these low mountain towns and swirled in the streets, causing people to walk around a bit friendlier and slightly dazed, as if in a dream. It was great for magic, and for prophecies. Today they were in Rottweil of the Black Forest, a healthy market town where burly black-and-brown dogs worked the stalls alongside people, greeting customers, guarding wares, and pulling laden carts through the streets. Mari found them delightful and threw them bread heels and sausage ends, even though Udo told her not to disturb them in their work.

Work. It suited Mari. She had no regrets about leaving the estate and joining Udo. They'd been together a fortnight, working small river markets, polishing their act for the major markets waiting along the Swiss Plateau. Today had been lucrative. Even now, late in the afternoon, the crowd remained thick and eager, and Mari's pocket was fat and heavy with silver. "Stop fondling your money," Udo said. "It makes you look like an amateur. Or a pervert."

Mari couldn't help herself; she'd never had so much money before. She enjoyed handling it, diddling with it, delighting in its physical properties—the ice-cold silver, the gay tinkle of coins. Most of all she treasured the satisfactions it brought: a sense of industry and achievement; the hitherto completely foreign concept of independence; feelings of confidence and security that increased in due proportion with the girth of her purse.

A young woman appeared before Mari, breathless, greatly pregnant. "They told me you were here," she said, furnishing two groschen. "I was afraid I'd miss you."

"Open your coat, fine lady," Mari said.

Mari laid her hand upon the orbing womb and gazed into the hills. Pregnancies were always a snap with their two straightforward choices. This one would be a boy, being it clearly the woman's first child, youthful as she was and without others in tow. She'd be hoping for a son, and Mari had decided early on to be a good-news prophet, harbinger of joyous weddings, strapping sons, and lucky swine back home in the cattle pens. "You should damp it down some," Udo once said. "Nobody's luck is that good." But Mari had already gotten hooked on their delighted faces, their profuse gratitude, their jaunty gait as they walked off with their good tidings. Once the silver started cascading in, Udo kept quiet and went about his magic.

"Did you feel that?" Mari asked. "He kicked."

"He?" The woman's face lit with joy. How Mari relished that look.

"Hearty and hale, he is. He'll grow up a farmer, or a builder."

"My husband will be pleased."

"Luck be with you and yours," Mari said. She watched the woman lumber away and hoped to God the baby didn't come before she and Udo left town in the morning. "We should travel a ways before we camp," she told him. "That child is due any moment. If she births a girl, someone might come looking for us."

By now Udo was inured to her worrying and indeed seemed entertained by the way her swift leaps of logic invariably hurtled her toward the worst-case scenario (unbearable suffering and untimely death) like a stone skipping on water. "Fine. We'll camp in the hills tonight," he said. "It's your turn to cook."

ᚱᚱ

They parked the coach under a forest canopy and supped fireside on cold pickled herring with onions and black bread. Mari ate well with Udo, being at the markets daily, with plenty of silver between them. They had meat in every stew and fresh butter on their bread almost nightly. Sometimes they roasted a small chicken and together picked it clean, followed by fig cakes, perhaps, or drunken pears, or redcurrant tart.

The benefits of Udo's confederacy went beyond gastro- and economical. In addition to his being a solution to Mari's problem of homelessness, pennilessness and loneliness, she'd been correct about the protection of ignoble company. There was refuge to be had in Udo's subtle danger: his dark eyes and thin scruples, the inherent nastiness of magical trickery, his knives and bodkins and other sharp implements, his knack for insulting customers without them realizing it. No one so much as snickered at Mari in the Legend's presence, so vaguely threatening was he, and, by association, she. Or maybe a dwarf with a magician just made sense to people in a way that failed to incite their cruelty.

Likewise, Udo's lazy confidence and male unflappability were as good a balm as any for Mari's crisp nerves. He never indulged her worries, which had become excessive even for her, as life on the road presented endless potential for danger—from spoiled food to unsafe bridges to the very real possibility of being caught in a false prophecy and whatever vengeance that might entail. At first Udo had challenged her with logic but then quickly realized the futility in doing so. Now he just dismissed her fears, scoffed at them, chuckled at them, and threw them back in her face once time and evidence rendered them baseless.

After dinner, Udo busied himself by boring a hole into a walnut with a red-hot bodkin, while Mari counted her money. "Twenty-four groschen," she said cheerily.

"Good girl. My purse is inside."

She climbed into the coach and put his money in his purse. They had negotiated a seventy-thirty percent split of her earnings. Udo got the seventy. With homelessness looming, desperation mounting, and her utter powerlessness in life a foregone conclusion, Mari had accepted the terms with tearful gratitude.

She returned fireside, her hips and knees aching dully, even as she tread the soft forest floor. It could only mean one thing. "Cover the horses tonight," she said. "There's a storm coming."

"If the lady insists." With impressive dexterity, he rolled a scrap of paper into a tiny scroll and threaded it through his walnut hole. "We'll travel south to Zurich tomorrow," he said. "We can be there in three days if the horses cooperate." He pulled his ever-present pot of red wax from his coat and used some to plug the hole. "I'd like to reach Geneva by early December and stay a few days. It's a big market with lots of travelers, and everyone will be in a festive mood for the Advent."

"I hope I'm ready." The thought of a big city market with clever, sophisticated people made her uneasy.

"You're ready." He rolled the walnut in the dirt and got up to cover the horses. "Twenty groschen if you can find that hole," he said, tossing it into Mari's lap.

They climbed into the coach to sleep, Udo on the truckle bed and Mari on her straw mattress, which the Legend himself had sewn with his nimble magician's fingers. Moments after they'd lain, thunder rumbled in the distance. Mari turned to gloat. Udo's eyes were closed, but he was smiling. She studied him for a few seconds. He was almost handsome without his foolish hat, with a long slender nose and enviable eyelashes.

After breakfast the next morning, Udo undressed the horses while Mari climbed back into the coach, hoping to sleep. The storm had kept her awake much of the night, startling her with its heart-splitting thunder, spooking the horses, and rocking the coach, while Udo slept like the dead.

She lay on her back, watching the lantern swing as Udo drove over the forest floor. She thought about the Countess. It was hard to believe she was really gone, that she wasn't back in Rottenburg carrying on as usual. Meanwhile, Mari's own life had ended and had been replaced with this one, which only weeks ago would have been unthinkable, laughable, deplorable. The lady had detested show-men—minstrels and magic-men who had so little to do with facts and numbers, who sniffed out her dwarfess at markets and festivals like blood-tracking wolves. But in truth, Udo's companionship felt much like the Countess's—she having had a mannish capacity for silent concentration and stifled emotion. Like Udo, she'd been a person of instruments and techniques, a possessor of uncommon knowledge, thus pedantic at times, and also queerly oblivious to her surround-ings—she in her science bubble just like Udo in his magic bubble.

Still, one painful, irreconcilable difference remained: Mari didn't belong to Udo. He didn't own her, value her, and he certainly didn't need her. In fact, he scarcely seemed to care about her beyond a basic threshold of human decency, or a thin gossamer of friendship that bonded them, ever so loosely. Mari might have managed to stave off aloneness, but she was still utterly unloved and could remain so for the rest of her life, which was too unbearable to consider right now.

Determined to win back twenty groschen, she pulled the walnut from her pocket and twiddled it like a squirrel, looking for the hole. In time she slept, spinning the walnut in her dreams all afternoon.

Chill on her face woke her. Udo stood in the open hatch, smiling sinisterly as frigid air filled Mari's cozy slumber chamber. "Switzerland," he said.

She joined him up front, and they rode through the woodland, their path spangled with the late-day sun shimmering through the trees. Then the forest thinned, revealing vast swells of frost-dusted hills beneath a lavender sky. It should have been breathtaking, but all Mari could think of were the many false prophecies she had littered about the lands—all those wrong-sex babies and no-show suitors; promises of health, wealth, and happiness cruelly supplanted by sickness, pennilessness, and despair. From there it was just a short logic-leap to Mari's own unbearable suffering and untimely death. If she were ever to pass through those towns again, she'd be greeted by angry mobs. They'd call her a fraud, a witch, put her on trial, burn her alive ...

"Do we plan on returning in the spring?" she asked.

"Only a fool would plan that far ahead," Udo said. Then, "Sure, maybe."

She'd try not to think about it. She pulled the walnut from her pocket and turned it in her fingers for probably the hundredth time. "I still haven't found the hole."

Udo pulled a walnut from his coat. "It's in this one."

"You're a wretch!" She whipped the walnuts into the forest. Udo threw his head back and chuckled into the trees. Birds scattered.

"I never said I wasn't." He sniggered to himself, and then, seeing how prickly she was, put his arm around her and kissed the top of her head.

෨෨

As Udo had promised, Geneva was packed with travelers for the Advent. Rows of lantern-lit stalls glowed in the morning mist, draped with Yule boughs and stocked with bells and candles, ribbons and wreaths, candied nuts and sugared fruits. Spruce trees had been

potted throughout the market square and garnished with apples, walnuts, pretzels, and paper flowers. The blended scent of spiced wine
and grilled meat hung thickly in the air, along with peals of bells
and laughter, merry lute music, and balladeers singing today's news.
Hordes of merry faces glowed pink with chill, spewing clouds of breath
into the cold air through wine-stained lips. People were speaking French
now, and Mari, who'd been educated by nobles and spoke the language
impeccably, was pleased to be better at something than Udo, whose
own French was sloppy and sometimes hilarious. Having traveled so
far in just a fortnight, she relished the thought of spending several days
here—several days of candlelit streets, jolly faces, and cascading silver.
Maybe she could talk Udo into staying the rest of the Yuletide.

They weren't the only performers profiting from the season's
mirth. There were fire-eaters and tumblers; puppeteers with bulbous-
nosed, red-cheeked, foul-mouthed marionettes; and a stilt walker,
who took a keen interest in Mari. "Hello down there!" he said as he
tread gingerly by in his long flowing breeches and pink greasepaint
cheeks. He introduced himself as "*Prince Nouille*"—Prince Noodle.

"Prince Noodle," Udo said as the man teetered away, barely out
of earshot. "What a horse's ass."

Minutes later the Prince was back, juggling ninepins and inviting Mari to walk with him around the market. "She's working," Udo
said, rolling the cork ball through his knuckles. The cork ball always
came out, Mari had noticed, when the Legend was feeling threatened, or superior, or when he was deep in thought. "Run along now.
Don't hurt yourself."

"Did you have to be so rude?" Mari said after the stilt walker
had ambled off.

"He's just using you to make himself look taller. Soon he'll be
propositioning you to run off and be his sidekick."

"I already have a sidekick." She turned away, smirking. She
wasn't one to flatter herself, but there was no mistaking it: the Legend was jealous. The cork ball bounced off the back of her head.

That afternoon a maiden asked Mari if she would ever find love. "Next Yuletide you'll have a man at your side and a child-seed in your womb," Mari said. "Sleep with a wooden spoon under your pillow for a girl, copper for a boy."

After the girl had gone, Mari noticed Udo just standing there, staring at her. "Spoon under the pillow," he said, weirdly expressionless. "Good one."

"Thanks." She couldn't tell if he was mocking her or not. She held out his coins.

"Keep them. You earned them."

"Are you all right? You're acting queer."

"I'm fine," he said, snapping to.

She set out to find those giant sugar biscuits she'd seen people walking around with all day. She walked along the shimmering wet cobblestones, weaving through the throng, exchanging greetings with a few drunken revelers. Something—she wasn't sure what— made her stop and look back. Udo was still staring at her down the crowded lane, as if they were the only two people on earth. She hoped she hadn't been waddling, or that her rear-end hadn't looked excessively wide. She smiled and waved. He tipped his hat. In his other hand, the cork ball rolled.

The next morning, he wanted to leave Geneva.

ဢ

Days later, they were greeted with a hefty toll at the French border. Still pouting over Udo's decision to leave the lucrative Geneva market after only one day, Mari made no overtures to help pay it. "The French are crooks," he said, tucking his purse beneath the seat. "You can buy me supper."

They reached Grenoble by nightfall and were soon savoring a tableside meal of lamb and wine and crêpes with summer berries in the dead of winter. The bill far exceeded the tolls Udo had paid and emaciated Mari's purse. She comforted herself with the promise of work tomorrow, in this town full of miners, vintners, fisher- and fer-rymen, and, hopefully, their many spendthrift wives.

After sleeping restfully from the hearty meal and relief of returning to work, Mari woke in darkness the next morning to the coach jerking into motion, and Udo speaking his butchered French to someone outside. Somebody had probably ordered him to move. Mari fell back into an onionskin of sleep, still conscious of the horses' hooves clip-clopping on the cobblestones.

She woke when the hoofing changed to muted thumping. They were on dirt. Mari opened the curtains to glaring daylight. Gone were apartment blocks and municipal buildings; a chateau drifted by, tiny and alone on a vast expanse of land. Mari's ears popped. They were heading into the mountains. Udo had left Grenoble.

She pounded on the wall behind the driver's bench. "Where are we going?" she shouted, but he pretended not to hear. Mari plunked down on the truckle bed and seethed.

When he stopped around midday, she threw open the hatch and tumbled out furiously.

"I would have helped you down," he said, taking her arm.

She jerked her arm away. "Where are we going?"

"I thought about it while you were sleeping. We need to take advantage of this good weather to get out of the mountains. We can't risk getting snowed in until spring."

"It's far too warm for snow here. We could have worked all day today and left in the morning. A lot richer!"

"Grenoble wasn't worth our time," he said, turning to the horses.

"That market was huge!"

"Yes, but the French are tough customers. Their hearts and minds aren't open to magic. Only things like bread and cheese."

"Then why are we in this country?"

He sprang forth and hugged her against his hip. "Why do you worry so much, Little Luck?"

"We haven't worked since Geneva. I'm running out of money."

"I won't let you run out of money. We'll work when we get to the seaport. Wait until you see all the travelers celebrating the New Year. Ships as big as castles, full of them. You'll have to buy a bigger purse. For now just relax and enjoy France. Who wants to work the Yuletide anyway?" He herded her to the coach. "Ride up front with me. You need some fresh air." Mari climbed up without protest. She wasn't livid so much as frustrated, confused. Her newfound confidence and security were rapidly diminishing with the girth of her purse, gains vanishing as quickly as they'd been won—loss of money, loss of control, loss of dignity, begging in the streets ... suffering ... death.

Udo plunked down beside her and squeezed her knee. "There. Better?" Not waiting for an answer, he snapped the horses' reins.

చచ

Somewhere along the Rhône River, Udo started insisting on staying in pensions—something to do with French crooks. Although sleeping in a real bed before a crackling hearth was a welcome change, it only hastened to slim Mari's purse. They lodged in separate rooms, with Udo nagging her to lock herself in at night, never failing to jiggle her door handle to check for himself. She'd have preferred to double up to save money—they'd long been sleeping cheek by jowl in the coach—but she didn't dare suggest it for fear of seeming eager to share a bed with the Legend.

In very truth, there was a disquieting part of her that was not entirely uneager to share a bed with the Legend. First she had tried to ignore it. Next she tried to explain it away, putting it down to her forced closeness with a man, who was neither unhandsome nor charmless, and the fact that they were basically living as man and wife in all ways but one. But ever since Geneva, when they'd looked at each other as if they were the only two people on the crowded lane, and also after Mari's tantrum over his leaving Grenoble—since which he'd been acting paternally calm and attentive toward her—Mari was finding it difficult to banish the hope that the Legend might actually care about her beyond the basic threshold of human decency, and even beyond friendship.

He always knocked on her door to collect her for breakfast. When he didn't show one morning, Mari defied his wishes and stepped out alone. She checked his room. He wasn't there. She went outside. The coach was there, but one of the horses was gone.

She was on her way to question the innkeeper when Udo came loping forth, bareback. She almost hadn't recognized him without his hat. "What are you doing out here?" he asked, throwing a suspicious look around the wagon lot. "Did anyone bother you?"

"I've only been out here a minute. Where were you?"

"I went to buy a coat. Does it suit me?" He tugged at the waist of his trim little coat, a radical departure from the long, slouchy coats he normally wore. It made his body look small and queer. He had also waxed and twirled his mustache and apparently washed the horse, which was several shades whiter than the other.

"Have you a Frenchwoman?" she asked, regretting it instantly and hoping it hadn't sounded like she cared one way or another.

He threw his head back and laughed loudly, spooking his horse. Udo regained control and jumped down. "You know how I feel about French women," he said. Just the other day he had said that all French women were "porcupines," and even the peasant girls were too big for their boots.

"Yes, I know. I just thought—"

"Remember what we talked about, Little Luck," he said, wagging a finger at her. The other night at dinner he had made her promise to stop thinking so much, about money and everything else.

She sighed. "Right."

He patted her head and started toward the inn. "Come on, I'll buy you breakfast."

ഇരു

In Arles, a tailor's shop near their pension put the idea in Udo's head that Mari needed a new dress. "You're a showman now," he said. "You need to dress with flair." Mari didn't know whether to be amused or annoyed that he of all people was offering fashion advice. When she balked at the expense, he offered to pay. When she pointed out that a dress for her would have to be custom-made, thus detaining them for a week or two, he said they were just killing time until the New Year anyway. So she got fitted for a dark green dress trimmed with silver ribbon, not realizing she would end up looking like a very small Yule tree.

The dress was delivered on Christmas Eve. Mari put it on with all due haste, whereupon Udo became the first man ever to tell her she looked beautiful. They went to evening mass, where she was struck by how passionately the Legend prayed and how beautifully he sang his Christmas hymns. Afterward, they supped in a warm, flickering tavern, where Mari was able to cast aside her financial worries and join Udo in foie gras with fig jelly, partridge pie, and a Three Kings cake dessert.

They returned to the pension at ten o'clock. Udo came into her room and put a fire in the hearth. "It feels early," Mari said. She didn't feel like being alone.

The fire ablaze, he sat on the bed beside her.

"I don't see why we can't just stay one more day," she said. They were but a day's travel from the coast, with the New Year still a week away.

"Yule is the perfect day to travel. There's no traffic, and the toll collectors get drunk and let people pass without paying."

She was willing to cut the Yule short to save a few coins.

"Get some rest," he said. "Tomorrow will be a long day."

She smiled, but he didn't smile back. He looked at her with such affection, such tenderness, it sent a swooping tickle through her gut. She had never seen a look like that before, but she knew exactly what it meant: something had changed in him, appeared in his heart just as suddenly and mysteriously as the coins and walnuts that appeared in his fingertips. This wasn't a look between confederates; this was a look a man gave a woman. His dark eyes trilled her heart and sent a swell of desire into her lap, a cresting wave refusing to break, deliciously cruel. Her head swirled with confusion, disbelief, euphoria, and a longing so intense it felt like dread. What was happening? Had the Legend put a spell on her?

He leaned in, pressing his lips to her forehead firmly and lingeringly, while her heart screamed. "*Joyeux noël,*" he said softly, in an odd display of exquisite French. Then he stood up. "Lock the door behind me."

She couldn't believe he was just leaving. Leaving her to make sense of *that.*

He paused in the doorway. "I'm coming early tomorrow, so be ready. Wear your new dress, so they can see how beautiful you are."

"I will," she managed.

He smiled, kindly, wistfully, beautifully. "Sleep well, Little Luck." He pointed to the bolt to remind her to lock it and closed the door. Mari floated across the room and locked up, still holding the handle as Udo jiggled it from outside.

She lay awake for hours, imagining the look, the kiss, over and over again. What would tomorrow bring? Were they supposed to carry on as usual? She almost dreaded seeing him again, and yet she could hardly wait. *Joyeux noël,* she would say, chirpily, as if she hadn't lain awake half the night. Then she'd steal a glimpse into his eyes, see if the look was still there, see if that brilliant, glinting coin of a thing was still in his heart, or if it had just as soon vanished.

The clock chimed down the hours. Sounds of intense revelry wafted up the stairwell: joyful eruptions, off-key caroling, crashing tins. Normally she'd have been vexed to heavens by the noise, but tonight she barely noticed as she lay pinned to the bed, watching the firelight flit about the room but seeing only the dark, depthless eyes of the Legend of the Harz.

Chapter 3

THE SPANIARDS

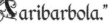aribarbola."

Mari stirred in her sleep.

"Wake up." A girl's voice. "It's almost noon."

Sleep forsook her, swiftly and cruelly. She opened her eyes to a roomful of revolting sunlight and quickly closed them again.

"Maribarbola?"

"What?" Mari mumbled, still half-asleep. "No." She had no idea what the girl had said, but occasionally she still came across a French word she didn't know. How rude of her to just barge—

Mari's eyes sprung open. "Wait. You mean Maria-Barbara?"

"Oh. It sounded like Maribarbola. They're hard to understand."

"Who's they?"

"Your party. They're waiting downstairs." She was barely a woman, thirteen or fourteen, wearing an apron and keyring, probably the innkeeper's daughter.

"You have the wrong person. I'm with the magician across the hall. It's just the two of us."

"Ugly hat? He left at sunup."

Mari shot up in bed. "Did he say where he was going? Or when he'd be back?"

"I don't think he's coming back. He paid his bill and left his key."

Mari's chest went leaden; her ears rang. She had a vague sense of not really being here, of watching this from elsewhere.

"They're asking for the dwarf."

Whoever they were, she wouldn't go. She still had enough money to get to the coast. She'd hire a wagon, work the seaport markets until she had enough money to get her back to Germ—

She snatched her knapsack from the bedside table and dumped it. Her purse was gone.

Mari covered her face and wept.

"Why are you crying?"

"He sold me," she said, chagrined by how pathetic she sounded. "I wasn't his to sell." Her foolishness was astounding, putting her trust—her very life!—in the hands of a professional trickster, a professional sneak. Of course he would do this. Of course he would. Now penniless, she had no choice but to go with them, whoever they were. The Legend had thought of everything. "I can't believe he took my purse!"

"I don't think you'll be needing it," the girl muttered from the window, looking down onto the street.

"And God only knows where they're taking me."

"I'd give an arm and a leg to go with you," the girl said dreamily. "Four handsome Spanish knights … "

Mari stopped crying. "What did you say?"

The girl tore her gaze from the window. "What? Here, come see."

44

Mari floated to the window on numb legs and peered over the sill. Horses, brown and shiny in the noon sun, lined up in twos before a splendid coach, a miniature palace of ivory and gold boiserie perched on large, gold-spoked wheels. There were four men standing by it, cloaked all in black except for spade-shaped white collars, sword hilts gleaming at their hips. Crowds had gathered on both sides of the street.

"There's another just like it around the corner," the girl said.

"Who in God's name are they?"

"That's a royal coach. Your magician sold you to a king."

෴

The crowd jubilated when Mari emerged stonefaced from the pension in her green dress. "¡Mariburbula!" one of the Spaniards flung into the air, and the men scattered in a cacophony of boot heels, pinging swords, and barking commands. The little ivory-and-gold doll box she had spied from the upstairs window was a towering edifice with gilded wheels taller than she. A heavy hand whisked her to the coach and folded warmly and firmly around hers as she mounted the steps. "Her Majesty will be pleased," he said in good German, basically to her rear-end, as she climbed inside.

Every inch of the interior was decked in sumptuous sky-blue silk. Mari took a soft seat. The man followed her in, slammed the door, and sat opposite her. "You should see your face," he said. Mari scarcely heard him through the ringing panic, the rush of blood in her ears. "Please know that we're all belted knights of the Military Order of Santiago."

"I have no idea what that means." She had no idea what anything meant; she was as blank-minded and horrorstruck as a seconds-old baby. She couldn't even derive a logic path to the worst-case scenario.

"It means you're very safe," he said kindly, but he had dark treacherous eyes like the Legend's. He pounded the ceiling with his fist, and the coach jerked into motion. "I'm Eduardo Francisco de María Ortega de Valencia de Salazar y Castellón, infantry officer of the Royal Guard to Her Majesty Queen Mariana of Spain, wife and consort to His Imperial and Royal Majesty Philip." A hint of good humor flickered in his eyes. "For time's sake, you may call me Lalo."

Mari studied him—the twirled black mustache, bluish shadow of a beard, white crescent scar under one eye. He was overwhelmingly manly, out of place in this elegant, tufted-silk chamber, his head framed by two plump ivory cherubs fixed to the wall behind him, staring at Mari with their dead, iris-less eyes.

"Your arrival in Madrid is much anticipated," he said. "Her Majesty is—"

"How much did the magician get for me?" The question flew from her mouth bitterly, involuntarily.

"I don't know the sum."

"Of course you don't."

"I do know that I could've just as easily fetched you myself, but it took four men to carry the chest of money."

"She's a fool, your queen. I'm not worth that much."

"She thinks you are."

"And how does she know I exist?"

"A broker from Barcelona came forth a couple of weeks ago bringing word of a dwarfess most intriguing."

Mari's chest went warm and heavy. What in God's name did Udo tell them?

"You hail from Austria," he said. "The Queen of Spain does also. Understandably she suffers from homesickness, so it seemed most fortuitous when a man appeared out of nowhere proffering a Germanic dwarfess, one who could speak to Her Majesty in her mother tongue."

"That's really not so fortuitous." They could have just plucked a German-tongued dwarf from a festival booth somewhere.

"Actually, you couldn't have come along at a better time. The Queen is also suffering a bout of heartache and misfortune. She recently birthed a womanchild who lived only a fortnight, her first pregnancy in five years."

Mari stared at him. She didn't see what any of this had to do with her.

"As you might imagine," he said, "Her Majesty was pleased to learn that this Germanic dwarfess is also a wise old seer and a purveyor of good fortune."

Mari felt like she was going to be sick. She glanced at the window, harboring vague notions of escape. Outside, building façades whizzed by.

"Our orders are to have you in Madrid by New Year's Eve. There's little for you to do now but rest." He stood up, stooping under the silk-tented ceiling. "Don't worry, I won't tell the Queen you called her a fool." Then he opened the door and stepped right out of the speeding coach.

Mari lunged to the window, expecting to see him lying dead in the road, but she just as soon heard him stomping on the roof, he and the driver flinging Spanish back and forth.

She spent the afternoon staring at the dead-eyed cherubs, ruminating on the Legend and his four-man chest of silver, trying not to retch. Everything made sense now: their rushing through France, skipping markets; his locking her up at night, paranoid about her being stolen; riding off that one morning in his queer little coat, probably dispatching a courier to that broker in Barcelona; and his insisting on a new dress for her ("So they can see how beautiful you are," he had said last night!). Even more sickening than his deception was her eagerness to be deceived. She had allowed him to trick her into thinking she could outrun her dwarf's fate, that she could provide for herself and not have to live at the mercy of others, when in truth she'd always be powerless, always stunted in all ways imaginable—a half-person living a half-life, a curiosity, sidekick, pawn, pet, chattel. Most cruel and humiliating of all was how he had preyed upon her lovelessness, daring her to believe she could be loved, romantically even, by a proper-sized man. The idiotic fantasies that kept her awake until dawn now rolled through her mind in a slow parade of embarrassments: the moonlit chase, the sunset proposal, the Alpine wedding. The wedding night. His inhumanly skilled hands …

Her very soul cringed.

They stopped after dark in a lazy French village. Townsfolk gathered around the splendid carriage. Mari drew the leather curtains. After a brusque knock, the door flung open, and there stood Lalo, his long black hair swirling in the breeze. "Care to join us for supper?"

The thought of food made her want to heave. She shook her head.

"We won't bite, I promise." A couple of lewd women traipsed by and suggested he take them for a ride. "You really want to sit alone on Christmas?"

She had forgotten it was Christmas. "I'm not hungry."

"Very well. Marco is right outside if you need anything." He hung a lantern and left.

The cherubs flickered demonically in the candlelight. Outside the crowd grew loud and eager, kept at bay only by Marco's rolling tongue and pinging sword. Mari lay on the seat and buried her face in the cushions, half-expecting to die from nerves alone, and half-hoping to.

ɷ

She woke the next morning in a pension bedroom, where the Spaniards had deposited her the night before. It was early; the room was tinged with pewter dawnlight. Just embers twinkled in the hearth. Mari's shock over Udo's betrayal had been dulled by sleep, but her feelings of helplessness and dread were unabated. Resigned by now to being in Spanish custody, she neatened herself and went downstairs to find her captors.

No sooner had she entered the crowded dining room than she heard an excessively jovial "*¡Maribarbola!*" chorus. The Spaniards were seated at a table by the hearth, dominating the room with their mustachioed handsomeness and aggressive good cheer.

They seated her with undue chivalry. "We were just fighting over who would get to wake you," Lalo said, apparently the only one of them who spoke German. He pulled some plates toward her with un-Spanish-like exigency. "Eat well and drink little. We're not stopping today. We need to stay on a strict timetable if we're going to have you in Madrid for the New Year's Jubilee."

New Year's Jubilee. She could kill Udo. "I don't mind missing it," she mumbled.

"The Queen minds. She wants you by her side as she passes into the New Year." He poured her a thin trickle of wine. "It must be true about you being good luck. Never have we had such easy passage through France. Usually Louis's boys go out of their way to give us a hard time."

"The Yule is the best day to travel," Mari said dully, and the Legend's words on her tongue put a flicker of rage in her breast. Legendary scoundrel. Whoreson. Dastardly swine. "How much money would you say was in that chest?" she asked, impelled by her schooled need for hard data, the better to quantify this staggering betrayal. "Approximately."

"Enough for him to live well for the rest of his life," Lalo said, busying with his meal.

"What did he say when you gave it to him?"

"Nothing. He just rode off like an imbecile." He glanced up. "You ask a lot of questions for a prophet."

"I hate him," Mari said, staring into the hearth fire like a vengeful witch.

"If only we'd known. We could have just killed him and saved the Queen a fortune."

There he might have been jesting, but Mari was finding Spaniards hard to read. As a German, she was wholly unaccustomed to their sustained levels of jolliness and enthusiasm.

෩

They spent the next few days barreling down the coast toward Barcelona. After they were safely out of French territory, Lalo let Mari ride outside, where she relished the lush green Pyrenees Mountains, the ocean air on her face. The villages, however, were nothing like the Spain she'd read about in books, where New World silver ships thronged the coastlines, and houses looked like churches with bell towers and stone saints in the courtyards, and every man, woman, and child was an able dancer and guitar virtuoso. The reality was rotting fishing boats, cottages crumbling from artillery damage, and gloomy looking people who seemed to be not so much living as existing. "Welcome to Catalonia," Lalo said, sensing her disenchantment. "Pawns in the endless war between Spain and France."

As they neared Barcelona, the Spain of Mari's fancies materialized. Dilapidated cottages gave way to proud Moorish villas nestled among slim cypresses and knotty fruit trees, and tall-masted boats bobbed on the sparkling sea.

They reached the city by dark. Ships rocked in the harbor like giant slumbering beasts. Bonfires danced like demons on the beach. The promenades became thick and frenzied with travelers and merrymakers. Coiling, teasing Spanish guitar melodies wafted from beachfront arcades, and the air stirred with the sweet zesty perfume of some oranges that had rolled away from the market and lay squashed in the street. They parked outside their pensión, a grand white edifice whose domed top looked like a marzipan cake, and climbed off the coach before a throng of excited onlookers who thought they were about to glimpse the Queen. "*La Reina no está,*" Lalo said, looking pleased to crush their hopes. When a groan of disappointment rippled through the crowd, he threw them a bone:

"*¡Maribarbola!*" he announced, Dwarfess to Her Royal Majesty. There were warm cheers, even some bows and curtsies. Mari felt silly, and oddly thrilled.

They dined in a courtyard tavern, under the boughs of an ancient fig tree, its fruits dangling over their heads like sacks of silver. A fountain trickled nearby, candle lights bobbing in paper boats. Parrots taunted diners from their leafy perches; fireflies winked from lush vines that bearded the stone walls. Mari realized she'd gone nearly an hour without thinking of Udo, and even now her hatred for him seemed to be changing, putrefying in the sweet balmy air. This was starting to feel less like a betrayal than some sort of depraved grand finale: the magician had turned her into that storied dwarf in a faraway land, where treasure ships slept in moonlit bays and fruits rolled fat and fresh in the streets; where treetops sighed in the warm winds of December; and birds didn't sing, but spoke.

After dinner they played Spanish cards. The men had been teaching Mari *Hombre*, the Queen's favorite game. Mari was struggling with the forty-card deck and its queer suits, *Hombre's* complicated rules and Spanish terms, and the unspoken protocols of playing against the Queen. "The key is to let her win without being obvious about it," Lalo said. He nodded at Mari's pathetic hand on the table. "Unlike what you just did there."

"That really was my best play."

"In that case, God help you."

God help her indeed. Now that they were nearing Madrid, reality was setting in: she was going to be expected to do the impossible. With every inbound mile her dread was intensifying. Eventually Lalo rejoined the others in Spanish, leaving her alone with her dark thoughts. Barcelona's magic turned hostile as her mood deteriorated. The fragrant air was suffocating; fireflies flashed bilious yellow-green light from walls that seemed to be closing in on her, like her fate. Her captors' tight, rapid speech rolled over her like a deluge of pebbles, with the occasional intelligible word leaping out: *imbécil, la corte, la*

Reina, and—this landing like cold rotten meat in her stomach—*la Inquisición*. The Inquisition. Unable to bear another moment of their jabber, or their rings pinging on their sword hilts, which they did constantly, or their frequent explosive laughter, which never failed to jolt her skittish heart, Mari scanned the courtyard with the brief delusion that she could escape them, four athletic, sworded men.

Sensing her agitation, Lalo replenished her wine.

Her fate hinged on but a single variable now: how the Queen of Spain would react when she discovered she'd been defrauded. Mari wished she could ask Lalo if he'd ever seen a dwarf imprisoned or executed in his lifetime. She hoped dwarfhood might mitigate her culpability in the same way it mitigated her humanity. She looked around the courtyard, wondering where exactly she was on that universal trajectory toward suffering and death and marveling at how a life could unravel so spectacularly in so short a time. Two months ago she was in Rottenburg watching the Countess die.

⁂

They spent their last night in the mountains, where the festive promenades and lush courtyards of Barcelona were forgotten among the goat paths and frosty junipers. Having nowhere to lodge, they camped streamside, roasting some pork and eggplant provided by a friendly goatherd. The night was cold but tranquil, the moonlight bright as twilight. Since Mari's bout of ill humor at dinner the other night, her captors had been spoiling her with wine and chivalry. Between the drink, the moon, and the mountains, she found herself strangely relaxed, despite being a day's travel from the Royal Alcázar in Madrid, and imagined herself having that beatific glow certain people purportedly got moments before being executed.

After supper they commenced cards—the German deck, which Mari had found at the bottom of her knapsack with a couple of Udo walnuts. "Pick a card," she said to Lalo. He went straight for the Queen. They always did.

"Why are you handing me a walnut?"

"Break it."

After several tries and much ridicule from the others, he broke it with his boot against a stone. "Queen of bells," he said, unfurling the scroll. Mari sat back smugly while they speculated on how she got the scroll inside. "Be sure to do that for the Queen," Lalo said. "She loves that kind of nonsense."

They climbed into the coaches to sleep. Lalo tucked Mari into her truckle bed as usual. "*Gracias, señor,*" she said. He smiled, patted her shoulder. He was a fatherly sort, though younger than Mari, with a wife and four daughters back in Madrid. This journey would have been unbearable if not for him. He had looked after her and protected her, not because she was the Queen's asset but because he was kind and chivalrous and probably saw how scared she was. Because he was the exact opposite man of Udo—Udo, who'd constantly had to be asked to slow down or reach something for her, and snickered for days after she had plowed eye-level into a woman's crotch, and told Mari her face looked like a horseman's buttocks after she'd gotten red and puffy from eating a cursed fish.

Udo, who had sold her like an animal to slaughter.

Lalo removed his sword and laid it, rather tenderly, beside his bed. The coach rocked as he plunked to his mattress. They lay in silence in the flickering lantern light. With a trepid heart, Mari spoke. "What's she like?" Until now she'd been afraid to ask about the Queen, lest she compound her dread.

"The Queen? I've never had a problem with her."

"Have others?"

After a harrowing half-second pause, he said, "Just do as she pleases, and you'll be fine."

And here she almost confessed that she wasn't a prophet or purveyor of fortune—the Queen of Spain had been duped by a two-groschen magician—but she didn't. Still, her ability to trust Lalo confounded her in the wake of Udo's betrayal. She didn't know whom to trust or what to believe anymore, including herself, and in that confusion opened a chink of hope, the possibility that maybe she was wrong about things, maybe something other than her demise awaited her in Madrid.

She recalled how desperate and alone she'd been when the estate turned her out, lying on the longhouse floor, facing a future without a noble lady to protect her. Her dearest wish from that night had been granted, on a scale so grand she'd nearly missed it. The noblest woman in the land had paid a four-man chest of silver and dispatched a small army to collect her. For the first time, Mari dared to hope she could please her new lady, this woman who wanted her, valued her, even if for false reasons. If the Queen wanted prophecies, Mari could dream up prophecies. If the Queen wanted lies, Mari could lie. If it was luck she wanted, luck would find her because now she'd be looking. The longer Mari could keep the deception going, the longer she had to endear herself, prove herself a loyal and worthy companion in her own right.

"I hope I can please her," she said quietly in the dark.

"You will," Lalo muttered from the edge of sleep. "*Buenas noches, damita.*" Little lady.

"*Buenas noches,*" Mari said in a voice brittle and childlike: thin with fear but hardened by determination. She lay on her back and stared, unseeing, at the candlelight playing on the tufted-silk walls. Tomorrow she would enter the service of Her Majesty.

❦

Chapter 4

THE ALCÁZAR

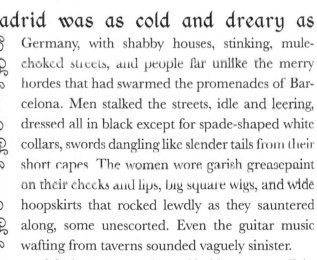

adrid was as cold and dreary as Germany, with shabby houses, stinking, mule-choked streets, and people far unlike the merry hordes that had swarmed the promenades of Barcelona. Men stalked the streets, idle and leering, dressed all in black except for spade-shaped white collars, swords dangling like slender tails from their short capes. The women wore garish greasepaint on their cheeks and lips, big square wigs, and wide hoopskirts that rocked lewdly as they sauntered along, some unescorted. Even the guitar music wafting from taverns sounded vaguely sinister.

Mari was rapt and mortified by a man soliciting a public woman in broad daylight, when Lalo nudged her. "There it is," he said. "*El Alcázar.*"

The Alcázar stood high upon a hill, veiled in haze, looking like a small city itself, a jumble of mismatched towers connected by long galleries.

Mari studied it through her optic tube. Some towers were modern and elegant with delicate spires and French windows; others looked ancient and militarized with their mealy, windowless stonework; others still, with their arched windows and red tile roofs, looked distinctly Spanish and woefully out of place against the cold gray sky. Mari lowered the scope with a pang of dread in her gut. Somewhere inside that rambling fortress the Queen sat, waiting for her.

They reached the hilltop at nightfall, the Alcázar looming colossally against a violet sky. Lalo navigated the coach through a mess of carriages and horsemen—bobbing lanterns and blazing torches, horses snorting and whinnying, Spanish rolling in all directions. He parked near the building, where a portly old woman stood. "*¡Por fin!*" she said, looking as cross as her plump, peachy face allowed.

"Traffic was horrendous," Lalo said in German.

"You knew it would be," she said, taking his language cue.

Dazed by nerves, Mari climbed down from the driver's bench, with Lalo's hand like a vise on her arm. "This is the dwarf," he said.

"I can see that, wiseacre." The woman waved Mari forth. "Come, let me get a look at you."

Mari stepped into the glow of the old frau's lantern. The woman had to be fifty years or more, though her cheeks looked fresh and rosy, and her gray hair was in looped plaits like a ten-year-old milk maiden's. "You stink," she said, wrinkling her nose. She swept her lantern over Mari's bedraggled travel companions. "You all stink. Hurry up and get washed. Don't you dare go near the Queen smelling like that!"

Allowing Mari not a moment to gird herself or say goodbye to her captors, the old frau whisked her into the Alcázar.

They navigated a maze of torchlit corridors, with the woman chattering and Mari struggling to keep pace. "Hurry. We don't have much time to pull you together." Mari caught little else; again she had a sense of not really being here, of watching this from elsewhere. She did catch the frau's name— Binnie—and that she was the assistant mistress of the Queen's bedchamber. "Which means I do everything around here."

They entered a large, humid chamber lit by a raging hearth fire. A copper bath gleamed in the halo of the blaze. Binnie snatched a mitten and pulled a kettle from the flames. "Get undressed," she said, tipping scalding water into the bath. Mari glanced around. A couple of maidservants fussed at the far end of the room. "Don't be shy. I've seen more nude dwarfs than I care to count."

No sooner had Mari's dress hit the floor than the maidservants were upon her, easing her, naked and abashed, into the bath. "Take this stinking rag up to Chita," Binnie told one of them, dangling Mari's week-old dress by the collar. "Tell her we'll be up shortly." She ladled water over Mari's head while Mari stared anxiously at the ceiling: a swirling melodrama of angels, trumpets, flowing robes, and rippled flesh. "They'll have to slap a wig on you," Binnie said, tugging Mari's snarled hair. "Soup starts at eight. We need to have you in your chest by a quarter of."

This jarred Mari to attention. "Chest?"

"You'll be brought to the Queen in a chest."

Mari looked to the door with vague ideas of escape, then realized she was nude, her dress gone.

"Don't worry, it's huge. It'll be a gymnasium for the likes of you." She dried her hands on her apron and went to an armoire chocked with bottles and jars. "They wanted to bury you in a cold pie and serve you to Her Majesty, but you were too late getting here."

"Shame," Mari mumbled.

Binnie returned tubside and uncorked a dark bottle. "Maybe next time." A cold trickle crept over Mari's scalp. The steam swirled with orange blossom perfume.

"How long will I have to be in it?" Mari asked, wincing as Binnie aggressively lathered her scalp.

"Just long enough for them to roll you up the aisle. Then they'll present you to the Queen, and you'll take your place by her side."

"I see. Sort of like a bride."

"Exactly like a bride. But instead of a marriage vow, you'll give her your prophecy."

Mari fell gravely silent, barely aware of Binnie's sloshing and trickling and manhandling, her displeasure about the chest eclipsed by concerns far more grievous. For all her worries this past week, it never crossed her mind that the Queen would expect a prophecy immediately.

She scarcely noticed as they dried her, smeared her with goose grease, misted her with lemon water, and wrapped her in warm linens. Still mute with worry, Mari followed Binnie to the office of doña Conchita Calderon, Mistress of the Wardrobe.

Magnificent chandeliers loomed in the Mistress's chamber, crystals shimmering like melting ice, flames quivering by the thousands. Below, chaos reigned. Maidservants dashed hither and thither with bolts of silk, their candelabras streaking through the stagnant, perfumed air. Seamstresses hunched like witches in ritual, toiling away with hooked fingers, sewing women into gowns so grand Mari wondered how anyone planned on exiting the room. Wigs spanned wider than wearers' shoulders; coils of hair spread out like sausages on a platter, garnished with ribbons, jewels, plumes, and furs. There was even a dwarf dressed like this, primped and fanned by servants, looking as bored and haughty as any tall woman ever looked.

"You're a healthy-sized dwarf," Mistress doña Chita said, peering at Mari over mannish spectacles. Then, to an assistant, "Bring me Inocencia's gown from the King's fiftieth. The Queen is also wearing red tonight."

They denuded her again, this time before the eyes of many. Mari hardly cared as her mind scrabbled for a prophecy, one that couldn't haunt her later by proving false. It had been easier when she and Udo were just passing through towns, never to be seen again. *Don't eat the custard, the eggs were spoiled. Don't eat the fish, you will surely die.* "What are they serving tonight?" she asked.

"The usual holiday fare," Binnie said, and that was that.

They caged her in whalebone hoops and cinched her into a rich red dress trimmed in braids of gold. *Beware the mustacheless man* (there had to be scant few in this country). *Beware of Frenchmen bearing cakes* (there were thousands of foreign tradesmen working in Madrid, she'd been told on the ride in). Now they were coming at her with rouge-dipped fingers, tickling her face with fur brushes. *Beware the red-hatted enemy.* No. Lalo and the other knights would know she was talking about Udo. Maybe she should just say she had no prophecy tonight. No news is good news, she could tell the Queen.

Last came the wig; she swayed under the weight of it.

"Good heavens," Mari said when they paraded her before a mirror. She looked like an angry marionette peeking out of the doorway of a house made of hair. Her cheeks blazed with rouge; her lips had been painted into a tart little sickle of a frown. Her hair spanned beyond her shoulders, curl after sausage-y curl, and a fat white foxtail draped atop, like a slipping mound of cream. Her hips were wider than she was tall. She looked like she should be standing unescorted on a corner down in Madrid. She had to exit the chamber sideways.

After another long, circuitous walk through the corridors, they entered a large chamber cluttered with stage machinery and props, the stuff of serious pageantry: winches and pulleys, painted backcloths, Grecian pillars, an enormous plaster bull on wheels, a treasure ship, a chariot. Workmen hustled about, shouting over the roaring din coming from the next chamber. The jubilee. "How many people?" Mari must have asked. She felt dazed and detached again.

"Fewer than a thousand," someone said.

The chest waited, on wheels, exquisitely carved and inlaid with egg-sized jewels. Binnie hadn't been jesting about the size of it. The front lay open like a drawbridge; Mari walked in and took a seat on a bench. "Good luck!" Binnie said from out of view.

The towering banquet hall doors stood directly ahead. Was it Mari's imagination, or were they actually pulsing? She should have fled from the knights when she had the chance, and there had been a couple of chances. Now the only way out of this was through it—through those quaking doors.

The drawbridge lifted, then a terse slam. Total darkness, latches locking, heart palpitations, nausea. Deep breaths. *Beware the mustacheless man.* That was going to have to be the prophecy. Outside, the workers' shouts intensified before being drowned out by joyous thunder as they opened the great hall doors. The chest jerked into motion.

Horns blared, torturously loudly, on either side of her. She had entered the hall. The cheer surged to deafening heights before collapsing into eerie silence. Blind, sweating, and on the precipice of panic, Mari rolled forth, in a box, to the Queen. The silence was embarrassingly tense: thick as soup, burbling with snorts and coughs, dashed by a whistle. A wheel squeaking below her sounded loud and close, a mouse in her wig.

The chest stopped. There were footfalls nearby, the solemn rhythm of monks ... a male whisper ... someone fiddling with the latches ...

The door fell. Mari winced in the abundant candlelight. Figures swarmed near. As her vision recovered she saw Lalo's face, then the others', her four-man army of captors—protectors—standing in precise formation. She wouldn't have recognized them if she had passed them on the street, so handsome were they with their fresh shaves and clean hair; so dashing in their knights' habits, their puffy sleeves and silk capes, red crosses emblazoned on their hearts; so official, so proper, so serious. They didn't even crack a smile when they saw her dressed like this. It rattled her, tendered her eyeballs with tears. Her amigos were acting like complete strangers, and right now she needed them more than ever.

The knights parted, and there Mari saw them: Their Royal Majesties, Philip and Mariana of Spain. They were unmistakable, seated up front, higher up. The Queen had a huge mushroom-shaped head, a wig like Mari's.

Lalo nodded, stern like a German, and held out his hand. He squeezed hard when she took it, a signal: he was still him, still in there behind the puffy sleeves and straight shiny hair. Tears hung in Mari's eyes as he walked her up to the Queen. Exactly like a bride.

"Your Majesty," he said, "I present your loyal dwarfess, Maribarbola." He bowed to the Queen so chivalrously it sent a chill up Mari's neck.

Mari wasn't sure what to do; Binnie hadn't briefed her on protocol. She dipped at the knees, a twitch of a curtsy, a twitch of a smile, her wicked marionette lips. The Queen lifted Mari's chin with a cool, gentle finger and said, "Heavens, what a face." Then she flung a lick of Spanish into the room, and a low rumble of laughter ensued. She turned to Mari, eyes lit. "You may submit your prophecy."

These proceedings were far more serious than Mari had imagined, Their Majesties' imperial presence so thick she could practically feel it on her skin. Beware the mustacheless man would be wildly inappropriate, she now knew—puerile and ridiculous, perhaps punishably so. She looked out into the room to buy some time. This was a mistake. Hundreds waited in breathless anticipation, unaware of the momentous failure they were about to witness. All those false prophecies she had peppered over the lands were avenging themselves at this very moment. This was God's justice.

She was about to tell the Queen there would be no prophecy tonight, no news was good news, when her eyes chanced upon the King sitting several feet away. In his fallen face, she saw the prophecy. This was God's mercy.

"Let no one unacquainted with sorrow enter here."

Her words vanished in awkward silence. The Queen squinched her brow.

A bellow of laughter exploded from a man nearby, probably a court jester with that floppy scalloped collar. It filled the hall, and the crowd erupted in kind, like a mass tickling. Laughter ripened to applause, cheers, whistles. A mime screwed his knuckles into his eyes, rubbing away invisible tears of sorrow. The Queen nodded. She accepted the prophecy. Lalo said something in the King's ear. He must have translated the prophecy because the King nodded at Mari. Warm heaviness flushed through her body and might have knocked her over if not for her whalebone cage: intense, blissful relief.

She was seated beside the Queen, thankfully too far away for conversation, and they started the snail soup. As her panic receded, Mari noticed she was ravenous. She cleaned her bowl and stared out into the banquet hall, awaiting the next course. By now the prophecy had been translated to Spanish and disseminated to the far corners of the room, and the mood was noticeably less jubilant. Many seemed to be hanging their heads over their soup bowls in sorrow. Melancholy guitar music wafted from the balcony. Maybe it was Mari's imagination, but it seemed like some merry-faced people were being escorted out.

The jester paced and babbled, clearly an idiot, occasionally slinging Spanish at the King and Queen, who ignored him. The next course arrived, a New World maize salad. Amid the swap of dishes Mari stole a glimpse of the Queen. She was a young woman, barely twenty, with dull eyes, a flesh-drip of a nose, and a jutting chin—not at all what Mari had imagined. Rather, the kind of woman Udo would have flirted with out of pity.

Course after course of gastronomic delights were paraded before the King and Queen. Mari devoured every morsel put before her: hare stew with pepper sauce, little pastries stuffed with pork sausage and garlic, knobs of veal fried in fat and sprinkled with cinnamon and sugar. For dessert they rolled out trays of rare fruits, brandy-slicked cakes of flan, fritters oozing with custard, and steaming cups of New World chocolate.

With every lard-laden bite Mari grew more fatigued. She couldn't wait to get this wig off and to go to bed, wherever that was. She had been so besieged by worry this past week, living so fully in the prison of her mind, that with this relief her bodily senses seemed to be avenging their neglect. The candles were legion—bright, hot, perfumy. The noise in the hall had crescendoed to an almost unbearable volume and stayed there. By now the jubilee had recovered its mirth; people were laughing, gesturing hugely, raising their cups. Mari spotted Lalo at a table of beautiful dark-haired women—his wife and four daughters, presumably. She looked down the royal table just in time to see the Queen sip from a tiny red cup and, to Mari's shock, chew off a piece of the rim.

The King was much older than his wife, fair-haired, dressed in black like all men here, with a thick gold chain slung across his breast. He had the longest, saddest face Mari had ever seen, his chin so large and stout it seemed to be pulling down the corners of his eyes.

Beyond him sat a young woman who looked just like the Queen, clearly their daughter. They did have children, Mari knew. She stole another glance at Her Majesty. No, she wasn't old enough to have a grown daughter. It must be her sister.

A change of music drove people from the floor, and dozens of dwarfs came out and danced for the King and Queen. Mari had never seen so many, forty or more, all in rich little clothes, toddling into sloppy figure-eight and cloverleaf formations, charmingly ungraceful and seemingly deaf to the merry flute music that was supposed to be timing their movement. Mari watched, mesmerized (Did she really look like that? Move like that?), as they whirled like tops, or the little wooden people she had once seen on a town hall clock in Switzerland. Some grimaced with the rheumatic pain that she herself knew well. She regarded them with a mixture of pity and envy, though not as brethren. She was not one of them; that was already clear by tonight's seating arrangement. Maribarbola was not here to dance.

The lackluster performance received a raucous ovation, and the dwarfs vanished into a dark arcade.

To thunderous applause, the mime stepped forth, stoking fury in the crowd by wiggling his white-gloved fingers. A dramatic hush fell as he bowed deeply and passionately to the King. In chilling silence, he stood before His Majesty. The King nodded, and the crowd erupted once again.

The mime held up ten fingers. "*¡Diez!*" the crowd shouted. The gloved hands blinked: nine fingers. "*¡Nueve!*" Eight fingers. "*¡Ocho!*"

Exhausted beyond caring, Mari wondered how far past midnight she was going to have to sit here when the buffoon barked in her ear, jolting her. "*¡Id a la reina!*"

She looked at him. "*¿Qué?*"

"*Go!*" he said in German, pointing to the Queen.

"*¡Cinco!*"

Confused, Mari slid off her chair and went to the Queen. Her Majesty watched the revelry, uncannily still and expressionless, doll-like. Her hand on her armrest was little and pretty, her ruby ring bright and glistening like a spot of jam.

"*¡Tres!*"

"*Eure Majestät?*" Mari said. The Queen turned her huge head.

"*¡Dos!*"

The Queen turned up her palm. Mari took the royal hand. It was soft and dry, a little bit cold. Mari prayed for the power to make this work, to please Her Majesty, to give her her four-man chest of silver's worth. Two months of vagrancy had utterly depleted her. She couldn't bear another mile of travel, another night on a truckle bed, another campfire meal, another moment of scraping by, changing hands, being bought and sold, rejected, betrayed, humiliated, shattered. In the Queen's grace was refuge, finally a home. Mari vowed to do whatever it took to stay here, because she'd sooner die than go back out there.

"*¡Uno!*"

Together they passed into the New Year, with the Queen's shy hand squeezing Mari's hard in the final moment, emboldened by a desperation that warmed Mari's heart and made her wonder if maybe the Queen needed her as much she needed the Queen.

"*¡Feliz Año Nuevo!*" The chapel bells gonged. The crowd thundered, drumming cups on tables. Musketeers shot glittering gold flakes from the balconies, showering the court. The music restarted, jollier than ever, and the dwarfs returned for another dance, this time with a few tall drunks in tow.

Mari placed the royal hand back on its armrest. "*Ein glückliches neues Jahr, Eure Majestät,*" she said, wishing the Queen a happy new year in their mother tongue.

"*Auf deine Gesundheit,*" said the Queen, a salute to Mari's health. Mari was heartened by her use of informal address. Maybe this wouldn't be so bad after all. Maybe everything was going to be all ri—

The side of Mari's face bristled, animated by dozens of tiny stings. The buffoon had whipped a fistful of rice at the King and Queen to the vast delight of the crowd. The Queen shook a few grains from her hand and, looking annoyed, raised her cup to the rabid revelers.

Mari looked to see the King's reaction. There was a boy sitting with him who hadn't been there before.

He was clearly a prince, dressed as he was, and seated in a little raised chair beside the King. He looked four or five years old, yet he was already breeched, wearing black like his father, but with a crisp white ruff. With a haughtiness unbecoming a child, he picked a grain of rice from his coat and flicked it out into the dancing dwarfs. He must have felt Mari looking; he turned and smiled sweetly. She smiled back.

To her relief, hornblowers came out and hushed the room, and the King and Queen stood to leave. They bowed to one another, joined hands, and walked out to the din of chafing fabric as the court genuflected en masse. The Queen's sister followed, then the Prince, walking with a confident little strut. Mari watched, vaguely unsettled, as he saluted the guards and strode out the door. So cocksure a lad she had never seen: a child king, bred to rule, already bearing the stamp of a military education, and clearly aware of his eminence, even at his age. He reminded Mari how serious her situation was, she being charged with an impossible task in this place where four-year-olds swaggered like tyrants and executions were ordered with the stroke of a pen.

As Mari had feared, her bedchamber was on the fourth floor of Torre de la Reina, upstairs from the Queen's apartment. "You'll get used to it," Binnie's voice shrilled in the stairwell. "It's good exercise for we old folk."

Mari's chamber was spacious but cozy, lit by twin crystal chandeliers suspended from a ceiling so high it vanished in darkness. A bank of French windows overlooked Madrid, now inky black and dappled with amber torchlight. The previous occupant must have been a child or very small dwarf; the furniture was all in miniature. Two maidservants busied about, drawing drapes and plumping pillows.

Binnie plunked Mari on a bench and removed her wig. "*Gracias a Dios*," Mari said, stretching her neck.

Binnie smiled and dipped a cloth in a pot of goose grease. "You did well tonight. Her Majesty seemed pleased."

"Thanks. It was hard to tell. They're so serious."

"Spanish sovereigns don't laugh in public." She scrubbed the rouge from Mari's cheeks with her usual heavy hand. "The Queen is gayer in private. You'll see."

"So many dwarfs," Mari said. "Two score at least."

"You won't see any in this tower. The Queen doesn't like them sneaking around. You're the exception."

The reminder that she was exceptional—and utterly alone in this—tempered Mari's relief from having had a successful first night. Already the pressure was mounting. "What will I be doing tomorrow?"

"I'll be back in the morning to dress you," Binnie said, toiling with Mari's bodice buttons. "Her Majesty has invited you to breakfast."

"It'll be my pleasure." Her first step in ingratiating herself to the Queen was to make a faultless impression with Her Majesty. "Perhaps you should brief me on protocol beforehand?"

"Dwarfs aren't bound by protocol. They do and say as they please. Be careful with the Queen though. She can be tetchy if you catch her on a bad day."

Mari wasn't too worried. She was nothing if not tactful. "What about the little Prince?" she asked as the arrogant tot swaggered through her memory. "Will he be there?"

Binnie stopped. Her peachy face turned grave. "There is no prince," she said in a prickly tone, as if Mari should have known better. "That's why you were brought here. To bless this marriage with a manchild. Bless Spain with an heir."

"Then who was that boy sitting with the King?"

Binnie's lips scrunched into a disapproving little worm. She resumed unbuttoning, harder and jerkier than before. "That was Nicolas, the King's most treasured fool. He's no prince, though he likes to think he is. And he's no more a boy than I'm a queen."

CŒ№ŋ

Chapter 5

THE KING'S FAVORITE

He was Nicolas Pertusato, Binnie explained the next morning, an Italian nobleman who had come to court with the Queen in 1650. According to legend, Her Majesty had carried him into the Alcázar herself. They had met when Mariana's wedding convoy from Austria passed through Nicolas's hometown in northern Italy. The two were introduced at a comedy, where the young Queen was delighted to learn that he whom she'd mistaken for a four-year-old boy was indeed a gentleman the same age as she. Charmed to heavens, she entered him into her service immediately.

The people of Madrid found him no less charming. Nicolasito, as he was affectionately called, was the most beloved courtier in Spain, more popular than the King even. His appearances drew enormous crowds. Women gushed over the tiny body and handsome little clothes.

Men looked upon him like a red-blooded son. Newssheets and ballads covered him copiously and endearingly. *El Principito España*, they sang—little Prince of Spain. *El Milagrito, el Tesorito*—little miracle, little treasure. A fleshly gem he was, rare even among dwarfs, precious and dazzling, divinely proportioned, the perfect man in miniature. "The Queen's best jewel, they used to call him," Binnie said as her plump, chapped hands cinched Mari into another elegant dwarf dress.

"But now he's the King's dwarf?"

"The King's *Validito*. His little favorite."

"Did something happen between him and the Queen?"

"Something happened, all right. They used to be bosom companions, but now they scarcely acknowledge one another. He used to live right here in your apartment. Then one day he was gone, dismissed from her company with little more than the clothes on his back."

"What did he do to displease her?"

"Good luck finding out," Binnie said. "The Queen's handmaidens from that time are all married and gone, and the Queen herself never speaks of it."

A cloud of worry drifted through Mari's mind. Whatever unspeakable thing he had done, she hoped herself incapable of doing the same. Given the task put upon her, the likelihood of displeasing the Queen was high, and unlike Nicolas, Mari was not so rare a jewel as to not find herself back on the streets (or rotting in an Inquisition dungeon) should she be banished from royal company.

೧೧

Her Majesty sat in her apartment near a bank of frosty French windows, awash in dull winter sunlight. She wore a resplendent dress, with a skirt wide enough to hide two dwarfs comfortably, and a hatched bodice that looked like a gold-dipped waffle. Her dull copper hair was in looped plaits like Binnie's (the wigs were only for special occasions, Mari had been relieved to learn). A lavish banquet decked her table: towers of buns and tartlets, artfully fashioned fruits, jewel-colored jams, a silver carousel of eggcups, a huge roseate pinwheel of meat slices. Several servants stood in wait against the gold-embossed curtains and giltwood serving tables. "Maribarbola," said the Queen, ignoring Binnie's impassioned curtsy, "you haven't been here a day and already you've made the news ballads."

"Your Majesty." Mari sank awkwardly in curtsy, nervous in the Queen's air-altering presence but encouraged by Her Majesty's seeming more relaxed and genial than she had last night.

No sooner had Mari been seated than the Queen dangled a sheet of paper at Binnie. "Sing it to her, Binnie."

With uncharacteristic delicateness, Binnie plucked the paper from the Queen's hands and studied it. She inflated her portly torso and, in a surprisingly tuneful voice, sang:

> *Let no one unacquainted with sorrow enter here*
> *With those words she killed the cheer*
> *But happy folks, ye needn't fret*
> *Plenty of sorrows await you yet*
>
> *Poverty, plague, and crippling taxes*
> *With every year Spain's misery waxes*
> *Industry in ruins, farmlands bare*
> *Thousands mired in hopelessness and despair*
>
> *Portugal claims herself a foreign soil*
> *Catalonia is on the brink of boil*
> *France's power meanwhile grows*
> *And now England, too, has joined our foes*

God preserves us, but only just
As this once-great nation crumbles to dust
With happiness a forlorn treasure
The Queen's old prophet seems sage in measure

With her rich notes still fading in memory, Binnie lowered the paper, her cheeks burning like a rose as she awaited the Queen's comment.

"Put it in the fire," said the Queen, buttering an egg. Mari sat stock-still and silent, wondering if she might eventually be held accountable for national calamities. The Queen laughed, a girlish snort. "Look at Maribarbola's face."

"You'll submit all further prophecies to Her Majesty in private," said a thin, waxen man seated nearby, clearly a German.

"Everardo doesn't see the fun in courting the press," the Queen said.

"Once again we see how even an insignificant remark can be misappropriated as ammunition against the Crown," he said.

"A prophecy is hardly insignificant," said the Queen. Then, to Mari, "Aren't you eating?" Mari made a hasty selection: crescent bun. "Speaking of prophecies, Maribarbola, when might I expec—"

"*Su Majestad.*" A page entered and sank to his knee. Mari blessed the timely interruption. "*Doñas Isabel y Agustina.*"

"Send them in."

Two maidens, barely just women, glided in and presented themselves to the Queen, who proffered a lazy hand and crunched into her toast while they took turns kissing it. They sat on an ornate French bench nearby, their silver skirts incandescing like fish scales and spreading like festival tents. "Did you see the fashion ballad this morning?" one of them asked. She looked the older of the two, very beautiful, with black hair knotted up like braided German bread.

"Chita warned her not to wear that dress," said the Queen.

"Oh, but she got what she wanted," the woman said with relish. "Three verses devoted entirely to her."

"I'm sure being likened to a stuffed chorizo was not what she'd had in mind," the Queen said, and everyone laughed, Mari too. Even Everardo suppressed a grin.

"A stuffed chorizo perched upon a 1630's Andalusian sofa," the younger, frizzy-haired girl said.

"Right," said the Queen, and sipped from her little red cup. Mari waited for her to bite into it, but she didn't. It was a *búcaro*, Binnie had explained, a cup of edible, scented clay that infused the water with fragrance.

"So, Maribarbola," said the Queen, "I was about to ask when I might hear your next pr—" Her gaze landed somewhere near Mari's mangled crescent bun. Any gaiety that had been in her face vanished. Mari's chest clenched in panic. Had she transgressed already?

"What is it?" the Queen said, seemingly to thin air.

Mari turned, and there she saw him: Nicolasito. He had slipped into the chamber like a cat.

"Your Majesty." He bowed at the waist, briefly disappearing below the tabletop. With a tiny hand on his heart, he bowed to Mari. "Maribarbola. My warmest welcome."

Mari sputtered a word of gratitude while trying not to stare. It was difficult.

"May I say," he said, "His Majesty found your prophecy most moving, and most fitting for this court."

"What do you want, Nicolas?" said the Queen.

"The King needs to know if you're available Sunday afternoon to receive the Viceroy of Naples and his wife. He suggests dinner and a comedy at the Buen Retiro."

"Let me guess," said the Queen. "He'll be hunting in the mountains."

"The Guadarrama bear struck again," Nicolas said. "This time it breached a sheepfold and killed the entire flock. His Majesty is determined to end the terror himself."

"Wouldn't that set the newssheets ablaze?" the Queen said. "'Guadarrama bear's reign of terror comes to bloody end via the King's own rifle.'"

"That is of course the point," Nicolas said. "So is that a yes for Sunday?"

The Queen rolled her eyes, nodded. Nicolas bowed swiftly. Mari got a strong whiff of vinegar and roses.

"May I?" he said, plucking a blackberry from the Queen's banquet. Mari watched him, uncomfortably mesmerized. What had been unsettling about him last night was even more so up close, in the unsparing daylight. His graceful, self-assured movement was so unnatural, so inappropriate for his child-sized body, it seemed almost demonic, like a doll bewitched to life and animated with a swordsman's swagger. His cheeks were pallid and babyishly round, and his voice had a stuck quality—stuck in pubescence, stuck in his throat—and a slight echo, as if an even tinier man had fallen down the well of his throat and was calling up from the bottom. He was exquisitely dressed in peacock blue silk, a crisp white ruff, and diamond-crusted slippers that twinkled fiercely with his every step.

"Did you see you got a mention in the fashion ballad?" the frizzy-haired handmaiden asked him.

"I did. The King and I shared a laugh over that this morning."

She made a face. "The King reads the fashion ballad?"

"If that is all, you may leave, Nicolas," said the Queen. "And take the back stairs. They'll be bringing Margarita up any moment."

"As you wish. *Feliz Año Nuevo a todas.*" The handmaidens reciprocated halfheartedly. The Queen crunched into her búcaro. He turned to Mari. "On behalf of His Majesty, *bienvenida.*" He bowed to the Queen and left, his little body striding mannishly out the doors.

"So now he's speaking on the King's behalf?" said the Queen to no one in particular. She wrinkled her nose. "Ugh. Fans please." A servant sprang forth and fanned the air.

"*Vinagrillo* cologne," Binnie explained to Mari. "He bathes in it. I've read he even washes his mouth with it."

"I know for a fact he does," said the Queen. "Who do think leaked that morsel to the newssheets?"

"Who is Margarita?" Mari asked.

"*Infanta* Margarita," Binnie said, scandalized. "Your Princess."

"My daughter," said the Queen. "She's frightened to death of Nicolas." She lowered her voice in earnest. "Children can sense when someone's not right."

"He just walks into your apartment unannounced?" Mari asked.

"Dwarfs aren't bound by protocols," Binnie reminded her. "They go where they please."

"Thanks for reminding me of that perk," said the Queen, punctuated by a click of her búcaro on its saucer. "Maribarbola, Friday night I'm going to send you into the King's bedchamber unannounced to see if he's sleeping alone these days, as he claims to be."

"I beg your pardon?" Mari hoped to God she'd heard that incorrectly.

"Your Majesty," Everardo said, "now is not the time to be playing ga—"

The Queen silenced him with a hand. "She's going."

"What should I say when he asks what I'm doing in there?"

The Queen shrugged. "Tell him you lost your way in this hideous maze."

"Won't he suspect you've sent me?"

"Of course he will."

"She should go in there with a question," the handmaiden with the braided-bread hair said. "That's usually Nicolas's excuse for coming in here, I've noticed."

"Good idea, Isabel," said the Queen. "I know. Ask him why his wife hasn't been out of the Alcázar in over a month now. Ask him when he's going to take his daughter to a magic lantern show, as he's been promising for weeks. Ask him if it's going to be four Saturdays

in a row he breaks her little heart to go hunting for that stupid bear."
She swirled her fragrant búcaro under her nose. "I should send Lalo
up there to kill it. Wouldn't that be funny?"

"Ask him if he'd like a copy of the latest fashion ballad," the
frizzy-haired maiden said—Agustina, Mari deduced. "Or ask him
how he can sit inhumanly still for hours on end. I was watching him
last night. It's astounding."

"That's easy. The man's half dead," said the Queen. Then she
added, "Take it from one who knows" in an evocative tone that
made the ladies giggle and caused Binnie's face to flush like water-
melon. Everardo shook his head.

The Queen sat back and gazed out at Madrid, looking pleased.
"It'll be nice to have a dwarf again," she said, in a mischievous tone
that unsettled Mari. Mischief verging on vengeance.

Chapter 6

THE SECOND PROPHECY

riday evening marked Mari's first full week at court. She supped alone in her apartment on fat white veal and warm buttered rolls, dabbing juice from her lips with a lace bib. Her drapes were open to the night, Madrid glowing with coach lanterns and street fires, the winter wind rattling Mari's delicate French windows. Her apartment, however, was toasty and bright, lit by dozens of fragrant candles and a raging hearth fire whose orange light danced on her gold candelabras and picture frames.

She was happier here than she had ever dared to imagine. The Spaniards had welcomed her, spoiled her. Nary an hour passed that some lovely young lady did not visit to freshen her fire or water basin, or carry her chamber pot away with a warm Spanish smile. Every meal was a sumptuous feast, every dish sweetly dressed, usually fatted and crisped with lard, thickened with cream, or sluiced with syrup. Mari had never slept better in her life, being on the fourth floor of a guarded tower in the capital city of the most militant nation on earth. The few dreams she had were mere recapitulations of what now constituted her normal day: mustachioed hidalgos, grandly dressed women, red-robed priests, dapper dwarfs, dogs in starched ruffs, plum-sized jewels, florid gold furniture, every edge of the Alcázar carved, corniced, gilded, garlanded, or bedizened with cherubs—and pictures, glorious pictures, hanging in frames, woven into tapestries, painted on walls and ceilings, on cabinets and chairs, on trinket boxes and cameos, even tiny, fully rendered pictures painted on walls of rooms inside other pictures.

With all these distractions Mari had thought little of Udo and even now it was less with hatred than a quiet shudder of disgust for the two months she'd spent with him, sleeping in a vehicle, eating off tinplate, washing in a cup, lifting her skirt in thickets, and trying to convince herself that she, noble bred, somehow belonged in Udo's sordid world of charlatans and thieves, drunkards and ruffians, grumpy innkeepers and stinky market folk. In fact now that she was relaxed and thinking clearly, she almost pitied him, his baseness and crookedness, his lack of proper education, his entire sad, itinerant life built on illusion, trickery, and lies.

It was the Countess who was most on her mind these days. The comfort and security of finally having a home again had evoked vivid memories of the lady. On quiet, contemplative evenings such as this, Mari sometimes felt a warm, benevolent presence, as if the lady were here, smiling, approving, perhaps even having machinated this whole thing, Udo and all, from her new celestial vantage of infinite wisdom.

Determined to live out the rest of her years here at the Alcázar (and perhaps be interred, amid the shedding of royal tears, in one of the lavish mausoleums), Mari was hopeful she could make this work. For one, the Queen was busy, verily so, with a thick schedule and an apartment always astir with visitors. If this week were any indication, Mari would be far from the ever-present companion she had imagined herself to be. The Queen had summoned her only twice so far; both visits had been brief and gay, and amid the bustle of servants, holy men and court officials, Mari had found it easy to deflect the Queen's inquiries about her next prophecy. Mari also reasoned that if the Countess's fever-deranged last words had passed for a legitimate prophecy around here, this job might not be so impossible after all, and she was now keeping a sharp lookout for anything cryptic, mystifying, foreboding, or inspiring enough to submit as her next prophecy.

Until then she was committed to proving herself a worthy companion in her own right and had so far presented herself to the Queen as a gentle and merry and most agreeable creature, laughing throatily at the Queen's jests, commiserating when the Queen complained (which was often), and humbling herself by asking for Her Majesty's help with Spanish grammar. Even better, the Queen seemed to have forgotten about sending her into the King's bed-chamber, not mentioning it again, even with some bitter remarks she had made about the King's marital and paternal negligence. Even Nicolas barging into her royal apartment, to confirm Sunday's agenda with the Viceroy of Naples, hadn't jogged her memory.

Her dishes cleared away, Mari had just relaxed by the fire with her Spanish and German Bibles, to study comparatively, when a sharp knock startled her. With cautious hope that it was an unusually late service call, she answered it.

It was Josefina, young page to the Queen. "Her Majesty calls," the girl said. "She told me to tell you to wear soft shoes."

ॐ

The Queen feasted alone in her apartment, her curtains open to the night. "Ah, there you are," she said when Mari moused in. Her table shimmered with candlelight and bright silver domes and dishes, and an exquisite saltcellar, an impish gold monkey balancing a jeweled salt bowl on its shoulder. She conjured a leaf of paper and slapped it on the table. "Here are directions to the King's bedchamber. I drew a map on the back in case you get lost. If anyone asks, tell them you're there on my orders."

Mari considered trying to plead her way out of this but reckoned it was too soon to come off as disobliging. "Just so I'm clear, I'm to walk into his bedroom, see if he's sleeping alone, and walk back out?"

"Yes. And if he's awake, make sure he sees you. Or you know what, if he's asleep, cough or something. Make sure he sees you regardless."

Mari had no intention of rousing the sleeping King. "All right. I'll be back shortly. I hope."

The Queen handed her a dripping candelabrum. "I anxiously await your word."

Mari ran into Binnie in the stairwell. "Where are you going at this hour?" Binnie asked.

Mari trudged past her, sour-faced. "The King's bedroom."

"*Ach. Es tut mir so leid.*" So very sorry.

Courtiers swarmed the Galería del Rey on this Friday night, their jolly Spanish filling the corridor like a deluge of bubbles. Careful not to set anyone ablaze, Mari threaded through the throng of doll-like women in huge wigs and sofa-sized skirts and black-caped gallants bearing slim swords and twirled mustaches. Having been torn only moments ago from her fireside studies, she hardly believed she was having to do this—spy on the King of Spain in his very bed. She'd be mortified if she weren't so annoyed—an annoyance much exacerbated by having to weave through all these tall, elegant, laughing people who, unlike her, probably didn't spend a moment of their lives being made to do things they didn't want to do. She stopped every few yards to squint at the Queen's directions, which saw her past the Royal Chapel, the Throne Room, the Room of Riches, the Hall of Princely Virtue, bringing her to the heavily guarded entrance of Torre Dorada—the Gilded Tower—where the King lived. *"Maribarbola, la profeta de la Reina,"* she said, and the guards parted like a crisp new deck of cards.

She plodded up the tower stairs, grimacing as hot wax dribbled onto her fist. The Flemish hunting tapestry, which the Queen had noted with underlines and exclamation points, undulated softly on a drafty third-floor landing. A guard stood nearby. *"Vengo en servicio de la Reina,"* Mari said, and he opened the door.

She entered a large antechamber with a glossy marble floor and fine pictures in stout gold frames. A pair of carved doors stood unattended. Mari checked the Queen's map and slipped into His Majesty's apartment.

The reception room was richly woodworked and appointed with more exquisite pictures and two enormous crystal chandeliers, looming and shimmering like flaming clouds of ice. A chamberlain tending the hearth didn't see her come in. Visualizing the Queen's map, Mari slinked down the hallway, past the King's breakfast room, his office, library, cabinet room, and—her heart quickening, face already flinching against the writhing tangle of flesh the Queen was expecting her to see—pushed through the doors of the royal bedroom.

A man stood at an armoire, his back to her, definitely not the fair-haired King. The royal bed lay in a dark alcove, blessedly vacant. The man turned. *"Buenas noches,"* Mari said, and hotfooted back out of the apartment.

She strode across the antechamber, impressed by her fortitude, relieved to be returning to the Queen with nothing unseemly to report. She was almost to the stairs when an odd voice spoke: "Maribarbola." Like a tiny man calling up from a well.

She turned to see Nicolas walking toward her, taking tidy little cat steps, wearing a child's lacy white nightgown. He looked like a lad who'd just been scrubbed squeaky clean at the hands of a German hausfrau; his hair was damp, and his cheeks shined like egg-washed bread. "What brings you to Torre Dorada at this hour?" he asked. Mari could smell the *vinagrillo*.

"I came to see the King."

He looked intrigued. "May I ask why?"

She had dreamt up the perfect excuse earlier in the week: "The Queen sent me to bestow good fortune upon him for Sunday."

Nicolas squiggled his brow in confusion.

"The bear hunt?" Mari said.

"Oh, right. How thoughtful of her. And yes, I do recall being told that you're a purveyor of fortune in addition to being a gifted oracle. What a worthy acquisition you are for the unlucky Queen, not to mention this godforsaken country. I'll pray hard for your success."

The Queen's displeasure with him notwithstanding, Mari found him genial and seemingly sincere. "Your prayers are appreciated." They exchanged courtly nods.

"The King is out tonight," he said, "but I'll be sure to tell him of your kindly intentions at the Queen's behest."

"May I know where he is? She might ask."

"She'll ask," he said dryly, and they shared a knowing chuckle at the Queen's expense. It heartened Mari and fomented the hope that maybe she wasn't utterly alone in this—maybe the dwarfs here were in a clandestine alliance, a low-lying parallel society marked by fellowship, favors, and subtle subversion. "Tell her he's at the theater," he said.

"Very well. *Gracias, señor.*"

"*El gusto es mío.*"

They bent necks and parted ways.

ಸಿ

The Queen was having her sweetmeats when Mari returned. "Well?"

Mari hobbled to the table. Her hips and knees weren't made for this kind of running. "He wasn't there."

"Was anyone there?"

"Just a couple of chamberlains."

The Queen pursed her lips and narrowed her eyes, thinking.

"May I?" Mari said, eyeing the plate of sweetmeats and a small opportunity to endear herself to the Queen by appealing to Her Majesty's generosity.

"By all means." She got up and went to the dark windows while Mari helped herself to a jam tart. "Where could he have gone at this hour?"

"He's at the theater," Mari said through a stuffed cheek.

The Queen whirled around, came closer. "What did you say?"

Mari hastened to swallow. "Sorry. He's at the theater."

The dull eyes glinted. The stout jaw hardened. The royal nostrils flared. Panic seized Mari's heart as she realized she'd said something horribly wrong. "Your Majesty, have I said someth—"

The Queen grabbed the plate of sweetmeats and smashed it down. Jam tarts and custard cups jumped and rolled like coins. "Your Majesty, wha—" Mari gasped as the royal hand snatched the monkey saltcellar. "Your Majesty, don't!" She spread her little hands in protest and cringed as the Queen hurled the heavy statue at the French windows. It shattered a pane and fell to the marble floor with a hideous clang. Mari rushed for the door, not waiting to be dismissed. Dwarfs weren't bound by protocol, and there were knives on that table.

Everardo appeared in his nightdress. "What in God's name ...?"

"It's starting again," said the Queen, pacing.

He looked at Mari. "I told her that the King was at the theater," she said.

He gave her an annoyed, reprimanding look. "Leave," he said. Mari gladly left.

৩৫৩

She found Binnie downstairs in the bath chamber, perfuming the Queen's lace. Mari shared every lurid detail: the Queen's face, the rolling sweetmeats, the flying monkey, Everardo in his nightgown. Binnie remained strangely tight-lipped, her ladle dunking and trickling, though she did pause and look when Mari told her about the King being at the theater. When the story ended, she stood and went to the cupboard without a word.

"Don't you find that queer?" Mari said over the clinking bottles. "Why would that set her off?"

Binnie returned tubside with a corked bottle. "You want to know why?" she said quietly. "I'll tell you why." She popped the cork and threw a furtive glance around the chamber. It was late; they were alone. "Let's just say … the King is a *very enthusiastic* supporter of the theater."

Mari knitted her brow. "So?"

"Hm, how shall I put this? The King is … an *ardent admirer* of theater performers."

"All right … ?"

Binnie threw another glance around the chamber and leaned in. "He likes to fornicate with actresses," she said in a harsh whisper.

"Ah … " It all came together like a snowflake.

"I've been here since the '30s," Binnie said. "It's always been a problem. Although I will say Mariana is far less tolerant of his adultery than her predecessor was." The Queen, Mari had already been told, was the King's second wife, hence the vast age difference. "She's much younger than the King's first wife. Immature. Splenetic. Full of resentment."

"Resentful of what?" Mari said. "They don't even live together. He's twice her age. It's not a normal marriage by any means."

"It's a political marriage, an alliance between Spain and Austria. There's a lot more than hurt feelings and wounded pride at stake. His indiscretions can create problems you and I would never dream of. The Queen understands the ramifications better than anyone."

"You mean Juan José?" Mari was talking about General Juan José, the King's illegitimate son from his first marriage, a great warrior and hero to the Spaniards. Lalo had spoken of him often and admiringly on the way here. He had also warned Mari never to speak his name to the Queen.

"Juan José is one of her problems, yes, and certainly not the least of them. The Spaniards worship him like a god, and rightly so. He quashed the Catalan revolt in Barcelona a few years ago, and now he's risking life and limb up in Flanders. It doesn't hurt that he's handsome like his mother." She gave Mari an ominous look. "She was an actress." She stirred the tub like a cauldron of broth, the Queen's handkerchiefs swimming like cabbage leaves. "He's the only bastard the King officially recognizes as his son."

"There are more?"

"There are many. So now you see why the Queen resents his late-night trips to the theater. The last thing she needs is another Juan José to plague her till the end of her days, reminding her how unpopular she is with her people and how vulnerable she'll be after the King dies, especially if she doesn't produce a son before then. You and I plan for tomorrow. These people plan for posterity."

"Why is she unpopular? She's not unlikeable."

"The Spaniards view her as an outsider—a cold German, not particularly loyal to Spain, nor particularly handsome. Their last queen, Isabel, was a great beauty and patriot, a fine Frenchwoman who sold her jewels to finance Spain's wars against her own coun trymen. We had a prince back then, too—Baltasar Carlos was his name, stout-hearted lad he was. Mariana was originally betrothed to him, but he fell ill and died, just as his mother had done two years earlier. The King was destroyed; he still is. All that's left of his former life is his seventeen-year-old daughter, the Infanta Teresa—you saw her; she sat beside him at the jubilee. His ministers persuaded him to wed Mariana himself, to strengthen ties with Austria, and to try for another son. Now the marriage is in its seventh year, and she's yet to give Spain a prince. So you see, she's been nothing but a disappointment so far."

Mari became uneasily silent. Again she was being reminded of why she was brought here, why the Queen had been desperate enough to pay a four-man chest of silver for her—money Spain didn't even have—and how Mari had better get busy reversing the Queen's fortunes.

"And if he is having another affair," Binnie said, "just wait until the gossips and satirists find out. They lick their chops over this sort of thing, not least because it's a chance to humiliate the Queen in the newssheets. But neither is the King immune to their poison pens. Thirty years he's been waging holy war against the Protestants, fighting heresy abroad, sending Spain's sons to die and bankrupting the country. But one need only parade a pretty young actress before his eyes and The Great Defender of the Catholic Faith is no better than the common adulterer soliciting women on the Plaza Mayor. His weakness creates trouble for everyone."

"Nicolas must have known how loaded that remark was," Mari thought aloud.

"No doubt he knew. And now you know he is not to be trusted."

Mari was angry at herself for having been so gullible—and with Udo's betrayal two weeks fresh. She had gotten too comfortable here, too taken in by the Spaniards and their hospitality, their warm smiles and jolly laughter, their guitars and roses and fried foods. Even more unsettling than her credulity was Nicolas's undue hostility toward her and the artfulness with which he had guiled her. Maybe the dwarfs here were the very opposite of gentle and merry. Maybe that low-lying society was not one of fellowship and favors but ruthless rivalry, played out unchecked, far below everyone else's noses.

"Little Prince of Spain my foot," Binnie said, with an angry plunk of her ladle. "Nicolas is a twenty-one-year-old man who can scheme with the best of them. Why do you think the King keeps him so close? It's not because His Majesty likes to play with dolls, I tell you."

"I still don't see what he had to gain by upsetting the Queen."

"It's what all the King's favorites do. You'll see. They keep the King as isolated as possible in order to maintain their tight sphere of influence over him. They all do it—his confessor, his cabinet ministers, and, yes, even his dwarf."

"Isolate him from his own wife?"

"Especially his wife. I told you what a disappointment she's been politically. I'm sure they'd love to get rid of her, but her father is the Holy Roman Emperor, and they wouldn't dare make an enemy out of him. That'd be the end of Spain. This makes Mariana extremely powerful, much to the dismay of the King's advisors. All they can do is try to minimize her influence, which they do by fostering distrust in the marriage. And the King's weak flesh makes it all too easy."

Selfishly, Mari tried to calculate how all of this might affect her and her tenure here. It seemed what the Queen really needed, more than a prophet, was a shrewd political advisor.

"So now you know why you're here," Binnie said, reading her thoughts. "Make her the mother of the future King of Spain, and all of this goes away. Just one prince is all it'll take to silence her naysayers forever."

A picture of Nicolas flashed in Mari's mind—his dimpled smirk, his duping delight. Mari vowed never again to play the dupe. The Legend had taught her better. Moreover, she now understood that there were two types of people in this world—pawns and players—and if she planned to be of use to the Queen, she'd better get on the correct side.

"She'll get her prince," Mari said, staring into the fire.

ೞೞ

She slept horribly that night, in fitful winks, writhing in pain as the Alcázar's miles of corridors and stairs took vengeance on her hips and knees. When the morning chambermaid came, Mari had her summon Binnie, who called a physician. Upon his orders, maidservants pressed packs of snow to Mari's throbbing joints, stopping periodically to pray over her. While their efforts numbed her skin and warmed her heart, they did little for the deep rheumatic pain, which gathered intensity as the day wore on.

All morning Mari lay shivering under the snow packs, watching a glazier dangle outside her window, repairing the Queen's damage from last night. She deliberated on Her Majesty's predicament, the intense pressure to deliver a prince, the quiet desperation she must be feeling. Mari longed to help, and not just to the selfish end of proving her worth and earning her keep. Since her conversation with Binnie last night, she felt more warmly toward the Queen, protective, and already bitterly adversarial toward Her Majesty's enemies. She understood the frustration and rage behind the flying monkey, the Queen's feelings of powerlessness, both in her marriage and at this foreign court. In fact, despite their vast differences in age, status, wealth, and height, Mari and her new lady were kindred in crucial ways. Like the Queen, who'd been a child bride, Mari, too, had been taken from her home at a young age and sent to live with strangers, as property. Both their fates had been sealed at birth, and they'd both been born into lives of extremely limited options.

Recalling the heartwarmingly desperate way the Queen had squeezed her hand as they passed into the New Year, Mari was now convinced that the Queen needed her as much as she needed the Queen, and less for prophecies than for loyalty, sympathy, confederacy, and friendship. With each having what the other needed, together they'd be stronger—symbionts, surviving and thriving as one. What Mari lacked in divine foresight she made up for in cleverness, logic, and reason. A cunning heart and laboratory-trained mind—who better to outfox the Queen's enemies?

Of course, Mari couldn't give her a prince; only the King could do that. To that end, maybe the way forward was to grease the wheels of this rusty marriage …

At midday, Binnie made her swallow a few spoonfuls of chicken custard. In the afternoon a page came bearing well wishes from the Queen—and a cup of strong sherry with orders to drink. Mari choked back what she could and was already tiddly as she flopped back on her pillow.

She woke hours later to what felt like an elephant sitting on her lower half. She had felt this sort of pressure before, but never to this magnitude. It could only mean one thing:

Through the tyranny of pain, a glimmer of opportunity.

A path forward for her and the Queen.

Ill-lit and possibly hazardous, but still, a path.

Dare she?

It was evening; Mari's drapes were drawn, her candles burning, her hearth roaring with fresh logs. Before she could think the better of it, she sat up, still giddy from the sherry, and worked up enough pluck to get across the room and back to ring the servant bell.

The girl-page Josefina answered as Mari was crawling back to bed. "Maribarbola! Why are you out of bed?" She helped her climb back in.

"Where's Binnie?" Mari asked.

"Supping. Should I get her?"

"No. Go to the King."

"*The King?*"

"Tell him to cancel his hunt. There's a great storm coming."

Josefina fled, her footfalls frantic in the stairwell.

Mari wasn't alone a minute when deep regret set in. What if no storm came? What if this joint pressure had to do with Madrid being dry, landlocked, elevated, or whatever? Or maybe it really was the Alcázar's corridors and stairs taking revenge. And she had told the King to cancel his plans! She propped herself up and took a throat-burning gulp of sherry.

She prayed he was the forgiving type. He was, after all, a paragon of Catholicism, militantly devoted to Christ. Of course the Queen wouldn't care one jot if the hunting trip were called off for no reason—she'd love it—but in her recklessness Mari had risked exposing herself as a fraud. Having witnessed Her Majesty's wrath last night, Mari was loath to even imagine how she might react if she found out she'd been duped. Horrors swirled: arrest, imprisonment, banishment. Inquisitors. Death?

Binnie returned with a tray of soup and bread. "Are your ears itching?" she said. "The entire court is talking about you."

Mari pretended to be too groggy to comprehend.

"They're putting the horses in the stables now," Binnie said, stirring the soup. The spoon clinking against the sides of the bowl chafed Mari's raw nerves. "They're going to send couriers down into the city with warning pamphlets. They're printing them as we speak. Residents along the river are being evacuated, His Majesty's orders."

Mari groaned and died inside.

"Poor thing. Get some rest." She left.

Mari lay steeped in pain and worry, angry at herself for adding yet another desperate predicament to the endless string of desperate predicaments that had become her life since the Countess died. She slept thinly, startled awake by every door slamming in the tower, seized by hope that it had been thunder. At dawn she hobbled to her wardrobe, dug out her optic tube, and scoured the sky for signs of a storm. There were none.

She crawled back into bed and contemplated going back to Rottenburg, back to the estate with her tail tucked, begging for shelter and forgiveness, or to her toll collector nephew in Vienna, his hungry children be damned. She received a small salary from the Queen's treasury; she could save for a couple of months and, come spring, if she wasn't rotting in an Inquisition dungeon, slip out through the orchards under the pretense of a stroll. There were plenty of idlers, ruffians, and thieves in Madrid who would put her on a mule for a few coins. She'd be outside the city walls before anyone noticed she was gone.

No. She needed to stop doing this—overthinking, overreacting, fixating on the worst-case scenario—goat logic, Udo had called it, due to her leaping and ruminating. A storm was coming, she could feel it, and if it didn't she would crumple at the Queen's feet and beg for mercy, explain how desperate and penniless she'd been, how lost and alone, how unfit and naïve for the sinister world, how easily swayed by the barest show of kindness, the promise of a mattress and steady meals—and *please* don't put her back out there, please let her stay and prove herself a worthy companion in her own right, a purveyor of warm friendship and humble counsel, or at least keep her on as the type of dwarf that danced jubilees. Mari could live with that. In fact she'd heard it was an endless party over in Torre de Carlos, where the dwarfs and buffoons and low-level staff lived.

Wrung out with worry, she finally slept and didn't hear the chambermaid come in to tend her hearth. She woke late in the morning to a sound so wondrous she'd surely dreamt it: explosive, heart-jarring, chamber-shaking thunder. Had it really been?

She waited. There was a low rumble that might have been thunder or maybe just someone rolling a cart through a corridor deep in the tower.

An ominous girl-voice floated up the stairwell, in German: "*Er kommt.*"

It's coming.

And so it came—not a great storm at first, but enough to make the prophecy true enough. Mari closed her eyes and savored the dense patter of rain hitting the tower, and thanked God. When the storm intensified, hurling violent sprays against her windows, she threw her head back and giggled madly and wondered if maybe she really was a prophet.

It wasn't long before Binnie strode in, looking pleased as a peach, as if she herself had cast the prophecy. "How does it feel to be a celebrity?" she said.

"For this?" Mari said, gesturing to the torrent-streaked windows.

"For saving the King's life. He would've caught the consumption and died or been buried alive up in the mountains."

Mari didn't argue. Binnie asked her what she wanted from the kitchen, anything at all—the Queen would see that it got made. Mari wanted pork sausage empanadas, hot fritters sprinkled with cinnamon and sugar, and a bottle of beer, preferably German.

It was on her bedside table within an hour, German beer and all. By now the rain had turned to sleet; it ticked against the window-panes like grains of rice. Mari stared at the gray windows and ate, unaware of the smug little smile on her face. Afterward, her body coursing with lard and joy, she fell into a deep, dreamless slumber.

She woke to a dozen maidservants in her chamber, cleaning fervently by candlelight. Mari propped herself up. "What's going on?"

Binnie's head popped up from behind a table. "Oh good, you're awake. Her Majesty will be up shortly."

Still groggy from sleep, Mari tried to ascertain whether this was good or bad.

Binnie came forth. "Did you hear me? The Queen is coming. You ought to look more excited than that."

"I'm excited."

"You darn well should be. A *dwarf* receiving the *Queen* in her bed-chamber? This is unheard of!" She ripped the coverlet and linens off Mari's body and took her sweet time replacing them with fresh ones.

Minutes later the Queen swept in, ignoring everyone's solemn curtsies. She wore a wide brown-and-silver brocade dress with a lace capelet, a huge mushroom-head wig, and a rare smile. With a flick of her hand, everyone filed out.

"His Majesty sends his regards," she said, taking a seat on the French bench that had been brought in for this visit. All of Mari's furniture was Nicolas-sized. This was his old room.

"You were with him today?"

"All afternoon." She went on and on about what a gay afternoon they'd had, her gayest in months. The Viceroy and his wife had braved the storm to get here and were dined by the entire royal family. "How charming to see the King dining with his daughters for a change!" the Queen said. Afterward they stood on the royal balcony and beheld the storm, and watched the dwarfs slip and slide on the courtyard and the buffoons carry out a fencing match on the ice. Then they retired to the Salón Grande, where, "Would you believe it? The King summoned the magic lantern people to the Alcázar for a surprise performance! I think he and the Viceroy enjoyed it even more than the little ones did." She chuckled at the fresh memory. "And of course Nicolas was barred from the festivities because Margarita was there. The day could not have been more perfect."

"I'm glad you enjoyed yourself," Mari said, fighting to stay awake, lulled by the rain and gentle thunder, her body heavy with peace and the satisfaction of having not only pulled off a prophecy, but also giving the Queen the small triumph of enjoying, publicly, the King's husbandly affection for a day. Then there was the added sweetness of Nicolas being banned and, Mari liked to imagine, pouting in his apartment all afternoon.

"Oh, by the way," said the Queen, "you'll be getting a twenty-ducat bonus next payday, compliments of the King." Mari's eyes popped open. "Don't worry, I'll wait until it's in your hands before I send you barging into his bedroom again." The afterglow of the fine afternoon faded from her face, and the usual icy glint returned to her eye. "I'm going to have you go later next time, midnight or one."

"Your Majesty. If I may speak."

For a second it seemed like she was going to say no. "You may speak."

"I've been thinking about your situation with the King, and … well, maybe the best course of action would be … inaction."

The Queen grimaced. "What's that supposed to mean?"

"What I mean is, sometimes the best way to secure a man's interest is to feign disinterest." The Countess's maidservants had constantly been cooking up these types of schemes to snare this young man or that. Mari didn't see why it couldn't work with the King. In any case, the Queen had been betrothed as a child and wedded at first bleed. She needed to be told these things.

"Is this your word?" the Queen asked.

"Not a prophecy. Just a humble grain of wisdom, I suppose."

The Queen scrunched her lips to one side and said, "Hm," like she would think about it. Her eyes locked on the near distance, calculating. After a couple of seconds she snapped to and surveyed Mari in all her pitifulness—crippled and buried in snow packs. The Queen smiled uncharacteristically sweetly and swept a gentle hand over Mari's forehead. Mari's flesh tingled at her lady's touch, a glorious Alpine chill, intensified by the snow packs. "Get some rest," said Her Majesty.

Chapter 7

THE SUGGESTION

ith the new year underway, it was back to business at the Alcázar, and securing the Crown's future was a desperate priority. To Mari's squirming discomfort, conversations had turned, with unbridled optimism, to the prospect of having a prince in the Alcázar in a year's time, which was, Mari was too often reminded, her chief reason for being here. To that end, the Queen's favorites gathered in her royal apartment one evening to escort her to Torre Dorada, where she and the King would lie in union for the first time in weeks. Doñas Isabel and Agustina briefed Mari on what to expect from her first coupling ceremony. "It'll be like a wedding," Isabel said, "only much shorter."

"And the bride and groom can't stand each other," Agustina said.

"Then they'll go off alone to his bedchamber," Isabel said.

"And you'll see her back in Torre de la Reina ten minutes later," Agustina said.

Outside, the chapel bells tolled seven. They were supposed to be in the King's reception room right now. "Mari, see what's keeping her," Binnie said.

The Queen sat alone in her bedchamber in an elegant gray satin dress. She had foregone the whalebone hoops tonight, and her body looked shockingly little without them. She cradled a cup in her lap.

"Your Majesty, it's seven."

"I'm almost ready." She swirled the cup too wildly; whatever was in it splashed on her hand. She looked at it for a moment and wiped it on her skirt.

"How much have you had to drink?" Mari asked, getting a whiff of sherry.

The Queen counted silently. "This many cups," she said, with a vague flourish of fingers.

Mari returned to the others. "She's soused as a pickle."

"Ah, fiddle," Binnie said, throwing up her hands. "She was fine twenty minutes ago."

"Can you blame her?" Agustina said. "She's about to go play hot cockles with her fifty-year-old uncle."

"Young lady!" Binnie said. Agustina shrugged.

"Look at Mari's face," Isabel said. "She didn't know."

Mari hadn't known.

"You didn't notice the family resemblance?" Agustina said, tapping her chin.

"The chin," Mari said in a flat, faraway voice. The chin.

"Yes, the chin," Binnie said. "And don't you dare mention it. She fancies herself a beauty."

A sound like crashing pans came from the Queen's bedroom. "*Dios mío,*" Binnie said and rushed into the chamber.

They wended down the tower stairs, the Queen's laughter chiming like Yule bells. She was a merry drunk, and remarkably steady on her feet. "Where's Mari?" she said. "Get me my Mari." Mari was whisked forth to the Queen's side and walked the entire Galería del Rey with the royal hand on her head. Since the storm prophecy, she had become the Queen's bosom favorite. Mari luxuriated in the attention, having just spent two months trying to claw out an existence in a world that cared not whether she were alive or dead, and indeed probably preferred her dead. Likewise, the Queen was as fine a successor as any to the Countess, a worthy receptacle for Mari's loyalty, which flowed forth like an avalanche toward Her Majesty. Being in the company of a lady again—a frosty German, no less, who sometimes reminded Mari of a younger, richer, more tempestuous version of the Countess—started to lift the weight of grief that had never fully unburdened Mari, that mountain of Alpine-snow love, softening and shifting toward the Queen.

The King and his favorites were already assembled in his reception room when the Queen ambled in tardily, petting Mari's head. Mari refused to look at Nicolas, but she could feel his smug amusement emanating like heat from his tiny presence by the King's leg. This was her first time seeing him since he told her the King was at the theater, a lie. The King had been in a meeting with his ministers that night. It had been reported in the newssheets, and the Queen had it confirmed by one of her own sources.

Mari hadn't seen the King since the jubilee; he rarely appeared in public. She had forgotten how long and sorrowful his face was, the downward pull of the chin, evoking thoughts of plunging and despairing. He acknowledged her with a nod. She bent her neck (dwarfs weren't bound by protocol, and the curtsy was hard on her knees). Two paydays had passed since she had saved his life, and she was still waiting on that twenty-ducat bonus.

Everardo, who was actually Padre Juan Everardo Nithard, Father Confessor to Her Majesty, stood in his red priest's coat and matching pie-shaped hat, surrounded by glowing tapers. The King and Queen joined hands before him, and all bowed their heads in prayer.

Although Mari's Spanish was improving quickly, most of the ceremony rolled by her. Everardo crossed the King and Queen, flicked holy water at them, read scripture in Spanish, sang in Latin. This went on for several cycles. The Queen hid her drunkenness impressively.

Mari's gaze drifted to the King's side of the room where his ministers and chamberlains stood, all wearing black like the King. Among them was don Luis de Haro, the King's chief minister, and, as such, a thorn in the Queen's eye. The handsome man beside him, with the silver-streaked hair and dark calculating stare, Mari recognized from his self-portrait in the Hall of Princely Virtue as maestro court painter don Diego Velázquez, whom the Queen also disliked on account of his giving her a fat neck in her official royal portrait. The King's older daughter was also there, the Infanta Teresa, his daughter from his previous life, the one Mari mistook for the Queen's sister at the jubilee. But they weren't sisters; they were cousins. The Queen had spoken bitterly of her as well.

Nicolas stood in front of the Infanta's huge skirt, looking deceptively precious from across the candlelit room. His ruff was enormous, the size of a cheese wheel, and starched and fluted so delicately it looked as though it could shatter. His white-stockinged legs were cute and slender like a child's, and his gem-crusted slippers crackled with color.

Everardo must have said something funny; polite laughter rustled through the chamber (the Queen cackled loudly). Mari watched Nicolas laugh, his cheeks dimpling, little double chin grazing his ruff. For a moment he was that four-year-old prince again, the one who had smiled sweetly at her at the jubilee. Then he shifted his weight mannishly and threw a bored, slightly annoyed glance around the chamber, and Mari was once again unsettled. She would never get used to it, those adult airs and movements in a child's body.

He felt her looking and turned. It was startling and eerie, but she did not flinch, she did not look away. He smiled. Mari nodded, no smile. Everyone else bowed their heads in prayer. Mari and Nicolas kept staring at each other. He was still smiling, but woodenly. A stranger happening upon the scene might have mistaken him for the Infanta's large, expensive doll. Mari narrowed her eyes, a message: she was on to his game. She was ready to play.

He looked away.

Mari's jaw clenched in steely satisfaction. It felt good to have graduated from pawn to player.

And then it was over. Everardo closed his Bible. Their Majesties turned to leave. The King ushered the Queen with a touch to her back. The room was silent, tense. Mari felt it now: the longing, the desperation, the hope so stale it had become a sad lie. Seven years of marriage and still they had no prince. They had palaces, churches, ships, armies, silver mines, mints, even a tiny man who looked like a doll, but they did not have what they needed most—could not get what money couldn't buy. They needed a son. Spain needed an heir. Otherwise this was all for nothing. All of it.

A voice punctured the solemn silence. "Your Majesties." Nicolas's voice, the man in the well. "May I offer a suggestion?"

He spoke in German. This was meant for Mari.

"Since Maribarbola is a purveyor of fortune," he said, "perhaps she, too, should enter the coupling chamber and be present for the conception."

Mari and the King locked gazes in horror.

"Good idea," said the tiddly Queen.

The King said something in Spanish, an objection, no doubt. He and Nicolas had a short, tense conversation. The Queen tried to interject, but they ignored her. Luis de Haro spoke, with a dismissive hand gesture in Mari's direction that made her hopeful he disapproved. Her heart quickened; her ears rang. She became hyperconscious of the hearth—enormous, raging, spewing hell-hot breath, softening her satin dress like lard. Dozens of stares fixed upon her, lit with intrigue and suppressed hilarity, smirks behind mustaches, even some of the priests, and Maestro Velázquez's artist's gaze boring, like a red-hot bodkin, into her very soul.

Then everything seemed to fall out of existence, except for the Queen's pretty little white hand, beckoning. "Mari. Come."

Mari's body did as it was told, an automaton. It went forth. It took the Queen's hand. She was going. Even worse than her murky understanding of the indignities she was about to witness was the unequivocal knowledge that she was still the pawn, still the dupe, and clearly Nicolas's new favorite victim.

"To the future," Nicolas said quietly as they passed. His face floated by Mari's, accompanied by an acid whiff of *vinagrillo*. "God be with you," he said, with relish in his eyes.

Mari floated down the hallway. Surely this wasn't happening; surely it must be a perverted dream. And yet here they were, entering the bedroom as three: uncle, niece, and dwarf.

Inside, Mari scanned the chamber with the desperate calculation of fleeing prey and set upon a chair in the farthest, darkest corner. "No. Here," said the Queen, herding her toward the bed in the alcove. Mari obeyed like a dumb sheep. "Can you make it?" said the Queen. "He can lift you." Mari scrabbled up the side of the bed, clawing the silks, using the fine wood carvings as footholds—whatever it took to avoid the King having to lift her from behind by her soaked armpits, because this was already going to be mortifying enough. She took her place among the gold-broidered pillows, sitting as far from the Queen as possible while still holding her hand, watching all of this from very far away, like from Jupiter, through an optic tube with a filthy lens.

The King, who by virtue of protocol moved as little as possible and had a reputation for being a human statue, now darted around the room with shocking nimbleness, dousing candles like a chamberlain. The Queen giggled at the sight, snorted into her hand. Mari blessed the gathering darkness, her near-total blindness. The King left a single candle burning far away, near the door.

His silhouette floated forth. He paused just long enough to stir hope in Mari's heart. Maybe he wouldn't go through with it. Maybe he would dismiss her, had left that candle by the door to light her way out.

He sat on the bed. Two clunks followed, his boots dropping. He stood up. There was elbow movement, the rustle of fabric, a tiny metal chime. He was undoing his trunks, the King of Spain.

The bed lurched, the feather mattress sighed, the support ropes creaked. Fabric whished—loud, hasty, serious—then an awkward pause, a puff of air, the Queen's skirt probably. The Queen's hand tightened around Mari's. Mari closed her eyes and prayed for a swift conclusion.

ಬಬ

The Queen went unseen for days—a mercy for Mari, who was keen to never have to face her again. Mari slept a lot, ate a lot, studied her Spanish Bible, built a house of cards—simple, wholesome activities to cleanse her mind of the coupling chamber. Nicolas sent a bouquet. His evil knew no bounds. He was like a bored child, but with adult faculties, who had fixed upon Mari as his new toy. And she was powerless against him, he being utterly entrenched here and knowing every machination of the court. Mari's only hope of defense was to learn quickly, rise in the ranks, and help the Queen regain her wifely influence with the King—use Her Majesty as the thin edge of a wedge to get between the King and his manipulators, including Nicolas.

She sat snuggled in a blanket by the windows, gazing out at Madrid, thinking how strange her life had become. She thought a lot about the Countess. Mari was losing her, couldn't quite remember her face, her ways. She was losing all of it—Rottenburg, the estate, the laboratory, Leviticus the Stoat, Karl the Clown. Her mind was too full of fiery jewels and glittering slippers, crystal chandeliers the size of treetops. Memories of her old life couldn't compete with this bombardment of riches, this blinding splendor to which she was rapidly becoming accustomed. Now chairs looked queer if they didn't have little gold faces peeking out of their armrests. Ceilings looked queer if they weren't swirling with angels. Stoat skins were used for wiping mirrors around here; the King and Queen kept elephants and tigers in their menagerie. They had a tower full of real clowns.

She fetched her knapsack to touch the few artifacts left of her previous life, to confirm it hadn't been a decades-long dream. The green dress Udo had bought for her now looked like a pauper's rag, balled up in her knapsack, unworthy of a hook. There was a deck of German cards, some brittle Black Forest pine cones, and the wool finger puppet Udo had procured at one of the Yule markets and sneaked into her pocket as a jest. She had one walnut left, unfinished, the hole unplugged, its edges blackened from Udo's hot bodkin. It was unlike him to be so slipshod, especially in his magic.

Very unlike him, in fact.

Her heart quickened. She turned the walnut in her fingers. "*Dios mío*," she whispered. Could it be?

He had been in her knapsack that final night to steal her purse. Had he made this walnut in haste and thrown it in there, a secret message, hidden from the Spaniards? Did this contain the Legend's last words?

She broke it under a chair leg and, hands shaking, unfurled the scroll.

Queen of Bells.

She flicked it into the fire, shaking off a twinge of embarrassment for having expected it to say *I'm sorry*, or, even more foolish, *I'm coming for you*. Not that she wanted him to. She could never go back out there now knowing what was in here. Like her twelve-year-old self spying Saturn through an optic tube and realizing she'd been theretofore living in blindness, she had undergone another personal renaissance during her time at the Alcázar. Just as her young self had understood she could never return to dolls and needlecraft, Mari now understood she could never return to her former life, that bleak world where there were no cherubs, no pictures, no rooms of riches or halls of princely virtue, no glory or satisfaction like that she had tasted during her short tenure as Maribarbola—and most of all no Queen who needed her, more than Her Majesty knew, and whose icy exterior belied a delicate, desperate soul with royal problems ripe for the solving. In her Mari had found not just a mistress and a home, but, for the first time in her life, a purpose.

༄

She caught up with Lalo for a night of cards. He couldn't believe how far she had come with her game and her Spanish. She told him about the coupling chamber—just enough to convey the horror, no details. Lalo was annoyingly unsympathetic, downright joyful even; she thought his jolly laughter and lewd musings would never cease. When he pressed for details she silenced him with a hand, and he told her she was starting to act like the Queen.

"Of all the people at this court," he said, his face still flushed with cheer, "Nicolas is the last one you should have provoked."

"I did nothing to provoke him."

"You're a threat. Nicolasito isn't used to being thrown into the shade. Your storm prophecy captured the attention of all of Spain. Now everyone's watching to see what Maribarbola is going to do next. And you can bet the King is watching, too."

"I'm sure the King has more important things to worry about."

"You don't understand how desperate he is. This country is falling apart. The Crown is losing its grip. If we don't get a prince in here soon, we'll all be speaking French in twenty years. That storm prophecy was the best thing to happen at this court in a long time. You've done wonders for public morale, not to mention the King's reputation." He was right. Weeks later, the newssheets were still carrying on about how expertly the King had handled the emergency with his warnings and evacuations, and how he'd spared the people of Madrid hundreds of thousands of ducats in property damage and, in some cases, their lives. "You can be sure his ministers are watching you closely now, wondering if we finally have a true prophet in our midst. God knows we've had our share of false ones."

"What do you mean?"

"Every dwarf here was thought to be a prophet at one time or another."

"Even Nicolas?"

"Especially Nicolas. Greatest false prophet of all time."

Mari waited with wide-eyed relish.

"I remember his harvest prophecy most vividly," Lalo said. "He had promised splendid bounty—those were his exact words, delivered to thousands of people on the Plaza Mayor." He tossed a silver *real* into the pot. "Turned out to be Spain's worst drought on record. We all lived on chicken custard that winter, even the King. To this day I can't stand the smell of it."

Mari chuckled with joy. She needed this.

"And then there was his prince prophecy," he said. Mari looked at him quizzically. "Margarita was supposed to have been a boy."

"*Dios mío.*" She didn't know which was more troubling: that Nicolas had had the iron nerve to make that gamble, or that he hadn't suffered any real consequences for making such a hideous blunder.

"Their Majesties were furious. They gave him so many chances. After a while it just became comedy."

Mari wondered if this was the incident that got him banished from the Queen's company, the shattering betrayal Binnie had mentioned. She hoped not. Inevitably she, too, would throw a false prophecy, and unlike Nicolasito, she didn't have the charms or knacks to secure favor elsewhere.

"So now you see why your success rankles him," Lalo said. "Sending you into the coupling chamber wasn't just about making you squirm, although I'm sure he enjoyed that. But now if the Queen doesn't bear a prince, he can accuse you of fraud." That word, spoken in Lalo's voice, landed like a stone in her stomach. She was a fraud. "And if she does have a prince, he can claim credit because it was his idea."

Mari's schadenfreude over Nicolas's failures evaporated. He was even more diabolically clever than she had thought, and court life was going to be more ruthless than she had ever imagined. Any confidence and gameness she'd had was unfounded; she was in over her head. She had thought she could treat the Alcázar like a giant laboratory, where problems could be solved methodically—only instead of larvae and bean sprouts, she'd be dealing with people, feeble-minded people who still believed the sun circled the earth and that women became witches by copulating with the Devil. But Mari's way of thinking had no currency here, she now realized. Courtiers were a different breed, governed not by logic and reason but by power and ambition. They sought not truth or knowledge but royal favor, nobility, tax exemptions, treasured objects, papal forgiveness, and, weirdly, physical proximity to the King. While Mari had been charting stars and dissecting insects, Nicolas had been honing the only skills that mattered here: scheming, manipulating, charming, cajoling, lying, gossiping, backstabbing. She was woefully unprepared for a game she scarcely understood but was being forced to play. There was no winning; that much she knew. The closest thing to winning was to stay and continue playing (and by that measure Nicolas was categorically winning). To lose was to perish from the court and join the ranks of faceless people Binnie whispered about in her cautionary tales, people who had been dismissed, destroyed, exiled, imprisoned, disappeared, disgraced, and banished.

Chapter 8

THE PERFORMANCE

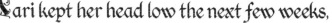ari kept her head low the next few weeks, studying Spanish in her apartment, occasionally surfacing to play cards with the Queen or wander through Torre de la Reina's candlelit corridors, indulging in court gossip with a pleasure and zeal that slightly shamed her, though not enough to stop. With no feasts or coupling ceremonies scheduled, she had been spared exposure to Nicolas except for distant sightings in the Royal Chapel, where the Queen's icy presence (or better, little Margarita's abject horror) repelled him by a wide radius.

"Ladies, I could use a change of air," the Queen announced one Friday morning, having summoned her favorites for breakfast. "Tonight we'll be attending a theater performance at the Buen Retiro."

Agustina perked in her chair. "A machine play?"

"Seven backcloths and a moving ship, I'm told."

The favorites stirred with excitement, Mari included. She had never seen a machine play; the Countess hadn't been a patron of the arts. She would also get to see the Buen Retiro, the King's magnificent leisure palace on the east side of Madrid.

Everardo looked up from the writing desk. "Surely you don't plan on appearing in public unescorted," he said.

"Lalo and Marco will take us," said the Queen. "They're belted knights." She set her búcaro on its saucer with a sharp click. "Problem solved."

"Surely you know that the King is your only worthy escort," Everardo said.

"And surely you know that the King has become quite the hermit in his old age. If I wait for him to take me out, I'll rot within these walls."

"You were just out with him two days ago."

"Lenten Mass at the Escorial. What a gay time that was." The ladies giggled.

"Perhaps Padre Juan and I can talk to His Majes—" Everardo said before she cut him off with her hand.

"You'll do nothing of the sort. I've come to realize that in dealing with the King, the best way to cultivate his interest is to feign disinterest." She threw a conspiratorial glance at Mari. "Let him read about our jaunt in the newssheets tomorrow. That'll get his attention."

Isabel's and Agustina's faces lit with intrigue. Mari pushed a blackberry around her plate. She could feel Everardo's eyes on her. Though pleased Her Majesty had found her advice helpful, Mari hadn't anticipated the Queen being like wax in her hands, or that the Queen might lack the womanly wiles to carry out Mari's plan subtly and effectively and without involving the newssheets, or that such antics might furrow the foreheads of the Queen's more legitimate handlers.

"Such games are beneath the dignity of your Crown," Everardo said.

"Having you and Padre Juan beg him to spend time with me would be beneath the dignity of any woman. Right, ladies?" All nodded vehemently, even the banquet maidens.

"Your Majesty," he said, struggling to contain his prickliness, "may I remind you we're talking about the most exalted man in the Western World and not some distracted schoolboy?"

The Queen threw her head back and chuckled loudly. "Ah, Padre, you are a wit." She nodded to the banquet maidens, who scurried forth and cleared her plates. "So then. You ladies have all day to make yourselves fashion ballad-worthy. You too, Mari. You've been tucked away for far too long. It's time the public feasts its eyes on the illustrious Maribarbola."

ૹૹ

Mari spent the entire day in the wardrobe chamber getting fitted for a dress that was to be, per the Queen, a precise replica of Her Majesty's, and thus had to be remade every time the Queen changed her mind about what to wear. Now girded and cinched into a whalebone cage draped with yards of heavy crimson brocade and trimmed in snowy white ostrich feathers that kept flying into her nostrils and getting stuck on her waxy red lips, Mari stood exhausted, sore, and irritable on the Queen's chilly wet plaza, wondering how her already tortured neck was supposed to hold up this wig for several more hours.

A thin crowd had come out to enjoy the cold drizzle and fog creeping down from the Sierra de Guadarrama. Plaza vendors set the night aglow with cookfires, sweetening the fog with caramel and cinnamon aromas. Chico the idiot buffoon was out, pacing the slick stones and clutching his pinwheel—the fool's wand—while a merry horde of Torre de Carlos dwarfs scattered over the plaza in search of sweetmeats, gossip, and petty amusements. Mari nodded to them, exchanging sororal smiles with a few of the women. All other contact was forbidden. The Queen didn't need them infiltrating her inner circle, reporting her every word and deed back to the King or, God forbid, the newssheets.

Anxiety rose in Mari's breast as Lalo and Marco wrestled the Queen's hoops through the coach door. Mari hadn't stepped foot outside the Alcázar since she arrived six weeks ago. Some courtiers hadn't been outside in years, and she was beginning to understand why. From up here, behind tower windows, Madrid seemed like just another of the King's fine pictures. But now they were going down there—into the cesspit, the Queen called it, with the prostitutes and thieves and baseborn rabble, the Queen called them—while the gossips and satirists lay in wait, poison pens dipped, eager to get their first look at the illustrious stormseer Maribarbola, who, in her feathers and greasepaint and garish red brocades, looked like a dwarf version of the unpopular Queen.

Nor had Binnie helped Mari's nerves. All afternoon she'd gone on about the Queen's arrogance and brazenness for appearing in public unescorted, and dressed like a harlot on a Lenten Friday, and no wonder she was so disliked, more than she would ever know, as the most scathing ballads and cartoons were dutifully banished to the nearest fire before her royal gaze chanced upon them. "Who the devil is advising her?" she had said at one point, and Mari had fallen silent.

Marco stuffed Agustina's skirt into the coach. "I have a bad feeling about this," Mari muttered as Lalo took her elbow.

"Is that a prophecy?" the Queen's muffled voice called out from deep within the tufted-silk interior. She had very keen ears, Mari had noticed.

Lalo herded her up the steps. "Just relax and have a good time." He stuffed her into the coach and practically slammed the door on her rear-end.

After an intensely cramped ride through the choked streets of Madrid, they parted the thick Friday-night crowd at the Buen Retiro Theater, with Mari grateful for her companions' billowing skirts, which hid her like a bug inside a great blooming flower. She could see little beyond the Queen's tawdry red dress (Binnie was right, not a good choice), but she could hear the whisper of chafing fabric as people bowed and curtsied en masse, and cheers and whistles and even a tiddly catcall, to which the Queen rolled off a retort in Spanish, filling the lobby with laughter.

Once seated, Mari was able to relax in the dark safety of the royal box and admire the King's theater from the balcony. Chandeliers hung from the great black void of a ceiling, throwing their ochre glow onto the stage, a stately marble façade of columns and arches garlanded with stone fruits and cherub faces. Candlelit theater boxes lined the walls like jewel chests stacked on shelves in a fancy shop, with tiny people sitting inside. The crowd on the main floor was mostly men, a swarming pool of black wool, white collars, and bald patches, with just a few women in the women's section, *la cazuela*, the Spaniards called it—the stew pan.

Mari was wishing she'd brought her optic tube when she thought she caught a whiff of *vinagrillo*. With horror in her heart, she turned to the Queen, her wig wobbling violently. The royal nose twitched.

No sooner had Mari parted her lips to speak than Nicolas appeared, bending to the Queen. "Your Majesty!" he said. "To what do we owe this pleasure?"

"Are you suggesting I should be required to explain my presence?"

"Of course not!" Mari had never seen him so jolly. As penance, he lifted the royal hand from its armrest and kissed the Queen's glove. "Maribarbola. Lovely as always." He lifted Mari's hand, her first occasion to touch him. His tiny hand was precious and tender, his kiss like a dewdrop on her glove. Satan's cherub. Mari managed a courtly nod, knowing the barest show of hostility would be deadly. She needed to impress nothing upon him whatsoever.

He bowed to Isabel and Agustina. "You all look ravishing," he said, with a flicker of enjoyment as his gaze swept Mari and the Queen in their feathers and sausage curls and red tent dresses.

Truth be told, he looked lovelier than all of them, even Isabel. He was dressed most tastefully, most Lent-appropriate in his deep violet doublet and thin, crispy ruff that looked like a giant Eucharist wafer.

"Are you here alone?" the Queen asked.

"No, I'm with the lovely Maria Montalvo." He gestured toward a young woman in a box across the way. "You might remember her as Helena in last summer's comedy on the lake?"

"Vaguely," said the Queen, throwing an acid glance at the woman.

"I was just speaking with one of your admirers down there," Nicolas said. "The Marquis of Villamirada is most eager to meet you. I told him I'd see if I could arrange it."

"Not tonight," said the Queen, fanning herself.

"As you wish." He waved to a man down on the floor, a gentleman of around five-and-twenty, with pale skin and raven hair, devastatingly handsome. Agustina even let out a little gasp. "I should try to crush him gently," Nicolas said.

But one look at the man was all it had taken to change the Queen's mind. "Tell him we'll receive him up here after the performance," she said. Isabel and Agustina stirred with coquettish excitement.

"He'll be overjoyed," Nicolas said.

"How is the King spending his evening?" the Queen asked, stealing another look at the Marquis of Villamirada.

"He's taking his art lesson with Maestro Velázquez," Nicolas said.

"He's still on that, is he?" said the Queen.

"Yes, and an obedient pupil he is. The Maestro had him sketching a plate of chicken gizzards when I left." They all chuckled at the King's expense, with the Queen taking care to hide behind her fan, so as not to be seen laughing in public. "Imagine," Nicolas said, "the most exalted man in the Western World, sketching a plate of chicken gizzards." He laughed heartily, cheeks plump with mirth, while the rest of them fell into frosty silence. Mari knew they all had to be thinking the same thing: either he had used Everardo's exact words by sheer coincidence, or he'd been listening to their conversation this morning.

"Well then," he said, picking a feather from his sleeve, "I'll give the Marquis the good news. Your Majesty, ladies, enjoy your evening. This performance should be quite the spectacle, I'm told." He bowed cleanly at the waist and vanished like a sprite.

"He's in a good mood," the Queen said suspiciously.

"Do you think he was spying on us this morning?" Mari asked.

"I don't know."

Moments later he appeared down on the main floor, marching in his virile little strut toward the Marquis, speed lifting his hair, leaving a trail of delighted faces in his wake. The Marquis bent low so Nicolas could speak in his ear, and, looking pleased, righted himself and bent afresh for the Queen. She nodded coolly.

Ushers doused the candles. People took their seats. Agustina leaned over and asked, "Remember when Nicolas appeared onstage as Cupid in that loincloth?"

The Queen's tart cackle filled the theater. Every head turned as she raised her fan to her face, much too late. She cursed quietly. That would definitely be in the newssheets tomorrow.

Clearly pleased to hear the Queen's laughter, the Marquis sent a dashing smile up to the royal box. "*Dios mío*," Isabel whispered. Mari had been thinking the same. So fine a man she'd never seen. Though there was something odd about him, she wasn't sure what.

As the darkness thickened, so did the silence and anticipation. Men lit the stage with silver lamps and wax torches. Under the cover of darkness, Mari rested her wig against her seatback and surrendered to the enchantment of the torchlit stage, its great crimson curtain rippling with secrets. She was glad she came. It felt good to be out of the Alcázar for a change.

As the silence became unbearably thick and tense and the red curtain heaved its last rippling sigh before disappearing, it dawned on Mari what was odd about the Marquis: "Beware the mustache-less man," she whispered in the dark, just to be funny.

"*Shh.*" The Queen.

The curtain rose on a guitar ensemble, whose long, somber melody nearly lulled Mari to sleep. Finally they disbanded, revealing a table with what was clearly a man lying upon it, covered in cloth. Mari thought little of it, figuring the story began with a death, a tale of vengeance perhaps. Then she noticed the drainage tube, the kind doctors used to bleed patients, and figured the play was about a physician, a plague drama perhaps. She wondered how and when the seven backcloths and the moving ship were supposed to come in, because right now there was none of that. There was only the table.

When two men came out and introduced themselves as the lector and incisor, a flutter of panic teased Mari's heart, because she realized they'd made a very foolish mistake coming here tonight—Nicolas *had* been listening this morning, and this would be a special performance just for the Queen, compliments of the King and his ministers.

"What play is this again?" Isabel whispered.

The Queen shrugged, shaking her head.

"This isn't a play," Mari whispered. "It's an anatomy dissection." The Countess had always wanted to travel to Italy to see one of these. Public dissections were popular in Italy.

"A what?" the Queen whispered.

But it became clear once they folded back the cloth on the cadaver, a freshly executed criminal, and promised a most fruitful excavation of the bodily cavities, a dizzying array of parts, and invited all those present to witness the glory of God in the human entrails.

So began four hours of slicing, flaying, snipping, sawing, and copious lecturing, with guitar players tickling out macabre melodies at apropos moments. Mari watched with an admixture of fascination and dread as they unraveled the bowels and stretched them twenty-two feet across the stage and slashed the stomach to determine the prisoner's last meal (bread and fish). She dared glimpse the Queen only once, when the incisor walked to the front of the stage and raised the heart to the royal box, where Her Majesty sat simmering with quiet rage, no doubt trying to calculate the political damage she would suffer for having attended this gruesome event. Mari prayed she herself would not bear any blame in the matter, her advice having prompted this outing in the first place.

She nodded off near the end, during a long-winded discussion of the bodily humors, and woke to hearty applause and the Queen saying, "Wake up, we're leaving."

Groggy and stiff, she struggled to keep pace as the furious Queen made a charge for the exit. Not a word was said about the Marquis of Villamirada, who'd been forgotten even before the incisor had made his first slice.

୧୧❋୨ୡ

Chapter 9

THE MARQUIS OF VILLAMIRADA

"**Mariana Takes Her Pleasure in Four-Hour** Medley of Horrors" was one of many damning headlines the next morning, as newswriters and satirists took their own rabid pleasure in exposing the Queen's taste for the macabre. In addition to her grisly appetites, the Queen was savaged for appearing unescorted in public, laughing in public, shedding feathers all over the public, and holding up traffic on the Calle Mayor, unforgivably delaying the bullfight. In a ballad that could not have pleased the King and his ministers, one acid-witted rhymester politicized the folly by suggesting the gore-loving Queen take her next holiday up in Flanders, where rivers ran red with Spanish blood and the streets were littered with the body parts of her countrymen.

"That ought to teach her to play with fire," Binnie said, tossing a wad of newssheets into the crackling hearth.

"It ought to," Mari said, but by now she suspected that the Queen was deaf to public opinion and had political instincts about as sharp as a spoon, which boded ill for Mari, she being tasked with reversing the Queen's political fortunes. This of course was in addition to Mari's being a false prophet, and the alleged barrenness of the Queen's womb, and the explicit antagonism coming from the King's ministers, and Mari's wholly unsolicited, undeserved feud with Nicolas, which had kept her awake last night, enumerating the many ways he could destroy her, knowing it wouldn't be that hard if he really wanted to.

At midday the Queen summoned. With trepidation Mari entered the royal apartment and was relieved to see Isabel and Agustina had been called as well. "I had horrid dreams last night," Isabel was saying. "I still couldn't eat this morning."

"At least you didn't have to spend your morning being lectured to by Everardo," said the Queen, gesturing for Mari to sit. She seemed relaxed and cheerful, even from behind a litter of newssheets.

"Has the King said anything?" Mari asked.

"He sent his regards," said the Queen. "And this." She snatched a paper from the table and held it up. It was the King's sketch, the chicken gizzards.

"He's actually a very good artist," Agustina said, tilting her head. The Queen shot her a look and slapped the paper back down.

"Your Majesty," Mari said, scanning the chamber, "we should be careful about what we say from now on." She herself had been chasing shadows in her apartment all morning, her nostrils fanned for *vinagrillo*.

"Mari's right," said the Queen. "We can never know when"— she raised her voice to the room—"the King's little footlicker is in here listening." She nodded to Mari. "And we must also heed Mari's word, always, especially when she says she has a bad feeling about something. That is, after all, the reason she's here."

Mari had forgotten about the remark she'd made to Lalo last night, when she'd been anxious about leaving the Alcázar. She gave the Queen her wise old prophet's nod, solemn and portentous, while inwardly she cheered the lucky coincidence.

"But enough about that," said the Queen. She swept a letter off the table and fanned herself with it teasingly. "Guess who called this morning."

"The Marquis?" Agustina said.

The Queen grinned and allowed everyone's excitement to bloom before she continued. "He's deeply disappointed by not having received his royal audience last night. He was hoping to talk to me about his charity."

"He has a charity?" Isabel asked.

"A children's charity," said the Queen, and watched them swoon with delight.

"Is he married?" Agustina asked.

"No."

Their excitement quickly devolved to girlish silliness. Even Mari was caught up in it.

"So, I've been thinking," said the Queen, "and I've invited him here tonight to see if he's a fit match for Isabel."

"Your Majesty!" Isabel shrieked, somewhat in horror.

"What? You're nearly sixteen. It's high time you wed." She relished their reactions from behind her búcaro—the blushing, the giggling, fanning one another in jest. "We'll receive him here at eight o'clock, nothing formal, just wine and biscuits. Agustina and Mari will be on hand to keep things gay. If you approve of him, and he of you, I'll speak to your father."

"The Honorable Marquesa de Villamirada," Mari said, bending her neck to Isabel. "Where is Villamirada?"

"Damned if I know," said the Queen.

❧

The Marquis disappointed no one when he called that evening; in fact, he was even handsomer up close, luminously pale, with shiny black hair and honey-brown eyes that reminded Mari of the Queen's tortoiseshell toilet cabinet from Paris. After allowing him to admire moonlit Madrid from her tower windows, the Queen invited him to sit on the sofa beside her, where she banqueted him with tarts and puffs, rare fruits, and sweet red wine.

"Refresh my memory as to the whereabouts of Villamirada," she said, accepting a dainty silver goblet from one of the inordinate number of banquet maidens on hand for this informal visit.

"I found myself saying the same thing to someone only recently," said the Marquis, and the room tinkled with feminine laughter. Mari had liked him instantly and found him charming, well-mannered, and just the right amount of jolly. "It's a tiny mountain province in the northeast, near the Catalonian border."

"Be careful up there," said the Queen. "The Catalans are reverting to their savage ways. It's only a matter of time before the entire region erupts."

"They're getting bolder, no doubt," said the Marquis.

"Are you far from Berga?" the Queen asked. The town of Berga had dominated the newssheets this week after an Inquisition raid on a humble mountain villa turned up a massive arms cache, all French made. The homeowner and his wife were tortured and executed on the spot.

"About a day's travel," he said. "Truth be told, I haven't been back there in a couple of years now." He explained that he was Marquis of Villamirada in name only, and that his mother and sisters were still there to handle the occasional petty official matter. He had assumed the marquisate at nineteen after his father died, for no better reason than none of his brothers had wanted it. Now he spent most of his time in Madrid. "Nothing against goats, but I much prefer the company of people."

This got them talking about Madrid's cultural scene—operas, comedies, poetry jousts, bullfights, and cane-tourneys—the Marquis enjoyed it all. The Queen did most of the talking; Isabel was mute, even Agustina was acting bashful, and Mari was content to just sit back and enjoy the view.

Conversation turned to last night's spectacle at the Buen Retiro. "And what did Her Majesty think of the performance?" he asked the Queen playfully, and most daringly. He had to have seen the news-sheets this morning.

Her response—a stony glare—drew chuckles from all around the room.

"I found it fascinating," said the Marquis. "Especially the part on bodily humors." This got him on the topic of his nonexistent mustache, almost unheard of for a Spaniard, which he attributed to a humor imbalance. "Too much blood and not enough bile," he explained to the rapt room.

"I'm sure your bodily composition is quite satisfactory," said the Queen, to a chorus of approving laughter.

But he continued to speak at great length about his mustache: the patchy growth he achieved if he stopped shaving, how it actually looked worse than nothing at all, the remedies he'd tried, the ridicule he'd suffered as a young man, the waiting and praying, even a desperate consultation with a witch, and how he ultimately made peace with that which was not there.

"Present in its absence," said the Queen, in a bored and rather conclusive tone. She didn't like it when people carried on about themselves. A brief, melancholy silence drifted through the room. "You wished to speak to me about your charity?"

"If I may." He spoke at great length again, this time about his charity: the mouths they'd fed, the backs they'd clothed, the staggering number of orphans in Madrid, starving and shivering in the shadow of the Alcázar, his deep moral and spiritual obligation to help the least fortunate among us, his begging missions and fund drives, as well as future plans and revenue goals. "So any support you could lend would be most humbly and gratefully accepted," he told the Queen, whose eyes had glazed over with boredom. "And it doesn't have to be monetary support either. For example, Nicolas has offered to make an appearance at our upcoming bread drive for the children of San Balbina."

This roused the Queen from her bored stupor. "Nicolas Pertusato? Really?"

"Yes, and he's promised unprecedented donations and press reportage. We're confident he'll deliver." He smiled fondly. "Indeed, is there a person alive who cannot be warmed to generosity by the charms of Nicolasito?"

"Indeed," said the Queen tartly, but so delighted was the Marquis with his thoughts of Nicolas that he didn't notice her sarcasm.

The Queen set her goblet down with an authoritative chink.

Clearly unwilling to be outdone by Nicolas, especially in matters of goodwill and moral uprightness, she pulled a ring from her finger and offered it to the Marquis. It was a lovely piece, one of Mari's favorites, a tiny gold cornucopia spilling a riot of jewels of every known type.

"Your Majesty," he said breathlessly.

"Take this jewel to the broker on the Puerta del Sol," she said. "Be sure to tell him who gave it to you. Use the money to buy meat and fruit for the children of San Balbina, lest they should tire of Nicolas's bread."

The Marquis clutched the ring to his heart and bowed deeply. Then, in a shockingly bold gesture, he lifted the royal hand to his lips and planted a lengthy kiss on the newly bare finger. "Your generosity befits your rank," he said softly. "And your beauty." Mari's eyes stretched in disbelief as he helped himself, flagrantly, to a heaping eyeful of the royal bosom.

The Queen dismissed him soon after, fanning herself as her cool gaze followed him out the door. Whether or not she found him a fit match for Isabel, Her Majesty never did say.

⟨✤⟩

Chapter 10

THE THIRD PROPHECY

The San Balbina orphans would eat like
kings for months. Mari had to read all about the
historic bread drive in the newssheets. "Nicolasito
Leads Charge against Hunger" one headline read,
with a cartoon of Nicolas riding a loaf of bread like
a horse, his sword raised in the fight against hunger. "Three Feet Tall, Heart of a Giant," another
read, in a sixteen-page booklet that recounted the
event in exhaustive detail: Nicolas arrived to a
packed plaza and a rabid welcome. The fashion
ballad lauded his tasteful decision to forgo the fine
silks and gem-crusted slippers in favor of simple
black wool and Italian leather boots. He began by
reading a statement from His Majesty, who issued
his heartfelt regrets for not being there, and led the
masses in prayer. Then, to the delight of all, he
donned a baker's cap and crisp little white apron
and spent several hours collecting bread with his

own precious hands—and live chickens, a swine, sacs of beans and grain heavier than he, sugar, potatoes, blankets and coats, socks and shoes, toys and games, firewood, candles, and upward of a thousand ducats in cash.

The Queen's donation got lost in the plenty, but the Marquis did thank her publicly for her generosity in a brief quote at the bottom of an obscure gazette, in a sentence that managed to get smudged by the printing press. However slim, the favorable reportage was encouraging for the Queen, who recognized an opportunity to refurbish her reputation. So the Marquis was back tonight, in the Queen's apartment, enjoying a lavish dinner with her and her advisors, to discuss her involvement in future charitable efforts.

Having supped alone in her apartment on *pescado frito*, Mari sat with a cup of chocolate by the windows, gazing at the stars, trying to remember their names—even if these days she scarcely remembered her own. Maria-Barbara. Haunsin. *Deutsche.* Dwarfess of Walther. That person she'd been before she became Udo's prophet, before she became Maribarbola of Spain. The person who had lived in solid comfort and quiet dignity and never dreamed she'd be forced to live a life of deception, be forced to play or perish. She was transmuting into someone else, the court player version of herself, who at times felt like an impostor and other times felt more genuinely her than she'd ever felt in her life. And darkly fascinating was how swiftly and thoroughly this new self was supplanting the old. She rolled her r's even in German now, and her face was fat and rosy from her new diet of lard and spice. Instead of science and astronomy pamphlets, she scoured the gossip sheets, relishing the tawdry ballads and cartoons. Whereas before she'd been motivated by curiosity and a respect for knowledge, the main thing driving her now was her ambition to stay here, and she lay awake nights trying to figure out how to do just that, how to help the Queen while minimizing her own exposure to Nicolas. Rather than facts and data, she found herself increasingly reliant on intuition, assumptions, gossip, and lies. The only use her optic tube ever got these days was to observe the King's late-night comings and goings at the Queen's behest. The Countess would be scandalized.

A strand of the Marquis's witty banter leached through the floor, followed by the Queen's shrill laughter. Mari was grateful for him; he'd been an unexpected boon during an otherwise troubling couple of weeks. By now the storm prophecy had faded from the Queen's memory, and she was pestering Mari for the next one. To that end, the Marquis was a blessed distraction of Her Majesty's attention while Mari fretted over what to do next.

The anatomy dissection had shaken Mari, and not because of the gore. What had clearly been meant as a harmless (and admittedly impressive) prank on the part of the King and his ministers betrayed something far more sinister. The coup had been chilling in its efficacy and threw into stark light the kind of organized ruthlessness the Queen was up against. In their arsenal they had Nicolas, whose talents for intrigue were painfully evident; they had the absolute power of His Majesty, who had likely usurped the theater performance with a scribbled note, and the Inquisition, who had likely supplied the corpse and—Mari shuddered to think—might have executed the man expressly for the occasion. Mari's original plan to have the Queen play coy with the King was, she now realized, woefully inadequate—a milkmaid's game, played against actual military commanders. These men were indomitable. They feared nothing under the heavens, and half the earth was their domain.

Mari's breath caught in her throat. Thrill spread like heat through her chest. Her gaze slid across the night sky.

They feared nothing *under* the heavens. But the heavens were Mari's domain.

She dashed to her wardrobe and fetched the box containing her optic tube. Heart pounding, she opened it in the firelight. Papers lined the box, ledger pages spattered with the Countess's notes and calculations, diagrams of star constellations, planets, orbits. Mari found the page she was looking for and unfolded it:

29 September 1651 — Penumbra

25 März 1652 — Partielle

17 September 1652 — Partielle

14 März 1653 — Totale

7 September 1653 — Totale

3 März 1654 — Partielle

27 August 1654 — Partielle

20 Februar 1655 — Penumbra

18 Juli 1655 — Penumbra

The dates went back nearly a decade and extended well into the next. The lady had become uncannily skilled in forecasting lunar eclipses, some down to the hour. Mari could see her perfectly now, she could hear her voice, droning on about cone shadows, draconic months, ecliptic planes. What she wouldn't give to hear that mind-numbing lecture one more time, stand outside in her nightgown one more time and see her lady puffed up with pride over the red disc in the sky, as if she, not God, had put it there.

Mari stared at the data, lips pursed and nostrils flared, fiendishly pleased for having remembered in time. "Play or perish," she said in a silky voice, with a rolled r.

A total eclipse stood weeks away.

ॐ

The timing of the March coupling ceremony could not have been better. It would provide a perfect forum for delivering the prophecy, solemn and spiritual, with both Their Majesties present.

Mari stood among the Queen's favorites in the King's reception room, barely conscious of Everardo's praying and singing and holy water flicking. They were near the end; she'd have to act soon but found herself paralyzed with trepidation. There were a lot of people here tonight, especially on the King's side. His officers and chamberlains formed a black woolen mass several men deep, with Nicolas nestled therein, shining like a coin in his gold-broidered vest and puffy little satin trunks. The King's older daughter Teresa was there, and Maestro Velázquez, his artist's gaze roving and probing, that soul-piercing, truth-seeing gaze that threatened to land on Mari and see her squarely for the fraud she was. Waiting until they got back to Torre de la Reina was an option, but Mari would hate to waste this prophecy on the Queen's ears alone.

No. She had to do this, not for herself but for the Queen, whose enemies were all conveniently amassed on the other side of the room. These men who antagonized her for sport were long overdue for a jolt. Mari wanted to put their teeth on edge, put the weight of worry in their hearts for once, allow them to witness firsthand what unearthly powers lurked in Torre de la Reina. They had their cunning and games and political influence, but the Queen had something incalculably more valuable: a True Prophet.

Everardo raised the holy cup. It was now or never.

Mari swayed in place and slumped to the floor like a noodle, using Agustina's hoopskirt to break her fall. Feminine gasps whooped through the Queen's side of the room. The King's side broke into baritone murmurs.

"*¿Qué ha pasado?*" Everardo said in his German accent.

"*No sé.*" A female hand touched her forehead, cool and gentle.

"*Se ha desmayado*"—she fainted. This was Agustina.

A pair of boot heels clopped forth from the King's side. A male hand took her pulse brusquely at the neck. It hurt. "*Está viva*," he said. She lives. Or *it* lives.

"*Padre, agua.*" This was unmistakably Nicolas, speaking with an urgency Mari found oddly touching.

There was rustling, murmuring, a metallic ping, the patter of tiny slippers coming closer. Someone lifted her head from the floor. This was going even better than she had planned. She would rouse to waking and deliver her prophecy the moment the holy water touched her tongue. His Catholic Majesty would love it. She parted her lips and waited for the holy cup's cold kiss ...

An angry sheet of water hit her face. It went up her nose, burned, and crept coldly under her collar. Shocked and annoyed, but determined to stay on task, she opened her eyes and blinked holy water from her lashes.

She saw Nicolas first, standing over her, his brow furrowed with concern, chalice dangling in hand. Behind him were the King's daughter, fingering her rosary; the Queen with her hand over her mouth and eyes laughing (she was tiddly again); and between them the King, wearing his usual mask of misery.

Ignoring that she was drenched, Mari met the King's gaze with a faraway stare. In the eeriest voice she could manage, and poetic meter, she delivered her prophecy to His Majesty, in a handy little couplet that had come to her in a flash of inspiration the night before:

> "*The red moon on the eve of morrow*
> *Bespeaks the end of Spain's great sorrow.*"

Her words were met with perfect silence, and then the rustle of wool as the King's men stirred with curiosity and confusion and perhaps a bit of unease. Nicolas raised his eyebrows at her, a look of sportly intrigue.

ཉༀ

Mari left her drapes open the next night and had the moon in sight as she climbed into bed. She had full faith in the Countess, but if it didn't happen tonight she could always say that the absence of the red moon was a harbinger of continued sorrow. Then if the eclipse did come tardily, everyone would be overcome with relief and unlikely to care about Maribarbola's lack of precision.

She lay awake for hours, checking the moon every couple of minutes. Eventually she slept and continued to watch the moon in her dreams.

A gunshot outside startled her awake. She sat up in bed and checked the moon. It was gone.

Another shot rang out, this one with a sizzly firework sound to it. Hope waxed in Mari's heart as she went to the window.

She looked westward, and there it loomed: the beautiful blushing moon. A deep blush, too, like the dark side of a peach. "Thank you," she whispered to it, her eyes tingling with tears, because she really felt like it was the Countess herself up there, smiling down upon her.

A door slammed somewhere in the tower; the Alcázar was stirring. She should probably go downstairs and wake the Queen, but she threw a fresh log on the fire and crawled back into bed. One of the pages would do it.

A sharp knock woke her. "Come in."

Binnie's candlelit head and shoulders floated forward in the dark. "Did you really think you'd be allowed to sleep through this?" she said.

"My work is done." Mari had earned the right to be smug.

"You're wanted on the King's Plaza."

"Send my regards, would you please?" She wasn't about to leave her warm bed to go revel outside at three a.m. with the Torre de Carlos fools. Besides, keeping a low profile was not a bad idea. Let the Queen's enemies wonder what Maribarbola was doing under the red moon.

"So I'm to tell His Majesty you can't be bothered?"

"The King?"

"Yes, the King. Standing outside in the middle of the night, waiting for you."

Minutes later Mari stepped out onto the royal balcony in her nightgown and coat to a thunderous ovation from the crowd below. She took her place at the Queen's hip and took the royal hand. To their left stood the King, with little Margarita drowsing on his shoulder and his other daughter Teresa beside them. He nodded to Mari. She responded in kind. Scores of cups rose from the crowd. "*¡Maribarbola!*" they shouted in a joyful, sloppy chorus. "*¡Brava!*" They raised their cups to the red moon. "*¡Luna roja!*" they shouted, and howled at it in jest.

Torches and braziers lit up the plaza, flames wild in the spring wind, setting merry cheeks and white nightgowns aglow. The crowd covered every last stone of the plaza—buffoons and dwarfs, handmaidens and chamberlains, cavaliers and clergymen—all nearly unrecognizable in their nightclothes, all equals under the red moon, laughing and dancing, raising cups to one another. Guitarists tickled festive melodies into the air; musketeers shot at the night sky.

The dwarf Manuelito rose above the crowd, perched upon the shoulders of Goliat, the six-and-a-half-foot buffoon. With the crowd's help he raised the Spanish flag, the Cross of Burgundy. It caught the wind and the torchlight and rippled gloriously in the night. The plaza erupted in joyous shouts: "*¡Viva España!*" Fireworks exploded overhead, showering sparks on the Alcázar.

Mari watched the revelry, sort of wishing she was down there, but mostly just praying. Praying that this would be a self-fulfilling prophecy, that things would start to turn around for them. She was starting to consider herself one of them.

She looked to her left. The King and Queen were holding hands, a rare sight. Rarer still, the King was smiling.

Her gaze landed on Nicolas down below, talking to a group of women, wearing a doublet unbuttoned over his lacy white nightgown, a red rose tucked behind his ear. He had his dog with him, a Spanish mastiff that walked as tall as he. Nicolas felt her staring and looked up. They beheld each other from this strange new vantage point—he down there in the crowd, she up here, with the King. Nicolas saluted her. Mari nodded coolly, tightened her grip on the Queen's hand. One of two things was going to happen now. He was either going to leave her alone, or he was going to hit back harder.

❧❀❧

Chapter 11

THE LOAN

he Queen sat among towers of buns and cakes, silver bowls of jam, and meat and egg slices fanned out on platters. She had summoned Mari to breakfast, apparently with just her and Everardo. "There you are," she said. She was reading a letter.

"Your Majesty. Padre." Mari took a seat.

The Queen folded the letter and slid it slowly through her fingers, looking pleased.

"Did the Marquis call?" Mari asked, reaching for a sheep cheese tartlet.

"No. This is from the King. It's a request for a loan."

Mari plopped a huge blob of red jam onto her plate. "The King needs a loan? From you? How much?"

The Queen and Everardo exchanged grins. "Not a monetary loan," said the Queen. "A staff loan."

133

"I see."

"He wants to borrow you."

"*Me?*"

"Yes." She relished Mari's horror before continuing. "Apparently his own oracles and astrologers and magi aren't pleasing him. He's asked me to lend you out for a horoscope, and any other divinations you can provide."

Mari's body became leaden, her appetite vanished. "When?"

"Whenever it's convenient for us, he says."

"When will that be?"

"We're not sure yet," said the Queen, glancing at Everardo. "We need some time to think about this."

Mari was relieved she wouldn't be meeting with the King right away, but the Queen's and Everardo's perversely cheery moods troubled her plenty. Clearly they were going to try to use her in some politically strategic way, and the Queen's political instincts were dubious to say the least.

The Queen tucked the letter under her plate. "Just be ready at any time."

തര

After her initial wave of dread dissipated, Mari resolved herself to advising the King and also recognized the opportunity to puff up the Queen in his eyes. The Countess had been a keen astrologer, though less so after she discovered the writings of Galilei, so Mari already knew that one needn't be clairvoyant to prepare a horoscope. She had a page fetch her an astrological almanac from the Queen's library and details of the King's birth from the palace archives.

His Majesty had been born at ten o'clock post meridiem on April 8, 1605, in Valladolid, Spain, which made him Aries ♈, ruled by Mars ♂, with a rising sign of Sagittarius ♐. He had no planets in the top half of his chart, the public half. This made sense; the Queen was always complaining about what a hermit he was.

Mari could suggest he heighten his visibility, do a banquet or masque maybe once a month. It would be good for public morale, she'd tell him, which was good for the Crown.

Unsurprisingly, the melancholy King had Saturn, the planet of pain and hardship, in his ascendant house. Mars, his ruling planet, lay in his fifth house, the house of recreation and lovers. This would explain his passions for hunting and riding, the arts, and of course actresses. Mari would stay away from that last part. She would, however, suggest he redirect some of that energy into neighboring houses, those of work and domesticity. She could encourage him to spend less time in the saddle and more on the throne, devote more time to the Queen and the girls. Balance is the key to happiness, she would tell him. Marriage is sacred. A good woman is worth her weight in rubies. A wife of noble character is her husband's crown.

She pondered his chart for several days, honing her analysis to the point where even she believed it. She told herself this was no different from the river market prophecies of her Udo days; if anything, it was easier because she knew far more about the King than she had those people. The fact that his life was vastly more complicated than the average person's meant the possibilities were endless, and any prognostications she made were bound to come true sooner or later. He was at war with half of Europe; if she promised victory was nigh, one was sure to occur on some battlefront somewhere, and the same could be said for crushing defeat. If she promised a splendid boon, she could count on his conquistadors to intercept a Dutch merchant vessel from East India, loaded with silks and spices and blue-and-white bowls. If she warned of pecuniary loss, a galleon carrying eighty tons of New World silver would sink in the Atlantic. These things happened every other week.

Still, one topic made her profoundly uneasy. Without a prince, the Crown's future remained uncertain, and Mari couldn't promise the fifty-one-year-old King that he wouldn't die without an heir, or that the next prince to live in the Alcázar wouldn't be a French dauphin. She prayed His Majesty wouldn't ask.

಄

She made it through the week without being summoned for the horoscope. The Queen hadn't said another word about it, and Mari wondered if she was going to be ungenerous and not loan her out after all. In any case, it was late Friday night, and the King would probably be hunting all day Saturday and praying on Sunday, so Mari savored having two worry-free days stretched out before her.

She had just put a fresh log on the fire and folded down her bedclothes when someone knocked.

"Come in."

Josefina, the young page, entered. Her rueful posture already had Mari worried. "Her Majesty told me to tell you it's time."

"Don't tell me—you mean the horoscope? Now?"

"Yes. I'm sorry."

Mari pinched her eyelids closed, shook her head. "Fine. Let's be done with it." She snatched her housecoat.

"You should probably dress," Josefina said.

"It's eleven o'clock. He can receive me in my nightgown."

"You're leaving the Alcázar."

"*What?*"

"Don't be angry with me, Mari! He's at the Buen Retiro."

Mari dressed and went downstairs. The Queen sat alone at her table, writing a letter over a late snack of chicken on toast. "Oh good, you're here," she said. "I'm sending you to the Retiro unannounced. Lalo's waiting downstairs."

"Jolly," Mari mumbled.

"Keep your eyes peeled the entire time. I'll want details. As for the horoscope, you're to tell him that Haro is an enemy and not to be trusted." She meant Luis de Haro, the King's chief minister, the second most powerful man in Spain.

"Isn't treachery punishable by execution?"

"Yes, by public burning," said the Queen, stirring a cup of chocolate.

"Your Majes—"

The Queen cut her off with the hand. "Haro would do the same to me if he could. He's been trying to get rid of me for years now. Did I tell you he secretly tried to have our marriage treaty nullified over some legal triviality? And just a few months ago, he made an overture to the Vatican about an annulment."

"I understand he's a threat, but it'll be obvious that the horoscope is a false one coming from you. A subtler approach is needed."

"Such as?"

"I'll keep it vague, say something like, 'An enemy is close.'"

"That could mean anything. Haro could turn it around and convince the King it's me."

"I'll specify it's a man."

The Queen shook her head. "No. I want Haro gone. We may not get another chance like this. Name him. I command you." She tickled the air with a finger. "See if you can make up a rhyme about it, like you did with the moon. It'll take you a good hour to get there."

Already sick with dread, Mari left without comment.

Lalo was waiting downstairs with the coach. "Advising the King," he said as he helped Mari up to the driver's bench. "Soon you'll be running the Spanish Empire."

"I have no wish to run the Spanish Empire."

"Only a madman would. Or a fool."

They inched along in heavy traffic; coach lanterns swarmed like fireflies on the Calle Mayor, the air thick and fetid with the stench of mule dung and the pork fire smoke of street vendors. Idlers and sinners mobbed the promenades, lurking in shadows or peacocking through the violent firelight and noxious smoke of coal braziers—sworded, caped men in plumed hats;

prostitutes in wide, rocking hoopskirts and black veils covering all but one eye.

Mari watched but saw little. Her mind was already at the Buen Retiro, bumbling through the King's horoscope. She barely listened as Lalo rambled on about everything from celebrity bullfighters to the various schemes he was concocting to keep suitors away from his daughters. Anxiety tickled her heart every time the coach trundled forward, closer to the Retiro, while intrusive thoughts of Luis de Haro burning to death on the Plaza Mayor threatened to plunge her into an irrevocable state of panic.

They reached the Retiro after midnight. There was a play tonight; the Queen no doubt wanted Mari to observe the King in the company of actresses to confirm her bitterest suspicions. Lalo spoke to a valet, who sent them around the back of the sprawling compound, another quarter-hour of travel through torchlit gardens and moonlit olive groves that would have been enchanting had it not been for Mari's frayed nerves.

Lalo steered the horses into a desolate courtyard darkened by a tower. Mari had that faraway, fragmented feeling again, as if half her consciousness had given up and left. "*La Profeta Maribarbola para el Rey,*" she heard Lalo say to the tower guards, and her numb body floated to the ground. She didn't hear him wish her "*Buena suerte*" or feel him squeeze her shoulder; she was already gone. Her heart beating in her throat, she followed two guards through a gaping black doorway.

She struggled to keep pace as they led her up the tower stairs, their curt boot heels echoing in the stone shaft and their shadows hulking and spreading over the torchlit walls. Every time Mari thought they had reached the top, they took another coiling turn and ascended into more darkness.

"*¿A dónde vamos?*" she asked. She heard voices and laughter, a muffled party.

"*A los aposentos del Rey.*" The King's apartment.

They entered a large, empty gallery. Massive chandeliers loomed, shimmering with candles and crystals. Party din wafted from some unseen chamber, cresting in jolly shouts and wicked laughter. Marble statues stood like frozen ghosts in candlelit alcoves, and magnificent oil pictures in gilt frames covered nearly every inch of wall: battle scenes and Bible scenes, bullfights and hunts, and portraits of prickly people, their heads sitting upon ruffs as thick as layer cakes. Mari finally understood why the Queen complained so much about the Alcázar, a dreary old dungeon compared to this young, elegantly appointed palace.

The guards clopped across the marble floor and opened a set of doors, releasing a puff of warm, perfumy air and revealing a raucous, decadent scene. Scores of people, mostly women, made themselves right at home in the King's apartment, lounging on cushions, their stockinged feet and powdered bosoms on full display, lips purpled with wine. They were theater types; Mari could tell by the white grease-paint faces and flaming pink cheeks—even the men, and their very un-Spanish-like pastel clothing, the better to catch the stage lights.

The guards led Mari through the tight maze of hoopskirts and outstretched limbs amid the cacophony of feminine debauchery: sugary voices and tart laughter, melodramatic whining, a few bars of rather good drunken singing, silver cups chinking daintily on jas-per tables. "*Es la Profeta Maribarbola,*" someone whispered. "*¡Holaaaa Maribarbolaaaa!*" a girlish voice sang as Mari receded down the hall-way with the guards.

They came to a door. One of the guards knocked.

"*¡Entre!*" Male voice.

They entered a dark, flickering chamber lit only by a hearth fire. A dozen or so black figures loitered about. As Mari's eyes adjusted, she recognized some of the King's ministers. One of them made eye contact with her, clearly befuddled by her presence, but said nothing.

The black forms shifted and parted, revealing His Majesty, sitting behind a desk, and Nicolas propped lazily beside him in his little chair. Nicolas perked up and squinted in the dark. "Mari, is that you? What are you doing here?"

Mari stepped forth and gave the King a rare, awkward curtsy. "I've come to discuss His Majesty's horoscope."

"*Dios mío*," Nicolas said. "I thought Mariana had died." Uneasy laughter rumbled through the chamber.

"Give thanks, the Queen is well."

"Thanks be," he said dryly, to more snickers.

"Please sit," the King said quietly. He had never spoken to her before. It was strange.

Mari sized up a chair, trying to calculate the indignity she would have to suffer as she struggled into it before a male audience. "*Un momento*," someone said, whisking past. She glanced around the King's study, a walnut-paneled chamber lined with bookcases and more fine pictures. The usual cohort of shadowy mustached figures lurked nearby, but there was also a woman sitting near the hearth, her ivory dress snatching up most of the firelight in the room.

The man returned with a stepstool and placed it before the chair. "*Gracias*," Mari said, accepting his hand.

"*Con gusto.*"

Mari looked up at the chivalrous helper. A pang of dread rippled through her gut. Luis de Haro nodded at her and retreated behind the King.

"What ill predictions do you bring me?" said the King in what sounded like a jest, though his face remained grave; indeed, his lips had barely moved.

Mari glanced at Haro standing wide in the corner, his hands clasped in front of his crotch. She wasn't about to start with that. "I'm concerned by the complete lack of planets in your public domain," she said in her clunky Spanish. "This is evident in your natural tendency toward reclusiveness."

The chamber rustled with knowing laughter. "Painfully evident," Nicolas said.

"Quiet, Nicolas," the King said softly.

"You mustn't overindulge your fondness for solitude," Mari said. "An invisible king is a weak king. Let yourself be seen. Dine ceremonially in public at least once a month, and attend vespers in a public church at least once a week."

The King nodded. His ministers smirked behind their mustaches. Apparently the Queen wasn't the only one vexed by his ever-worsening hermitism. Nicolas reached out and patted the King's chest, two cavernous thumps. "I'll get him to some comedies on the lake this summer."

More actresses was not what Mari had had in mind. Now was as good a time as any to address the King's wayward appetites. "You are a man of great passions," she said. "Your devotion to Christ is unparalleled, your horsemanship and marksmanship are legendary, and your picture collection is a matchless marvel. It will be the envy of kings twenty generations hence." She paused for a moment, letting the silence percolate. She rather enjoyed having command of the room. "These passions must be tamed, however, lest they overtake you."

Nicolas knitted his brow. In his shadowy corner, Haro nodded.

"Neglect not your duties as governor and father," Mari said, with a righteous finger in the air. "Those soils too need nourishing, lest their gardens wither."

An awkward silence bloomed. Nicolas lazed in his chair like a bored tot.

"Balance is the key to happiness."

"It is indeed," Nicolas said. Was he mocking her?

"A wife of noble character is her husband's crown."

"But she that maketh him ashamed is like rot in his bones." Yes, he was definitely mocking her. The King looked at him. "Proverbs," Nicolas said. "Right, Mari?"

Mari glowered at him before continuing. "Aries is his own worst enemy," she told the King, "headstrong and impulsive. You must grab the ram by the horns and keep your grip ever firm. Only then can you be your own true master." Panic fluttered in her breast as she realized her blunder. "Aside from God, that is." She scanned the vicinity for Inquisitors.

The King nodded. Mari took an overdue breath. Stalling before she had to finger Haro as a traitor, she rambled on about random benign things. She advised the King to get more walks and eat more fish, add sage and wormwood to his baths for improved virility (she had read this in one of the medical pamphlets), and carry an ox bone rosary on his person to protect against the evil eye (Binnie swore by hers).

"What of Bragança?" the King asked, startling her.

This was a city in northern Portugal. He was probably planning on attacking it or something. "Let God handle Bragança," Mari said. The King seemed satisfied with this answer.

She could no longer delay. She glanced at Haro. He stared back, his dark mustache climbing high up his cheeks, pointy as pitchfork prongs. "There's one more thing," she said, squeezing the words through her constricted throat. "A wicked one is near."

Nicolas lifted his head from his languor. Silence gathered as they waited for her to continue, but she could hardly manage another breath, let alone a sentence.

"Who is it?" Nicolas finally said.

Mari gave up. Stopped lying to herself. She couldn't do it. The Queen's wrath was vastly preferable to sending a man to his fiery death; this she'd known all along. "His identity eludes me."

"Is it someone in this room?" Nicolas said.

Mari's gaze pivoted and landed on him like a clock hand to midnight, striking fear in his huge Italian eyes as they both realized she held the power to destroy him with her next breath. The possibility burgeoned between them, their gazes locked so intensely Mari felt as if their minds had merged. *Dare she?* they wondered. In the space of a few seconds, she catalogued his every evil deed—his perverted games, the lies, the mockery, the coupling chamber—and now the thrill of vengeance quickened her heart, his eyes pleading for mercy, while a life less troubled stretched out before her, a life in which Nicolas had been scrubbed from existence, her biggest problem at the court solved.

She savored his name on her tongue, the almost-comical desperation in his eyes as she parted her lips to speak. "I don't know who it is," she said. Alas, she wasn't cruel like he was. "I only know His Majesty has placed his trust in someone who plots against him." Nicolas's jeweled coat buttons spread as he breathed with relief. His lips tightened in smug satisfaction, though his eyes shot Mari a rattled look which she loosely interpreted as gratitude.

The room stood in bleak silence, firelight flitting across grave faces, everyone looking around at each other, dark eyes shifting, fear and distrust looming like a giant poisonous mushroom. With a sickening swell of regret, Mari realized she'd just endangered every man here. The Inquisition was world-renowned for its torture methods.

"I always had my doubts about you, Haro," Nicolas said, and the tension dissolved into uneasy chuckles.

"And I you," Haro said.

The horoscope concluded, Mari stood to leave, already plagued by the fresh dread of having to go home and face the Queen. "Anyone need a glimpse of the future while Mari's here?" Nicolas said, raising his man-in-the-well voice. "Octavio, you should have her look at that rash and tell us if it really is smallpox." The chamber erupted in hearty laughter. "How about you, Roberta?" he called to the woman by the fire. "You're awfully quiet over there."

The woman hid behind her fan in jest.

"You're an actress, how can you be shy?" Nicolas said. "Come, let me introduce you to Maribarbola before she leaves." He squinted at the lantern clock. "Good of Mariana to send an old woman out at one in the morning," he said to no one in particular.

The woman floated forth like a spirit in her white dress. She was a beauty, with honey-colored hair and ivory skin, face and breast plump with youth, and lips as red and succulent as a New World strawberry. "Mari, I present the lovely Roberta Rosado," Nicolas said. "Of course the venerable Maribarbola needs no introduction. I'm sure you've read all about her in the papers."

The actress smiled warmly and curtsied. Mari reciprocated; then she witnessed a violation of protocol so shocking, so brazen, she had to avert her eyes. Roberta touched the King. Caressed the royal shoulder. Let her ungloved hand slither lovingly and sensually upon it. Not even the Queen was permitted to touch him like that, certainly not in a roomful of men.

Nicolas glimpsed the lewd gesture and raised an eyebrow cutely. "Please give Mariana our regards," he said.

"God preserve you," said the corpselike King. Mari couldn't tell if that was remorse in his face, or just his face. Still trying to process what she just saw, she bent her neck and left quickly.

తువు

It was three a.m. by the time Mari trudged up the stairs of Torre de la Reina, praying the Queen was asleep so all these ill tidings could wait until tomorrow, after breakfast, with the Queen rested, full of bread and jam and warmed by the grid of gold sunlight that streamed through her French windows these spring mornings.

On the way home, Mari had prepared a few arguments to hopefully mitigate the Queen's anger over her Haro failure. As for the actress Roberta's explicit gesture, she wasn't sure how or when—or even if—she should tell Her Majesty. To say nothing would spare the Queen no small sum of anger and humiliation, but then Mari would be burdened with the fear of the Queen eventually finding out about the woman and the fact that Mari hadn't told her. Roberta's message had been clear: she was the King's mistress, and she wanted Mari to know it. It was only a matter of time before the King's cronies made sure the Queen found out, if for the sheer pleasure of reminding her how inadequate and powerless she was in her marriage.

They were also probably going to be watching closely to see how Mari handled this to ascertain her level of discretion and the strength of her devotion to the Queen. If she chose to protect the Queen's feelings by not telling her, they might interpret that as a show of disloyalty and, Heaven forbid, try to exploit Mari in their efforts to subvert the Queen. There was also the King to consider; tattling on him would land Mari in his ill graces. That is, if she was even important enough to incur his ill graces. She'd been at the court three months before he'd uttered a single word to her.

Too exhausted to care anymore, she entered the Queen's apartment. The reception room was deserted. Hoping the Queen was asleep, Mari plodded down the hall and poked her head into the royal bedchamber.

Only a few candles burned. The fire looked fresh. The Queen's bed was empty. Mari had no idea where she could be at this hour, nor cared. She was about to leave when she heard the Queen speak from some dark pocket of the room. "Come in, Mari."

Mari lifted a candlestick and walked toward the voice. She found the Queen in a fireside chair in an elegant nightgown, cradling a búcaro in her lap. Her hair was pinned back, and her face shimmered with goose grease. "What did he say when you told him?" she said.

"I couldn't do it."

"What do you mean you couldn't do it?"

"Haro was there with him."

"Even better!"

"Your Majesty—"

"When I command you to do something, you're to obey. I'd have thought that was obvious." The glimmering goose grease seemed to magnify the anger in her face.

"Please just hear what I have to say," Mari said, holding up a little hand. "Didn't you say we must always honor my prophet's intuition? My instincts implored me to refrain. The timing just wasn't right."

The Queen eyed her stonily.

"They would have known you put me up to it. The King would have dismissed the accusation and resented your trying to manipulate him. Haro would retaliate against you. He's already tried to have your marriage nullified twice. Do you really wish to reignite his interest in having you gone?"

The Queen shifted her glare to the fire. Mari was getting through.

"Trust me, it's better this way," Mari said in a silky, conspiratorial tone that surprised even her. The Queen's eyes shifted to her coolly. "I warned the King—before a roomful of his ministers, mind you—that an enemy is in his ranks. Now every one of those men is suspect and in turn suspects every other. The King's entire cabinet now operates under a web of paranoia and distrust." A lump of dread jellied in her gut as she heard her own words, realized what she had done, the game she was in. These men controlled half of the western hemisphere. Stakes didn't get any higher than this.

"Their power structure will weaken," Mari continued. "They'll be so preoccupied with their internal intrigues, they'll have neither the time nor inclination to concern themselves with you. As the King becomes increasingly isolated and paranoid, you'll be able to reestablish yourself as the supportive wife and trusted political ally."

The Queen sipped from her búcaro and stared into the fire. "Were there women there?" she asked wearily.

Now was not the time for that conversation. "There was a party in his apartment. Women and men alike. Theater people, drinking and loafing about. The King stayed in his study the whole time I was there."

The Queen rested her head against her chair and closed her eyes. "Go to bed."

ლელ

Mari slept poorly and woke early the next morning. Feeling hollow and jittery from lack of sleep, she breakfasted alone to the sound of the Queen and Everardo murmuring downstairs, though she could make out little apart from their German cadence and dry, mirthless tone. They spoke for much of the morning, until Binnie's shrill old lady voice sliced in out of nowhere and killed the conversation.

When she hadn't been called by midday, Mari figured the Queen was letting her rest. But she couldn't rest; she was consumed with worry over the King's alleged affair. His infidelity was the most toxic of subjects with the Queen, causing her not only public humiliation but the far more serious problem of bastard sons—among them the great General Juan José—to challenge the Crown after the King died. With the flying monkey episode still fresh in mind, Mari dreaded tempting the Queen's wrath, but knew the longer she waited, the worse it would be for everyone when she finally did tell her. And she now knew that she must. Neutral was not an option, not for someone in her position. She was the Queen's asset, the Queen's sworn ally and staunchest supporter, and most importantly, the Queen's best hope for outflanking her enemies and reversing her political fortunes.

Last night's excursion had troubled Mari anew—she having witnessed the men of Torre Dorada in their natural element, huddled around the King's desk in his shadowy office, where they plotted their endless conquests and wars. The air had been thick with manly humors: power, aggression, greed, arrogance. These men were used to taking what they wanted with impunity, confiscating land, homes, businesses, money in the form of taxes, treasured objects, actual human bodies, entire continents and oceans. They were master takers and claim-stakers, but they could not take the Queen's God-given power, and they certainly could not appropriate the Prophet Maribarbola for the King's better use. For anyone interested in knowing the strength and direction of Maribarbola's loyalty, she would make it abundantly clear: her allegiance was unshakably to the Queen. A four-man chest of silver should at least buy that.

Still, an ember of hope glimmered in the ash heap of worry. Last night she had brought Nicolas within a hairbreadth of his life before conferring grace upon him. Would he, quid pro quo, desist from antagonizing her now?

Another day passed before Mari found herself alone in the royal apartment with a reasonably relaxed Queen, looking ahead to a night of cards. Madrid sprawled beneath her eternal haze of brazier and pork fire smoke, a vast jumble of church towers and clay rooftops tinged golden-pink by the setting sun. The Queen had just drained a cup of sherry and asked Mari to pour another. Feeling the moment was as right as any would ever be, Mari eased into the conversation with a hypothetical: "If two parties enter an agreement, and one violates the conditions of that agreement, does that not put the other party in a position of advantage?"

"It depends," said the Queen. "Is it a legally binding agreement?"

"Yes. Most definitely. Sanctioned by the law of the land and in the eyes of God."

The Queen knitted her brow. "What kind of agreement are you talking about?"

Mari hesitated. "A marriage treaty."

The Queen's face hardened. "What are you getting at?"

Mari sighed and let the words tumble from her lips: "I think the King has a mistress."

The Queen's eyes bulged. "You think?"

"There was this woman the other night ... " She told the Queen about Roberta and the lewd caress. She demonstrated on a sofa cushion.

"And you're just telling me now?"

"I didn't want to upset you. I'm not sure I would want to know myself."

"I want to know everything," the Queen snapped, "before it happens, which is the reason you're here."

Mari bowed repentantly, but the gesture went unseen. The Queen's furious gaze was out in Madrid somewhere. Her lips pursed into an angry little bud. The royal nostrils flared.

She stamped her goblet on the table, stood up, and went to her writing desk. Her skirt puffed up with air as she dropped into the chair. She brandished a leaf of vellum from a drawer and slapped it down in front of her.

"Your Majesty, what are you doing?"

"Writing my father."

"The Emperor?"

"That is my father." She whisked a second sheet of vellum from the drawer and slapped it down. "And the Holy Father."

"You mean the Pope?"

"I mean the Pope." She dipped her pen.

Mari dashed to the desk and blocked the fine calfskin paper with her hand. "Perhaps ... we ought not pull this loaf from the fire before it fully cooks."

The Queen eyed her. "Meaning?"

Having deliberated on this matter exhaustively for the past forty-eight hours, Mari finally concluded that the Queen's problem was less about the King's behavior than the Queen's inability to maximize his weakness to her advantage. She needed to stop taking umbrage and start taking action. "Getting back to my original question," Mari said, "the King's infidelity puts him in clear violation of your marriage treaty, certainly your marriage vows. Does that not afford you a certain amount of ... leverage?"

The Queen squinted. She wasn't following the logic.

"It's the King's nature to do as he pleases," Mari said. "I doubt that even an admonishment from the Pope could curb his sins of the flesh. Rather than waste your energy trying to control his behavior, perhaps it would be wiser to ... exploit his guilt to your advantage."

"And how do you suggest I do that?" The Queen's tone was acid, but her eyes blazed with interest.

"Request an audience with His Majesty right away, but don't say what it's about. He and his ministers will assume you mean to confront him about what I witnessed the other night. When you meet with him, invoke my name right away. Tell him I shared a most scrupulous account of my visit to the Buen Retiro, unsparing in its detail. Tell him what a delightful and loyal companion you've found in me, and that we have no secrets between us, you and I. By then it'll be obvious that you know. Pause. Let him simmer in his discomfort."

The Queen narrowed her eyes, seeming to relish the thought.

"Then tell him the Emperor sends his regards," Mari added, with patent glee. She was made for this. Palace intrigue. She should have been a court dwarf her whole life. "After that, you'll discuss the real reason for your wanting to meet with him, which is, you're going to ask him for something. It doesn't matter what, but make it substantial—like a staff increase, or a new coach, or a Pacific island in your name."

"He's nearly bankrupt."

"Not your concern. The point is to make your message clear: you're willing to turn a blind eye to his lechery, for a price. We'll see just how far he's willing to go to appease you. You may even be able to negotiate Haro's dismissal over this. Eventually, I mean. Don't open with that."

Mari removed her hand from the paper.

The Queen stared at the blank sheet, pursing her lips.

She tapped the ink from her pen and parked it in its holder.

ᗉᏽᏽᗉ

Chapter 12

THE QUEEN'S PLEASURE

ari's first springtime in Spain was the finest of her life. The sun returned to Madrid with a cheery vengeance, slicing through palace chambers in wide sashes of light, burning off the stale winter chill and at least some of the Alcázar's pervasive gloom. The days stretched longer, and Mari's habitat wider as she enjoyed many afternoons exploring palace grounds. Stone paths led ambling courtiers to pleasure gardens of lush green lawns, placid pools, and topiary shaped with godlike precision into balls and spirals and giant cakes. Mari stayed clear of the box-hedge maze, a stamping ground for small animals and randy couples, for fear of chancing upon something vulgar or getting lost and panicking in there. She preferred the pools and their splendid marble fountains—Triton blowing his shell trumpet, Neptune on his seahorse-drawn chariot, a ring of cherubs frozen in a tiptoed prance—where she could sit on a sunbaked stone bench, listen to their sweet, soothing gurgle, and throw crusts of bread to the swans.

Weeks ago, heeding Mari's advice, the Queen had demanded a meeting with the King and Haro both, during which she alluded to the King's incurable lechery and, bearing newssheets, rattled off a list of political items that could displease Spain's foremost ally, her father, Ferdinand III, by the grace of God elected Holy Roman Emperor, King of Germany, Hungary, Croatia, Bohemia, Bulgaria, Serbia, et al., Archduke of Austria, crowned and consecrated Supreme Protector of the Catholic Church by His Holiness, Pope Alexander VII. Then she asked for a ten-percent increase to her household budget—and got it.

She spread the wealth and good cheer top to bottom through Torre de la Reina, raising salaries and fattening provisions tower-wide. Staff enjoyed greater bakery rations, extra candles from the wax station, and treats from the Queen, such as flowers, a cake of fragrant soap, or a spice bun and cup of chocolate before bed. Mari received four new dresses and a wig in one of the newer styles, saw her first machine play at the Buen Retiro, and enjoyed jaunts in countryside with the surprisingly rustic Queen, often with little Margarita in tow, in Her Majesty's luxurious new coach.

Meanwhile, a couple of high-ranking dismissals in the King's cabinet suggested the web of suspicion Mari had cast over them was working, and the Queen's involvement with the Marquis of Villamirada's children's charity finally netted Her Majesty some favorable press. When she hosted the San Balbina orphans at the Alcázar, where she (in absentia) lavished them with a hearty chicken feast and magic lantern show in the Salón Grande, the Marquis coordinated a press campaign across several high-circulation newssheets, garnering her most flattering reportage since her 1649 wedding.

Mari hadn't felt this content since the Countess was alive and relished the satisfaction of having engineered the Queen's reversal of fortune, thereby rescuing her from the political impotence in which she'd been mired for years. Mari no longer fretted about proving her worth; her worth was evident in the Queen's newfound swagger, her quick laughter, the largess she showered upon her household, the soaring morale in Torre de la Reina. Aside from Her Majesty's disobliging womb, Mari's foremost concern these days was whether to make her next prophecy foreboding or inspiring, cryptic or plainspoken. Even then she was unhurried; she was still enjoying the trailing ends of success from the red moon, nearly two months later.

She found even greater relief in having neutralized Nicolas. Since that night at the Buen Retiro, when she struck terror in his heart before sparing him, he had ceased all deviltry against her. Thenceforth their dealings had been blessedly banal: courtly nods at coupling ceremonies; awkward kisses of peace in church. Beneath this new veneer of cordiality Mari's old resentments still chafed, but she played along, grateful to be in a truce and comforted in knowing that even Nicolasito could be counted on to abide by some loose code of human decency, if pushed far enough.

ॐ

One perfect May evening, Mari waited until seven o'clock for a royal summons, and when none came she crept down the tower stairs as the chapel bells tolled. She strode out to the Queen's Plaza at a good clip, her speed fanning the little flame of hope that had been burning in her chest since late afternoon, when it started looking as though she might have another evening to herself, her third this week.

The plaza bustled with activity under a mellow sunset. Guitar players plucked out festive melodies. Savory-sweet aromas infused the air: cinnamon and pork, chocolate and garlic, fried meat and warm candied figs. Noblemen haggled with farmers and tradesmen. Buffoons and male dwarfs flirted with fair-faced peasant girls.

153

Pigeons and orphans begged. Mari threaded through the crowd, bought a paper cone of hot fritters, and kept walking.

The pleasure gardens were deserted; the Torre de Carlos dwarfs and buffoons were performing a comedy tonight on the King's Plaza. The sun hung low and red over the orchards, throwing syrupy light and long shadows onto the land. Feminine laughter rang out in the distance, and the maze spit out a relaxed, frolicsome couple. Mari sat on the sun-warmed rim of the cherub pool and let the fountain's sweet one-note song and her bottomless cone of fritters lull her into a blissful trance.

Everardo appeared in the distance, in his red priest's frock and matching tartlet-shaped hat, probably coming from vespers in the royal chapel. He trod the footpath with nary a glance at the majestic roses that garnished his way, or the incandescent pink sky reigning to his left, or the orange cat that had stretched out in his path and squirmed playfully as he strode callously by. Mari figured he was going to make a quick circuit through the maze, as the priests sometimes did, to discourage fornicators and prescribe atonements on the spot. But he didn't go to the maze; he took a hard right at the cherub pool and walked straight toward her.

"Her Majesty wishes to see me?" Mari asked, with shattering hopes for a quiet, selfish evening.

"No. I wish to see you."

Mari rolled up her fritters and offered him a seat. He declined.

"The Queen is dining with the Marquis of Villamirada tonight," he said. "This is the third night this week he's paid her court."

Mari already understood where this was going. Gossip had been spreading through Torre de la Reina like pox.

"She's been quite cavalier about matters of propriety," Everardo said. "I'm told she dismissed her attendants and sat alone with him in her apartment for nearly three hours the other night." Mari threw an uneasy glance around the garden. The Queen would not be pleased by this conversation. "Surely you must be as astonished as I am by this man's excessive daring in courting the Queen."

"I wouldn't call it courting," Mari said. "More like a strategic partnership. And one of great mutual benefit. I've never seen Her Majesty so pleased."

He gave her a dry look.

"Padre! That's not what I meant! What I meant was, she's found great satisfaction in helping Madrid's children."

"The Queen of Spain must receive a man in her apartment thrice weekly to coordinate bread deliveries to orphanages?"

"There's great need out there."

"And what of the flowers and sweetmeats he brings with him every time?"

"She's the Queen," Mari said lamely.

"And the drunken lute serenade wafting from her chamber the other night?"

Mari had been wondering what that was. She thought the Queen had been bored and called in one of the buffoons to entertain her.

"Surely your prophet's eye can see the danger she puts herself in by tempting the King's wrath. Her political standing is precarious, to say the least. She cannot afford even a breath of scandal."

"The King himself hardly sets a good example in matters of marital propriety," Mari said, shocked and thrilled by her own impudence.

Impatience played on Everardo's face. "The King himself is beyond reproach; Mariana is not. Her presuming herself to be held to the same standard is foolish and indeed very dangerous. As hopes for a prince diminish, the threat of her dethronement grows. We can be certain Haro is entertaining his options."

"But her father—"

"The Emperor's reach is not nearly as long as she seems to think it is and certainly does not extend to matters of his daughter's marriage. His supremacy endows her with a false sense of security more than anything else."

Mari, who'd been enjoying her own false sense of security commensurate with the Queen's, was crestfallen to hear this. "Have you discussed this with her?" she asked.

"Yes."

"So I guess you want me to talk to her."

"You're the only one she seems willing to listen to these days."

Mari looked around. Dusk had fallen. A monk was lighting the floating prayer candles at the far end of the pool. She resented Everardo for troubling her. One niggling dilemma was all it took to spoil an enchanted evening.

"Her indiscretion puts us all at risk," he said, "and the Marquis as well."

"I'll try."

ཉཉ

The Queen accosted her in the stairwell a few days later. Mari was surprised to see her walking alone, a violation of protocol. "I need you on hand tonight," said the Queen. "Cristofer is coming over so I can help him prepare a tax-exempt petition to submit to the King. I can't have attendants standing around ogling him all night. He's very self-conscious about his mustache."

"Yes, of course."

"I'm going to have you meet him by the north entrance and bring him up the service stairs. Don't let anyone see you. Everardo has taken to lurking in the hallway outside my apartment to observe his comings and goings."

"Your Majesty,"—now was the time—"Padre's concerns are valid. You know how freely gossip spreads. You don't want to give anyone reason to accuse you of impropriety. As always, we must assume the King's ministers are watching."

"Good. Let them watch. If His Majesty should take an interest in my social appointments, I'd be happy to negotiate some rules that we can both carry out in good faith. Until then, I may see whomever I choose, whenever I choose—as the King does."

"Your Majesty … " She hated to play her prophet card again—she needed to keep its edges sharp and corners crisp—but Everardo was right, this was getting out of hand. They were finally reaping the sweet fruits of Mari's success; if left to the Queen, it would all go to rot. "I have a bad feeling about this."

"You have a bad feeling about feeding orphans?" said the Queen, and whisked off in her giant skirt.

Her swift, dainty footsteps climbed two flights and exited a door with a slam. Mari stood silent, watching a torch flame dance wildly on the landing below. Maybe her mind was playing tricks on her, but she thought she smelled *vinagrillo*.

తఙ

Mari sat on a cushion in the Queen's apartment, sipping sherry and admiring the Marquis's unassailable facial geometry. "Forgive me for asking," said the Queen from her writing desk, "but you are of pure ancestry, right?"

"Yes, of course," he said, stroking his nonexistent mustache. He did that a lot, Mari had noticed. "Well, I may have a drop of Moorish blood in me, but that's going back generations."

"I'll pretend I didn't hear that," said the Queen. "You're going to have a hard enough time getting this approved. The King's granting very few exemptions these days. He's already raiding church coffers to pay for Flanders, and now God is telling him to take back Portugal and reunite the peninsula before he dies."

"How is he going to pay for another war?" said the Marquis.

"He can't," said the Queen. "He's squeezed every last peso out of the populace, and Cromwell's cruisers keep seizing his silver imports. But of course he's not going to let a silly thing like bankruptcy get in the way of his plans."

The Marquis turned to Mari. "You should talk some sense into him," he said. "I'm told you have his ear these days."

"I don't meddle in warfare."

"Perhaps you should."

The Queen fanned the ink. "It's done. I'll have Everardo file it tomorrow."

"I'm unworthy of your kindness," said the Marquis, bowing from the sofa. "Maybe Maribarbola should cast an enchantment on it, to better my chances."

"She's a prophet, not a witch," said the Queen, and they all laughed.

"So tell me, prophet," he said, "will His Majesty approve?"

"Yes," Mari said, an easy call. The Queen was sponsoring him, and she basically got everything she asked for these days.

The Queen sat down beside him, and they talked politics while he gazed upon the royal bosom and compulsively topped off everyone's sherry goblets. His drop of Moorish blood notwithstanding, the Marquis was a firm Catholic and patriot who supported the King's efforts abroad, though he did fear that a full-scale war with Portugal would plunge Spain into even greater penury, leaving thousands more children breadless. "The situation in Catalonia is especially dire," he said. Mari recalled Catalonia from her inbound journey—the crumbling cottages, the dejected people.

His concerns rolled over the Queen like fog on ice. "Their misery is owed entirely to their loyalty to the French," she said of the Catalans.

"Don't you fear another revolt?" said the Marquis.

"Let them revolt. They'll be quashed harder this time. Philip would sooner pull Juan José out of Flanders and let the Netherlands fall than lose Barcelona again." Mari was surprised to hear her acknowledge the importance of her bastardly stepson, whom she despised.

"Perhaps we ought to send some bread carts up there in your name," said the Marquis, "as a show of good faith."

The Queen batted down the idea with a hand. "They're on the coast. They can eat fish."

Soon the evening turned to cards. Apparently nobody had told the Marquis about the unspoken rule of letting the Queen win; he bested her repeatedly, with relish and gloating, while she glared at him and threatened to burn his tax-exempt petition.

At one point, when it was his turn to deal, he did a slick little card move that reminded Mari of Udo and plunged her into deep thought about the Legend. By now months had passed; time had diluted her anger and allowed for some detached reflection on the matter. She finally saw his last feat, the one that made him rich and her Maribarbola of Spain, for what it was: a perfect exchange. The stuff of folk rhymes, beer songs. The stuff of legend. How had he done it? How had he known, for example, that the Queen of Spain had been lonely and desperately unlucky? Had his travels brought him here once?

"You're awfully quiet over there," said the Queen.

"Was there ever a magician here in a big puffy red hat? Like a giant red pepper?" She gestured about her head. She was tiddly; they all were.

"Sounds ravishing," said the Marquis.

"No," said the Queen, picking through her cards. "If there were I'd have burned that hat myself on the Plaza Mayor, with his head still in it." Here the Marquis made a jest about her cold German heart, and she gave him a flirty little look that, if anyone else had witnessed it, would have done nothing to squelch those impropriety rumors.

The rest of the night careened by in a noxious, woolen-mouthed, sherry-vapor haze. Their card game deteriorated. A candle tipped over, and the Marquis doused the flame with his bare hand. Mari ended up alone on a sofa, propped up like an idle marionette, dozing, while the Queen and Marquis huddled nearby, whispering and tittering, his arm around her shoulders in full violation of protocol.

Mari wanted nothing more than a cup of juice and her own bed, but she still had to escort the Marquis out through the back corridors.

She woke at some unknown hour, still upright, feeling dreadful, in silence and darkness, alone. She wondered if the Marquis had left and the Queen had gone to bed without waking her. The thought of relocating was too cumbrous to entertain, so she curled up on the couch and fell back to sleep.

A gentle hand shook her. Mari woke to the Queen's and Marquis's candlelit faces, he holding a candelabrum in his bandaged hand. "Wake up," the Queen whispered. Mari peeled herself off the couch.

"Don't let anyone see you," the Queen hissed through a crack in her apartment door as Mari and the Marquis set out into the cold dark bowels of the Alcázar.

There was no danger of being seen at this hour. They plodded along in awkward silence. Mari's mouth was desiccated, pasted shut with something dreadful. Her head felt like a rotting pumpkin, her stomach a sloshing sac of putrid black bile. Somehow she saw the Marquis to the little-used north exit, where he was greeted by bird-song in the silver light of morning.

✿

Chapter 13

THE PAINTING OF THE PAINTING

mboldened by her improved political standing, the Queen began shirking duties with impunity. These included sitting for her official royal portrait with Maestro Velázquez. "Tell him to copy my last portrait and just freshen up the costume a bit," she said when Everardo brought it up. "How much can I have changed in four years?"

Nobody challenged her, but only because the Maestro had had a radical—and bizarre—change of plans. He would proceed with the royal portrait; indeed, it would be a portrait of the King and Queen together. Their Majesties, however, would not be in it.

"He's going to paint himself painting what would have been your royal portrait," Nicolas explained, having barged into the Queen's apartment under the pretext of borrowing a jewel. "A painting of a painting, if you will."

"So he's basically going to paint a picture of himself," Agustina said, "and call it a royal portrait."

"Basically," Nicolas said.

"That's awfully bold," Mari said.

"I don't care what he does," said the Queen, "as long as I don't have to sit for it."

The artist's plan soon became the talk of the court. Many were baffled and feared the Maestro had lost his mind. Others lauded the idea as brilliant, daring, cleverly ironic, a portrait of the King and Queen that did not show the King and Queen—a picture of absence itself. Only a genius would dare dream it, let alone attempt it.

By now even the Queen was intrigued and sought to inject her will into the matter. She understood that she could not be in the picture—that would ruin the whole concept—but she did insist that her daughter be in it.

Nobody balked. In fact, the King so liked the idea of having his little girl in the painting, he decided it should hang in his apartment when finished. Perhaps thinking it unseemly to have just himself and five-year-old Margarita in the picture, the Maestro decided to include some handmaidens and invited the young ladies of the court to a model study in the Galería del Rey.

"Get down there, all of you," said the Queen on the afternoon of the study. "You too, Mari. I want to know which of those court hussies they choose to grace the wall of my husband's bedroom."

The galería was swarmed with bell-shaped lovelies, their delicate necks balancing huge wigs, rouged cheeks and lips garish in the sun-soaked chamber. Sweet voices flittered through the atrium like a legion of butterflies, and hope hung in the air like an overeager splash of perfume. Beyond the shifting mass of satin skirts and voluminous dark curls (the artist had specified no blondes), a cluster of black-clad figures stood at the edge of the gallery: the Maestro and his assistants, talking among themselves, paying scant attention to the throng of peacocks thickening before them.

Mari, Isabel, and Agustina squeezed in by a window and surveyed the scene with smug amusement. Mari recognized María
Concepción de Mora, darling of the fashion ballads, and the low-
born Cristina María Reynoso, whose banker father had bought her
a place on the court. María del Campo y Salvo, a sixteen-year-old
who recently wed one of the King's gray-haired ministers, was there,
as was María Milagra Guzman, the tall handsome daughter of two
Torre de Carlos dwarfs. And no gaze could go unsnagged by Gabriela Castellón—*Gabi la Hechizada*, she was called, Gabi the Hexed.
Too beautiful for her own good, she would never be accepted into
the jealous Queen's ranks or know true female friendship. Even her
sisters avoided standing next to her in the presence of eligible men—
though men, for their part, seemed content to admire her from afar.
Lalo, her father, made sure of it.

There were gasps, a shriek. The room hushed, and the throng
collapsed in a sloppy, murmuring wave, a mass curtsy. The King had
entered the gallery.

Flanked by ministers, His Majesty ambled through the crowd,
nodding to ladies, honoring a lucky few with words, sending ripples
of giggles through the chamber. This was the most relaxed Mari had
ever seen him. He actually looked happy. It was infectious; the mood
in the galería turned gay and airy, percolating with girlish silliness.
Mari caught herself smiling for no reason.

He pivoted toward the window, catching Mari in his royal gaze.
Looking pleased to recognize her, the King came forth. Behind her,
Isabel and Agustina sank in reverence. Mari bent her neck. The
King came unnervingly close, rested his hand on her head, and stole
a glimpse out the sunny window. With the royal hand heavy upon
her head, Mari made a funny, mortified face, setting off chimes of
feminine laughter.

The King moved on to the next cluster of admirers.

The Maestro, who'd been watching from across the room, kept
staring at them.

ཙེ

"We are the hussies!" Agustina said after they'd raced upstairs to tell the Queen. "The Maestro chose us!"

"You jest," said the Queen.

"It's true!" Isabel said. "He saw the three of us standing by the window, and, for whatever reason, he wants us!"

"Even Mari?"

"Even Mari!" Agustina said. "José too!" Oddly, the artist had plucked Jose Nieto, the Queen's quartermaster, from the crowd as he happened to pass through the galería.

"Really?"

"Really!"

The Queen threw her head back and let rip a wicked, self-satisfied chuckle. Everyone shared in her shrewish delight. Such irony that the Queen's favorites should be chosen to hang in the King's apartment and have their watchful eyes upon him every second he was in there. "Ah, God," said the Queen, wiping the corners of her eyes with her fingers. "I love it."

ཙེ

Their excitement wilted once they realized what the commitment required of them. Even before the ten-foot canvas was stretched, they were made to endure endless wardrobe fittings. The Maestro was fickler than the ficklest of women, unhealthily preoccupied with colors and textures, and thought nothing of having a dress torn apart and rebuilt even after the last of its trimmings had been painstakingly stitched into place.

Meanwhile, the King decided that Nicolasito should be in the picture. Nicolas agreed, but only if his dog could be in it with him. Since he and Margarita couldn't be in the same room together, they posed in small groups, a tedious process that dragged on for weeks. Isabel was made to hold a curtsy, but Agustina by far suffered the worst: the artist put her on her knees, pitched forward, offering a búcaro to the Infanta, who at five years old wanted no part of standing still for hours on end.

When it was her turn to sit, Mari reported to the Maestro's atelier eager to please. Nicolas was already there with his mastiff, Feroce, arguing with the Maestro in the kind of fierce, *rapido* Spanish Mari still found difficult to follow. Nicolas was miffed about the clothes he'd been made to wear: a child's red playsuit with a clownish white collar and cuffs, and slippers he claimed he wouldn't wear to clean a horse stable. The Maestro told him he was lucky to be breeched at all and had, in fact, come close to wearing a boy's dress.

The Maestro welcomed Mari with a curt nod and herded them to the window, where her black dress wasted no time soaking up the summer sun. Nicolas was still sulky about the playsuit. "Thank God this picture is meant for the King's private study," he said in German so the Maestro couldn't hear. "Few will ever have to see it."

To Mari's quiet satisfaction, the Maestro put Nicolas in a difficult, silly pose, with a foot on Feroce's haunch and his hands raised in childlike whimsy. Nicolas mockingly complied. The Maestro took Mari by the shoulders and (a bit roughly) moved her toward Nicolas. Her scalp tingled as he arranged her hair. "*Perfecto*," he said sternly. He was not a man of mirth. Then he backed away slowly, unnerving her with that trenchant, computing gaze of his, and said, "Now show me your heart."

Mari's cheek twitched in visceral discomfort. Germans didn't show their hearts.

Nicolas sniggered. "He didn't ask to see my heart."

Mari resisted the temptation to remark upon his not having one. She didn't want to disrupt their delicate truce.

A long couple of minutes passed. The Maestro's tools clicked and chinked as he mixed paint. "This is excruciating," Nicolas said, staring at Feroce's back.

Mari ignored him, staring obediently ahead.

"At least the money's good," he said.

"You're being paid for this?"

"Of course. Aren't you?"

Mari fell silent. The Maestro had picked up his brushes.

"You should talk to Mariana," Nicolas said. "Twenty ducats is reasonable for something like this."

They stood in deep silence. Mari didn't know how she'd be able to endure several weeks of this. The Maestro's dark eyes roved every God-given inch of her, anatomizing her like a chicken gizzard. It was mortifying. Never had she felt so self-conscious, so profoundly short and misshapen, yet paradoxically huge beside Nicolasito. She tried to show the Maestro her heart while keeping hidden the dark truth festering therein: she was a fraud, a false prophet, a purveyor of lies. Now in the hostage of the artist's vivisecting gaze, she feared he might *see* her and, God forbid, expose her on his ten-foot canvas. With panic kindling in her breast, she scavenged her heart for random benign cherishables: babies, kittens, snowfalls, or the Queen's earsplitting laughter last night when Mari, mimicking the Marquis, quipped a witty retort in Spanish and stroked her nonexistent mustache.

After several agonizing minutes, she was almost relieved when Nicolas spoke. "I saw the Marquis of Villamirada at the bullfight the other night," he said with calculated airiness. "He had an odd glow about him."

Mari said nothing, refusing his bait.

"Oh, and just a tip—the Reina north entrance can get busy on summer nights with the river path right there. Carlos south is best for those wanting to come and go unseen."

She shot him a sideways glare.

"Don't worry," he said. "Her secret is safe with me."

"What secret? If you're suggesting what I think you are, Her Majesty would never be so foolish as to court such scandal."

"Who said anything about scandal?"

Mari rolled her eyes. "As if Haro isn't licking his chops over the possibilities. The Queen of Spain and the unsparingly handsome nobleman. Wouldn't that set every newssheet in Europe ablaze?"

"Is the Marquis really that handsome? I don't think I've ever really looked at him … "

"And speaking of scandal," Mari said, "how is the King's … " She flourished a hand in disgust.

"Mistress. Roberta. She's well."

"I suppose the foolish woman fancies herself the future Queen of Spain."

"Spain already has her Queen."

"And we both know how determined Haro is to one day see the back of her. Do you really think she'd make it easy for him by committing a moral turpitude?"

Nicolas laughed quietly. "You may be an oracle, Mari, but you know nothing of politics. Mariana's not going anywhere. Everyone here accepts that, including Haro."

"The Emperor's reach is not as long as you suggest, and Her Majesty is well aware of it."

He thought about this for a moment. "No. It really is."

"And if a man were to plant his bastard seed in the Queen's womb?" She could hardly believe she was speaking these fears aloud—to Nicolas! "You're saying Haro wouldn't sink to his knees in gratitude before driving her from the court in shame, or having her slaughtered on the Plaza Mayor?"

"An extremely far-fetched idea, dreamt up by someone with way too much time on her hands. You should take up a hobby or something—that is, in addition to your prolific prophesying. There's good money in stitchery."

"*Silencio*," said the Maestro.

"Besides," Nicolas whispered, "I don't think we need to worry about anyone planting anything in the Queen's womb. And if she did birth a bastard, who would even know?"

"If the baby were handsome," Mari hissed, "everyone would know."

Nicolas let out a thundering chuckle that sounded like it came from a full-sized man.

"*Quiet, fool!*" The Maestro's roar shook Mari's heart.

The sittings dragged on for weeks, during which Mari and Nicolas's relationship took on a strange new character in their forced company. In the atelier, any ill will he harbored toward her was supplanted by his evident dislike for the Maestro ("the King's *true* favorite," Binnie had explained). In German, with the Maestro working only feet away, Nicolas gossiped shamelessly about the artist's exorbitant salary, his controlling personality, and the secret nude he had painted for Haro's sleazy son. With the Maestro apparently unneedful of things like rest or nourishment, Nicolas and Mari bonded in misery over their slavish circumstances, with Nicolas negotiating hard for occasional stingy breaks, usually on account of Mari's being "a crippled old woman." Sometimes his ad hoc friendliness took on a pushy, paternal tone ("Did you talk to Mariana about payment, like I told you to?") or mild flirtation ("He's quite taken with you," he said when Mari spent a particularly long, torturous afternoon in the artist's undivided gaze. "You might be the most important person in this picture, besides himself.")

Sometimes the King visited, taking a chair to watch. Once the Maestro even let him paint a couple of strokes. "He'll scrape it off as soon as he leaves," Nicolas said in German. With His Majesty sitting feet away, Nicolas entertained Mari with stories of the King's misguided artistic endeavors, including a Guadarrama mountain scene that looked like hills of vomit, and a portrait of his mistress so unflattering the King was forced to repent with diamonds. "He thinks he's an artist born mistakenly into kinghood," Nicolas said as the King took his leave. "He stares at pictures all day while the country goes to hell." Uneased by his brazen criticism, and not entirely certain the Maestro wasn't a German-eared spy, Mari said nothing. "But life is not a picture," Nicolas said loudly in Spanish. "Is it, don Diego?"

"Life is *only* a picture," said the Maestro, scraping away the King's effort.

One afternoon Mari reported to the atelier to find Isabel instead of Nicolas. Without warning, her sessions with him had come to an end. The sittings were thenceforth even more unbearable, Isabel being an earnest, obedient sitter who didn't speak. As Mari stood for hours in excruciating silence, encroached upon by Isabel's giant hoopskirt and driven to near-madness by the Maestro's tools clicking and chinking and scraping, she was surprised and baffled to find herself actually missing Nicolasito's company.

To the displeasure of no one, the painting of the painting was eventually finished and put on temporary display in the Room of Riches. The King proclaimed it a masterpiece, the finest ever to leave the Maestro's easel. It was indeed shatteringly magnificent, enormous and radiant, cunning and wizardly—though odd in the way it beheld the beholder. And for all those tedious philosophical debates about presence versus absence, the Maestro did end up showing the King and Queen, tiny and blurry in a mirror on the back wall.

Mari regarded the picture as the most beautiful lie ever told, with the King and Queen shown happily together in the mirror, little Margarita standing but a horse-length away from Nicolas, and he looking like a sprightly, harmless lad in his playsuit. Mari's fears of being exposed had been unfounded. Her calm, sunlit self blended handily into the scene, a false prophet looking right at home in the false moment, hiding in plain view. And yet, through the Maestro's lie shone a brilliant, radiant truth. Mari needed look no further than her own eyes, gazing with love and loyalty at her Queen, who had never stepped foot in the atelier but was, by now, in Mari's heart. The Maestro had seen her heart.

෴

Soon after, Mari found herself with some unexpected time off. The King and Queen had retired to the Escorial, the royal monastery in San Lorenzo, for an official mourning period. A letter had come from Vienna. The Emperor had died.

The mood in Torre de la Reina turned somber, not with grief but with worry for the Queen. "This weakens her politically," Binnie said against the trickle of her laundry ladle. Mari watched the perfumed steam curl, the Queen's lace swirl. "Her situation just went from bad to worse."

"But her brother will be crowned Emperor," Mari said.

"A brother is not a father. Besides, he's only seventeen. He'll be Emperor in name only."

Mari kept quiet. Binnie didn't know the full story. At the moment Mari was sworn to secrecy, but soon news would break that would change everything. The Queen hadn't bled for nearly four moons now and was almost certainly pregnant.

Chapter 14

THE FOURTH PROPHECY

August in Madrid was harsh. Mari spent her days in the Queen's dark apartment, where she and others cooled the pregnant Queen with fans, snow packs, sugar-lime ices, and strawberry water, while pages fielded Her Majesty's insatiable demands for chilled prawns, cold muskmelon soup, and peach tartlets. A brutal heat spell drove them underground for a week, to a dank but richly appointed parlor, where they sat on velvet cushions and played cards and dice by candlelight and became melancholy for want of daylight.

Their first morning back upstairs, the Queen invited her favorites to breakfast against the view of sunny Madrid. They read the newssheets while they ate. "Oh look," said the Queen mockingly, "Inocencia is the latest of the King's soothsayers to announce the sex of the baby." Inocencia was a Torre de Carlos dwarf who still had a shred of credibility as a prophet due to her knack for calling bullfights and cane-tourneys. "She's predicting a prince, of course."

"Would anyone dare tell the King otherwise?" Isabel asked.

"Good question," said the Queen. "Mari, if your prophet's eye told you I was carrying another womanchild, would you shatter the King's heart now or later?"

Mari had been trifling with her custard, pretending not to listen. This topic was on everyone's lips these days, such that she had started avoiding people and quit reading the newssheets. Since the pregnancy had been made public, all eyes were on Maribarbola—not just in Madrid but all of Spain and other parts of Europe, even the New World. The very thought struck panic in her heart and filled her gut with dread. She didn't know how much longer she could avoid being dragged into this high-stakes guessing game. So far the Queen had left her alone, having more or less accepted Mari's explanation that prophecies cannot be conjured at will, but it was only a matter of time before someone important—like Haro, or the King himself—tried to corner her for her word.

"The truth must be spoken as known," Mari said dully. "'Twould be a sin to do otherwise."

The Queen flicked the newssheet aside. "Inocencia's word is worthless anyway. She's a gambler masquerading as a prophet."

"I wonder if Nicolas is going to make a public prediction," Isabel said.

"I'm sure by now he's learned to keep his mouth shut," Mari said, eager to keep the conversation on Nicolas, whose faults always fruited much discussion.

"He has nothing to lose by trying," Isabel said. "His reputation as a prophet couldn't sink any lower."

"Let him try," said the Queen. "It'll be amusing to watch."

"Well, according to this," Agustina said, dangling a newssheet, "there's only one opinion that matters, and we've yet to hear it."

"Who on earth could they be talking about?" said the Queen, and they all laughed, except Mari, who had stuffed herself silent with a giant strawberry.

The Queen sensed her discomfort and threw her a crumb of mercy. "No news is good news, right, Mari?" Mari nodded. "The matter will be settled one way or another, eventually. Until then, I say keep them guessing. It's good press."

ന്ന

As the Queen's figure waxed evermore buxomly, the Marquis paid court several times a week. "There is naught so lovely as a woman with child," he said, not for the first time, to the Queen's copious bosom. Mari knew what was coming next; the Marquis was one of the people she'd been trying to avoid these days. "Did I miss any prophetic words while I was gone?"

"Leave her alone, Cristofer," the Queen said. "She doesn't do well with pressure."

"Oh, no pressure," he said cheerily. "Only half the world waits." His contrived charm and jocularity were starting to annoy Mari. "Just yesterday I had in my hands a newssheet from Jamaica, written in English, but I was able to make out one word: Maribarbola."

"Stop," said the Queen, whacking him gently with her fan. Mari wondered how much longer she could count on the Queen to keep saving her like this. Her Majesty's benevolence had its limits. "Being that you're so interested in the matter, you should know by now that every one of the King's soothsayers is predicting a prince."

"Yes, well, nobody cares about them," he said.

"Apparently the King does," said the Queen. "He's already drafting new policy under the assumption that we'll have an heir soon. A full-scale assault on Portugal could come next spring, and I'm told he's trying to secure a loan for Teresa's dowry." Teresa was the King's older daughter from his previous marriage.

173

"Teresa's getting married?" Mari asked, eager to steer the conversation away from the pregnancy. "To whom?"

"I imagine she'll be offered to Leopold," said the Queen. Leopold was the Queen's brother, the Holy Roman Emperor-elect. "Spanish princesses are betrothed to Austria, Austrian princesses to Spain. That's the arrangement."

"When?" Mari asked, wondering if the King might put her on the wedding convoy to Vienna, for good luck and protection. She'd not seen her fatherland in thirty years.

"Next year," said the Queen, "and not a moment too soon." It was no secret that she bore no love for her stepdaughter-cousin and would be glad to see the back of her. "But of course everything hinges on this little one." She stroked the satin half-ball that was her abdomen. Conversation never failed to return to the pregnancy. "Did I mention they're saying November now?"

"Let's hope he's a punctual sort," the Marquis said, beaming at the tidy mound.

"Let's hope he's healthy and happy and not at all like his father," said the Queen, and they all chuckled at the King's expense, though it quickly dissolved into uneasy silence. Mari knew they all had to be thinking the same thing. She herself had been trying to remember when the last coupling ceremony had been, when the Marquis started staying until sunrise, and when the Queen stopped bleeding. Surely others around here wondered the same, though no one dared speak it—not even Binnie, the most egregious of the gossipmongers. But that didn't make the possibility any less troubling, or the threat any less real: male or female, a dark handsome baby would bring a world of misery upon this tower.

※

September brought its own grand affair when María Concepción de Mora, lady-in-waiting and darling of the fashion ballads, married the second son of the most noble and venerable Duke of Alba.

Nearly a thousand courtiers packed into the Salón Grande for a night of feasting and dancing in the blessed presence of the King, who'd been making more of an effort to show himself in public, though looking everywhile miserable.

Mari sat beside the Queen at the royal table watching the mass of merrymakers shift and swirl in a mosaic of black wool and bright silks. Guitarists played tirelessly from the balcony, though their passionate performance was swallowed by the thundering din of the crowd. Goliat, the six-and-a-half-foot buffoon, lumbered across the dance floor with Churro the dwarf—a tiny fritter of a man with a sweet, delicate disposition perched on his shoulder, while Mudo the mime slinked through the crowd like a silk thread, sneaking up on clusters of young ladies, who shrieked in horror at the sight of his white lead-powdered face.

There were newswriters here, with ink-blackened fingers and pens dancing on parchment pads, scratching out their usual blather and acid. Many were probably enumerating every braid and bauble on the bride's sofa-sized dress, though Mari also felt the occasional vulturine gaze land upon herself and was grateful that protocol prevented any mortal from coming within yards of the royal table without the explicit consent of His Majesty, which he gave almost never.

Tonight's banquet had included squab and pheasant in savory sauce, potato sheep cheese pie, red wine punch, and caramel crème cake spiked with rumbullion. The Queen had eaten greedily, having kept at it long after everyone else's plates disappeared, and even now grazed from a cornucopia that was clearly meant as a decoration. With two months left of her pregnancy, she had practically doubled her girth in a handful of weeks. Even the flesh-loving Marquis had curtailed his visits and begged off with a supposed fever every night this week. Mari hardly blamed him. Though Reina staff were working round the clock to indulge Her Majesty's every caprice, their efforts did little to mitigate the crabbiness and laziness to which she was prone even under the best of conditions, and morale sagged tower-wide.

Nicolas lazed in his little chair beside the King looking sweet and adorable in the soft light of a gourd lantern. His collateral presence with the King's at public events was, Mari suspected, an act of calculated pageantry: his boyish figure served as an ersatz prince to a people who desperately needed a real one, while making His Majesty appear virile and fatherly, not to mention physically huge. Nicolas was dressed exquisitely tonight, with his usual air of effortlessness, in a silk doublet the color of blackberries and dotted with freshwater pearls, snug as a fruitskin against his tiny torso, and a ruff so crisply starched and diaphanous it looked to have been spun from sugar. He hated banquets, it was well known, and looked about as happy to be there as the King did. At forty-five pounds, he couldn't drink alcohol and ate little more than a cat, and during their sittings with the Maestro he had told Mari he'd rather be disemboweled with a spoon than participate in a dwarf dance.

The Queen yawned, a welcome sign. It was late, Mari had a wig-induced headache, and she'd had enough of Chico the Idiot, who was in an agitated, food-flinging mood. She was pleased when the hornblowers silenced the crowd and stole a last sip of punch as she waited for the King and Queen to rise from the table.

They were taking forever. The crowd rustled with restlessness. Then came the whisper, multiplying and dispersing like windborne seeds. Mari had only just become aware of it when it burrowed through her wig and slipped into her ear: *Nicolasito tiene unas palabras.*

Nicolasito has words.

Mari sat back and took another drink of punch. This should be amusing. Maybe he was going to issue his prophecy on the sex of the baby.

Nicolas slid off his chair and stepped center stage before an adoring crowd. "Please join me in offering heartfelt congratulations to Pedro and María," he said. "Pedro, María, may God bless your union with health, wealth, and happiness, and many heirs to the noble House of Alba."

A smattering of applause bloomed to a hearty ovation. Nicolas waited for it to die and continued: "Speaking of heirs ... " He turned to the Queen. He and she exchanged tart smiles, and the crowd rumbled with laughter. "As the Queen's body waxes double and her shadow threatens to darken half of Madrid"—there was more laughter, and a hilariously frosty glare from the Queen—"so grow our faith in the Almighty God and our hope for the future of this great nation.

"This child-blessing comes not a moment too soon, as its joyful promise slathers a much-needed balm upon the festering soul of this tortured realm." He paced as he spoke, slippers crackling light and color, his gait vaguely feline—dainty and soundless and slightly stalking—his Italian hands flying, his man-in-the-well voice surprisingly acoustic and filling the hall. He spoke at length about Spain's hardships, which included, in addition to Her Majesty's infertility, war, plague, poverty, moral decay, and a sickly economy owing to the rampant debasement of the currency and shameful obliteration of nearly every Spanish industry. "That very cloth upon your back," he said in a rather scolding tone to the ill-at-ease audience, "was almost certainly made by Dutch hands." Mari turned to see Their Majesties' reactions. The Queen looked bored as she plucked a chestnut from the cornucopia and swilled it down with a drink of punch. The King was his usual corpselike self.

"But with this child," Nicolas said, softening his tone, "the well of hope springs anew." People in the audience nodded. A drunken whistle pierced the silence. "Perhaps this really could be the end of sorrow we were promised"—he looked at Mari in a way that made her stomach lurch—"on that long-ago night under a red moon."

The crowd broke into applause spiced with howls and whistles. Boots drummed the floor. A warm heaviness spread through Mari's chest, down her arms, and up into her throat. There hadn't been a truce. That had been him lying in wait.

"Maribarbola," he said, stalking toward Mari, his eyes alight with wicked pleasure. "It's been a while since we've heard from you.

How've you been?" The audience laughed warmly. The Queen laughed also. Mari stared at him blankly from what felt like a great distance. She wasn't sure this was really happening, that she wouldn't wake upstairs with her teeth clenched and nightgown drenched. "Surely you know that every ear in the land stands keenly pricked as we await your answer to the only question on anyone's lips these days." Then all geniality vanished from his face, and he adopted the scolding tone again: "The very question which, I might add, tortures His Majesty every moment of every hour, such that those around him fear his heart may succumb to the weight of worry."

The room fell horrifically, sickeningly silent. Mari felt nauseated. Her face burned beneath its powder finish. Nicolas was publicly shaming her and doing a fine job of it. She actually felt tears coming on.

"Forgive me for saying what everyone else is thinking," he said, "but your enduring silence in this matter seems unintentionally cruel." *He*, accusing *her* of cruelty! But she looked around and saw the irony was lost on all. "I'm sure I'm not the only one who finds it hard to believe that the greatest prophet in the land, who sees far into the heavens and beyond time itself, cannot see into the womb bulging only feet away from her." He turned to the crowd and shrugged. "Surely you must know something the rest of us don't." People were nodding vigorously.

"I therefore beseech you," he said, raising a tiny finger. "I beg you, in the presence of the Almighty God and His Most Excellent Majesty, the Queen, and the many noble men and women here tonight. Tell us, dear prophet, once and for all." He gestured to the portly Queen. "What in God's name is that blessed child?"

Thick, woolly silence filled the hall. Mari's heart thumped in her ears, alarmingly sluggish. She couldn't feel her body, nor the two-pound wig on her head. She turned to the Queen with meager hopes of salvation, but apparently this was the moment the Queen stopped coming to her rescue. Her Majesty waited along with everyone else.

Mari took a long overdue breath and reminded herself she had a plan in place. She'd always known someone would force her hand in this matter eventually, although she did acidly resent that it was Nicolas and in such a public way.

Tonight Maribarbola would issue her prophecy on the sex of the royal baby. She had spent many sleepless nights thinking it through, weighing the risks and rewards, the probabilities and possibilities. Pregnancies had always been a snap in her Udo days with their two clear choices. Boy or girl. Play or perish. Mari had gambled with the storm and the red moon and won. She couldn't fold now even if she wanted to, nor did she want to. If she were right this time, her powers would be unassailable. The Queen would be untouchable against her enemies. Mari would be invulnerable to the whims of Nicolas. Torre Dorada would be neutered from top to bottom.

The consequences if she were wrong were murkier and ranged anywhere from the Queen being really mad at her and perhaps reducing her pay and perquisites to burning to death on the Plaza Mayor. The gamut between those two extremes included banishment to Torre de Carlos or the streets, imprisonment, torture, slave labor in the cesspits (which often resulted in putrid gas asphyxiation), or drowning in a dive capsule while she pawed for sunken treasure. Mari could only pray that the Queen—one, cared about her enough not to allow the worst of those things to happen; and two, was powerful enough to protect Mari against the Inquisition. I did it for you, Mari would tell her if it should, God forbid, come to that. Gambled my very life for your political advantage.

Mari looked into His Majesty's eyes and almost lost her nerve when a memory sprang up in her mind like a fresh green sprout: that night in the coupling chamber, the indignities she had witnessed. Not the actual coupling; that had been over in the turn of a hand. It was the King afterward, in a mound on the floor, quaking, crying, begging, *cursing* the Lord to give him another son—not even to carry the Crown, but to stanch the fount of despair left by Baltasar

Carlos, the son he had lost. So pitiful was the sight, even the Queen had wept.

She had a fifty-fifty chance. Mari raised her cup to the King.

There were gasps, murmurs, a premature shriek of joy. In her Maribarbola voice, she spoke:

"*Dios le va a dar un príncipe.*"

God will give you a prince.

And the Salón Grande shook with joyous thunder.

ℜℜ

Weeks later, celebration still raged uninterrupted. Every meal was a sumptuous feast, every evening an occasion of great pomp and splendor. There were pageants and comedies, balls and masques, bullfights and cane-tourneys, carnivals, a horse ballet, and torch-light processions down the Calle Mayor. Fireworks crackled over Madrid even as the sun rose, while people danced and staggered in the streets, and public fountains ran red with wine.

After Maribarbola had submitted her prophecy to the King that night, His Majesty baffled everyone by standing up and leaving while the Salón Grande rumbled with cheer. A near-riot broke out as revelers fled to see where he had gone. They spilled out onto the King's Plaza, and there they saw him, trotting across the courtyard on his Neapolitan charger. With braziers blazing on every side of him, he reared his horse and let rip a joyous howl (now jestingly known as The Sound Never before Heard on Earth). Then he charged through the streets of Madrid, relaying the glorious news to dumbstruck citizens with his own royal tongue.

Only then had Mari understood the weight of her word, the wickedness of this game she was playing, and the sickening truth that, come November, the sight of a screaming pink womanchild could very well kill him, in which case she could be charged with regicide, a crime for which the Devil himself could not design a punishment more horrific than what the Inquisition would do to her.

She had packed her knapsack that night. The problem was, she had nowhere to go, and a winged horse could more easily hide on the streets of Madrid than a fugitive dwarf. So she stayed and lived in abject misery while the court reveled in the lap of pleasure. She looked on, quiet and sober, while everyone sang and danced and got tiddly; sat stone-faced in the audience of sidesplitting comedies; and waned ever thinner as banquets grew ever lavisher.

Tonight was a grand water party on the Manzanares River behind the Alcázar. There had been a mock naval battle earlier, with theatrical warships built for the occasion, and now revelers were enjoying fireworks, bonfires, and pontoon rides. It was Oktober; the night was crisp and swirling with fog, the gardens were dying, the last of the orchard fruits had dropped. Next week would bring Hallowtide. Next month, the baby.

Mari stood at the orchard's edge nursing a cup of chocolate, looking down the riverbank at the festive scene. The riverfront twinkled with torchlights and teemed with revelers, their laughter and music filling the night. Floating lanterns dotted the black water with amber light—an enchanting procession of tiny boats, each carrying a candle and a prayer through the fog courtesy of some hardworking monks upriver. Every few minutes a dwarf or buffoon floated by in a coracle, raising raucous cheers from the crowd. Even the King had ridden through on his horse earlier, and to the delight of all, dismounted to take a spin on the sea beast carousel with a group of lucky children.

The last time Mari saw the Queen, Her Majesty was being helped aboard a gilded gondola, which had rocked violently under her girth and made onlookers cover their mouths in horror as the future King came within a whisker of drowning. The Spanish Ambassador to the Republic of Venice had sent the gondola, a token of congratulations. By now Maribarbola's prince prophecy had spread across Europe and would soon reach the New World colonies. Lavish gifts were already trickling in, including a magnificent silver bedstead shipped from the Netherlands by the great General Juan José for his half-brother-to-be, the future King. The Queen's brother Leopold, heir to the Holy Roman Empire, sent a solid gold rattle topped with a clear glass orb filled with diamonds. The Viceroy of Naples sent the unborn prince his first servant, a handsome young dwarf named Carlo. Even the French had sent a baby gift.

Mari's mental state had stabilized, albeit in a dark, hollow place. She was now consistently despondent or, on good days, dead inside. She wasn't sure she'd last long enough to see the birth; she might panic and flee in the night, or her own heart might succumb to the weight of worry. It was as if the moment she had given the King the prophecy, she had taken on his boundless misery as her own—into a body half the size.

She felt a diminutive presence and turned to see Nicolas standing beside her, looking down the riverbank, eating a finger cake. He was dressed mannishly tonight, in a wool tunic and worn leather boots, and had a couple of lewd greasepaint kisses on his jaw. "Don't you wonder how he's paying for all of this?" he said. This was their first exchange since María Concepción's wedding. They'd been avoiding each other.

Mari didn't reply.

Then he took another bite of finger cake and said, through a stuffed cheek: "Wouldn't it be funny if it turned out to be a girl?"

It took everything she had to walk away without killing him.

She cut through the orchards, her path lit by paper lanterns dangling from the tree canopy, the smell of rotting fruit sweetening the cold air, patches of fog wafting across the footpath like vagrant ghosts. Deep in the woodlet, a young couple threaded through the trees in a romantic chase. Mari plodded forth, deadened to the magic all around her.

She went to the royal chapel. It was always empty this time of night and early morning before the priests woke. Mari knew; she'd been coming thrice daily. "Aren't you the pious one these days?" the

Queen had jested a couple of weeks ago. "You make the rest of us look like heathens."

She slipped into a pew and winced in agony as she sank to her arthritic, bruised knees. She prayed that if and when she were exposed as the disgraceful lying fraud she was, she'd be shown more mercy than she deserved. And she would be exposed, eventually. This game couldn't go on forever; she was old and tired and couldn't keep this up for much longer. Clawing out an existence was exhausting, as was constantly trying to prove one's worth. Or rather, desperately trying to conceal one's worthlessness. Because the cold truth was: without Maribarbola, she was nothing. Without Maribarbola there'd have been no buyers, no takers, no sane, decent person looking to acquire an elderly crippled dwarf who had naught to offer but her own neediness. She was as helpless and burdensome as a child only without the preciousness and innocence that made children worth their keep; indeed she was hideous, and a criminal. The Queen had paid a four-man chest of silver for just another parasite to feast from the royal hand. Mari had only her loyalty to extend in return, and loyalty by itself was intrinsically worthless.

Exhausted and slumped between the pews, Mari asked God to bestow His mercy upon her, forgive her lies, or, better yet, render them true. For the hundredth time today alone she begged Him for a prince and offered her very life in exchange.

Her shameful, festering lie of a life.

⟨❊✤❊⟩

PART II

Chapter 15

THE DECREE

Icy winds nipped Mari's cheeks as her squire steered the horses through Madrid's city gates. Snow flurries prettified the otherwise gloomy urban landscape. Winter had been mild when they left, the day after the New Year's Jubilee. "*¿Cuál es la fecha de hoy?*" Mari asked. She hadn't seen a calendar in weeks.

"*El cinco o seis de febrero,*" the squire said.

The Alcázar sat high on its hill above the city, a heartwarming sight. Mari was surprised by how homesick she'd been and how passionately she had missed the Queen. She had received but one letter from Her Majesty in the weeks she'd been gone. Everyone was doing as well as could be expected, it had said. Everardo was driving her mad. She had undertaken a slimming regimen, something involving goose grease and turpentine. Already she was feeling pressure from the King's side to return to the coupling chamber, to try again. *Don't come back without my case of Pla de Bages!* she had written. *By the time you read this, I will have drunk my last bottle.*

They reached the Alcázar by nightfall amid the usual crush of coaches and horses. Mari's lap was littered with sweetmeats and paper flowers, and her hand was blackened from touching the masses who'd swarmed her coach as it inched up the Calle Mayor. She hadn't the heart to deny anyone the hope of good fortune and had touched some very filthy, sickly people in her travels. Still, she marveled at how her reputation hadn't suffered one tittle, even after the most important prophecy of her career had turned out to be spectacularly wrong.

"You were foolish enough to return," Lalo said as they pulled up to Reina south.

"Did you miss me?" Mari said.

"Do we look like we've had time to miss you?" Binnie shrilled from the shadows.

Lalo helped her down and hugged her against his hip. Binnie swept a lantern near Mari's plump, tanned cheeks. "I'm glad somebody looks rested," she said. "I reckon the food was good in Barcelona?"

The Alcázar's ancient, musty smell welcomed Mari as she walked with Binnie through the torchlit corridors. She raved about her trip: her luxurious pensión, the ocean views from her terrace, warm breezy nights filled with wine and music and card games, and many, many chicken-chorizo empanadas. "I can barely button my coat."

"I'm glad one of us is fat and happy," Binnie said. "It's been nothing but chaos here. You couldn't have picked a better time to leave."

"How's the Queen coping?"

"The Queen's like a cat in cream. It's the rest of us who are running mad. Those nursemaids, God bless 'em, they don't get a wink of sleep." They climbed the stairs to Mari's apartment. Mari had

forgotten about the stairs. This extra weight wasn't helping. "I suppose you want supper and a bath."

"Later. I want to go downstairs and surprise the Queen first."

"She knows you're here; the watchmen spotted you an hour ago.
She's slimming tonight. Stay away, unless you want to see her naked
and slicked up like a ham."

"No. I don't want that."

"You can breakfast with her tomorrow." She fished a key from
her apron and opened Mari's apartment.

The new furniture overwhelmed. Mari hadn't gotten used to it
before she left. Gone were Nicolas's child-sized furnishings. She now
had elegant giltwood tables and chairs custom made for her height,
a chest of drawers inlaid with mother-of-pearl, and a canopy bedstead with velvet brocade curtains. "How are the—" she had started
to ask, when a large form waddled into her peripheral vision.

She turned to see Bosco, the Torre de Carlos dwarf with the
high boxy shoulders and rosy alcohol cheeks. "Welcome home,
señora," he said, bowing deeply.

"I forgot to tell you," Binnie said. "You have your own dwarf
now." She rolled her eyes and left.

"It's an honor to serve you," Bosco said.

"Who sent you?"

"I'm a gift from His Majesty."

"How long have you been in here?"

"Just a couple of weeks."

"A couple of *weeks*?"

"What will you have me do, señora? Anything at all. I've already
fixed your clock. And organized your chest of drawers."

Mari dismissed him immediately, sending him back to Torre de
Carlos to resume his dwarfery or buffoonery or whatever it was he
did before. She couldn't believe that had gotten past the Queen.

She plunked on the bed and surveyed her furniture and curios,
all ornate gilt edges and dark bulbous jewels, pictures and tapestries,

gem-crusted trinket boxes, solid gold candlesticks. No sooner had she lain to rest than the automaton clock shocked her heart with its loud, tinny chime. The tinkly music started; it was supposed to be gay, but Mari found it vaguely sinister. She sat up, annoyed, and watched the little pageant people come out of their door—the king, the queen, jesters, and jousters—and glide jerkily by before disappearing through the other door. Every hour they did this. Mari had purposely jammed the gears with a pen within hours of receiving it. It had been a Yule gift from the King. Most of the riches in here were gifts from the King.

The Queen was thankfully more practical, raising Mari's salary five ducats per month and fattening her provisions. Mari's dining table was as crowded and colorful as the Queen's these days, her hearth raged afresh every hour, and her washstand always stood watered and fragrant. She received a snow ration now too, a four-pound chest delivered daily, for preserving milk and cheese and fruits. The Queen bought her a new winter coat, warm and stylish, French-made and lined with white beaver, a very rare New World treasure. And then, shortly after midnight at the New Year's Jubilee, before the entire court, the Queen surprised Mari by telling her she'd be leaving for Barcelona that very day in Her Majesty's own travel coach. "I think a holiday is well-deserved," the Queen had said, and the Salón Grande thundered with cheer. Even the King had clapped.

Nobody seemed to notice or care that the prophecy had been technically—and gloriously—wrong. One thing was clear, however: Maribarbola's powers to purvey fortune could never again be doubted.

Spain hadn't gotten a prince. She had gotten two.

Two princely cherubs: Prospero and Ferdinand. Mari had been praying in the chapel when she heard and wept with joy. She burst out onto the King's Plaza, where two months of sickening worry lifted in the cold afternoon like steam from a broken fritter. She laughed for the first time in weeks, danced for the first time in probably decades, guzzled way too much wine, and gave lucky Maribarbola hugs to all who asked, from nuns to Inquisitors and everyone in between.

December celebrations had been rampant and rabid. There was Prospero's christening as the future King of Spain, the Queen's twenty-second birthday jubilee, and Yule festivities. Mari relished every moment, feasted greedily, raised her cup at every toast and jest. One drunken night even saw her mired in a dwarf dance with Nicolas. The red moon prophecy was coming to fruition. Everyone felt it. Everyone believed it. Even Mari believed it.

Now she lay on her back, staring up at her gold-fringed canopy. She could hear the Queen downstairs, speaking with the airy confidence of a woman beyond reproach. Even as her staff martyred themselves in thankless childcare, the tower was infused with a peace and complacency that definitely hadn't been there before. With two princes in the cot, the Queen was politically unassailable. The King's ministers were finally showing her due respect, publicly praising her, lavishing her with gifts, indulging her every budgetary whim despite the Crown's looming bankruptcy. Public support was emphatically on her side; even Nicolasito's reputation had lost some shine as old grievances between him and the Queen were raked up in the gossip sheets. As one writer put it, a new era was dawning upon the court: the rise of Torre de la Reina.

For the first time in her life, Mari felt powerful, effective, dangerously invincible. She wondered if this was how proper-sized people felt all the time, and if so, she considered all the clawing and scheming it took just to get on equal footing and was angered on behalf of all dwarfs everywhere. All dwarfs except Nicolas, that is.

God had given her a second chance. She vowed not to let it slip through her fingers. She had gambled thrice now and won. It was time to fold—retire Maribarbola, quietly and gradually, without anyone noticing. There would be no more high-stakes prophecies concerning the fate of the Empire; Mari's foolhardiness was spent. She would dust off her old river market self, proto-Maribarbola with her vague promises of true love and triumph over hardship. She would avoid speaking in public, especially to the King, and if pressed she would speak in riddles—or better yet, worn-out axioms, rejiggered Bible verses. God willing, she would bore Spain into leaving her alone.

At this point she couldn't convince the Queen she was a fraud even if she confessed outright. Mari's work was done, her worth proven, her station secured. Her only ambition now was to uphold her end of the divine bargain she had struck a thousand times over on the chapel floor: live virtuously, in humble gratitude for the mercy she'd been given; renounce all lies and schemes; and abstain from all deeds rash and stupid.

⚕

"There's my lucky charm," said the Queen when Mari breezed into breakfast the next morning. Mari kissed the royal hand and shared a warm embrace with the Queen. The slimming regimen was working; she was not far off from her original well-turned self. "Did the Catalans give you any trouble?"

"No. They were lovely." She shared an awkward half-hug with Everardo.

"That's surprising," said the Queen.

Mari told them about her trip, deemphasizing the drinking and gambling for Padre's sake. There was no denying her gluttony, however.

"I can see you're fat as a goose," said the Queen. "It pleases me to see you looking well again."

They discussed Prospero and Ferdinand. "Scrawny but ravenous," said the Queen of the princes. She invited Mari to visit them in their apartment later. Mari had seen them several times before she left. They were handsome lads, but not so much as to raise suspicion. "Already His Majesty wants to start trying for a third. Easy for him, right?" She brought Mari abreast on court gossip. María Concepción was conspicuously pregnant just four months after her wedding. Mudo the mime had been caught with a prostitute and was doing forty days' penance at the monastery upriver, King's

192

orders. "Oh, and you'll enjoy this," said the Queen. "I'm told Nicolas is lobbying hard to be appointed Prospero's chamberlain."

Mari stopped eating. "You jest."

"Apparently he's tired of being a dwarf. Says he wants more responsibility."

They all chuckled at the thought of Nicolas looking after the infant king. "Whatever brought this on?" Mari asked, caring little. His channeling his ambitions into something other than tormenting her was further evidence of her having neutered Torre Dorada top to bottom.

The Queen and Everardo exchanged glances. "I think I have an idea," the Queen said. She nodded to Everardo. "Padre, would you please? It's on my desk."

Everardo went to the desk and returned with a scroll.

"The King issued his annual New Year's decree while you were gone," said the Queen. "I've a copy of it here." She flourished it teasingly. "There's a part about you."

Panic crept into Mari's chest. Two months of blissful relaxation obliterated in an instant. "What does it say?"

"Don't look so frightened. He has only the highest praise for you." She unfurled the scroll. "Let's see, he writes, 'Maribarbola Haunsin'—he even spelled your name right—'is hereby confirmed a True Prophet.' He says your gift of foresight is 'demonstrably infallible, conferred by God, and hereby officially recognized as such.' He goes on to say that all prophecies and horoscopes rendered by The True Prophet Maribarbola shall supersede any other prophecies and horoscopes submitted to the court by lesser prophets and shall henceforth be considered word of law."

"*Word of law?*"

"Signed, *Yo, el Rey*." I, the King. She seemed to enjoy Mari's horror. "Why that look? You should be pleased."

"I'm just—" Whatever she felt, it definitely wasn't pleased. "To what purpose?"

"We have our theories," said the Queen. "I personally think he and Haro are pandering to the public by giving you official recognition. Let's face it—you're even more beloved than Nicolasito these days, and I'm sure it irks Haro to no end that you belong to me. But Padre has other ideas."

"I suspect they're going to start consulting you in matters of policy," Everardo said.

"Policy?" Mari said. "As in war and peace?"

"And domestic affairs," said the Queen.

"They may also try to use your word to sway public opinion," Everardo said, "and justify unpopular policies."

"Like these twenty-four new taxes, tariffs, and levies," said the Queen, dangling the decree.

"Furthermore," Everardo said, "his officiating your status as supreme prophet of the court puts you directly under his royal command, which means he can summon you at will, without Her Majesty's consent."

"We'll see about that," said the Queen.

Mari's plans for a humble, virtuous life evaporated. She was doomed to a life of lying and gaming, a life of constant worry and dread. No good could come of her working under the King's command; in fact, this seemed the surest way to land her in an Inquisition torture chamber. Having to transact with high-ranking officials would only make her more vulnerable, more desperate to keep weaving her tapestry of lies, more likely to panic and misstep and expose herself as a fraud.

"Why so glum?" said the Queen. "You have the King's ear and, according to him, your word is as good as law. What more could you want?"

"I'm unworthy of the King's ear. I know nothing of policy." All she had wanted was to be the quiet force behind the Queen.

"You're more worthy than half the fools in his cabinet," said the Queen, and she and Everardo exchanged smirks. Seeing Mari was still vexed, she added, "Don't worry, I know enough about policy for the both of us." Then she gazed out at Madrid, looking relaxed and pleased and clearly musing about something.

※

After the Queen dismissed her, Mari went outside and found Lalo on guard duty, eating chestnuts surreptitiously from his pocket. "You're practically as powerful as the Pope," he said after she complained about the decree.

"I don't want to be as powerful as the Pope."

"Better to be powerful than powerless."

Mari would have debated this if she'd had the energy. She stared out at the dead winter gardens, entranced with worry. She was a victim of her own success. Having no prior experience with power, she hadn't known that power compounded itself by sniffing out and consolidating with other powers—which meant the King and his ministers couldn't allow Maribarbola to frivol away her talents in Torre de la Reina forever.

Lalo chucked a chestnut at her, rousing her from her trance. "You should see your face," he said. "Remember when we first met? That's exactly how you look right now."

When they first met. When Udo's betrayal was ten minutes fresh. When she'd just discovered how truly powerless she was, a pawn in someone else's game. Lalo was right—it was better to be powerful than powerless. The problem was, she was still the latter. Torre Dorada planned to exploit her for political gain. The Queen planned to exploit her to counter-exploit Torre Dorada. Mari was still the pawn, would never not be the pawn. To be fair, no one could be blamed for overestimating Maribarbola's capabilities; her knack for deception shocked even her. But all this time, she'd just as easily been deceiving herself. She may not be a Torre de Carlos dwarf, but, like everyone here, she was still going to have to dance for the King.

Chapter 16

THE WOLF

The red moon's promise was tested by two crushing defeats abroad. The Crown now secured, the King ordered 18,000 troops, led by Haro himself, into the Portuguese city of Elvas. His Majesty had greatly underestimated his westerly enemy, now well-armed by her French and English allies, and the brutal battle ended with the Spaniards retreating in panic. Only a third of them made it back alive.

Meanwhile, General Juan José held down the Spanish Netherlands, but even he could not stave off a vicious attack by the French and English on the port city of Dunkirk, a Spanish privateering base. Dunkirk fell to the French, a devastating strategic loss. In the east, the Catalans were no doubt feeling emboldened by these developments. Spain's enemies lay in wait on every side of her.

Having dominated the known world for centuries, the Spaniards were unaccustomed to feeling vulnerable, and unease swathed the Alcázar like an ill-fitting coat. The jolly laughter that normally filled the galerías became thin and polite, the feasts lean and sober, the music somber, the buffoons tiresome, the dwarfs pesky and always underfoot. Women thronged the royal chapel, which twinkled thickly with prayer candles at all hours, and men who had never seen battle in their lives strutted through the galerías looking ready to fight. Even Nicolasito had taken to wearing a dagger.

If the Queen was fearful, she hid it well. In fact the only thing that seemed to bother her was that for all the carnage Spain had recently suffered, neither Haro nor Juan José had managed to get slain in battle. Mari was less concerned about the vague threats of far-flung enemies than she was the very real and immediate threat of the King soliciting her advice on how to save his collapsing empire. She read every newssheet and sought advice from Lalo and the surprisingly astute Binnie, whose gossipmongering and strong opinions also extended to world affairs. But despite her efforts, Mari still felt as uninformed and confused as ever. The decades-long wars, the ever-shifting borders, the fickle alliances and broken treaties, dynastic feuds and incestuous marriages, centuries of Philips, Charleses, Ferdinands and Louises—the situation was almost too complicated for a single mind to comprehend.

Mari was about to settle into bed with a military treatise and cup of warm sheep's milk late one night when Josefina knocked. She was calling on behalf of the Queen.

"What does she want at this hour?" Mari asked.

"She means to discuss something with you. I've no idea what."

Mari went downstairs. The Queen was propped up in bed, sinking into a wall of pillows, her goose-greased face glimmering by candlelight. "Oh good, you're awake," she said.

"You wanted to discuss something with me?"

"Yes. I dined with the King tonight. He asked about your availability this week." Mari's heart tripped. "Everardo was right," said the Queen, shaking her pen. "They're going to start using you to inform their policy decisions. I've never seen them so desperate."

"*Dios mío.* Did you tell him I know nothing of warfare?"

"Relax. I doubt he's foolish enough to seek your advice on military strategy."

"What then?"

"I overheard him telling someone he's close to securing a loan for Teresa's dowry. He's going to offer her hand in marriage in the coming weeks. I suspect he's going to solicit your opinion in the matter."

"What is my opinion?"

"She should be given to my brother, of course. We have a longstanding arrangement with Austria. Nothing else even bears contemplating."

"That's what I thought," Mari said, her panic retreating. This sounded like an easy one.

"Good. We're in full agreement." She dismissed Mari and bade her goodnight.

ⓡⓒ

The King didn't call that week. Even better, he left on a hunting expedition Friday, reprieving Mari for a couple of days. On Saturday the Queen took Margarita to a puppet show, leaving Mari with a day to herself, which she intended to fritter away in her apartment.

Midmorning, a gruff, masculine knock on her door nearly stopped her heart. Praying it was only Everardo or the odd male page, she answered it.

"*Buenas tardes,*" Nicolas said in a businesslike tone, looking boyish and innocent in the ill-lit vestibule. "May I come in?"

Mari hesitated but stepped aside.

He glided in swiftly and soundlessly, like a cat to a dish of cream, and went deeper into the room than was polite. He was dressed plainly, in a belted wool tunic and leather slippers, and his hair was tied back in a silk snood. "It's strange being in here," he said, looking around.

"Why are you in here?"

"Haro was hoping to have a word with you." He eyed her mess of newssheets and cheese rinds on the dining table.

"On behalf of whom?"

"Haro."

"I have no business with him," Mari said.

"It's not about business. He just wants to have a friendly chat." He wandered over to her automaton clock and peered inside at the jammed pageant people. Mari was regretting letting him in when he turned to her, smirking, and said, "She's made you bitter and paranoid, like herself."

That deserved retaliation. "I'm sorry about the chamberlain position," Mari said coolly. He hadn't gotten it. "I know how badly you wanted it."

He shrugged. "I suppose there's always a job waiting for me in Torre de Carlos if I get desperate enough."

"Must be tiresome being the King's favorite."

"The idle soul shalt suffer hunger," Nicolas said. "Just think how bored you'd be if you didn't have all those prophecies to keep you busy." He was mocking her, of course, and reciting Bible verse in the same breath. "Talk to Haro, Mari. You don't even have to talk, just listen. He's quite genial once you get to know him. I can only imagine what Mariana has told you about him, but I'm sure it's wildly exaggerated."

He took one more sweeping appraisal of the furniture and came back toward her, his dainty steps, his slippered feet. "Ignorance has never served anyone," he said.

"Actually, it has."

"Out there maybe," he said, bucking his chin at Madrid. "But not in here."

He was right—she didn't have the luxury of ignorance. Soon she'd be advising the King; she should hear what Haro had to say. Admittedly she was curious, especially since he had chosen today, with both Their Majesties gone. "Alright. Fine."

She and Nicolas crossed the Galería del Rey together, ignoring the murmurs and playful taunts of courtiers who were no doubt baffled to see Maribarbola and Nicolasito walking abreast given the animus between them that had played out in the gossip sheets after he had publicly shamed her at María Concepción's wedding.

Nicolas saluted the guards as they entered Torre Dorada. Mari started to turn up the stairs. "This way," he said. They were going downstairs, into the coldest, darkest bowels of the Alcázar.

They descended several flights. Mari had been to the Queen's underground chambers before, but the King's catacombs lay much deeper in the earth and spread far wider in a rambling stone maze, cramped even for dwarfs, cold and dank and feebly lit by the silent orange laughter of torchlight. "Haro's an extreme choleric type," Nicolas said, a reference to the bodily humors. His voice sounded especially man-in-the-well-ish down here. "You can always find him down here, even in winter."

As they forged deeper into the minatory maze, Mari regretted having allowed Nicolas to lure her here. "We're almost there," he said, sensing her discomfort as she eyed his dagger. They had come very far and were probably no longer beneath the Alcázar.

They stopped at a door lit by a single torch that had not been mounted with dwarfs in mind and threw stingy winks of light onto their faces far below. Nicolas knocked startlingly hard, as if possessed of strength freakishly disproportionate to his size.

"¡Entre!" Haro said within.

Nicolas turned to her. He may have been smiling; it was hard to tell in the dark. He leaned so close Mari stepped back—she could smell his *vinagrillo* breath, and for the queerest, most confusing second of her life she thought he was going to try to kiss her. *"Einen Wolf gibt es da drinnen,"* he whispered. Then he backed away and vanished into the darkness, leaving her alone.

There's a wolf in there.

Was that a warning, or was this another one of his ambushes?

"¡Entre!" Haro said.

Mari entered.

"Maribarbola!" he said. "Good of you to come. Please, sit." A step stool already waited by a chair. Mari took a seat and glanced around. His office was cold and lair-like, his desk filling half the small chamber. Mirrored sconces gave off brilliant, sparkling light with only half the heat. Among the mess of books and papers on Haro's desk a bottle of beer nestled in a small chest of snow.

"Thank you for coming," he said. "I've an important matter I'd like to discuss with you."

Mari nodded, determined to keep her words to a minimum.

The wolf smelled her fear and threw her a false scrap of reassurance: "Of course, whatever you say in here shall remain confidential."

Mari didn't believe it for a second. Nicolas was right—the Queen had made her bitter and paranoid, and thank God for that. She laced her fingers in her lap and waited.

Haro smiled, the twin pitchfork prongs that were his mustache twitching on his cheeks. He parked his pen and leaned back in his chair. "Wise is the man who seeks the wisdom of others," he said. "The King is a very wise man, as I'm sure you're aware, and soon he'll be seeking your prophetic insight into the matter of Teresa's betrothal and how he may marry her most advantageously."

"Do we not have a matrimonial agreement with Austria?"

"We have. However, these are challenging times, Maribarbola. Strange times. The world changes as we speak. What worked in the past may not bode well for the future. I'm sure that you, in your divine wisdom, would agree." Mari nodded. "Recent events have forced His Majesty to consider options hitherto unthinkable."

"Such as?"

Haro's dark eyes locked on her. "The King of France has extended his hand in earnest."

"*Dios mío*," Mari said, despite herself. King Louis XIV wanted Teresa as his bride? She was the daughter of his archenemy, and, truth be told, homely and melancholy, just like her father.

"The French are vehemently interested in a peace treaty consummated by the marriage of their King and our worthy Infanta, whose virtue is known far and wide. Given the worsening violence between our nations, their offer deserves careful consideration, wouldn't you agree?"

Mari agreed.

He snatched his beer from the snow and took a long pull before continuing. "I sit before you a changed man, Maribarbola. A haunted man. I saw things in Portugal I wish with all my heart I could unsee." He spoke at length about all the carnage he'd seen: vast fields soaked with blood and littered with bodies; limbs and entrails of thousands of men, some just fifteen and sixteen years old. "I wouldn't have believed what a musket could do had I not seen it with my own eyes." He added that, in the Netherlands, the dunes of Dunkirk had been painted red with Spanish blood—two thousand of Spain's sons slaughtered or maimed at the hands of the French, and another four thousand captured and imprisoned. "No house in this land remains untouched by the atrocities of war. A treaty would bring a suspension of hostilities, peace for the first time in most men's memories."

He took another drink. Mari waited.

"Naturally Her Majesty is allegiant to the House of Austria," he continued, stifling a belch. "While her loyalty is admirable, I fear it prevents her from seeing the situation objectively. Of course, your loyalty to Her Majesty is also admirable, but I daresay you possess a measure of wisdom and good sense that the Queen, frankly, does not." He smiled wolfishly. "Which is why I've summoned you here today."

"I'll speak to her," Mari said. "She's nothing if not reasonable."

"Her Majesty's opinion is irrelevant. The King is interested in your opinion, Maribarbola, and will be asking for it in the coming days."

Mari understood now. He was asking her to betray the Queen.

"In any case," he said, "I thought you should have this information before you advise His Majesty."

"Agreed. Thank you." Thinking they were done, she slid forth in her chair.

Haro halted her with a hand. "One more thing, if you don't mind."

He stood up and pulled a box from a shelf—a wooden chest, the size of a breadbox, chunkily carved and secured with a silver latch. He placed it on the desk and sat. "I dined with the Inquisitor General the other night."

Mari went warm and heavy in her chair.

"He asked me if I believed Maribarbola is indeed a true prophet. I said, 'Why, of course she is. His Majesty has decreed it so.'"

A sick, shivery feeling spread through Mari's trunk. She felt her flesh turn dough-like—cold, pale, sticky.

"Let's put the Inquisitor's mind at ease, shall we?" Haro said. "We wouldn't want him to feel the need to launch a sorcery investigation against you. His interrogation measures can be quite brutal." He slid the chest forward with a slow, ominous scrape. "Surely The Prophet Maribarbola can see into this box, no? After all, one would hope that she who is deemed fit to advise the King of Spain in his worldly affairs would be able to accomplish this relatively simple feat."

Mari prayed he couldn't hear her heart thumping or see the cold sheen of sweat forming on her face. She calculated her cruel options. Not answering would all but confirm she was a fraud—or worse, a sorceress—and see her lying on the Inquisition's torture rack before sundown. And yet, the only way to hazard an answer was to put all of her trust in the very person she trusted least, her life in his hands, and lay bare—to him!—her desperation and impotence. At best it'd be a staggering defeat, a forfeiture of power from which she'd never recover. At worst, unknowing his intentions, it could be suicide.

"Tell me please," Haro said, with an edge of impatience. "What's in the box?"

As always, the choice had already been made for her by someone who was not her. She couldn't even begin to calculate what this would cost her. Favors didn't come free at this court, and favors from enemies were dearest of all.

"There's a wolf in there," Mari said.

Haro smiled. He popped the latch with a loud silver kiss, raised the lid, and reached inside. Mari's heart pounded; her laced hands were slick with sweat. He pulled out an oblong white object, irregularly shaped, ridged and cratered. He turned it to face her: a smiling skull, with a bony snout and deadly sharp canines.

"I slaughtered this wolf myself," he said, clearly pleased by the bloody memory. "She attacked me as I played in the wood near my home. I'll never forget my mother's face when I walked in, bloodied head to toe, holding the bitch's head by the ear." The pitchfork prongs twitched into a smile. His dark eyes shimmered in the ambient light. "I was eight."

రచ

Shaken, she returned to Torre de la Reina. Every man had looked like an Inquisitor on the walk back. Crossing her apartment vestibule, she was annoyed to find Nicolas perched on her sofa holding her favorite trinket box, the silver one with an enamel top and a snowy Alpine village painted on it. It was the one gift from the King she truly treasured. "I picked this out," he said, staring into the box. "I told His Majesty it was very Maribarbola, and he agreed." He let the lid drop with a clap. "So? How did it go with Haro?"

"Fine."

"Wolf?"

"Yes."

A snide little laugh escaped his nose. "He gave me that same prophet's test, so long ago he obviously doesn't remember. I failed." He set the box down with care. "Of course, I hadn't meant to imply that the Great Maribarbola should need my help solving Haro's trifling riddles. I suppose that was just my way of saying, 'Let's start afresh, you and I.'"

"All right," Mari said, knowing neither of them had any intention whatsoever of starting afresh.

"Don't worry," he said, sensing her wariness. "I'm not about to tell you how you should advise the King. You've got plenty of others to do that." He slipped off the sofa and stepped toward her. "It'll be good for Philip to have a True Prophet on hand. You'll bring him comfort in his decision-making. God knows he could use some peace of mind." He ambled over to a console table and surveyed the rich curios. "Of course, Mariana always has her own best interests at heart, which could make things sticky for you." He smirked. "But I'm sure your inviolable wisdom will prevail."

His gaze drifted up the wall. "It brings back memories being in here," he said. "I can't say I miss those days." He started walking again, thankfully toward the door. "Is Mariana driving you mad yet?" His cheeks dimpled in a wry smile. "You know we've got bets going as to how long you'll last."

"Who's we?"

"Just a few of us. Myself, Octavio, Sergio, the King."

The King? "I have no intentions of leaving her company," Mari said.

"That's what I said, in the beginning."

Actually, it was the Queen who had banished him, but Mari kept quiet.

He paused in the vestibule to admire some gold candlesticks. "Handsome candleholders." Mari didn't care for them; she couldn't tell if they were supposed to be cherubs or nude dwarfs. She kept them in the vestibule so she didn't have to look at them. "Let me know if you tire of them. My broker in Toledo can fetch you top ducat for the pair." He sauntered toward the door. "Let's face it—a dwarf's salary doesn't go far these days, especially the way he likes to debase the coinage with his New World silver. You know a loaf of bread costs almost two *reales* now? A pound of cheese will set you back three." He paused at the threshold. "You are saving, right? I hope you're saving."

"Of course I am." Even with her fritter and gambling habits, she had still managed to stash a few coins away, somewhere ...

"Put away as much as you can. In a bank outside the Alcázar, preferably outside of Spain." He raised his eyebrows. "These are interesting times. Nobody knows quite how this is going to end. We're just one coup away from being out on the street, and then what?"

Finally he stepped into the corridor. "This is good," he said of their blossoming friendliness. "I should take you out on my horse when the weather breaks. He seats two dwarfs comfortably—rides like a royal coach."

"Splendid," Mari said dully. Two dwarfs on a horse.

Nicolas just laughed and disappeared down the tower stairs.

Mari closed her door and stood staring at it. She didn't know what to make of Nicolas's sudden show of goodwill other than there having to be an ulterior motive. He wanted something from her, and she had better figure out what it was before she inadvertently handed it to him. Power compounded itself by sniffing out and consolidating with other powers. Now that she had the King's ear, maybe he had concluded it would be wiser to work with her than against her. Or maybe he was still against her.

That wolf tip had been less an olive branch than his maneuvering her into a situation where she had no choice but to trust him—an act to demonstrate to her how powerful he was, how valuable an ally he could be. She couldn't afford to reject his overtures outright. Haro had made himself clear: unless she cooperated, he would set the Inquisition upon her. Mari needed every advantage she could get, and Nicolas knew this court like the inside of his pocket—and probably hoarded more damning secrets than all confessional priests here combined. At this point, a fake friendship with him seemed vastly preferable to remaining active enemies.

These were challenging times, Haro had said, strange times. Mortal enemies were extending their hands under the guise of friendship, forging alliances hitherto unthinkable.

Chapter 17

THE HEARTBREAK

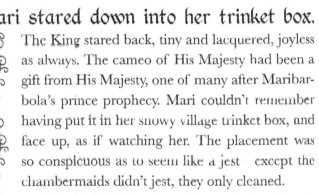

ari stared down into her trinket box. The King stared back, tiny and lacquered, joyless as always. The cameo of His Majesty had been a gift from His Majesty, one of many after Maribarbola's prince prophecy. Mari couldn't remember having put it in her snowy village trinket box, and face up, as if watching her. The placement was so conspicuous as to seem like a jest — except the chambermaids didn't jest, they only cleaned.

She buried the cameo in prayer beads and slapped the box shut, then plucked a hair from her head and lay it over the top. Since her meeting with Haro the other day, she'd been tracking objects in her apartment with excessive vigilance. *She's made you bitter and paranoid, like herself.* But she had to consider she was being watched and might have been for some time. Bosco had spent a fortnight alone in her apartment while she was in Barcelona, ostensibly as a servant sent by the King. Now Mari was convinced he'd been less a gift than a Torre Dorada spy.

She dumped her knapsack on the bed and opened the box containing her optic tube. Panic seized her heart as she riffled through the Countess's papers, seeing them for the first time through Inquisition eyes: symbols that looked like satanic runes; blasphemous diagrams of the earth orbiting the sun; notes declaring *that which is not observable does not exist* and other such heresies, the very mildest of which would be more than damning enough to see Mari aflame on the Plaza Mayor.

Quickly, before sentimentality got the better of her, she chucked the papers into the fire. Through a sheen of tears she watched them burn—her lady's handwriting, decades of painstaking observations and calculations, small astronomical triumphs, those rare glimmers of the lady's joy and passion, now curling and dripping to ash in a fireplace in Spain, as if none of it ever were. And as the papers disappeared, Maria-Barbara disappeared a little more with them, yet more precious evidence of her destroyed— that person who had lived humbly and worthily, now all but unobservable, nonexistent.

తాత

As the Queen's fine figure reappeared, so did the Marquis, looking handsomer than anyone remembered. He came bearing silk dresses and jeweled daggers for Prospero and Ferdinand and was invited to stay for a courtly meal and months-overdue *Hombre* rematch with Mari and the Queen.

"What are the stakes, ladies?" he said, cutting the deck. "*Reales?* Pesos? It's yours to lose."

Mari glanced at the Queen, hoping she would handle this.

"She says she's not gambling anymore," said the Queen.

"*What?*" he said.

"She says it's a waste of money."

"The San Balbina children don't think it's a waste of money." Mari knew he would play that card. Supposedly he gave all of his winnings to his charity. "What's the fun in playing if there are no stakes?"

"I thought maybe we could play for beans," Mari said, fondling the sac of beans she'd brought.

"*Beans?*" said the Marquis.

"Alright, maravedis then," Mari said. This was the lowest Spanish coin, basically worthless.

"Beans would be more exciting," he said. "What's gotten into you, Mari? You've never been one to pass on a bet."

As if Haro's Inquisition threat hadn't been enough, Nicolas had put the fear of God in her with his talk of runaway inflation and their being just one coup away from living on the streets.

"She gets on these jags," said the Queen. "A few months ago she was on a prayer binge—thought she was going straight to hell." The Marquis chuckled. "Now she thinks she's going to end up destitute somehow."

"Imagine that," he said. "The King's prophet, destitute."

"I beg your pardon?" said the Queen. "She's my prophet."

They played for beans. Conversation turned to Teresa's betrothal, which was always on the Queen's mind these days. Mari had told her all about the meeting with Haro, including the part about the Inquisitor General asking if she were a true prophet. To that the Queen had pointed out that Mari was indeed a true prophet and therefore had nothing to worry about.

"Haro was emasculated in Portugal," said the Queen, "so now he's trying to cement his legacy as some sort of peacemaker." She was on her third cup of sherry, and her lips were loose. "But I can't believe the King is actually considering it. Never mind the political consequences, which would be dire, but to send his own daughter to live with those wretched people? You know those French kings parade their mistresses around in plain view? Have them living right there in the palace, right under the queen's nose. It's vile."

"I suppose it shows how desperate he is," said the Marquis carefully, "if he's willing to sacrifice his own daughter in that regard."

The Queen plucked a card from her hand and slapped it down. "Foulest people on earth, the French … godless, lecherous, filthy lazy drunks … I've heard stories of their debauchery that would make a whore cringe. Teresa wouldn't last a day up there, pious as she is. Poor girl will probably die of syphilis, if she doesn't throw herself off a tower first." She peered over her cards at Mari. "Be sure to tell him that, Mari, when you meet with him."

Mari nodded and rearranged her cards.

The Queen took another sip and stamped her cup down. "And what of the flagrant disrespect for my brother? Spain's greatest ally! Do they honestly think that such a grave insult to the Emperor and the House of Austria would go unpunished?"

"No doubt they've considered that," said the Marquis. "But Leopold's young yet. He needn't marry right away. Perhaps the King intends to betroth Margarita to him someday."

"*No!*" said the Queen, so ferociously that Mari's heart jumped.

A horrid silence fell. Mari and the Marquis exchanged mortified glances. The Queen pressed her fingers to her lips and closed her eyes. The Marquis reached out and squeezed her shoulder, a violation of protocol. "Your Majesty, forgive me," he said softly. The Queen held up a hand, forgiving him.

Mari stared at her cards but didn't see them, and she felt sick because it all made sense now—the way the Queen drank four or five cups of sherry before every coupling ceremony, the way she always returned afterward looking vacant and despondent and wanting to be alone, the way her fingernails had dug into Mari's palm that night when her fifty-year-old uncle climbed atop her. This wasn't about her loyalty to Austria; it was about her love for her daughter. She wanted her stepdaughter to marry her brother so her own daughter wouldn't have to. She wanted to spare Margarita the quiet horror of having to marry her uncle—and bed her uncle—the way she herself had to.

No house in this land remained untouched by the atrocities of war, and that the Queen would sooner allow decades of bloodshed to continue than consign Margarita to a similar fate spoke volumes of the Queen's true feelings about her unnatural marriage and the fierce love she had for her daughter. To the King's ministers, her opposition to a French treaty probably looked like a selfish political maneuver, a power play for its own sake, a man's game. But Mari understood now: this was a mother's game. The Queen was desperate and ferocious, and it was as heartbreaking as it was scary.

The Queen recovered quickly, and they continued their game. The Marquis won handily, amassing a huge pile of beans. Mari dozed on the sofa while they sequestered themselves in the royal bedroom and was made to walk him out at his usual ungodly hour.

They plodded through the corridors in sleeplorn silence, with the Marquis seeming vaguely bashful and apologetic like he always did on these walks. A tinkling leather pouch in his hand turned Mari's head. "She bought my beans for a ducat apiece," he said. "This'll feed a dozen orphans for six months." Mari nodded, careful not to encourage him on the topic of his charity, which would keep him talking until sunup. "Of course she forbade me to inform my press contacts. God forbid anyone should know how big her heart truly is."

If they knew they would use it against her, to destroy her. For all the time he spent in the Queen's bed, he should know that.

They reached the deserted Carlos south entrance. The Marquis opened the door to the usual chorus of birdsong that sang him off after a night of sin with the Queen. He hesitated at the threshold. "She's in knots over this marriage," he said. "I've never seen her this upset. She thinks everyone's against her. Your loyalty means the world to her." Mari nodded, expressionless. "Well, goodnight." He stepped into the pewter dawnlight. "Or, I guess I should say, good morning."

Mari watched him tread the footpath. She resented his presuming to be the only one who knew the true size of the Queen's heart, even if he was the only one, and his presuming to tell her what her loyalty meant to the Queen, which was really just a pitifully transparent attempt to manipulate her into doing what the Queen wanted her to do while allowing himself to think he had held sway in the matter.

Behind every smile, every word, every deed, a motive. Mari would never hear another sincere word spoken again as long as she lived. She was incapable now. Maybe the world had always been like this, self-serving and disingenuous, a world of Udos, differing only in their bags of tricks and degrees of skillfulness, and this court had finally forced her to see it.

ᘏᘏ

Mari gazed out her windows at Madrid, gold and hazy in the setting sun. She'd been told today would be the day and had been sitting here all afternoon in a good dress, waiting. Right now she was thinking about the Legend, that night in Geneva when they had camped by the grand lake—the way his hot bodkin made orange squiggles in the dark, and the snowflakes gathered in the folds of his pepper hat. He had entertained her with stories of his travels that night, tales of mischief and magic and shockingly gullible women, while Mari had laughed and snorted and counted her coins.

She tried to remember if there was ever a time she'd been in control of her life, but she could not recall any such time. A knock on her door interrupted her thoughts. "Enter," she said. Two shadowy mustached figures darkened her threshold. Maribarbola rose from her chair and went with them.

His Majesty had agreed to her terms, she was told as they climbed the Torre Dorada stairs. She would speak to him alone under the condition of confidentiality.

The King received her in his study and acknowledged her with a nod. With his falling face and leaden eyes, he awaited her word. Behind him, his realm sprawled: twilit Madrid, her street fires ablaze and taverns ringing with mirth, and beyond, mountains rising, hazy and ghostlike, across the vast Castilian plain. That night in Geneva, Udo had told her the story of a little girl who had come to him with a fistful of pfennigs and asked him to cast a spell to grow her father's arm back. The man had lost it fighting the Catholics at Nördlingen. Mari had scarcely realized it at the time, but by Catholics Udo had meant the Spaniards, who crushed the Swedish and German Protestant armies in that bloody 1634 battle and still commemorated the victory every September here in Madrid, with fireworks and a hundred-pig stew on the Plaza Mayor.

Mari reminded herself of the one-armed man, and Haro's dead fifteen-year-old soldiers, as she stood before the King. That she was using carnage to comfort herself only proved how twisted her life had become and also marked a shameful new low in her attempts at self-rationalization. In truth, ending a war was a tangential concern; the only life she had come here to save was her worthless own. The threat of being burned or buried alive was real now. It was real. As always, the choice had been made for her, another non-choice cruelly disguised as choice, the better to plague her wretched conscience. Haro had known exactly what to say, exactly how to yank her puppet strings, to make Maribarbola dance for the King. "You can bestow no greater honor upon your daughter," she said, her voice cracking because her heart was breaking, "than to offer her hand in peace to your enemy."

His Majesty received her word with a solemn nod. Having no desire to linger in his presence, Mari bent her neck and made to leave but paused at the painting of the painting, looming hugely in the King's study, beholding the beholder. She locked gazes with her former self, that person she had been when the Maestro painted her—the one who no longer existed, in the black dress that no longer fit her, showing him her heart that was no longer in her, so quietly resolute, so utterly, foolishly convinced she would sooner die than betray her Queen.

She couldn't look at Margarita.

જીજી

The Infanta Teresa was betrothed to King Louis XIV of France, and Haro and his French counterpart began negotiating the thorny preliminaries of a peace treaty. To appease his closest ally, Philip offered Emperor Leopold the Infanta Margarita, the younger and fairer of Spain's royal daughters. Leopold accepted his niece's hand but agreed the girl should be kept in Spain until first bleed.

Mari braced herself for a day of reckoning with the Queen, but that day didn't come. The King and Haro apparently upheld their end of the confidentiality agreement, which only compounded Mari's guilt. As if betraying the Queen were not enough, she now got to share the filthy secret of it with Haro. He had sent a note, which Mari swiftly burned, thanking her for her cooperation along with another unwanted cameo of His Majesty, lest she forget her true master, and a bouquet of irises, lest she forget they were watching her. She was under Torre Dorada's thumb now, not only useless to the Queen but potentially dangerous. Haro had neutralized Maribarbola, paralyzed her, and quite possibly weaponized her.

When Mari's guilt threatened to get the better of her, she began rehearsing her confession to the Queen. She would confess all of it, everything, starting with Udo. Then she would tearfully plead for mercy, beg the Queen to banish her to the streets, let her leave with her life.

But she didn't confess; she never got the chance. A fresh sorrow befell the Crown and eclipsed all other cares, driving Their Majesties, united in grief, to the Escorial monastery in San Lorenzo for an official mourning period.

Baby Ferdinand had suffered a massive fit and died.

જીજી

Chapter 18

THE KING'S JUNKET

In the spring His Majesty left for the French frontier, in a twenty-mile-long caravan of thousands of diplomats and servants, to deliver Teresa to her bridegroom and sign the peace treaty with the House of Bourbon. The Queen stayed behind to serve as regent in his stead, a role she did not relish, and threw herself into the tedium of governing. This included a slew of paperwork and daily council meetings, and sitting on the throne several hours a week to hear petitions from random citizens on things like building permits and wagon ordinances—even a mule dung dispute, which, according to one newssheet, Her Majesty quashed with a flick of the hand.

One morning shortly after the King's departure, there came a spirited knock on Mari's door. She answered it and was shocked to see Nicolas, whom she'd assumed the King had taken on his diplomatic junket to dazzle the Frenchmen with his tiny charms. "*Buenos días,*" he said. "May I come in?"

She let him in. Since he had saved her life with the wolf tip several weeks ago, she'd felt obligated to participate in this pantomime of friendship—the starting afresh, as it were—except to Mari it felt more like a hostage-taking, with she bound by her indebtedness to him. Though she had never actually thanked him, her grudging gratitude now thickened the very ether between them, tincturing their every interaction. Again she found herself on the wrong end of a gross power imbalance, forced to endure his unbidden visits, his every smirk and jest, condescension and insincerity, fiction and flattery, and the self-satisfied air of saviorship he now wielded over her, which was especially irritating coming from a man three feet tall.

He sauntered to her automaton clock and peered in at the pageant people, while Mari quietly enjoyed how he looked like a little girl peeking into a dollhouse. "I'm surprised to see you," she said. "I assumed you'd gone with the King."

"He invited don Diego Velázquez to ride with him. You know the artist doesn't care for me much." He ambled toward her, and she waited for the inevitable invitation to go for a turn in the countryside on his horse, which she'd twice now declined. She wasn't about to put her rear-end in his sidesaddle, her life in his reins. "I come bearing news," he said. "You remember Roberta Rosado? The actress?"

"The King's mistress? I remember."

"She's pregnant."

Mari was careful not to react as she tried to calculate the emotional and political repercussions for the Queen. "Has Her Majesty been told?"

"Not yet. Nobody wants to do it. They're having a card tournament Friday night. Whoever loses has to tell her." He ran his tiny finger along the edge of a console table. Mari glowered at him, outraged on the Queen's behalf. How repugnant of them to make a sport out of her humiliation. "So that's why I'm here," he said, brushing imaginary dust from his fingers. "I thought you might like to tell her yourself."

"Why in God's name would you think that?"

"You could frame it as a prophecy," he said. Mari snorted. "No, think about it. It would give her time to get used to the idea before she gets the official word, and you could add it to your growing list of successes."

"The King should be the one to tell her."

"He's too cowardly. He waited until he'd be gone to have somebody else tell her. Roberta is rather far along. He's installed her in an apartment at the Buen Retiro." He raised his eyebrows. "Let's face it, this should come as no surprise to anyone. He's quite virile."

"So I've heard." Approximately thirty, Binnie once told her. Thirty bastards. Only General Juan José had been legitimized, however, decreed the King's own. The rest had been tucked away in private homes or convents, unaware of their parentage.

"It would be easier for her to hear it coming from you," Nicolas said.

"No. I don't want any part of this."

"It's your decision. You still have a few days to change your mind."

On his way out he suggested they see a comedy together at the Buen Retiro; he'd have a lot of time on his hands with the King being gone, and boredom and idleness never failed to drive him crazy. Mari told him she'd check her schedule and get back to him.

৩৩

All week Mari fretted over whether or not to tell the Queen about Roberta's pregnancy and resented Nicolas for burdening her with the dilemma. With Haro having lain bare his ambition to cripple Maribarbola, she also had to consider that Roberta might not be pregnant—that this might be a ruse to lure Maribarbola into a false prophecy. With the King gone the next several weeks, lies, intrigues, and power plays would be rampant, and already Mari had a vague sense of being circled by wolves. Foremostly suspicious was Nicolas's conveying the pregnancy news, ostensibly as a favor, after having maneuvered her into a counterfeit friendship so deftly and sneakily she now wondered if he and Haro had set her up with the wolf together.

She would play it safe and keep quiet. Any move she made, no matter how measured and discreet, might trigger a counter-move from Torre Dorada setting off a chain of events that could too-easily end in a hail of threats against her. If Roberta really was pregnant, the Queen would find out eventually. Besides, Her Majesty was so busy running Spain these days, Mari saw her only briefly a couple of times during the week, and both times she seemed frazzled and annoyed and still heartsick over the loss of Ferdinand.

On Friday morning the Queen summoned her. Mari found her in her heretofore little-used study behind a torrent of paperwork, scratching away with her pen, a pair of black-rimmed spectacles straddling her nose. Mari chuckled at the sight. The Queen looked up and plucked off the spectacles in one swift, Udo-esque sweep. Mari's smile vanished when she saw the look on her face.

"Octavio Barón was just here," said the Queen. This was one of the King's equerries. "I'm told the King's wench is pregnant."

Mari's eyes widened; her lips parted in genuine shock. Their card game was supposed to be tonight.

"Don't act surprised," said the Queen. "He said you knew."

"Your Majesty ... " Mari grappled for words. "Nicolas told me, but I thought he might be lying. I didn't want to trouble you unless I knew for sure."

"You should have told me regardless."

"You're right, I should have. Please forgive me." She bent her neck with humble hopes of mercy.

The Queen stared her down for an excruciating couple of seconds. Through her icy glare glimmered something Mari had never quite seen in her before: genuine hurt. "I should banish you from my company for such a betrayal," she said.

"And stand alone against your enemies?"

"I must ask myself if I already do." This she said with enough sadness and loathing to make Mari wonder if she was really talking about the Margarita betrayal—as if the Queen had known all along, perhaps even orchestrated it herself as a test. The possibility made Mari physically ill.

"Your Majes—"

"You're dismissed." She dipped her pen and returned to her papers.

Stunned and sick with shame, Mari left.

ɷ

If those Torre Dorada snakes were trying to drive a wedge between her and the Queen, it was working. The two avoided each other all week, with Mari absenting herself to her apartment, waiting for the Queen to summon her, forgive her, scream at her, box her ears, anything. But the Queen only ignored her, leaving Mari to ruminate on her failures, her disloyalty, her unfitness to serve. As the estrangement lengthened, fears of banishment intensified. Mari wondered if this was what had befallen Nicolas, the alleged unspeakable betrayal, and was chagrined by a newfound sympathy for him. Maybe serving the Queen was impossible, abject failure inevitable.

By week's end, self-loathing gave way to angry self-rationalization. By now Mari was certain Haro hadn't divulged her filthy secret; he wouldn't snip that puppet string without good reason. That meant the Queen was basically making an elephant out of a midge, punishing Mari unfairly, *infuriating* her with the suggestion that she, the Queen, stood alone against her enemies! But apparently Mari's efforts hadn't been enough. The storm, the red moon, the rise of Torre de la Reina—not enough. All that clawing and scheming and life-gambling, not enough. And if a prince in the cot didn't please her, nothing Mari did would ever please her. Sustained loyalty to such a person was futile, like tossing water into the ocean—not to mention unrequited. Surely the Queen wouldn't hesitate to throw Mari to the wolves should the need ever arise.

Mari was forced to contemplate a Queenless future, a move to Torre Dorada, perhaps, as Nicolas had done. If she were honest, the Queen was hardly worth the trouble anymore. Mari was starting to think she'd been shackled to the wrong royal, that the King was her better destiny, defection to Torre Dorada necessary to preserve her sanity. Yes, His Majesty had problems—huge, abstract problems that played out on maps on tables, his nearest formidable enemy four hundred miles away, in Portugal. The foremost benefit, however, was his Absolute Power, which for Mari meant absolute protection against the Inquisition—freedom from fear, from panic, every time she heard boots in the stairwell or got the urge to duck behind galería columns at the sight of every ministerial-looking man.

She imagined herself reaping the spoils of the King's favor: a spacious apartment, her own coach, dogs, horses—one of those Torre Dorada lackeys even had a pet monkey—a magnificent wardrobe, rich and beautiful toys, pictures painted by the Maestro's own hand, bullfights, comedies, machine plays, operas, poetry jousts, weekend hunting trips in the Guadarramas. She had heard that the King liked to sleep in the open air, under the stars, and that he could be warm and funny in private. Mari could accompany him on his expeditions for good luck and protection. She could tend the fire, fill the wineskins, cook the game, and share in the jolly laughter and hearty meals of men. She was so sick of salads and jams. So sick of cards and dice, and sherry and biscuits, and Binnie's voice shrilling in the stairwell, and frittering her life away in the Queen's apartment, which always smelled faintly of overripe melon even though there were no melons, and the pointless gossip, the who wore what and who was courting whom, the clay-on-clay sound of the Queen's búcaro clattering on its saucer, and—good God—the way she'd nibble off a piece and crunch it in her teeth. It was maddening.

On Friday night the Marquis paid court. Mari could hear them downstairs, bantering to the tinkle of dinnerware and coquettish laughter. The Queen liked to watch him flirt with the maidservants, the way they fumbled the silver, the way their cheeks blushed, even the old hens. Soon they'd retire to the sofa to talk news or politics, and she'd go off on some long, boring tangent while he gazed at her bosom, pretending to listen.

Mari half-expected Josefina to call, to tell her she was wanted downstairs. The Queen always invited her when the Marquis came to maintain a façade of propriety and have her on hand for *Hombre*, a three-man game. It was also Mari's job to lubricate the conversation and keep things gay, and to make the Queen look tall and beautiful beside her. Surely by now the Marquis had asked where she was, and, depending on the Queen's mood, might have dared to exact his manly logic upon her, telling her she was being unreasonable, she couldn't ask for a more faithful servant, and she ought to accept Mari back into her company immediately, to put an end to this nonsense.

Mari wouldn't answer. She'd pretend to be asleep. Or maybe she should leave, go downstairs and pester Binnie. But then Binnie would ask why she wasn't with the Queen tonight, and Mari didn't feel like explaining that she was no longer trusted, her services no longer needed, and that one false step was all it had taken to slip from the Queen's good graces, permanently apparently.

Josefina didn't call, and as the night dragged on, and the Queen's laughter grew louder and shriller and evermore annoying, Mari made the spiteful decision to contact Nicolas in the morning to see if he was still up for that comedy. The gossip sheets would be on fire if Maribarbola and Nicolasito stepped out in public together, the press having (accurately) pitted them against one another after he'd shamed her at Maria Concepción's wedding. "An End of Hostilities," they'd write, an equivoque on the treaty with the French. There'd be cartoons of her and Nicolas with doves and olive sprigs, white flags.

Wouldn't that get the Queen's blood up!

Mari woke the next morning still committed to the idea and scratched out a courtly letter to "don Nicolas" inquiring about his availability that evening. She didn't want to have a page deliver it and risk having the Queen told that she was messaging Nicolas, so she sealed it and put on her coat to post it outside. She flung open the door and was startled to see Binnie, her fist raised to knock and her peachy face looking very grave.

ಚ

Mari entered the Queen's dark, chilly apartment. The drapes were drawn. Only a loaf of ash lay in the grate. The sherry bottle and cups from her evening with the Marquis stood forlornly on the reception room table. Please get down there, Binnie had said. Her Majesty was refusing to see anyone. She had been alone nearly three hours now; people were starting to worry. Mari was the only one who could barge in and check on her, the only Reina staffer not bound by protocol.

She walked down the hall to the royal bedroom and nudged the door open. The Queen lay on the bed in a slender heap, unmoving.

Mari went to her. The Queen's eyes were closed. She clutched a balled-up handkerchief to her heart. Mari touched her in a panic—she thought she was dead—but she wasn't dead. She opened her eyes, closed them again, and began quaking with sorrow.

Prospero had suffered a fit that morning.

Mari stayed with her, wiped the Queen's tears, held the Queen's hand, spoon-fed her broth, and tried in vain to cheer her. She promised her everything was going to be all right, he was going to be all right. God be thanked, it was just a small one. And he was alert now, looking around, an excellent sign. He would live, Mari promised. He would live to be King. Heaven had ordained it.

When the Queen finally slept, Mari stayed at her bedside, too heavyhearted to move, too vividly reminded of her last days with the Countess, the helplessness and sorrow of watching her lady suffer. She was shamed by her childish fantasies of defecting to Torre Dorada. She would never, could never, leave her. Silently, as if in prayer, Mari pledged her loyalty to the sleeping Queen. Loyalty itself might be intrinsically worthless, but it was all she had left to give, the only thing left of her she was certain was real. She may be shackled to the wrong royal, but the Queen was the best thing she had, her home and refuge, the one who had snatched her up when no one else wanted her, needed her when the cruel world was trying hard to dispose of her. That alone was worth more than the King's protection, more than the sum of all the King's riches.

The silent avowal brought Mari a few breaths of peace, the promise she'd never again have to suffer a week like this, deprived of the Queen's affection, sickened by the Queen's disappointment. Never again would she have to see that look in Her Majesty's eyes when she had wondered aloud if she stood alone against her enemies. Of all Mari's harrowing moments at this court, that one had been the worst. The moment she thought she had lost the Queen.

ॐ

A few weeks later, Mari stood cowering between Isabel's and Agustina's skirts, hiding from the venom, the airborne poison. It emanated from the Queen like quivering licks of heat and filled the King's reception room like a sweltering stench. She was stone sober for this one.

Mari peeked out at the King's side. Yes, they felt it too. Mari would have reveled in their discomfort if she herself weren't so uncomfortable. The Maestro was there, his dark gaze roving and probing as usual, objectifying everyone and everything in its path. Beside him, Haro—the Prince of Peace, the newssheets were calling him—hung his head in prayer, probably praying this would end soon.

Below, nestled in the forest of black legs, a shock of peacock blue: Nicolas in a sumptuous little suit, staring uncomfortably at the floor.

Outside, a firework whistled up over the city and detonated in a lame crackle. Celebrating the King's safe return.

He had gotten back that afternoon, looking more morose than ever. Binnie had already procured the story from someone who'd been there: the cunning Frenchmen had taken full advantage of Spain's political and economic desperation and strong-armed Philip into making concessions hitherto unthinkable. In addition to handing over Teresa—with a half-million escudo dowry, which he still hadn't secured—he was forced to concede vast territories of Catalonia and Flanders. The Spanish-French border had been redrawn. Spain had been castrated.

The trip had put the fear of God into His Majesty, allowing him to gaze upon the very flesh of his mortal enemies: so stout and hale they were, so great in number, so tall and elegant in their high-heeled shoes and curly wigs, such beautiful, round, fertile young women. An army of kings and kingmakers, with their every eye on the Spanish Crown. And then to be greeted by the devastating news that Prospero was not the sturdy little prince everyone thought he was.

So as Madrid blazed and crackled with joy over the return of her lord, and the Salón Grande thundered with mirth downstairs, the favorites had been summoned to the King's apartment for this emergency coupling ceremony and were now made to suffer the horrific awkwardness of being present for Their Majesties' first contact since the Queen had been so chickenheartedly informed of Roberta's pregnancy.

The blessed end neared. Everardo flicked them with holy water. Mari swore she heard a sizzle when it hit the Queen. She caught Nicolas's eye from across the room. He threw her a look, uncomfortably amused.

Their Majesties started down the hall. The Queen strode briskly, stirring the air with her angry wind, slicing through her rage with yet more rage, walking way ahead of him, an egregious violation of protocol. Mari's anxiety mounted with the Queen's fury. Even more distressing to witness than Her Majesty's humiliation was her dangerous obliviousness, her unquestioned belief that she could flaunt her rage with impunity—that she was still politically unassailable with her prince and her prophet, as if Prospero weren't sickly, as if Maribarbola hadn't been crippled by enemy threats.

Haro, meanwhile, stood on the King's side of the room, looking unaffected by his historic victory, calm and focused in a way that frightened Mari. He had just negotiated an end to a thirty-year war; he could find a way to end this marriage if he really wanted to. Feeling Mari's stare, his gaze locked upon hers and lingered disturbingly, as if daring her to act, knowing Maribarbola's next move could subject her to life-threatening Inquisition scrutiny and bring down Torre de la Reina all the more quickly. All she could do was stand by helpless—she and her worthless loyalty, hiding like a child between the skirts, as impotent as on the day Udo sold her, having to bear the merciless degradation of being a dwarf cut off at the knees.

The royal footsteps faded. His bedroom door closed. Woe be unto any child who should take seed in that acid womb tonight.

The Queen's hostility lingered thickly in the reception room. They all stood paralyzed by it, eyes scanning one another, smirks blossoming behind mustaches, igniting rage in Mari's breast.

"That was painful," Nicolas said.

♥♥♥

Chapter 19

THE PLOT

eeks after returning from the French frontier, don Diego Rodríguez de Silva y Velázquez, belted knight of the Military Order of Santiago, Senior Chamberlain and firm friend to His Majesty, Curator of Royal Pictures and Tapestries, and himself the greatest painter of all time, fell ill and died. The King nearly sank to the grave brokenhearted, such that even the Queen's bitter heart sweetened with pity. Though sharing in the general sadness that befell the court at the Maestro's passing, Mari was more troubled to learn of the King's debilitating grief, as his melancholy never served anyone but his highhanded ministers, who ruled unchecked while the King retreated in misery.

His Majesty's summer worsened yet. A cache of explosives was found hidden beneath the stage machinery at the Buen Retiro in what was being investigated as a foiled attempt on the King's life. The newssheets blazed with conjecture. The principal suspicion was that the evildoers, encouraged by reports of Prospero's ill health, had sought to kill the King before he could seed another, thus paving the way for a coup. His Majesty threw the full power of the Inquisition behind the investigation, and their arm of torture reached far and wide across the land.

Inquisitors could have spared their victims agony untold by simply asking the Queen. "It was Catalan rebels," she said, punctuated by the chink of her cup on the table. The Marquis was visiting, and they'd just eaten a summer meal of cucumber soup and cold lamb pie. "They've been emboldened by the concessions he made to the French, which is exactly what I said would happen. Now watch, that entire region is going to erupt. It'll be 1640 all over again, only this time he's bankrupt and his army is spread even thinner."

"I hope you're wrong," said the Marquis.

Mari hoped to God she was wrong. Between her Inquisition fears and Torre Dorada's insidious games, her nerves couldn't withstand another threat. Until now, the possibility of another Catalan uprising had been the least of Spain's problems, a fly on the King's cheek. If the Queen was correct, that meant Catalan rebels had taken their fight to Madrid, the seat of the Crown. Just one coup is all it would take to put Mari back on the streets, living on nothing but sweet memories.

"The investigation will prove me right," said the Queen. "The whole thing reeks of Catalan barbarity. Only they would be savage enough to blow up an entire theater of innocents along with the King. Or who knows? Maybe I was their intended target."

"I'm sure it was the King," said the Marquis, clearly thinking aloud.

"Are you suggesting I'm not important enough?"

"What? No, of course not!" He laughed uncomfortably, but she wasn't jesting, she was serious. "You're absolutely worthy of being assassinated."

This hung awkwardly in the air for a moment, but the Queen let it go.

ဘာ

Later that week, with the King and Queen down in Madrid for a public mass, Mari's quiet afternoon was interrupted by a curt knock on her door. Assuming it was just another unwanted visit from Nicolas, she flung open the door and found herself staring, with nascent horror, at an abdominal expanse of ministerial black wool.

"*Buenas tardes*, Maribarbola," Haro said. "May we speak?"

Mari stepped aside.

He traversed the vestibule with that self-important stride all the men of Torre Dorada had and winced at Mari's sunny windows like a person who kept his office far below the earth. Mortified by the sight of Haro in her apartment and dreading whatever reason had brought him here, Mari half-consciously offered him a seat in one of her dwarf chairs. The minister declined.

"I won't take up much of your time," he said, eyeing her florid gold curios with the contempt of a man who oversaw the palace books. "Now that the business of the treaty is behind us, I've returned my attention to pecuniary matters," he whisked a letter from his coat and handed it to her, "such as this one."

Mari unfolded the paper with tremulous hands, somehow expecting it to pertain to her—the expenses she'd incurred in Barcelona, for example, or that twenty-ducat bonus from the storm prophecy, which the King never did pay. When she saw the name *Cristofer Sandoval* in the Queen's elegant handwriting, she recognized the document instantly: the Marquis's tax-exempt petition, which apparently had been languishing in the backlogs all this time.

"A cursory audit of the Queen's budget revealed a bequest of over two thousand ducats to this man in the past year alone."

Despite herself, Mari's eyes bulged. She wouldn't have guessed the Marquis's gambling winnings had amounted to that much. "He has an orphans' charity," she explained. "The Queen is his chief benefactress."

"Even if the Crown weren't nearly bankrupt, two thousand ducats is an exorbitant sum, wouldn't you agree?"

After a stretch of dense silence, Mari said, "She has a big heart."

"So she must. Or perhaps this Marquis of Villamirada is an extraordinarily persuasive sort."

"Not really," Mari mumbled.

"What do we know of his politics?"

We. So apparently she was a Torre Dorada informant now. "Staunch loyalist. Devout Catholic." This was actually true. "He's been nothing but a firm supporter of Her Majesty, and the Crown in general."

"For two thousand ducats," Haro said dryly, "he must be a firm young man indeed."

Mari's cheeks blazed. She handed the petition back to him.

"Surely you, with your divine foresight, recognize the danger in getting involved in something unseemly," he said. "You wouldn't want to be caught standing too close to Her Majesty if she should be burned by scandal."

Burned. Mari shook her head.

With that, he bade her good wishes and took his leave, pausing at the threshold to tell her the Inquisitor General sent his regards.

※

Haro's visit all but confirmed Mari's direst fears. Emboldened by his treaty triumph, the King's chief minister had revived his long-standing ambition to unseat the Queen. He and the other Torre Dorada jackals no doubt had their eyes on the not-too-distant future, in which the elderly King lay cold in his crypt, leaving behind a child successor and Mariana ruling as regent until the boy came of age, which could mean a decade or more of absolute power for the Queen. Such an arrangement would shake the court to its very marrow, reducing the men of Torre Dorada to stable boys if not heaps of ashes on the Plaza Mayor. If Mari could envision such an outcome, clearly they had, too, and would be taking aggressive measures to try to prevent it. This put Mari in the agonizing position of knowing the Queen was in political danger but being helpless to intervene. Indeed, if she so much as uttered her theory aloud, the ever-unsubtle Queen would send Maribarbola marching into the King's office with some cack-handed prophecy about Haro being a traitor, impelling Haro to retaliate with Inquisition force.

Furthering Mari's suspicions, Nicolas called the following Saturday morning, bearing a vessel of chocolate from the King's breakfast. By now she anticipated his visits, though his motives remained dubious as ever and frustratingly well-hidden. It made her long for the days of yore, when his old brand of overt antagonism seemed downright sportly compared to this subtle-manipulation thing he was doing now.

She let him in. It was a sweltering day, but Nicolasito didn't sweat, Mari had noticed, and in his tailored indigo suit looked as fresh and crisp and richly clad as a summer plum. After his requisite check of the automaton clock ("They never move," he said of the pageant people), he sat on the sofa and even accepted the chilled peach she offered from her snow chest, though, just like a tot, he lost interest after two small bites, leaving Mari to lament the waste.

"I'm worried about Philip," he said. "This bomb plot has left him shaken." He told Mari that, although the King had publicly shrugged off the assassination attempt as cowardly, foolhardy, and bearing the stamp of amateurs, privately he was acting like a man who had come within an inch of his life. "You should talk to him, assure him that everything will be all right. He'll listen to you."

"I can't assure him that."

"Sure you can." This led to an annoying philosophical debate on the nature of truth and when it might be considered morally acceptable to gloss the facts or even outrightwardly lie, "which I'm not asking you to do anyway," Nicolas said. He insisted that Philip's worst enemy was not the Catalans, the Portuguese, the English, or the French, but rather himself—his own stubbornness and short-sightedness, his blind loyalty to Rome, his overfondness of pleasures, his fetishism for pictures, his indulgence in melancholy, and his failed policies and impotence as a leader, as evidenced by Spain's recent humiliations abroad, her ruined economy, staggering debt, soaring inflation, and her proud, lazy, morally degenerate populace, most of whom were not clever enough to build machines, but also not humble enough to shovel mule dung off the streets. "Thank God the Moors are still willing to do it," he said.

As she half-listened to his rant, Mari was struck by how alike he and the Queen were. A couple of twenty-two-year-old sauceboxes, but correct much of the time. They must have been quite the duo, back when they were bosom companions.

Finally he stopped talking. He scrunched his lips and inspected his tiny fingernails, looking slightly embarrassed by his harangue. It was cute.

"Have you shared these insights with His Majesty?" Mari said, a jest.

"Many times." That was the thing with dwarfs and buffoons; not bound by protocol, they were permitted, encouraged even, to speak boldly to the King.

Conversation returned to the Retiro plot. A prominent newssheet was speculating it had been a rogue assassin, a rabid nationalist who'd been outraged by the King's prostrating himself at the feet of the French. "The Queen is convinced it was the Catalans," Mari said.

"Or maybe she's just trying to convince everyone it was the work of rebels and not an inside job."

A fertile silence fell. Nicolas wore the dimpled smirk of a lad gone too far.

Mari reminded herself to be careful, that she was being spied on in plain view. "What are you suggesting?"

"All I'm saying is, I'm not convinced of the purported political motivations behind the plot, or even that His Majesty was the intended target."

"You're saying the Queen may have been the intended target?" Nicolas snorted. "Who would care enough to kill her?"

"I can think of a couple of people," Mari mumbled offhandedly.

The remark wasn't lost on Nicolas. He hurled his man-in-the-well chuckle into every dark corner of the chamber. Mari really hoped the Queen wasn't downstairs. "Yes, I'm sure Haro would love to kill Mariana, but she's not worth blowing up the Retiro for. It'd be a lot less messy to just petition the Pope for an annulment."

Mari hated the Torre Dorada arrogance with which he said this—as if they were just a dispatch away from ousting the Queen, and only but by their grace and benevolence did she still sit upon her throne. In truth, Haro had already tried that tack and failed.

Nicolas cocked an eyebrow, his usual foretokening of intrigue. Mari regretted letting him in. "Being that the explosives were found beneath the stage," he said, "wouldn't it make sense that the target may have been one of the performers?"

She saw what he was doing now. So clearly, in fact, she was almost disappointed that Nicolas could be so transparent. Maybe she had overestimated him, just as he had clearly underestimated her.

"Don't tell me it hasn't crossed your mind," he said.

When the details of the Retiro plot first leaked, it actually had crossed Mari's mind, briefly, that the unexploded cache beneath the stage—practically beneath the actresses' skirts—seemed like some bungling attempt to implicate the Queen. The timing was especially suspect, she having flaunted her rage over the King's improprieties at that still much-discussed coupling ceremony only weeks before. "I can't imagine Roberta would be performing in her condition," Mari said carefully.

"She's not." He fiddled with a tassel on his breeches, clearly hesitating about something. "In fact, she's not even at the Retiro anymore. He's moved her here, for her safety and so his doctors can keep a close eye on her."

"*Dios mío*," Mari whispered, despite herself. If he was telling the truth—if the King really was keeping his mistress under the Queen's roof, like a vile French king—the Queen would be red-eyed with fury. She'd blow up the Alcázar and everyone in it. Maybe that's what they were trying to do—incite her to a state of rage in hopes that she'd retaliate in some scandalous, self-destructive way. "In Torre Dorada?"

"No. He would never be that brazen. He's installed her in one of the underground apartments, and just as well. Imagine being pregnant in this heat. You should see her. She's huge."

Mari narrowed her eyes at him. "Did he and Haro put you up to telling me this?" By now she knew how those cowards operated, and that they would thenceforth try to make Maribarbola the bearer of all bad news to the Queen.

"Not at all. In fact, they're going to great lengths to keep this secret. Poor Roberta hasn't seen daylight in weeks. Do what you wish with the information, but whatever you decide, please leave my name out of it."

Though skeptical of his claims, Mari resented his coming in here and lobbing another powder keg into her lap. The last time he did this, she and the Queen didn't speak for a week. "The Queen isn't capable of murder," she said firmly. "And even if she were, that trifling woman and her misbegotten child are hardly worth the trouble."

"His twenty-eighth misbegotten child. Haro keeps count. And those are the ones we know of." He cocked an eyebrow. "Or who knows? Maybe the King was her intended target. Now that would be a scandal."

꧁❀꧂

Chapter 20

THE QUEEN'S JOY

ne advantage to having Torre Dorada in
her head was that Mari could see their game more
clearly with every play, like a picture emerging from
an aggregate of sketchy brushstrokes. In hind-
sight, Mari had taken the Queen too high, made
her too powerful for her own good. The men of
Torre Dorada didn't tolerate threats to their hege-
mony gladly, and the Queen had become just that.

Their quiet assault had probably begun
shortly after the rise of Torre de la Reina. Mari
had returned from Barcelona to a spy in her apartment and a decree appropriating Maribarbola for
the King's better use. Thence the real chicanery
began: Nicolas, the most legendary and unapologetic of the Queen's betrayers, had guiled Mari
into a spurious friendship, saving her life only to
extort her with her own gratitude. Meanwhile,
Haro, who'd been taking the heads off bitches

since he was eight and would probably love a queen's skull for his office treasure chest, had basically terrorized Mari into betraying the Queen.

This was all part of a plan to poach Maribarbola from the Queen, strip the Queen of her best asset, and render her defenseless against a barrage of attacks that were already underway: pecuniary audits, preposterous allegations, defamations, provocations, humiliations. They were going to try to kill her with scandal. This was precisely the deviltry that had caused the desperate Queen to gamble a four-man chest of silver on the hope of gaining an advantage over her enemies. The malice had always been there, but Mari hadn't noticed in the early days because she'd been too busy being ambushed by Nicolas—which, too, may have been part of a larger Torre Dorada strategy. And as long as Haro held the threat of Inquisition torture over her, Mari couldn't retaliate. These men were so skilled in the game of personal destruction they had preemptively thwarted Maribarbola from thwarting their attacks.

Unwilling to risk another breach of trust with the Queen, however, Mari decided to tell her about Roberta's alleged change of residence immediately. "Your Majesty," she said one morning at breakfast, "I've heard some disturbing news from one of the other dwarfs."

The Queen looked up from her newssheet. "You've been fraternizing with other dwarfs?"

"Only politely."

The Queen didn't press the issue. "So what is your disturbing news," she said, returning to her newssheet.

"Please withhold your reaction until I'm done speaking."

That caught her attention. She looked up. Mari softened the command with a slight bow.

"Go on," said the Queen.

"Out of concern for her health and safety," Mari said, in her calm, sagacious Maribarbola voice, "His Majesty has moved his pregnant mistress to a chamber far below the earth, into the cold-est, darkest bowels of the Alcázar." The Queen's jaw hardened; her nostrils flared. "She's been entombed there for several weeks, hiding from the scorching heat and eyes of God, having no human contact but for the servants who wash and feed her, the King's probing doc-tors, and the priests who try in vain to pray away her stain of sin."

The Queen squinched her brow. Encouraged, Mari continued. "She's not seen daylight in weeks and has plunged into a state of melancholy so severe as to make His Majesty seem as jolly and zestful as a lad at a bullfight." The Queen's eyes bulged. "But the brave wench does not weep. She does not complain. She accepts her adulteress' fate and is content to spend her days sprawled in darkness like a shade-seeking swine—you should see her, she's huge—saying her beads as the churchmen prescribe and praying for the soul of her bastard child and for the blessed end of her own wretched days."

A couple of beats of silence passed. By now the Queen was winc-ing in disgust, or perhaps pity. Whatever it was, she shook free the feeling, made an incredulous face, and returned to her paper. "How very chivalrous of him." Then, seized by a thought, she looked up. "Perhaps I should intervene on her behalf."

"A noble thought," Mari said, "but only God can intervene at this point."

※

A knock on Mari's door jolted her awake. She lay pinned and stu-pefied, trying to anchor herself in reality. Her apartment was dark but for a lone candle in the vestibule. It had to be the middle of the night. She was concluding she had dreamt the knock when another came, sharp and impatient. It startled her anew and set her cogs of panic and dread into quick motion. Was this the coup?

They pounded again as she staggered through the vestibule. "¡Dios mío! I'm coming!" She flung open the door.

It was one of the King's pages, just a glowing face and torch-bearing hand looming in darkness. Horacio was his name, a handsome lad in the bloom of manhood, much discussed among Reina's younger staff. "What in God's name?" Mari said.

"His Majesty wishes to see you."

"What time is it?"

"Four."

"What does he want?" She hoped to God he wasn't looking for a prophecy.

"He has something to tell you."

"It can't wait until morning?"

"He's rather eager."

Mari pinched her eyes closed and shook her head. "Alright. Let me dress."

"You needn't dress. He's in a leisurely state."

She winced in confusion but didn't ask. She tied on a housecoat and went with him.

A handful of revelers still loitered in the Galería del Rey at this hour, reaping the last vestiges of merriment from the stale night. "*¡Maribarbola!*" they said with wilted cheer as Mari trudged by in her housecoat and snarled hair, ignoring them. "*¡Reveladnos una prophecía!*"

They went to the King's apartment. The reception room stood deserted. Horacio led her down the hall, past the King's office, library, cabinet room, and royal bedroom, taking her deeper than she'd ever been inside His Majesty's living quarters. Rowdy male banter wafted from some unseen chamber, bursts of drunken bravado and riotous laughter. "Look at him, he wants a rematch!" someone shouted, followed by hearty laughter. "What kind of king doesn't follow his own rules?"

"A typical one," somebody answered.

Horacio opened a heavy carved-wood door, and they stepped into a candlelit parlor peopled by a dozen or so men. It was the King's game room, Mari deduced from the polished wood card tables and green wool billiard boards. A hideous wild boar's head smiled above the hearth, one of the fabled thousands of beasts, Mari presumed, to have been slain by the King's unerring rifle. Cream-fleshed goddesses graced the walls, startlingly nude. The air was sultry with New World tobacco smoke and the sweet, yeasty smell of drink.

"Maribarbola!" Haro cleaved himself from a small pack of men. "What brings you here at this hour?"

"His Majesty sent for me."

With this the room exploded in theatrical outrage, howling disapproval. Octavio Barón shot up from a chair. "You're going to have Maribarbola do it?" he shouted across the room. "You niddering snake!" The chamber roared with drunken hilarity. In the corner— Mari could hardly believe her eyes—the King sat at a table, sloped easily in his chair, like a normal man, laughing.

"He's over there," Octavio said, "sulking in the corner."

"You were supposed to let him win, fool," someone said.

Annoyed, Mari wove through them, taking in as much as she could, knowing the Queen would want details. She rounded a sofa and was surprised to see Nicolas stretched upon it, tangled in a linen, sleeping soundly through all of this, like a lad defeated by a long day of play, Ferocc the mastiff slumbering on the cool marble floor beside him.

Mari presented herself to His Majesty. He acknowledged her with a nod, looking relaxed and bleary eyed behind a mess of cards and coins. "He's really going to do it," someone said.

"You had something to tell me?" she said, with a prickly edge to her voice. Nicolas was right. He was a coward.

His face had reverted to its usual mask of sorrow, but his eyes were still alight with the dying embers of laughter. "Roberta had a son," he said. "Please tell my niece."

Mari bowed her head stiffly and exaggeratedly, her disgust on full display, and threaded her way back out of the room.

"He was supposed to tell her himself," Octavio said in the tone of a mother shaming a child.

"He's a dastardly swine." This had to be a buffoon talking. "No wonder this country has gone to wrack and ruin."

"Poor Maribarbola, summoned in the night!"

"While Nicolasito sleeps like an angel." A froth of jolly laughter filled the room.

"Stay for a beer, Maribarbola?"

Mari let the door slam behind her.

She walked back to Reina, alone. The Alcázar was quiet; only monks and watchmen were awake at this hour—and Binnie, who thrived on little sleep. Mari crossed the deserted Galería del Rey in the ochre glow of dying chandeliers, her slippers pattering on the marble floor. Her blood was up; she was awake for the day, and just as well. She would need these hours before breakfast to craft her words for the Queen.

She stepped outside to savor a few breaths of cool air before returning to her fourth-floor bread oven of an apartment. The dark orchards chittered with birdsong as the new day blanched the horizon. Madrid slept below, dark but for the eternal flames of church courtyards, motionless but for the smoke swirling from bakehouse chimneys.

Mari wandered to the cherub pool, where the floating prayer candles still burned in the gloam of morning and the fountain sounded deafening at this desolate hour. She sat for a long time, watching the sun rise over the easterly plain and Madrid waking toyishly below: tiny wagons and tiny people, sprung to motion, inching blithely along. She would keep it to the barest facts with the Queen. The child itself was a stale concern at this point, not likely to stir the Queen's blood, though she'd be peeved that it was a boy. That was all she needed to know. She needn't know about the card game or the mockery and flippancy with which this news was being delivered, the flagrant disrespect for her as Queen Consort and mother of the future King. That would rile her needlessly. It would hurt her. Mari would keep it to herself, simmer in quiet rage on the Queen's behalf, shoulder the worries alone, and sit with the troubling knowledge that, whatever Torre Dorada was doing, it was working, they were winning. Her Majesty's political capital was falling, and fast.

It was his choice of words that bothered her most.

My niece, he had said. Not my wife. Not the Queen.

ೞ

"I'm told he's a handsome child," the Queen said to the Marquis days later. "Imagine that."

"Where is the boy now?" said the Marquis, with minimal interest, to her bosom.

"He and the mother are being kept at the monastery across the river. She'll be allowed to nurse him for a few days until they figure out what to do with him."

"Poor thing," said the Marquis. "Torn from his mother's breast so soon."

"He'll be better off," said the Queen. "He needn't know the baseness and depravity of which he was conceived, or that his mother is a woman of inferior stamp. The humane thing to do is put him in the care of another and let him grow up thinking he's a normal, virtuous boy, perfectly worthy in the eyes of God."

"I believe he is," the Marquis said quietly. If the Queen heard, she ignored this.

"I'm sure the King will put him in good care," Mari said to keep it gay.

"He'll be raised by nuns," said the Queen, "or simple mountain folk." She swirled her búcaro under her nose. "Gypsies," she added with acid amusement. "Wolves." Mari snickered dutifully, while the Marquis sat quiet and cheerless, as if still pondering the child's worth in the eyes of God. "If he even lives," she said, way too gaily. "I'm told he's scrawny and sallow and feeds badly."

243

Her words hung cheerily in the silence that followed. She nibbled off a piece of her búcaro and crunched the clay excruciatingly loudly.

The Marquis begged off early that night, claiming he felt unwell. "Poor thing," said the Queen as she and Mari watched him slip into the vestibule. "He did seem unwell."

He went unseen in the weeks thereafter. Mari suspected his heart had gone cold toward the Queen, that he of children's charities had been shocked and offended that a child's ill health could please her so vastly. Haro's having denied his tax-exempt petition may also have contributed to his vanishing.

If the Queen felt jilted she didn't show it, nor could she have lamented for long. Torre de la Reina had been touched anew by a spirit of hope and joy which little could dampen. Roberta's baby was soon forgotten, and Prospero grew haler by the day: plump, red-cheeked, and insatiable, just like his mother. The Queen was pregnant again.

❦

Chapter 21

THE INVITATION

utumn came tardily but swiftly, cooling the scorched plains and driving courtiers out of doors to rediscover the forgotten pleasures of crisp air, cold rains, and the scent of wet dead leaves and fallen apples. As the gardens withered the plazas flourished, blazing with cookfires and brewing with Hallowtide cheer. Courtiers strolled in coats and capes of the latest fall fashions, clutching steaming cups of chocolate and paper cones of coal-roasted chestnuts. The King was gone hunting more often than not, and the court relaxed in his absence. Protocols slackened, rituals were shirked, chapel services ran half empty. Meanwhile, the Queen fattened like a harvest lamb, devouring the season's delicacies with unabashed zeal: savory partridge pie, chorizo-chestnut empanadas, fried olives, creamy apple tartlets, pumpkin flan. But even as the newssheets waxed joyous over the pregnancy and the royal bosom strained the Queen's bodices to the brink of rupture, the Marquis did not pay court, leaving Mari to conclude, with relief, that the illicit romance was finally over.

One brisk Saturday morning saw Mari alone at the cherub pool, washing some apples she had scavenged from the orchard floor. She glanced up and saw Nicolas's head skimming along a short stone wall in the distance, his hair jouncing in the breeze. She figured he must be on the hunt for a late-blooming rose with which to garnish himself, something he did, admittedly, to exquisite effect.

He emerged in full from behind the wall, took a surprise turn, and strode toward her. He was dressed for sport in a wool tunic and leather gloves and looked like a stouthearted little prince coming fresh from a horse lesson. "*Buenos días*," Mari said warily as he neared.

"*Buenos días*. Mariana told me I'd find you here."

Mari didn't like him asking the Queen where she was. She and the Queen rarely discussed Mari's relations with Nicolas. Her Majesty didn't concern herself in the affairs of dwarfs, and given the Queen and Nicolas's fractured history, he was a delicate topic. "What can I do for you?"

"I'd like to invite you to dinner in the city tonight, at the House of Seven Chimneys in the old merchant district. There are some people I'd like you to meet."

"What kind of people?"

"People completely unaffiliated with this court. People with fresh and interesting perspectives on things."

"That doesn't tell me much."

"It should be enough to entice you, no? Please, join us. It'll be a lovely time."

"Is there a reason you're inviting me?"

Nicolas shrugged cheerily. "I suppose I feel a need to atone for my past pranks against you, which I can do by looking out for your interests as I would my own. I also judge you the type who can keep a secret, especially when it's to your own better advantage."

Mari was barely listening. She was still hung up on the word "pranks." Is that what those had been in his mind? The coupling chamber, Maria Concepción's wedding? Pranks?

"Just come and hear what they have to say," Nicolas said. "It's healthy to mingle with people outside of your own sphere. When was the last time you had a conversation with a court outsider? And the fritter man doesn't count."

Mari glared at him. It was truly disturbing how much he knew. He leveled his naughty-lad smirk at her. She had never seen him out of doors in broad daylight before. He had murky blue eyes, she noticed for the first time, and dazzling copper strands in his otherwise dull brown hair. "You'll feast well tonight," he said. "They are most eager to impress you."

So whatever he was up to, he had promised whomever he was consorting with that he would bring the Prophet Maribarbola to the table. "Sounds illicit," Mari said.

Nicolas laughed. "Yes, I suppose it is. So are you coming?"

Certain that this was just another Torre Dorada bid to undermine the Queen, Mari said, "No. Thank you."

His good humor vanished in an instant. He rested his hand on his dagger and eyed her with disappointment, pity even. He turned away and paced a few steps, his boot heels like baby lamb hooves on the stones. They were quiet for a few moments and watched with vague awkwardness as a couple swanned out of the distant maze in a clear state of postcoital bliss.

"Your loyalty to her is admirable," he said. "And also foolish."

Mari looked at him.

"I felt that way about her once," he said. "About them, the Crown in general. Sometimes I still do. But eventually I came to realize, just as you will someday, that blind loyalty is worthless to he who confers it, and indeed very dangerous. I've seen people burn to death on the Plaza Mayor for misplaced loyalties."

"They sooner burn for treason."

"I'm not up to treason. This is about protecting ourselves, having a contingency plan."

"Are you telling me I should be worried?"

Sensing her anxiety, he shook his head. "Believe me, when it's time to worry, you'll know."

Mari tried to think of an excuse to leave. This conversation was making her anxious and angry. Her loyalty to the Queen was sacrosanct—by now that should be obvious to him—and yet he kept trying to subvert it, over and over again. It was insulting.

"There's a sea change out there," Nicolas said, lifting his face to a well-timed breeze. "The power balance in Europe has shifted. Spain is no longer the great nation she once was. Of course Philip will always see himself as the center of the universe. It's a fatal flaw all kings share." Mari braced for another of his political rants. "His conceit will be his undoing. Anything can happen at any time. Just look at the Retiro plot."

"I thought you were blaming the Queen for that."

At this he just laughed. "All I'm saying is, we need to be prepared for anything. Even the noblemen are uneasy, and they can flee to their country estates if Madrid is sieged. But what about us dwarfs and buffoons? We wouldn't survive without the protection of the court. Out there people like you and I are treated like animals, playthings, objects of ridicule. We get laughed at, spat on, picked up and tossed."

"You're highborn," Mari said, annoyed. Nicolas came from a noble family near the Italian Alps and was apparently too precious even for them, hence his consignment to royalty. He'd been swaddled in luxury and adoration since birth and would continue to be as long as he lived, which, at the rate he aged, could be till the twelfth of never.

"True, but what about you? You especially need to double down on your security, which is why I'm asking you to join me tonight. Think of it as a survival strategy. You can bet Mariana's looking out for her own interests; you need to start looking out for yours. Do you really want to spend the rest of your life in her service?"

"Yes," Mari said, staring into space. He was going to badger her regardless.

"Well, see?" He threw up a hand. "That's what they do. It's the genius of power. They convince you that you need them more than they need you." He paused to wave at a pair of young lovelies on a distant footpath. Mari hoped this chat was nearing its blessed end. "We've been isolated for too long. There's a world of new ideas out there. Philip can't keep them out forever. Truth always finds a way."

Mari snorted undetectably. Nicolas, espousing the virtue of truth.

"So? Are you coming?" he said.

She shook her head.

"Fine. I'm leaving at eight if you change your mind." He tipped his head and left in a small huff.

She watched him leave, his boot heels heavier now, ram hooves—his lank hair lifting in the wind of his stride. She was angry at herself for having once again sat and listened obediently while he spewed his cynicism and stoked her fears. So obnoxious he was, so overbearing; if he were a full-sized man he'd be an insufferable tyrant. She should have pointed out the fact that while he had been a two-pound baby suckling cream from a silk rag, or a lad wearing Italian lace dresses and playing with gold jacks, or a grown man living the life of a pampered cat—while he had been on his journey from rich to richer, from precious runt to national treasure—Mari had been out there in the hostile world, surviving well enough without the protection of the court.

Survival strategy, he had said. If he had spent but a day of his life out in the real world, living hand to mouth, being feared and ridiculed and pelted with liquids, being exploited and sold, maybe then he would understand Mari's loyalty to the last person on earth who had wanted her, the woman who kept her and fed her and seemed to care whether she lived or died. He didn't understand loyalty because he'd never had to, never had any use for it. The world always fell into place for Nicolasito. He'd never know what it was like to be dispossessed, homeless and frightened, unwanted, unadored. Oh, and the Countess had lived on the very edge of that world of new ideas of which he spoke but knew absolutely nothing!—that rolling boil of curiosity and dangerous new opinions, truths finding their way. Mari had read the words for which Galilei died imprisoned, the ones that refuted scripture and ignited hellfire within the Catholic Church. She had believed them, repeated them even, spread the blasphemy with her own tongue. She had devoured those very books the Inquisition burned.

How she wished she could have said this, but she only just remembered it. That part of her life was buried so deep it hardly felt real anymore. She'd been living this Maribarbola lie for so long as to invert reality, alchemize a new truth. And that was why she despised Nicolas so much for trying to subvert her loyalty. Devotion to her lady was pretty much all she'd retained of her former life, the only part of Maria-Barbara that had been transferable. And here he was trying to take it, flippantly, as if it were a prize in a game, not the only thing left of her she was certain was real.

⟨⟨❧⟩⟩

Chapter 22

THE FATHER CONFESSOR

fter his shadowy dinner invitation, Mari avoided Nicolas. She made it a point to leave her apartment Saturday mornings, his usual calling time, and hide downstairs in the Queen's apartment, where he was generally unwelcome. Whatever he was up to, she wanted no part of it and was keen to end their sham friendship, which had only brought her anxiety, irritation, and information she didn't want to know. As far as she was concerned, she had repaid her debt of gratitude with interest, having suffered months of his unwelcome visits, his unsolicited gossip and political opinions, and his dastardly attempts to turn her against the Queen. The more Mari got to know him, the more she disliked him. In addition to his disloyalty and insincerity, his arrogance and pushiness, she especially resented his untortured ways: his psychological immunity to the kinds of threats that kept her awake at night; the way he reveled in intrigue while giving the impression he was floating above it, playing the game while pretending there was no game; his tall-person confidence, his physical grace and impeccable attire, his inability to sweat.

On one of her Saturday avoidance maneuvers, Mari strode into the Queen's apartment nearly tingling with cheer, having just read a glorious ditty in that morning's gossip sheet, which detailed a night of shocking debauchery at the Buen Retiro involving a bevy of eager young actresses and one very depraved high-ranking official, unnamed but thinly veiled and unmistakably Haro. Eager to commence the cringing and lewd musings and wicked delight, Mari was disappointed to find the Queen's reception room empty.

"Good morning, Mari," Everardo said from the writing desk, startling her.

"Good morning, Padre. Is Her Majesty here?"

"She went downstairs for a dress fitting. She'll be back shortly." He gestured for her to sit.

Mari sat and folded the gossip sheet in her lap. She was dying to discuss it, but not with a priest.

"I'm glad to have you alone," Everardo said, parking his pen. "I was hoping to persuade you to have a word with Her Majesty about her near-nightly outings." Since the Marquis had vanished, the Queen was going out several nights a week. Ostensibly she had rediscovered the rich pleasures of the theater, but Mari suspected she was hoping to chance upon the Marquis. "Given recent events, her parading herself through the Retiro night after night leaves the impression that she is little concerned for the safety of her unborn. And one needn't mention the dreadful inconvenience her travel inflicts upon the public. Every time she steps out of the Alcázar she courts public wrath."

"I can speak with her," Mari said. "I'll make it clear that many are concerned for her safety." The Queen would be flattered somebody deemed her assassination-worthy.

"And of course," Everardo said carefully, "there is also the deli-cate matter of her appearance."

He was talking about her weight, which had become a national obsession. Nary a day passed without a merciless ballad or cartoon—or even serious political analysis on the matter—basically scathing the Queen for stepping out fatter every night and never in the same dress twice, while children all over Spain lay hungry in their cots. "I think the safety issue should be enough to convince her," Mari said.

"Very well." He nodded and returned to his writing.

Mari listened to the gentle scratching of his pen while he busied himself in one of his Everardo drudgeries: letter writing, petition fil-ing, budget requests. Given his unquestionable loyalty to the Queen, and a cunning and ambition only barely concealed by his priest's collar, Mari often wondered why Everardo wasn't more politically aggressive. Had Torre Dorada neutered him, too?

"Padre?"

"Yes?"

Her heart quickened at what she was about to do. Months of silence and impotence under Torre Dorada's quiet tyranny was kill-ing her from within. For one blessed moment she wanted to feel the rush of power that came from speaking the unspeakable, the thrill of telling, the power of words. And lo, here she sat, alone with a confessional priest. "I think Torre Dorada is trying to ensnare her in scandal, with the aim of destroying her." It sounded so silly when spoken aloud in her timorous voice. Had Torre Dorada made her crazy? Everardo's look of comic curiosity wasn't helping. "Nicolas outrightly alleged that the Queen ordered the Retiro plot"—she was aware she sounded like a tattling child—"as retribution to the King's ... actress."

Everardo smiled wearily. "There was never any question as to who was behind the Retiro plot. The perpetrators made their iden-tities very clear. One of the powder kegs had the Bars of Aragon painted on the side." This was the red-and-gold-striped Catalan flag, the rebel insignia. Mari had never heard this part of the story. "A stagehand was arrested and interrogated and admitted to having rebel ties. The Crown is keeping it quiet so as not to incite sympathizers."

Mari was stunned. What else was the Queen not telling her?

"If Nicolas is looking to impeach the Queen," Everardo said, "I'm afraid he'll have to come up with something cleverer than that. Whether or not the King's infidelity can inspire her to murderous rage remains to be seen, but if it does, I can assure you, she would never resort to the crudity of gunpowder and a slow match. Her Majesty is many things, but an amateur she is not."

"No. Definitely not." They shared a light chuckle. Encouraged by his rare display of levity and candor, Mari asked, "Was their marriage ever good?"

He plucked off his spectacles and leaned back. "I suppose in the beginning it was good enough. Certainly better than it is now. Cordial. Somewhat affectionate. But Mariana was a child, mind you. She came to Spain pious and dutiful, eager to please. The King, too, put his best foot forward and appeared to be faithful for a while. But as everyone knows, he is a very sick man and soon reverted to his true ways, leaving Mariana to grow up quickly. But she was always a shrewd and ambitious young lady and took to her role as Queen like a fish to the sea. And of course back then she had a staunch ally in Nicolas, who is every bit as shrewd and ambitious as she is."

"How did Nicolas betray her?"

"As I remember it, he didn't so much betray her as abandon her. Mariana can be selfish at times, demanding. This was especially true in the early years of her reign. She was a child queen testing her authority, desperately homesick, and having to come to terms with the unpleasant realities of life as royal consort. Those early years were filled with tears and tantrums. Nicolas had finally had enough and decided to do what was best for him."

"As Nicolas always does."

"One can hardly blame him," Everardo said. "Too often Mariana treated him like a doll or a child. She didn't respect his manhood."

Mari snorted. Nicolas. Manhood. If she lived a hundred years she'd never reconcile the two.

"He didn't care to sit in her apartment all day," Everardo said, "listening to her and the handmaidens talk about dresses and babies, or rank the knights from most to least handsome. Life with the King promised bullfights, hunting trips, an ever-changing assortment of beautiful eager young women. There's not a man alive who wouldn't have done the same."

"So he just switched to the King's side? Just like that?"

"They had a corner apartment waiting for him in Torre Dorada. Haro had been courting him for quite some time." So they had poached him, just as they had tried to poach Maribarbola. God forbid the Queen should be allowed to have an asset they didn't. "This was at the height of Spain's Nicolasito mania. He was worth tenfold his weight in gold, and he leveraged it to his utmost advantage. He gets paid better than most chamberlains, for doing absolutely nothing, in addition to the luxuries and privileges he enjoys as the King's favorite—still while collecting a pension from the Queen's coffer." Mari's eyes bulged. "Never in my life have I seen anyone so well mastered in the art of having it both ways."

"*Dios mío*," Mari said. She hadn't known the Queen was pensioning him. That must have been painful for Her Majesty. It was painful for Mari, who hadn't seen a raise since Prospero and Ferdinand were born.

"His move hurt Mariana," Everardo said, "personally and politically. The entire saga played out in the newssheets, and of course the public sided with Nicolasito. Mariana was vilified and reviled, in the press and by her people. They raked her over the coals for everything, from her political foibles to the size of her chin. On top of that there were several miscarriages and another

Infanta who died in the cot. It was a dark and lonely time for the Queen. Nicolas wasn't there for her, and, worse, as the King's ministers became increasingly antagonistic, he did nothing to intervene on her behalf. That probably hurt her more than anything."

By now Mari's blood was up, her nostrils flared.

Everardo's demeanor lightened. "Then one day a broker from Barcelona presented himself in this very room and spoke of a German dwarfess most intriguing."

Mari forced a tight smile. A wistful silence drifted through the room. "I wish I could bring her the good fortune she deserves," she said.

"I'd say you've done well by her. She has a prince in the cot, hopefully another in the womb. She certainly feels less alone in the world with you by her side. What more could you do?"

"I've done nothing to improve Spain's fortunes. As long as the people suffer, the Crown will also suffer."

"There is no fortune to be had in Spain. If you want to see what Spain has left to offer her people, steel yourself and look no further than the harrowing depths of His Majesty's eyes. He knows better than anyone how dire the situation is and that he's powerless to correct it. Don't blame yourself for problems a century in the making. In fact, if you had a drop of good fortune in you, you'd have ended up anywhere but here."

"What keeps you here, Padre?"

"I'm here to protect the interests of the Austrian Crown." His unapologetic candor shocked Mari. "Oh, don't look so astonished, Maria-Barbara," he said in sudden German. "Just as you've learned to contentedly masquerade as Maribarbola of Spain, so too have I, Father Johann Eberhard Nithard, as Padre Juan Everardo Nithard, Father Confessor to Her Majesty."

Mari smiled sadly. He was right. This court was a huge, glittering masquerade ball, where every guest's overriding agenda was to keep the party going for himself for as long as possible. Even the priests and monks and nuns were keen to feast on the fat of these godforsaken lands and dance like devils on the slanting deck of this sinking treasure ship. But eventually the sun would come up, and the sweet winey haze would burn away, leaving misery and regret to rule the day.

There were elephantine footsteps in the vestibule, and the Queen lumbered in belly first, cursing under her breath. She eyed them suspiciously when she noticed them sitting there together, smiling at her. She looked like a harvest gourd in her gold pleated dress—enormous and radiant, with a thick, tough rind.

༓

Several nights later, the chapel bell jarred Mari awake: a single, ominous gong, baritone and dissonant, fading to silence. Then another.

The death knell.

Mari thought little of it; today was All Souls' Day. Still, she didn't appreciate being wrenched from sleep in the predawn hours. Some of those monks were wicked.

After a few minutes, the last bell had tolled, and she sank back into a soft loam of sleep. Seconds passed.

She woke again to a horrific wail in the stairwell. She lay pinned in bed, heart thumping in her ears. Another wretched, billowing wail filled the tower.

The Queen.

Mari slipped out of bed and listened through the door. An urgent clatter of boot heels and men's voices echoed in the stone shaft, along with the Queen, shrieking and moaning, as if dying. With horror in her heart, Mari ripped open her door and ran barefoot down the stairs.

She waited in the shadows outside the Queen's apartment. Men were barking orders in Spanish, praying in Latin. The Queen's moans became so loud and gut-wrenching, Mari covered her ears.

The cohort bumbled into view on the stairs, with the Queen floating, horizontal and nightgowned, in the hands of four guards. Several priests followed, chanting and raising crosses.

"Padre!" Mari cried as they passed. Everardo broke his prayer trance and turned. "Please tell me what's happening!"

But her heart already knew.

Chapter 23

THE FUTURE KING

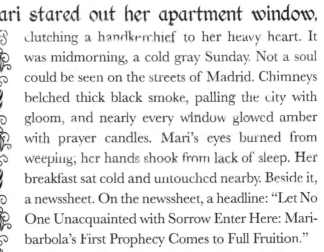ari stared out her apartment window, clutching a handkerchief to her heavy heart. It was midmorning, a cold gray Sunday. Not a soul could be seen on the streets of Madrid. Chimneys belched thick black smoke, palling the city with gloom, and nearly every window glowed amber with prayer candles. Mari's eyes burned from weeping; her hands shook from lack of sleep. Her breakfast sat cold and untouched nearby. Beside it, a newssheet. On the newssheet, a headline: "Let No One Unacquainted with Sorrow Enter Here: Maribarbola's First Prophecy Comes to Full Fruition."

Sorrow had fallen thick and fast, with every last mote of hope and joy carried away by the November winds. Prospero, and with him Spain's future, lay cold in his crypt at the Escorial in San Lorenzo. He had died five days ago of a massive fit. And now the Queen herself lay dying, her grief having spurred her to an early, violent labor. All night Mari had lain awake tormented by Her Majesty's bloodcurdling screams, the sinister clangs of medical instruments, the grave murmur of doctors, and the eerie incantations of bedside priests.

But now there was only sickening silence.

A timid knock on Mari's door jangled her taut nerves. She crossed the room leadenly, at nightmare speed, and answered it.

It was Binnie, looking sallow and vacant, a bloodless peach. "It was a boy," she said in a queer, flat voice, her gaze just skimming Mari's head. "It is a boy."

"How is she?"

Binnie shook her head.

"Don't!" Binnie said as Mari pushed past her and dashed to the stairwell.

Dazed and detached, Mari floated down the stairs, not knowing or caring what horrors awaited her in the royal apartment. She only knew she had to see the Queen.

Lalo and Marco stood guard outside the royal apartment, an unsettlingly abnormal sight. "No entry," Marco said, but Lalo, hanging his head, opened the door for her.

Mari floated through the vestibule and into the reception room. It stood sunless and cheerless, silent but for the snapping hearth fire, empty but for two maidservants on a bench, their faces splotched and puffy with tears, rosaries cutting into their fists. No sooner had Mari opened her mouth to speak than the young women were startled to their feet by boot heels coming from the Queen's bedroom, and sank to half their height in curtsy.

Mari turned, and there she saw him. His Majesty, the King. Here. In Torre de la Reina. Under any other circumstances she'd have laughed aloud at the very sight, but now it registered like a hand around her throat.

He emerged from the corridor with Haro and Padre Juan Martinez, his Father Confessor, walking two paces behind. Mari stood dumbstruck in their path. The King walked straight to her and stopped a couple of feet away. Gone was his usual mask of misery. In its place was a look of sheer horror.

"Your Majesty ... " Mari whispered and reached out to touch him, but stopped herself before her hand connected with the royal body. She looked to Haro for explanation. The wolf's eyes were red-rimmed and varnished with tears—yet another bizarre sight that Mari's splintered consciousness could barely process.

The King stared down at her, his gaze somehow missing her, and in a flat voice uttered the longest sentence Mari had ever heard him speak: "The punishment God lays upon these realms is rightly laid upon me." Then they walked out.

Numb and stupefied, Mari continued to the royal bedroom.

The door was closed. There was rustling within, feathery female voices. Mari entered.

Nurses and maidservants moved hither and thither about the chamber, carrying linens and kettles and bowls of snow. A small group of doctors and holy men convened near the hearth, the priests' red silk frocks flashing in the firelight. Everardo's face was hung with grief. A console table twinkled fiercely with vigil lights. The Queen lay tucked in bed, either dead or unconscious, Mari didn't know which.

Mari started for the bed. She needed to touch the Queen, feel for herself what warmth and life remained in the royal body. She was halfway there when a strange, duck-like sound arrested her in her path. She stood dumb and frozen, a tiny pageanter in a jammed automaton clock. Several nurses swarmed the sound, clustering around it, bending their necks over it, intensely interested in what-ever had caused it.

A couple of them cleaved away, and there it was: the little white bundle, smaller than a bread loaf. It was a boy, Binnie had said. It *is* a boy. He lived yet! Mari's heart pulled toward him; she started moving again, her gears unstuck, oiled by hope and joy. She forgot the Queen and went to the white bundle, went to the miracle like a moth to the light. As she neared, the nurse holding him turned her body and angled the tidy loaf in the crook of her arm.

Mari covered her mouth when she saw his face.

He was a grotesque, misshapen child, with a puckered, bean-shaped head and the face of a hymnbook devil. That he was Philip and Mariana's progeny there could be no doubt; the family chin was gruesomely manifest, and if the Queen lay dead it was surely because that monstrous part of him had torn her asunder. From the warped cleft that was his mouth came another tiny, animal-like cronk.

Mari watched in horror as they took him away, to the royal chapel for an urgent baptism, she was told. The King was gravely concerned for the child's soul. Already the whispers were starting, right there in the birth chamber: "*Hechizado*." Hexed. Mari needed no convincing. She was also certain the wretched soul had been seeded in the Queen's acid womb on that acid night, during the venomous coupling ceremony that had them all staring at the floor and praying for the blessed end.

Conceived of hatred, born of sorrow. Not expected to see the morrow, the child was christened immediately as Charles, heir apparent to the Spanish Crown.

ૹ

Three evenings later Mari sat in her apartment, staring into the fire, occasionally glancing over at Binnie in the opposite chair—another bizarre, unprecedented sight. Binnie never sat. For the moment Torre de la Reina stood thickly silent and slenderly at peace. The horrors of the past week had relented, and the suffocating sorrow was lifting on a rising crest of delicate hope. To everyone's astonishment and boundless gratitude, the Queen had dismissed death with a flick of the hand and now lay in a fragile state of recovery. Today they had her propped up in bed, sipping broth. She was alert and asking for her children. Margarita and the baby. So far Charles had defied everyone's grim expectations and round-the-clock prayers for a swift release from his earthly misery. Still, no one hoped for his survival, and right now a decision was being made as to whether or not the unfit Queen should be allowed to gaze upon her son's face before he died.

Binnie broke the silence. "From my lips to God's ears," she said quietly, "they're getting what they deserve." She was talking about the incest. No one dared speak of it, but the fact of it now thickened the very air. She raised a plump finger, pointing to a higher truth. "It defies nature," she said in a fervent whisper. "It defies God."

Mari said nothing. The whole situation made her flesh creep.

"But those poor babies——" Binnie said, her voice breaking. She covered her mouth and closed her eyes to keep the tears in.

Mari's gaze drifted back to the fire. The babies. She, too, had been thinking about them these past few days, and Binnie's words only affirmed the quiet fear simmering in her heart ever since she'd beheld the wretched Baby Charles. It was now clear that Margarita, their only hale child, was profoundly abnormal in that regard. Sick babies were the rule around here. Degenerate babies. Miscarried babies. Convulsing babies. Hideously misshapen babies. Dead babies. Maybe the King and Queen really were getting what they deserved. The punishment God laid upon these realms, the King had said in that harrowing moment of truth, was rightly laid upon him. He had bedded a fabled several thousand women—including a nun, if rumors could be believed—and yet the one who seemed to anger God most was she who lay with him in holy matrimony: his niece.

With two princes in the crypt and a third soon to follow, this family would go no further. Philip would be the last of his kin to enflesh the Spanish Throne. The next King of Spain would inherit the Empire not by right of blood but by force of will. Spain's enemies need only sit back and wait. In this incestuous union, the ruin of the realm was already wrought.

It didn't take a prophet to see it. This marriage was damned, and if matters remained thus, Spain, too, was damned. If Haro was looking for a reason to get rid of the Queen, he'd just been handed one from Heaven. A more dire warning of Spain's bleak future God could not have sent than that wretched child dying downstairs. The Queen had but one job—to produce heirs—and she was failing gruesomely. Her enemies would be coming for her now, ruthlessly. Even Mari could see the senselessness of keeping her on the throne. This wasn't a game anymore; it wasn't even about power. This was about saving the Empire.

The child was sure to die within days, leaving the Queen without a prince to protect her anymore. She'd be facing the political fight of her life with but a single blunt, rusty weapon in her arsenal: the Prophet Maribarbola. Mari could no longer remain latent, no longer hide in her apartment hoping the Inquisitor General had forgotten about her. She had pledged loyalty to the Queen, and loyalty, she was being forced to realize, was not sympathy or well-wishing or praying. It wasn't hand-wringing or worrying or seething in anger on the Queen's behalf. It wasn't even love or friendship. It was a willingness to *fight* for the Queen. Die, even, for the Queen. Anything less was an implicit betrayal. Anything else was disloyalty, which would rank Mari among the Nicolases and Udos of the world and mean the last real thing about her was in fact not real at all.

They were symbionts, she and the Queen, thriving and dying together, and that meant fighting together. Already the Queen was doing her part, batting down death with a hand, just another pesky enemy trying and failing to get rid of her. From the moment she'd arrived in Spain, she'd been forced to defend her God-given sovereignty. The King had married her reluctantly, for want of a better strategic option, and stuck his people with his homely, hard-hearted niece as their queen, the Austrian ambassador that Spain never wanted. She'd been defying her adversaries ever since: Torre Dorada, the savage press, ill-wishers and naysayers, Death, and now

God Himself. She wasn't going to abdicate quietly. Anyone who wanted to be rid of her would have to pry her crown from her cold dead fingers.

And here all this time Mari thought she'd been shackled to the wrong royal.

It took almost losing the Queen twice for Mari to see how right the royal she was—a better mistress than Mari ever could have wished for, certainly better than she deserved. The Queen of Spain had never mistreated her, abused her, unduly pressured her, degraded her, dressed her up and made her dance in public, and never once, to Mari's knowledge, betrayed her. And yet, ever since Mari had stepped foot in the Alcázar, she'd been almost singularly focused on saving herself, keeping herself here, maintaining this pampered existence. She'd been trying to outrun her dwarf's fate, a fate of powerlessness and unimportance, of being used by proper-sized people as proper-sized people saw fit. But she finally understood: her power and importance must come not from outrunning her fate, but by surrendering to it.

Mari had always known this day would come, the day she'd be expected to earn out that four-man chest of silver. The Queen had paid an exorbitant sum for her and thusly owned her, body and soul. She owned Mari's very life, so it seemed only fair that Mari should be prepared to give it. This life of cowardice was hardly worth living anymore. This person she'd become was hardly worth saving. Loyalty by itself might be intrinsically worthless, but loyalty plus courage was priceless to someone who needed it, and the Queen was going to need it.

Binnie's hand danced in her peripheral vision. Mari turned. "Heavens," Binnie said, "I thought you left us."

On the contrary, Mari felt like she'd been gone for months and only just returned.

She gazed into the fire, its flash and warmth matching the strange new feeling flickering within her: the flame of courage, the light of power. But this was a new and different kind of power, the kind that cannot be given by others and therefore can never be taken away. It self-ignites in the heart and engulfs the soul, and, once burning, can only be doused by death.

❧

PART III

Chapter 24

THE QUEEN'S PLAN

he Queen left her sickbed sooner than anyone expected, though looking wan and frail and
already thinner. She'd been heartened by a swell
of public support: city windows glowed day and
night with vigil lights, miles of prayer beads had
been fingered in her name, and the Alcázar post
was deluged with letters and packages offering
prayers and talismans, all but burying the Queen
in crosses, pocket Bibles, and other odd tokens
and amulets. The Marquis sending roses with a
chivalrous note also surely gladdened her, as did
the King's stating publicly that she had borne her
blows as a true Christian.

She had greater reason to mend quickly:
two children needed their mother's love, one of
them critically. To everyone's astonishment, Baby
Charles lived yet, and while few hoped for his
long-term survival, some had started praying for

his health rather than his swift return to Heaven. His hideous face made him no less loved by all, indeed more so. News of the hexed child pricked every heart in Spain and rallied yet more goodwill from the populace. Children were enchanted by the legend of the monster Prince, and just about every hag in Madrid appeared at the Alcázar bearing stones and herbs meant to reverse the cruel hex. Mari, too, felt warmheartedly toward the unsightly lad, she being well-acquainted with the plight of misshapenness.

The Queen told Mari that on the cusp of death she'd had an epiphany. It was basically the same realization Mari had come to about the Crown's bleak future; surely Baby Charles's wretchedness could not have failed to drive the lesson home. But rather than wallow in hopelessness and grief, the Queen was beset by determination that bordered on maniacal. These mornings she rose early, breakfasted barely, and took to her writing desk to scratch out impassioned pleas to her brother Leopold, Pope Alexander, bishops and cardinals, marquises and viceroys, and anyone else who might be of use to her. She was going to launch an aggressive campaign to pressure His Majesty to change his will and name Margarita heiress presumptive to the Crown. "Look at the English with their great matriarchs," she said, writing feverishly, her scrawny body hunched most unroyally at her desk. "We'd be wise to take a leaf out of their book, no?"

Mari nodded uneasily. When she had resolved to fight to the death for the Queen, she hadn't considered the potential for the Queen's exceptionally bad political instincts to hasten that outcome.

"It is God's will," said the Queen, shaking a finger heavenward. She seemed stricken by a religious fervor that hadn't been there before. "He cannot have made Himself any plainer."

Admittedly, it was not the worst idea ever conceived, nor impossible under Spanish law. Teresa had been heiress presumptive during the King's sonless years, and Haro wisely negotiated her forfeiture of all rights of succession in her marriage treaty with the French. Spain, however—with her bullfighters and swaggerers and endless bloody wars—was unready for a female sovereign, and surely the men of Torre Dorada were least ready of anyone. Not only was the Queen's plan a flagrant power grab, but her underhandedly beseeching of allies for support would be an egregious affront to His Majesty.

Mari, meanwhile, had been plotting Torre de la Reina's resurrection to power, beginning with the resuscitation of Maribarbola's flagging career. She'd been bandying ideas for a comeback prophecy, something joyful and uplifting—momentous enough to garner major press attention, but benign enough not to rouse Inquisition interest. If successful, it would provide a solid foothold in what Mari hoped would be a slow, strategic climb back to the top, the same careful scheming that had worked all too well before. For now, the Queen was safe. No one could touch her while Baby Charles was still alive, and this latest outpouring of public support afforded her yet another sheath of protection. The King's ministers wouldn't dare set upon her now—she fresh off her deathbed and emitting the saintly aura of tragedy—lest they expose themselves as the Godless swine they really were.

But alas, the Queen's desperation trumped all caution and reason. Josefina called late one night as Mari turned down her bedclothes; Her Majesty needed an urgent favor. Mari went downstairs and found the Queen in her study, bespectacled, sitting among stacks of dusty tomes. "Your Majesty?"

"I think I've found a loophole," said the Queen, beckoning with an ink-blackened finger. "I've been reading up on the law of the *Cortes Generales*, and the wording in volume eighteen, section two hundred sixty-seven is highly ambiguous and could potentially allow for a just and legal disruption of the natural order of succession under certain circumstances. Here, listen ... "

Mari stood bleary eyed and lead-limbed, staring at an ink smudge on the Queen's nose, as the Queen read several pages from the centuries-old law book.

The Queen peered over her spectacles like a scholarly old man. "Is that not open to interpretation?"

Mari hadn't heard a word of it. "It is indeed."

"An unequivocal equivocality, if you will." She chuckled as one does on the edge of madness.

"You need sleep."

"I'll sleep better knowing this is in the King's hands." She shoved a large cylindrical object at Mari.

"*Dios mío*," Mari said, realizing what it was: a vellum scroll, fat and heavy as a fire log.

"I copied that section for him and added some annotations of my own." Mari's eyes widened. She must have been writing, uninterrupted, for days. "Go now and give it to him, along with your prophecy. You know what to say. Make sure you put the scroll directly in his hands. Anyone else is liable to toss it on the fire the moment you turn your back."

Mari tucked the scroll under her arm. It was pointless to try to reason with her.

"Tell him it's God's will!" the Queen barked at her receding back. "Tell him she's Spain's only hope!"

Mari dragged herself downstairs, already embarrassed by the Queen's obese scroll, the sheer girth of which, never mind the manic contents, would betray her impendent insanity and give Haro yet another reason to get rid of her. Though still of a mind to sacrifice herself for the Queen, Mari wasn't prepared to do it tonight and certainly not for such a hopeless cause. Of all the prophecies she could submit to the King, her marching into his apartment and appointing the Heir to the Empire was about the most hideously brazen thing imaginable, the surest way to pitch Haro and the Inquisition against her. She was on a suicide mission, basically, and a pointless one at that.

Her long, heavy-footed walk to Torre Dorada allowed ample time to contemplate the horrors she could unleash upon herself by following the Queen's orders. Mari could defy her, of course, exercise her own better judgement. As sage and seer, part of her duty was to protect the Queen from the Queen's self, which Mari could only do by keeping her own self alive.

She entered the King's apartment. It was late; the reception room was deserted. Surely the obnoxious timing of this delivery was meant to surprise him at his bedtime exploits, although the devastated father was supposedly in a severe melancholic and hermitic state, and Mari more so dreaded finding him alone and weeping inconsolably than she did finding him stark nude in a salad of actresses.

She went gingerly down the hall. The door to his study stood ajar. She nudged it open and peered inside.

The King sat in a fireside chair, his back to the door. Mari entered.

The room flashed gently with firelight and smelled of leather and beeswax. Only the King's hair could be seen crowning over the seatback, and the royal hand, corpselike on its armrest. The Maestro's painting loomed ten feet tall on the wall in front of him, overbearing in its splendor, tyrannizing the room with its majesty. Mari stepped forth, still not knowing if she was going to lay down her life tonight or retreat into her cocoon of fear and let the Queen fight one more battle alone, until the next one.

Clearing her throat so as not to startle him, she rounded the chair and presented herself to His Majesty.

He was asleep, bolt upright in his chair. Mari froze and studied him. He looked like a wax effigy, stiff and morbid, face melting in sorrow. The punishment God laid upon these realms was bearing down on him with all the weight of a collapsing empire—centuries of conquest and world domination, all crashing down on this single man in his fireside chair. Where was Nicolas? Where was Haro? Where were the parasites when the King needed comfort?

The royal eyes opened without warning, sending a ripple of panic through Mari's chest. She stood helpless in the King's befuddled gaze. His eyes flickered with recognition as they puzzled out her form in the firelight. He glanced at the painting of the painting as if to validate who she was—as if the Maestro's picture were the truest and most reliable version of her, her living flesh a mere copy.

Not knowing what to do, Mari turned to the picture, and obeying the ten-foot tyrant, fed it her gaze. The painting gazed back in its eerie way, beholding the beholder. Mari wondered if the King spent most of his days in locked gazes with it, longing to enter that perfect world of beauty and symmetry and sunlight, the Maestro's atelier, one of His Majesty's few joys on earth. They all looked so hopeful and innocent back then, two dead princes ago. Mari's perfect-world self stared back at her, the very picture of allegiance and obedience with her hand over her heart, and Nicolas beside her, in his own selfish little world. How wise the Maestro had been, a True Prophet. He had seen their hearts; he was showing them to Mari now, showing anyone who looked, for all posterity. People centuries hence would gaze upon this picture and see Maribarbola, the dwarfess willing to die for her Queen. That person on the wall really was the truest and most reliable version of her, and this weak, cowardly flesh just an inferior copy.

Mari turned to His Majesty.

She beseeched God to protect her in the days and weeks to come. "There is but one worthy successor to your Crown," she began.

It wasn't a prophecy, Maribarbola could always tell her Inquisitors. Just sage advice.

෴

Chapter 25

THE MAN IN THE MOONLIGHT

wo sleepless days passed without Mari being snatched by the Inquisition, and then came such a boon as to leave little doubt God had intervened on her behalf: the King left Madrid for a spiritual retreat in the mountains, leaving the Queen to rule as regent, which put the Inquisition under her command. Temporarily swaddled in absolute protection, Mari hadn't felt this confident or hopeful since the rise of Torre de la Reina. After months of paralytic fear, Maribarbola was back—and angry over all the time she'd lost, sickened by how far the Queen had fallen without her. Reina was poised to rise from the flames, and Heaven help her enemies this second time around.

Mari had doubled down with the King that night, admonishing him—with cool Maribarbola certitude, and the child herself flickering beatifically in the dead center of the Maestro's hallowed masterpiece—that Margarita must be named heiress presumptive. It was God's will, Spain's only hope, and any other course of action would be fully equal to consorting with the devil. Then she had shoved the Queen's scroll at him and marched out on jellied legs.

Torre de la Reina received the news of the King's spiritual retreat with runaway optimism; surely he was praying over Maribarbola's prophecy and would see the divine logic thereof. For Mari, the many-sided implications of the Queen's proposal, and Mari's role in executing it, fit together like the facets of a gem: divine, brilliant, perfect. This had never been about the Queen protecting herself politically, Mari knew in her heart. This was still the mother's game. The Queen had never stopped playing. She was trying to reverse Margarita's fate, nullify the girl's betrothal to her uncle, sparing her a perverse marriage and—more urgent than ever now—the horror of bearing degenerate babies. God was giving Mari yet another second chance she didn't deserve: the chance to join the Queen's fight, save Margarita, and reverse Mari's betrayal, her biggest regret since she'd stepped foot in the Alcázar. Indeed, the biggest regret of her life.

Meanwhile the Queen, eager to demonstrate her worth, threw herself into her regency. She went little seen as she spent her days in the hostage of councilors and diplomats, or on the throne hearing burgher petitions, with evenings holed up in her study, slogging through backlogs late into the night—signing off on building permits, livestock ordinances, prison sentences, even armament requests from commanders at war. And somehow she still found time to run the Alcázar like a German: rituals were upheld and executed with gemmy precision, no meal or mail delivery ever came tardily, and every cranny of the Alcázar dazzled with cleanliness.

One blessedly dull evening saw Mari perched at the top of Torre de la Reina, in the fifth-floor chamber with the unglazed windows and tight swirling winds. It was a warm, balmy freak of a night, as if lazy Barcelona had yawned wide and stretched her arm across the peninsula. Below, Madrid blazed with firelight and dinned with tavern music and bursts of courtyard revelry. Above, the stars dazzled like a spilled pouch of diamonds. Mari roved the sky with her optic tube, naming constellations in her mother tongue: *"Orion. Zwillinge. Löwe. Krebs. Wasserschlange. Sextant. Luchs. Einhorn."* The words sounded almost as queer and meaningless as witch incantations to her now-Spanish ears.

Faint girlish laughter fluttered through the night. Two figures trod the distant footpath, silhouetted in torchlight: a skirted woman and a small breeched boy. An impossibly surefooted lad.

Mari pointed her optic tube at them. The woman stood out in the dark like a milk-fleshed goddess in one of the King's nocturne paintings. Her face glowed like the moon itself; her ropy golden hair flailed in the wind. Mari recognized her instantly, from that long-ago night at the Buen Retiro. It was unmistakably she.

She lowered the scope and watched them pass. Unintelligible snatches of their conversation flittered up—the man in the well, her sweet theater voice. She was caped and gloved, a thickset woman. Philip likes them plump, Nicolas once said back when he and Mari were pretending to be friends, and from there he had punted into some backhanded remark about the Queen, who was not plump and clearly not to her uncle's pleasing.

He took his companion's hand as they navigated an uneven section of footpath. They made a darling sight: a miniature squire and his lady, or a virtuous lad caring for his mother. Mari watched, with fading interest, as they headed out to the gardens.

They went to the maze. Mari raised her optic tube.

The maze was only ever used for one thing around here: fornication.

They drifted asunder at the mouth of the maze, still speaking from yards apart. Nicolas's Italian hands flew in the night. Roberta held up a finger haltingly, twirled it. He turned his back to her, and she vanished into the maze.

Nicolas stood alone in the moonlit circle of Mari's optic tube. He walked a few steps, kicked at something in the grass, picked it up, examined it, tossed it. He looked up at the moon and rolled his gaze across the starry sky. He lost interest in the heavens and started pacing, slow and gainly, stalking the box hedges like a big cat, hungry but patient. He paused and lifted his face to a balmy wind, hair swirling about his shoulders. When the wind died he hung his head and resumed pacing, hand on dagger, skulking and elegant, his slouching back, his feline grace, *ein Löwe, un león*.

Like a raptor, Mari watched him. As he stood alone in the moonlight, alone in the circle, with no one and nothing nearby to scale him, she finally saw him for what he was: a man. A real one. A tall one. In a 1:4 scale body. He was all of it: red-blooded, overconfident, swaggering, lustful, overbearing, self-righteous, wolfishly acquisitive, surefooted and sturdy, gracefully athletic, charming and funny when he wanted to be, caring if it served him. All those things that made men men, concentrated in miniature. Somehow he had managed to escape the mental prison of dwarfhood, going forth in life with all the agency and options of a full-sized man, including the full-sized women. He had leveraged the only conceivable advantages of dwarfhood—cuteness and rarity—while rejecting the innumerable catastrophic negatives: powerlessness, insignificance, subjugation, abuse, ridicule, self-loathing, arthritis. The master of having it both ways: a servant without the loyalty, a prince without the duties, a dwarf and not a dwarf, an adult male enjoying the kind of preciousness and latitude usually only given to small children or beautiful women. He was a living testament to what one could achieve when one had no conscience or scruples holding one back. And that was the real reason Mari despised him. She envied him. He had outrun his dwarf's fate, simply let himself out of his cage, while people like Mari and Bosco and Churro were all dying in theirs. Mari had never even fathomed that a key to the cage existed, but apparently one did. Nicolas had used it for himself and then swallowed it. He had left them all behind—a traitor through and through, even to his own kind.

With a brandish of his dagger, he cut a winter rose from a bush, sniffed it. Behind him, the Guadarramas hulked in silhouette against the royal-purple horizon. Somewhere in those black hills, His Majesty cloistered himself in prayer.

The master of having it both ways stepped into the maze.

༺༻

Mari breakfasted by her window, watching Madrid wake beneath a haze of winter fog and chimney smoke. The cold had returned in full. Mari's hearth blazed with timber and baskets of olive stones, and still half the room steeped in chill. It was an otherwise untroubled morning, the start of another day off. Having thumbed through the newssheets, she sipped chocolate and let her thoughts wander. She wondered how the Queen's wastewater and mule dung meeting had gone yesterday, and what might be served for dinner later, and why more things weren't fried in lard. She wondered if Udo was still alive, still wearing the hat, and how the King could not have syphilis after decades of lying with slatternly women. Inevitably she found herself wondering what in Satan's name would make a young, beautiful, proper-sized woman wish to be hunted in the maze by Nicolasito.

Mari hadn't told anyone about him and Roberta; she didn't want anything to flare up from the firesticks just yet. The Queen would be incapable of keeping such gossip on the backstairs; she'd leak it to the newssheets before the next morning's print run. What a waste of a scandal that would be. So sharp a weapon must be kept sheathed. With the Queen's political fate hanging in the balance, they never knew when they might need Nicolas's compliance in some future matter.

Mari's attention drifted back to the newssheets. Every headline waxed joyous: Juan José was on his way home. With Flanders falling like a house of cards and the French clearly undefeatable, the King was recommitted to unifying the peninsula before he died. To that end, Spain's greatest general and his men were being rerouted to the western front, whence they would launch a full-scale assault on Portugal and submit the Portuguese once and for all to their natural Sovereign. The General's boots on Spanish soil would also put the fear of God into the Catalans, whom he had pacified years ago, but who had grown increasingly bold while he'd been away.

Spain cheered the homecoming of her favorite son, who was expected in Madrid in less than a fortnight. A great feast would be given in his honor, followed by a jag of rabid revelry and manly indulgences: bullfights, cane-tourneys, beast combats, public executions, hunting expeditions, a hundred-beast stew on the Plaza Mayor, equestrian parades, pageants, masques, and many debauched nights at the theater in the eager company of actresses. Already the Calle Mayor was being swept and garnished, with grand stone façades covering shabby cob-and-timber houses and taverns and orange and scarlet ribbons streaming from the balconies.

A gunshot cracked the sky over Madrid. Mari looked up from her newssheet, her cup halted near her lips. Another shot rang out, somewhere in the east, then a hail's worth. A firework whistled up over the city and exploded in a small shower of white light. It was 8 a.m.

The King had reentered Madrid.

ন্তন্ত

No sooner had His Majesty stepped into the Alcázar than rumors spread like blight: the King of Spain had retreated as a humble monk, rising in darkness, dressing in rags, sustaining himself on bread and broth, and spending entire days upon his knees, praying, it was said, as many beads as would circle the earth. Although few had seen him since his return, he was rumored to be thinner, his flesh radiant with the grace of God. Moreover, whatever divine revelations he had sought had been given to him. He had purportedly made a momentous decision, to be announced in the coming days.

The air in Torre de la Reina crackled with excitement as the Queen's supporters conjectured he was a hairbreadth away from naming Margarita heiress presumptive. Though the Queen herself was not the sort to be effusive with her emotions and usually feigned disinterest in rumors concerning the King, this rumor could not have failed to please her. Mari, too, was solidly optimistic, having seen how hopeless and defeated the King had looked that night in his chair. Surely he must be desperate enough to take unprecedented measures to save the Empire, and Maribarbola had only voiced what he already knew in his heart must be done.

One morning after the King's return, the Queen's apartment chirped with activity: maidservants bustled, Binnie had come by to submit her urgent opinion on some trifling household matter, Everardo read the newssheets, and the favorites gathered about the Queen, finally off regent duty, to revel in her company and bring her abreast on all the gossip she had missed while running the Empire. The topic on everyone's lips these days was the return of Juan José.

"He was near Paris last I heard," said the Queen. "He should be here in a week if the French don't figure out who he is and kill him first." Her eyes blazed with relish at the very thought.

"'Twould be a shame," Mari said, matching the Queen's sportive tone. "Many women are praying for his safe return."

The Queen knitted her brow. "Is that why the chapel is so full of women these days? And stinks of roses and rancid goose grease?" The room chimed with laughter. How gay it was to have the Queen back.

"The wardrobe chamber as well," Agustina said. The ladies of the court were sparing no effort in preening themselves for the unwed hero's homecoming. "And there's not a pot of lead to be found on store shelves. All beauty aids have been sold out."

"Even the old married hens are hoping to catch his eye," said Binnie, busying nearby.

"Well," said the Queen wistfully, with a sad, gentle click of her búcaro, "I'm afraid there are going to be a lot of disappointed women around here. He's not nearly as handsome as his picture."

The chamber erupted in wicked laughter. Everardo shook his head. The Queen sat back, smirking. This was the most contented Mari had seen her in weeks. There was plenty to be hopeful about. Baby Charles had at last taken the breast, and the softhearted public continued to cheer his progress and inundate his household with toys, talismans, prayers, and spells. Public support for the Queen was soaring; her latest regency had left few unimpressed, and scattered among the Juan José articles were commentaries lauding her administrative talents and calling upon His Majesty to put her to better use. Moreover, the female contingent of the court seemed overwhelmingly in favor of having Margarita as their next ruler. Even the return of Juan José could not dampen the Queen's cheer. She seemed to be looking forward to the festivities as much as anyone and was no doubt thinking how satisfying it would be to see the haughty bastard drop to his knee before his precious angel of a half-sister, his future Sovereign and commander at war.

"In any case," said the Queen, "he's certainly n—"

A girl's shriek in the tower froze everyone in place. They looked to the vestibule in bewilderment. Mari's heart thumped as frantic footfalls rose in the stairwell, bringing forth some fresh calamity.

The apartment door clunked, and the girl-page Inmaculada shot through the vestibule, her breath short and cheeks flushed. She took a moment to curtsy. "What on earth is it?" snapped the Queen.

"The King is coming!"

The maidservants scurried out the service door as if the chamber were ablaze, while the pages lined up, giggling and squealing, near the entryway. Everardo stood and fussed with his frock. Isabel and Agustina scrambled to their feet and arranged themselves behind the Queen. Mari smoothed her skirt and folded her hands in her lap. Binnie flitted about in a last-minute tidying frenzy.

The curt patter of boot heels rose in the stairwell.

One of the pages made an odd little squeak, and the girls sank in a sloppy line of curtsies. His Majesty and Haro stepped through the doorway.

"This is an unexpected pleasure," said the Queen.

"Your Majesty." Haro sank to his knee and kissed her hand. The King acknowledged her with a nod. He perhaps looked thinner, but he by no means glowed with the grace of God, and whatever peace of mind he had found on his retreat he had clearly just as soon lost. He held a scroll to his breast. A decree.

With a flick of the hand, the Queen dismissed all but Everardo from her company.

Mari joined the horde of pages and handmaidens gathered outside the apartment, their sweet voices and effervescent laughter filling the corridor. After the barest amount of coaxing, Mari pressed her ear to the door.

"What are they saying?" someone whispered.

Mari shook her head. She could only tell that Haro was doing most of the talking.

The sound of boots tickled her heart, and she peeled her ear from the door. All stood poised for the King's exit.

The door clicked open. With a great satin whoosh, the throng of lovelies sank in reverence. The King and Haro strode by with nary a glance and disappeared down the tower stairs.

The ladies stormed the Queen's reception room, a frenzied clatter of pretty shoes on marble. Mari was among the first to reach the Queen, the first to notice Her Majesty's vacant stare and face white as quicklime. "Your Majesty?" The Queen closed her eyes. Mari looked up at Everardo. His face etched with disgust, he nodded to the scroll crushed in the Queen's fist. Mari pried it gently from the royal hand.

She read in silence while the others thronged around her, heating her with their breath. "What is it, Mari?" The written words slipped down her gullet and settled in her stomach like chunks of spoiled meat: *Por la presente declaro … el niño … mi hijo natural … llevará el título de don José Roberto de Toledo …*

"Tell us, Mari!"

Yo, el Rey.

Mari lowered the paper. So this was the big announcement, his divine revelation. "He's going to legitimize Roberta's bastard."

Chapter 26

THE COAT

ays later, the humiliated Queen was forced to attend a public feast in honor of the heavy artillery battalion leaving for the Portuguese front ahead of Juan José. By now news of the King's plan to legitimize another left-handed son had rippled through Spain, and the Spaniards, gripped by Juan José mania, rejoiced at the prospect of having another baseborn prince. Newswriters and balladeers rhapsodized over the King's growing army of bastards, who, having everything to prove, were Spain's best hope for a return to her former glory. Scant regard was paid to the Queen's wounded honor, or the long-term political repercussions for her and her children, who would reap the whirlwind of this decision long after the King's death. Surely one or both of these bastards would make a grab for the Crown eventually.

Mari sat beside Her Majesty at the royal table, staring out at the Salón Grande, now packed with feasting courtiers and warriors. Red silks and palm wreaths festooned the balconies, and great flags bearing the Cross of Burgundy undulated gloriously in the ceiling vaults. The arcades lining the hall twinkled with prayer candles for the departing battalioneers, and many a concerned young lady made a grand show of crossing the room in her high jingling pattens and sofa-sized skirt to light another, no doubt hoping to impress the fashion pundits and the soldiers themselves, the fiercest and most valiant of whom would be awarded marquisates and dukedoms, or maybe a viceroyalty of some palmy island paradise in the New World, if they were lucky enough to return.

The royal table shimmered like treasure with candles and silver bowls and heaps of polished fruit. Tonight's banquet included almond milk soup with garlic and grapes, wide red ribbons of black hoof ham, fried black pudding with pumpkin slices, and one of Mari's favorites, *rosquillas*—rings of fried dough topped with sugar and cherries.

Her appetite long since glutted, Mari tore into her third rosquilla. She was in a foul mood, made fouler by the thick froth of jolly patriotism filling the banquet hall. She and the Queen stewed alone in the bitter juice of defeat. The rest of the Queen's so-called loyalists had sulked and pouted over the King's decision for a couple of days, but then two hours ago giggled and swooned like milkmaids in a knights' billet when His Majesty, in a very rare display of humor, suggested to Maripaz Echevarria that her wig might not make it through the Salón doors.

His refusal to name Margarita heiress presumptive had crushed Mari the hardest. Not only had she failed to protect the Queen politically, she had failed to reverse Margarita's fate and, with it, Mari's unspeakable betrayal. Furthermore, the Infanta really had been Spain's best hope for a peaceful, stable future. The problem was, the King and his ministers didn't want peace and stability—only glory and victory, new dominions, new people to tax and subjugate and unite in Christendom, and new silver mines to finance it all.

Mari looked down at the scores of soldiers feasting and drinking, basking in His Excellency's favor. Half of them would spill their steaming innards on some frozen battlefield in Portugal this winter—baby-faced men with weeks to live, fifteen and sixteen year olds who had already seen their last springtime, their last blossoming tree and cool fountain, lived their last summer of sugar-lime ices and heat quivering over sunbaked rooftops, breathed their last breath of rich autumn air. And actually, Maribarbola had played a hand in hastening their deaths. As part of Teresa's marriage treaty, the French had agreed to withdraw their support from Portugal, reigniting the King's hopes of conquest. Thus the fighting would continue. The killing and conquering would continue. There was naught on earth so reliable as war. Any power or efficacy Mari had felt at the height of Maribarbola's success had been illusory. She was, and always had been, a pawn—a tiny cog in the vast unstoppable machine that was this court, the seat of the Spanish Empire, which had swallowed up half of the western world and was now devouring itself. And just as Mari had feasted at this court, the court had feasted on her. Maria-Barbara with her optic tube and noble intentions was gone; this court had eaten her—eaten her honesty, her integrity, her hopes for a simple, virtuous life, her naïve belief that goodness generally prevailed, and the very last shred of her ability to trust after being sold by Udo.

She blinked away a glaze of tears and chugged a full cup of wine. In the corner of her eye, the Queen's huge wig turned toward her, either in curiosity or disapproval. Mari ignored her and summoned a servant to pour another. She wasn't about to sit through a dwarf dance or buffoon battle of wits sober.

The drink failed to cheer her, and as the night dragged on, she kept checking the King for signs of weariness, hoping they'd soon leave. Nicolas was sitting beside him, in his little chair, watching the dwarfs dance with smug amusement, utterly convinced he was not one of them. This being the first public feast since Spain buried Prospero and welcomed the dying Baby Charles, Nicolas was taking his role as ersatz prince most seriously tonight. At a court where physical proximity to the King was seen as a direct bestowal of God's grace—and even the Queen had to keep a ceremonial distance—Nicolas flaunted his closeness to His Majesty (another dwarf advantage he fully exploited: he never held himself to protocols). The crowd heaved a sentimental moan every time he held the King's hand, kissed the royal cheek, or planted a tiny, jocular slap on the King's chest. *Nicolasito!* one of the popular ballads went. Spain's *Tesorito*, King's *Validito*, a slice of sunshine through His Majesty's dark cloud. Then a particularly annoying line about his having the heart of a giant and kisses as sweet and grand as Italian confections. That was another thing Mari envied: the ease with which Spaniards and Italians showed their affection, while she and the Queen sat fixed in frost, the world never knowing their true hearts—that inner fire which, if unleashed, would burn down the Alcázar. Nicolas was the exact opposite: warmly demonstrative but cold and empty on the inside. In fact, he was the very embodiment of this court: outwardly exquisite, dazzling, and bankrupt to the soul.

Having had enough of the false pageantry, Mari decided to go downstairs and light a candle for the soldiers and walk off some of this wine. Ignoring the Queen's quizzical look, she slid off her chair and went down to the main floor, where the Carlos dwarfs had just delighted the crowd by toddling into a Cross of Burgundy formation.

She slipped into the arcade and walked along the marble corridor, thousands of candles twinkling in neat rows to her right, the Salón raging through the open archways to her left.

Mari stood swaying at a votive rack, watching the flames dance through unfocused eyes, transfixed by their beauty. She hadn't realized how drunk she was. Behind her, the raging crowd and music faded further and further from her consciousness until there was no feast, no Alcázar, no Spain, no world. Just she and the candle flames, wavering as one.

"*Buenas noches.*"

She turned to see Nicolas, standing a polite distance away, candlelight flickering on his gold-broidered coat and cherub cheeks. He reached for a match. "*Buenas noches,*" Mari slurred. She ruffled through the matchsticks with a drunken hand.

Nicolas lit his votive and laced his hands in prayer, while watching Mari fumble her match from the corner of his eye. "Allow me," he said, with an edge of impatience. He took her hand roughly in his and plucked the match from her fingers like an angry father. "Are you drunk?"

"What? No!"

He clearly didn't believe her but said nothing more of it.

As he lit her match, Mari's boozy gaze got lost in his coat, splendid even for him: a doublet of sumptuous brown brocade shot with gold, a mesmerizing pattern of lambs and olive trees and rippling ribands of Latin writing, trimmed with blinding gold buttons and a crisp sugary ruff. "Handsome coat."

"Thanks. Philip brought it back from his travels."

He was talking about the King's retreat. "They make coats like that in the mountains?"

"Of course not. It's Italian-made. His Majesty dispatched a naval galleon to Rome while he was away."

"For a dwarf coat?"

"It's a prince's coat." He doused the match in a cup of sand and knitted his lips into a polite non-smile. "There you are then."

"Thanks." By now her unsubtle severance of their friendship was a firm fact between them. There was an awkward pause as she waited for a sardonic remark, a cryptic threat, a powder keg of gossip that would plunge her into moral turmoil, anything. But Nicolas only stood there, looking at her with an odd blankness, a polite neutrality she'd never seen in him before. It unsettled her in the same way the King laughing might unsettle her, or Binnie lounging on a couch.

"Don't burn this place down," he said, not jestingly.

"I shan't."

She watched him walk away in his coat from Rome.

He strode to the far end of the Salón, where the low-ranking courtiers always sat, farthest from the King—the armpit of the court, the Queen called that section. Curious as to what business Nicolasito could have in that part of the room, Mari wandered down to investigate.

Eventually she spotted him in the crowd, standing on a chair, surrounded by mushroom-wigged beauties, his hands flying while the women fanned their cheeks and laughed. He held out his arm, and they took turns feeling his coat.

Mari's gaze landed on Octavio Barón and Sergio Mora, the King's equerries, also hunting in the armpit tonight—little surprise, given Torre Dorada's excessive taste for lower-class women. Octavio spotted her as she stared drunkenly from the arcade. He spoke to Sergio, and Sergio looked her way. They nodded to her; she nodded back. The men huddled, smirking. It was then Mari saw her, poorly disguised in a black wig—the alabaster skin, the strawberry lips, the portly figure that so pleased His Majesty. How dare they bring her into this room? How dare they parade her before the Queen's unsuspecting eyes, allow her to feast from the Queen's banquet, breathe the Queen's air? They were even more brazen than Mari had thought. More blackhearted and indecent than Mari had thought.

Octavio saw that Mari saw her and turned away—typical Torre Dorada coward. Nicolas, oblivious to the matter, jumped off his chair and disappeared like a stone in water.

Mari looked back at the royal table, where the Queen sat with that wooden posture she had to maintain in public, tricked out in too many charms and jewels, her cheeks rouged like a puppet. All of Mari's fears for her had already come true. Her reign was effectively over; she was Queen in name only. Her arm of power did not even reach to this end of the room. All this time Mari had been searching the sky for a devil's chariot but ignoring danger on the ground. The Queen's demise need not be spectacular or dramatic. It needn't come as a coup, an explosive scandal, or her untimely death. It wouldn't look like Mari's blackest fears. It would look like this: a slow, steady slide to the bottom.

And they were already at the bottom; Nicolas's blank stare had confirmed it. He'd been looking through her, with patent disinterest. Mari, too, was impotent now—a non-threat, non-player, non-entity—not worth his time, his games, not even a prank. She and the Queen had been reduced to a couple of ghosts, a couple of shrews, marinating in their own bitterness while the court reveled on. Mari couldn't even get the Inquisition interested in her anymore. She had prepared herself to die only to find, embarrassingly, she was too insignificant to murder. And now she understood why the men of Torre Dorada so viciously defended their power. Once one's had it, it was almost unbearable to lose it. Unbearable to have been something and now be nothing.

Staring at the Queen on the stage, Mari remembered her first night here, the New Year's Jubilee, when she and the Queen had grasped hands and passed, full of desperate hope, into the future. Each had been thinking the other had what she needed in order to survive and thrive, when in truth they'd always been sinking together. The rise of Torre de la Reina had been a chimera, Mari now realized—a delusion. There had never been any game because the Queen had never had a chance, not at this court. Any political gains she made, her enemies would combine to reverse them. In fact, Mari's presence had probably only hastened Her Majesty's decline, dragged her down, entangled her in Mari's own pathetic destiny—a destiny of powerlessness and insignificance, of ridicule and laughter, disrespect. In all ways but bodily, the Queen of Spain was now living the life of a dwarf.

Fueled by fury and drunken bravado, Mari plunged headlong into the crowd.

She was used to ridicule and disrespect—all dwarfs were—but, Devil help her, she was not going to allow these swine to belittle the Queen. There may be no hope left for the rise of Reina, but there was still plenty of room for Dorada to fall. Mari had been looking at things wrongly. The power inequity between the Queen and her enemies would have to be reconciled not by elevating the Queen but by destroying her enemies, which could be only accomplished with sheer nastiness. And how convenient that this court had devoured Mari's every last shred of virtue. She wouldn't be needing it anymore.

Dodging legs and ramming skirts, she cut an angry swath through the crowd. They had gotten way too comfortable over in Torre Dorada. They needed a reminder that no one was safe—that utter ruin was but a whisper away, even for the King's favorite. The world had fallen too tidily into place for Nicolasito. It was time he was made to defend his pampered existence, claw out a life just like everyone else on this earth.

Mari spotted him several bodies away, in his coat from Rome that was filling her with dread—the dwarf coat that rode in on a warship. She sneaked up and took hold of his childly arm; so weirdly deceptive it was, mannishly hard, she almost lost her nerve. He turned. She leaned in too close, a drunken miscalculation, her face burrowing into his warm, *vinagrillo*-scented hair, and hissed in his ear: "I trust you kept Roberta well-attended in His Majesty's absence?"

She backed away, enjoying his reaction, the way it blossomed and ripened like a flowering fruit tree—so many colors, so many layers and textures: shock, confusion, a dash of annoyance, a flicker of defiance, then acceptance, guilt, sheepishness, a boy caught with his hand in the sweetmeats, the naughty-lad smirk, a plea for mercy in those round Italian eyes.

Mari bent her neck and walked away. She returned to the royal table, at last sharing in the fighting spirit that infused the Salón Grande tonight.

Chapter 27

THE WATERSHED

ari woke in misery the next morning, parched, queasy, shaky, thoroughly debauched. She had kept drinking last night, right up until the end. Memories of her antics assailed her in shards: grabbing Nicolas's arm and burrowing her nose into his ear like a randy whore, singing Spanish battle songs with her fist in the air, tossing a palm wreath onto Haro's head as he sat in serious discussion with a war general, walking face-first into the royal buttock during the exit procession. The King's.

She sent the smirking chambermaid away and spent the morning writhing in darkness, sipping tepid water and praying for mercy, which did come in the form of sleep. She woke in the afternoon feeling well enough for bread and broth and ate gingerly while ruminating on her conclusions from last night. Though her ambitions to annihilate Torre Dorada were tempered by sobriety, she was still committed to making life as miserable as possible for as many of them as possible. She compiled a mental list of aspersions: Haro's night of shocking debauchery, which had been hinted at in that lone ditty before being mysteriously and firmly squelched; Sergio Mora's mother smuggling high-tax imports like chocolate and French wines (the Queen was an enthusiastic customer); those persistent venereal pox rumors that plagued an otherwise healthy-looking Octavio Barón.

It wasn't much, but it was a start, and Mari fully intended to extort Nicolas for more. Surely he was sitting on an explosive scandal or two, just as Mari was sitting on one about him and Roberta. Doing nothing was not an option. The Queen's situation was deteriorating. Since Baby Charles's birth, Torre Dorada had become alarmingly bold. There was a new bastard prince to worry about, and the King's mistress was parading herself around like a legitimate member of the court. Roberta herself was no threat; it would be beneath the Queen's dignity to be offended by so inferior a woman. But the King's ministers had long wished Mariana gone, and Mari feared they were closer than ever to having it so. It was the contempt, the arrogance, the *lese majesty* coming from Torre Dorada that troubled her most. That, and Nicolas's coat.

Mari went outside for some air and found Lalo in the stable, trimming his horse for Juan José's homecoming parade. The General was expected in Madrid any day now. "If you were the King," she asked, watching Lalo braid a red ribbon into his horse's forelock, "what reason might you have for dispatching a naval galleon to Rome?"

Lalo thought about it, shrugged. "Send an urgent message to the Pope?"

"That's exactly what I was thinking."

"So?" he said, absorbed in his task.

"So I'm worried."

"You're always worried."

It felt different this time. The King had dispatched a naval galleon, quietly, to Rome, after having had some sort of prayer-induced epiphany. Mari feared he had come to the same realization she herself had shortly after Baby Charles's birth: in this incestuous union, the fate of the Empire was sealed. Spain's best hope for survival was to dissolve the royal marriage now, while the King was still alive and virile. Hence the urgent message to the Pope. He was seeking an annulment. He finally understood his niece must go.

ॐ

Unable to keep her fears to herself any longer, Mari went downstairs that evening to warn the Queen and implore her not to respond rashly. Eager to commence what was likely to be a tense conversation, she stepped through the vestibule and was surprised and annoyed to see the Marquis, sitting on the sofa beside the Queen, gazing upon the royal bosom as if no time had passed. Mari retreated, but the Queen saw her. "Come in, Mari."

She joined them in delicate silence, taking note of the lilies and sweetmeats on the table. The Marquis beamed at her like a pleased parent as she hoisted herself onto the opposite sofa. She hadn't seen him in months, and his merciless beauty assailed her afresh. The Queen fiddled with a handkerchief. She'd been crying.

Mari and the Marquis exchanged courtly nods. "I read about your impassioned performance of *Glory Glory* in the paper today," he said, with the same stale grin she'd received from countless others today. "How I wish I'd been there."

The Queen threw her a crust of mercy: "Cristofer's been in Villamirada these past several months, caring for his sick mother."

"She is reunited with the Lord," he added serenely.

Mari sputtered out a condolence. She still couldn't believe he was here.

"Thank you. It was womb cancer. Too much black bile."

He spoke at length about his mother's demise—the suffering she'd endured, how bravely she'd fought—at one point choking on his grief. The Queen reached forth and squeezed his hand. He cheered himself with a hardy breath. "I still have to go back and tie up her affairs. I thought I'd return to Madrid for the homecoming festivities. Heaven knows I could use some frivolity in my life."

"You'll attend the feast as my guest," said the Queen. "I'll have you seated a cat's leap from the King. Perhaps I can get you an audience with the General, depending on his mood. He's a fickle sort."

"I'm undeserving of your kindness." He bowed his head deeply, his dark shiny hair skimming forward.

The Queen turned to Mari. "Cristofer has decided to join the army."

They both enjoyed her stunned reaction. "Whatever brought this on?" Mari asked.

"I suppose you could say I'm a changed man."

He spoke at great length about how his mother's death had forced him to take inventory of his own life, which was little more than an aimless pursuit of pleasure and leisure. He said he'd had his fill of bullfights and comedies and charity fundraisers; a proper life, he now realized, was not centered on frolic and frivolity but, rather, honor, duty, courage, God, and country. "Devotion," he added, looking tenderly at the Queen. He said he'd not gone anywhere or done anything truly significant and would like to see the New World before he died—Florida or Mexico, he had read about the lovely beaches there.

Mari kept waiting for the Queen to exercise her unequaled talent for curtailing people's selfish monologues, but she allowed him to prattle on, fanning herself dreamily as he spoke of his desire to live honorably and fearlessly and how he hadn't known what bravery was until he watched his mother die, and how, at twenty-six years old, he finally understood what it meant to be a man, "and it took my mother dying of womb cancer to show me."

At long last, silence fell.

The Queen emerged from her doting trance. "I suppose God does have a sense of irony."

"She certainly does," said the Marquis. The Queen chuckled shrilly and condemned his blasphemy with a whack of her fan. He stroked his nonexistent mustache, pleased with himself.

Mari stared at him. Really studied him. His exquisite face. His lemon-oiled hair. His elegant hands. The thought of this man in the army was only less preposterous than that of a woman in the army.

In the corner of Mari's eye, the Queen was looking at her. "Something wrong over there?"

"No, Your Majesty." Her flat Maribarbola voice.

"Forgive her," said the Queen. "She had a rough night."

"I imagine today was rougher," he said.

The two shared an airy laugh, and then went on to discuss the Marquis's military career options. The Queen would sooner have him join the navy and work the silver fleets. "You'll be safer out in the middle of the ocean," she said, clearly aware of his unfitness for battle. When he tired of seafaring—"and your New World beaches," she added dully—she would appoint him to her Royal Guard. Eventually (i.e., when the King died) she would award him a dukedom, and not some far-flung goat province either. It would be here in central Spain, near the seat of the Crown.

"Please use me in any way you see fit," he said.

"I shall."

They exchanged a brief, naughty look.

Mari watched them, her blank gaze roving back and forth from him to her, back to him again—his sublime face, too delicate for a man, too chiseled for a woman, perfect and sexless as a flower. And then there was the Queen, with her bored eyes, her flesh-drip nose, the chin they wrote about in the papers. Having not seen them side by side for so long, Mari could see now how odd a couple they were, how woefully mismatched. "Are you alright?" the Queen asked, getting annoyed now. Mari nodded.

In fairness, the Queen was not without her charms. She was like a walnut, Mari had noticed, hard and unlovely, with a rancid, bitter heart, yet oddly appealing. But what men desired she did not possess. She was not particularly kind or softhearted, and she was even less sweet than she was beautiful. She wasn't selfless, indeed quite the opposite. And yet this jewel of a man kept coming back, sneaking in and out at profane hours to seduce the King's wife, risking his life every time. He was either unspeakably foolish, mad, or both, though to Mari he seemed neither. Granted, he was a parasite; they all were, Mari included. But for all the time and energy he had spent courting the Queen, he had naught to show for it but her charity donations (which she had since wisely retrenched) and her flimsy promises of far-in-the-future dukedom.

He was speaking to Mari now, something about a card rematch. " ... still not gambling?"

"She's gambling," said the Queen. "Back with a vengeance."

Before, Mari had more or less regarded him through the distorted lens of Maria-Barbara's vestigial goodness. Now that she was utterly virtueless and down in the dirt, however, she had a clear, snake's-eye view of him: this suspiciously timed visit, his harebrained military ambitions, the heart-stirring tale about his mother, the nonexistent tear he had wiped away while baring his grief. No doubt he was a fraud; by now Mari could spot her own kind. The question was, why was he here? Or, rather, for whom? With her fears of a plot against the Queen intensifying, Mari was loath to dismiss this sudden reappearance as mere coincidence.

He was telling Mari she was lucky he couldn't stay—he had to meet some elderly duchess at the opera tonight, a benefactress of his charity. "Perhaps next weekend?" he said, looking hopefully to the Queen.

She made him wait while she sipped her búcaro. "You may call next weekend."

She had Mari walk him out. He chattered genially all the way, oblivious to Mari's nascent hostility toward him. It was a respectable hour, so she let him out through the front entrance, where Lalo was on duty. They watched the Marquis walk elegantly down the foot-path and, with uncharacteristic boorishness, whistle for his coach.

"These liaisons need to end," Mari said, staring at the Marquis's slim back. "She's putting herself at great risk."

Lalo was unfazed. "This kind of thing has been going on since the beginning of time."

"And heads have been rolling over this kind of thing since the beginning of time."

"The King's too busy with his own liaisons to even notice."

"He'll notice." Mari bucked her chin at the distant Marquis. "This one's working for Haro."

Lalo looked at her.

"I need you to follow him, Lalo. Please. I need to know if he meets an old noblewoman at the opera, as he says he's going to. Just one lie is all I need to convince the Queen he's an enemy."

Lalo hesitated, but it was a dull night at the Alcázar. Most courtiers were down in the city, celebrating ahead of Juan José. "If you insist."

"Remove your habit and stay in the shadows."

Minutes later, Mari watched the Marquis's coach trundle down the winding hillside, with Lalo's horse trotting a quarter mile behind, barely visible in the night.

❧✦☙

Chapter 28

THE LETTER

he chapel bell struck six a.m. Mari sat by the frigid window, on the precipice of panic, shaking from cold and lack of sleep. Outside, Madrid lay eerily still. Even the Juan José revelers had surrendered to the hour. Mari could see the opera house from here, a gray cube with faintly glowing arcades. A ride there and back should have taken an hour. Lalo had been gone for ten now.

After he had ridden away last night, Mari had marched upstairs feeling clever and daring for having launched her first spy operation. She was starting to think like Torre Dorada, play the game like a proper snake. She returned to the royal apartment, where she and the Queen spoke about how well the Marquis looked, how surprising it was to see him again, how sad about his mother. The Queen said he'd make a lousy soldier but good enough sailor. They laughed and snorted at the thought of him in battle.

After the Queen had dismissed her, Mari rushed downstairs to get Lalo's report. He hadn't returned. Mari blamed the traffic. By midnight she was worried, though the guards jested that he was probably enjoying the opera or slopped in a tavern somewhere. At two a.m. she sent a squire to the opera house. He was back in forty minutes, no sign of Lalo. At four a.m. they checked Lalo's apartment, so now his wife and daughters were also sick with worry. If he wasn't back by sunrise, one of the watchmen said, someone would have to go upstairs and tell the Queen one of her senior infantry officers had vanished.

Now, as the new day perched in the east, Mari feared the worst. Lalo had been ununiformed on a royal horse. He may have been mistaken for a thief and right now be hanging by his thumbs at the Grand Inquisitor's office. Or else he was dead in a ditch somewhere, in which case Mari had basically killed him.

Binnie's voice leached through the floor. The Queen's morning routine was underway. Mari could hear washbasins pinging, wardrobes opening and closing, and the Queen ordering her servants around with lethargic, single-word commands.

Outside, a tiny figure caught Mari's eye. A horseman, riding uphill to the Alcázar. Mari sprung to her feet and scanned the hillside with her optic tube. "Please," she said, a pathetic whimper.

It was a mail courier. Mari plunked down and sobbed uncontrollably. She needed sleep. She needed to know Lalo was alive. If she didn't get those two things very soon, she herself would die.

She listened for the Queen to be left alone with her búcaro and newssheets. Mari would have to go downstairs and tell her everything. She'd have to tell her she had presumed to have the Marquis followed, that she suspected he was working for Torre Dorada— with the implication that his affection for Her Majesty was otherwise inexplicable—and that her reckless judgment might have killed

Lalo. She would prostrate herself and beg for forgiveness, soak the Queen's carpet with tears.

When the royal apartment fell silent, Mari went downstairs.

She passed an unfamiliar page exiting the Queen's apartment, a young man not of Reina. Mari floated through the vestibule. The Queen sat alone in the glow of a fresh fire, tented in red satin, the color of blood and victory. Maybe she had decided to attend Juan José's homecoming parade after all.

She was reading a letter.

"Your Majesty?" Mari's voice quivered.

The Queen held up a hand and kept reading. Mari stepped closer. The Queen's eyes oscillated frantically, her brow squinched in concentration.

The royal nostrils flared.

Panic rose in Mari's breast. "Who is that letter from?"

"Lalo."

"*Thank God!* Where is he?"

"Guadalajara," the Queen muttered, not looking up.

"Guadalajara?" Guadalajara lay forty miles to the north-east. Lalo must have ridden half the night. "What on earth is he doing there?"

"He's wounded."

"Wounded?" Mari leapt forth and startled the Queen, who seemed surprised and confused to see Mari standing there. "Badly?"

"Go to your room and lock your door."

Mari thought she was jesting. "Are you ser—"

"*Do as you're told!*"

Mari backed away slowly, the Queen's bloodcurdling command still hanging in the air. Even Her Majesty seemed shocked and horrified by it.

Mari turned and left, breaking into a run.

She locked her apartment door and stood pinned against it, breathless, heart thumping in her ears. She couldn't enjoy the news that Lalo was alive. Something dreadful was afoot. She had seen the terror in the Queen's eyes, heard it in the Queen's voice.

When it's time to worry, Nicolas once said, you'll know.

This was it. This was the coup.

Chapter 29

THE MESSAGE

A thunderclap of artillery fire shattered Mari's thin sleep. She checked the clock; it was midmorning. Was the enemy invading already? Dazed and jittery, she left her bed and went to the window. The Alcázar's front courtyard lay nearly empty. Beyond, the Calle Mayor looked like a miles-long swarm of red beetles: thousands of people, dressed for victory. Red silks streamed from balconies. Crosses of Burgundy rippled in the cold wind.

Two Reina guards flirted with some young women near the tower entrance. Churro the dwarf waddled toward them with a palm wreath on his head, red ribbons dragging behind him. In the center of the courtyard, a mounted guard performed horse ballet moves while his comrades laughed.

Another explosion rang out in the distance: cannon fire, followed by a crackle of gunshots.

The crowd on the Calle Mayor teemed and stirred. Mari could hear their shrill din through the glass. A bouquet of fireworks exploded over the east edge of the city. General don Juan José was in Madrid.

Mari relaxed. This wasn't the coup, not yet at least, and the General's presence already made her feel safer. She finally understood the adulation, all those women praying and preening.

Figuring the Queen had calmed by now, Mari decided to go downstairs and ask her what Lalo was doing in Guadalajara, how he'd been wounded, and what he had written to upset Her Majesty.

Mari was a dozen feet from her own apartment when a guard stopped her. "Get back in there," he said.

Figuring security was heightened for the General's arrival, she thought little of it. "I'm going downstairs to see Her Majesty." She started to go around him. He blocked her path. Mari looked up at him incredulously. Did he not know who she was?

He pointed to her apartment. "*Geh.*"

Go. In deadly serious German.

"*Ich bin die Prophetin Maribarbola.*"

"*Kein Durchgang. Befehle Ihrer Majestät.*"

No passage. Her Majesty's orders.

With fresh fears of a palace siege, Mari returned to her apartment and locked her door. She put a log on and crawled into bed. As she lay staring at the canopy, a crop of new worries bloomed. Maybe this wasn't a security matter. Maybe the Queen was furious with her for having had the Marquis followed, for acting above her station and issuing an order to a knight—which had really just been she asking Lalo for a favor, but the Queen wouldn't see it that way. Was Mari under house arrest?

No. The Queen would have reprimanded her this morning. And that wasn't fury Mari had seen in Her Majesty's eyes. It was terror.

Then it came to her in a flash: Lalo had been kidnapped by rebels! That letter was a ransom note. They had wounded him and were threatening to kill him if the Crown didn't cooperate. Maybe they had threatened to snatch others as well—the Prophet Maribar-bola!—which was why the Queen was keeping her under lock and guard. It made perfect sense.

Feeling safe for now, Mari dozed and woke in the afternoon. She could hear the Queen and Everardo speaking downstairs, a grave, murmuring conversation fretted by long pauses. Mari left her bed and cracked her apartment door. The guard turned toward her and planted himself. *Kein Durchgang.*

She fetched her optic tube and went to the window. The parade was fervently underway. The General's convoy lined the Calle Mayor, two dozen coaches with soldiers crammed atop like pigeons in black leather capes and sugarloaf hats, waving to the crowd. Some sliced at the flailing streamers with their swords. Roses and laurel wreaths leapt from crowd to convoy like New World popcorn springing from a kettle. Mari wished she were down there to see all those Spanish soldiers up close, with their raven hair and roses tucked behind their ears, smiles flashing through dark beards. But she hadn't planned on going anyway; the Queen would've taken it as an act of betrayal. Mari had long ago learned to feign disinterest in all matters Juan José.

She noticed she was ravaged. She hadn't gotten breakfast, or firewood or mail deliveries for that matter—even water and waste service. Nor had she heard Binnie's caws in the stairwell today or the squeals of girl pages. Was all of Reina confined to quarters? The Queen would not have given everyone the day off to stand on the street and froth over Juan José. Would she?

Having foraged some sweetmeats and an old pouch of cocoa from her cupboard, Mari ate by the window, staring at the parade, absorbed in worry. Reina's silence filled her ears like wool. Now that she'd noticed it, she couldn't ignore it. They were in some sort of quiet state of emergency. Tower operations had ceased. Nobody was coming in or going out down below. Whatever Lalo had written in that letter had plunged the Queen into a panic. And the Queen was not a panicky sort.

And what of the Marquis? Did he figure into this in any way?

The convoy inched down the Calle Mayor at a near standstill. It would be late at night before Juan José presented himself at the Alcázar. Torchlight dotted the twilit city, amassing thickly on the Calle Mayor, an enchanting sight. Fireworks detonated against the blackening sky. The crowd din surged to new volumes. Night never failed to intoxicate the Spaniards.

Mari was debating whether she should try to talk her way past the guard or at least pester him for information, when she heard ladylike footsteps skittering outside her apartment. She was already lunging through the vestibule, when a sharp knock met her door. "Coming!"

It was Lalo's daughter, Gabriela.

"*Dios mío*," Mari exhaled. "Where is he?"

"He got back a couple of hours ago," Gabi said furtively. The guard was watching them from a few yards away.

"He's wounded?"

"He was in a duel."

"A duel?" Mari said, too loudly. "With whom?"

Gabi's eyes slid askance. The guard took a couple of paces toward them. Some leather part of his habit made an intimidating squeak.

"How did you get past the guards?" Mari whispered, realizing only then what a foolish question it was. This was *Gabi la Hechizada*—Gabi the Hexed, the one too beautiful for her own good. Lalo must have known they'd let her pass. Beauty like that was above earthly law.

"My father … " the girl said modestly. She swung something at Mari. "He wanted me to bring this to you."

Mari winced in confusion. "A fruit basket? What on earth—"

Then she saw it, perched atop, nestled between two oranges. A walnut.

"Thank you. I'm starving."

Gabi nodded and scurried away.

Mari locked her door and, knees quivering, carried the basket into the firelight. She broke the walnut under a chair leg and, with shaking hands, unfurled the scroll:

He's a rebel. So is the King's mistress. Leave _NOW_. Get out of Spain. You don't want to be anywhere near this scandal when it explodes!

❧❀☙

Chapter 30

THE KNIGHT-ERRANT

She would go secretly by night.

When darkness fell, Mari put on a black coat and the black veil she never wore because it made her look like a very short prostitute. She stepped out of her apartment and, with the guard in the corner of her eye, darted for the stairs.

"Halt!" he barked, and intercepted her with just a few strides.

Never mind her prophet card; Maribarbola played her witch card. "Let me pass or I'll curse you," she said calmly, to his groin.

He hesitated and stepped aside.

Mari crept down the stairs and through the corridors to the sparely used Reina east entrance. She cracked the door and peeked out. A mounted guard stood a few yards away, smoking a New World tobacco roll, watching the torchlights coalesce and swirl on the Calle Mayor. Mari waited, and when a round of fireworks crackled over the Puerta del Sol, she slipped outside and hotfooted toward the river path.

The night was cold and smelled of fallen leaves and brazier smoke. Mari scuttled down the riverbank, scanning the dark for murderous figures or the rogues and bullies that lurked here in fairer weather, picking pockets and snatching capes or pinching fruits and sweets from the hands of children. But they were all down in the city tonight, hiding among the rabble of peasants and beggars, idlers and loafers, gapers and gossips. Mari trod swiftly, her steps crunching the cold grass, the river sprawling like a swath of black glass. She followed it northward, to the dependent buildings where the knights lived.

A guard stood sentry outside Lalo's building, another in the stairwell on his landing, and another in the hall outside his apartment. One by one, Maribarbola calmly threatened to wither their loins and watched them step aside.

She rapped on Lalo's door. His wife answered. "How is he?" Mari barked at her. Doña Castellón looked baffled to see her standing there, cloaked and veiled, a miniature black phantom. She glanced at the guard but didn't ask.

"He's resting," she said, stepping aside.

Mari swept through the vestibule and into the reception room. She had been here before, for birthday parties and card nights. It was a four-story apartment, well-furnished and staffed with servants. Belted knights enjoyed hefty salaries and tax exemptions as it were, and the handsome, valiant Lalo was a firm favorite of the Queen.

A quartet of raven-haired beauties sitting on cushions near the hearth shot up when they saw Mari. "Mari!" Gabi said. "How did you get past the guards?"

Mari tore off her veil. "They were open to reason."

"You have to leave, Mari!" Magdalena said. "Father is worried for your safety!"

"Go back to Germany!" Claudia, the youngest, said. "You can have my horse!"

Mari hushed them with a hand and turned to doña Castellón. "Where is he?"

A maidservant saw her to a second-floor bedchamber. Lalo lay asleep under a brocade canopy, his lacy white nightgown soaking up the firelight and sweat-matted hair creeping over his unshaven neck. The chamber was strewn with medical implements and smelled of boiled wine and vinegar. He opened his eyes, saw Mari, and closed them again. "I hope you're here to say goodbye," he mumbled.

"I'm here to find out what the hell is going on."

"He's a traitor. The Queen is in big trouble, and so are you if you don't get out of here." He propped himself up, wincing in agony.

Mari poured him a cup of wine. "How bad is it?" Pale, watery blood seeped through his nightgown over his ribs.

"I'll live."

She made him drink. "Tell me what happened."

"He didn't go to the opera. He went to a tavern on Toledo and Jerónima."

"That's ten minutes away. You were gone eighteen hours."

"Listen. There's more." He gestured to the bedside chair. Mari hoisted herself into it. "Within minutes Roberta arrived in Nicolas's coach."

"Was Nicolas with her?"

"If he was, he stayed in the coach. Their meeting was brief. Roberta left only minutes later. The Marquis left soon after and traveled north. It was clear he had no intentions of going to the opera, so I followed him. We left the city and rode for nearly two hours, to a villa in the countryside. It was a private residence, but there were armed guards at the door. Some of them wore the Bars of Aragon."

"*Dios mío*," Mari whispered. This was the Catalan rebel insignia, the one painted on the powder keg found beneath the stage at the Buen Retiro.

"The Marquis was permitted easy entry."

Mari's jaw hardened; her nostrils flared. All those card games. All his charm and geniality, the flowers, the sweetmeats, the fritters for Mari; all those tiddly nights in the Queen's apartment, the clowning and jesting, the sunrise goodbyes; all that talk of honor, duty, God, and country. He was a dastardly swine, with a tiny black peppercorn for a heart—a rebel snake who had slithered as deep as one could get inside the Alcázar: into the Queen's very body.

"How did you get hurt?" Mari asked.

"One of their men ambushed me from behind. I was able to escape, but not before he cut me. I couldn't mount my horse, so I footed to the nearest town. A landlady took me in and called a barber to sew me. I sent a letter to Her Majesty as soon as I was able. They've infiltrated the Alcázar and are no doubt planning an attack. I think they're waiting to get the King and Juan José under the same roof so they can assassinate them together."

"My God. The feast." The Queen had promised to seat him a cat's leap from the King. "How much does the Queen know?"

"Everything. She just left here a couple of hours ago."

"She's put all of Reina on lockdown."

"She's trying to contain this," Lalo said. "She has good reason to panic. The Queen has gotten herself into an impossible situation. The King must be told about Roberta immediately; as long as she's in the Alcázar, he remains a breath away from death. Once Roberta's arrested and interrogated, the Queen's association with the Marquis will be brought to light. She'll be executed alongside them as a traitor."

Mari covered her mouth, willing herself not to be sick. This was the boon the King's ministers had been waiting for. The Queen could not have made it more convenient for them, morally, legally, or politically. Once her close confederation with a known traitor was brought to light, Torre Dorada need only sit back and watch her lurid demise. The newssheets would savage her. The

Pope would proclaim her an adulteress and a heretic and sanction her execution. Even her brother Leopold would be loath to intervene. The Spaniards would rally around their King and watch with rabid pleasure as his false-hearted wife burned to death on the Plaza Mayor.

"In her desperation she might try to negotiate with the rebels," Lalo said, "endangering the Crown even further. I'm bound by oath to obey her, but you're not. Before you leave, you must let someone else know that the King is in grave danger."

"I'm not leaving."

"You must! Do you think this scandal won't touch you, as close as you are to the Queen? You'll be one of the first interrogated. I've seen the Inquisition's handiwork, and, believe me, there's no worse fate to be had on earth—not even burning at the stake, which is also a possibility for you!"

"I can get her out of this." Mari still had the King's ear; her word was still law. Any shred of self-worth she still had was inextricably invested in the Queen. Abandoning her now would be an unforgivable betrayal, rendering Mari soulless and purposeless—not to mention homeless—and plagued by a lifelong mental anguish that no Inquisition torment could match.

"You flatter yourself," Lalo said. "The only way to get her out of this is to put her on a horse and send her far away, never to be seen again. There's no way this can end well for the Queen. All you can do is make sure you don't go down with her. Hire a horseman and leave tonight. You'll be halfway to Barcelona before anyone notices you're gone. Don't stay and make a martyr of yourself. A martyr is a glorified fool. If you don't believe that now, you will when you're lying on the torture rack!"

He winced in pain.

The chamber fell silent. Mari's gaze landed on his bloodied nightshirt. "I shouldn't have asked you to go alone," she said.

"Thank God you asked me to go at all. Imagine if we hadn't known until it was too late."

Mari nodded, still staring at the stain.

"It looks worse than it is," he said of the wound.

Already his brow glistened with fever.

Chapter 31

THE PROMISE

ari entered the royal apartment. The Queen stood looking out the window, still in the red dress, her back as slim as a child's. It was late; the General's convoy was at last climbing the hill toward the Alcázar. The crowd had spilled onto the palace plazas. Music and laughter and jolly chants seeped easily through the Queen's windows. Below, the courtyard blazed with dancing torchlights and twirling sticks of fire. Mari's reflection appeared behind the Queen's in the dark glass.

"Why aren't you in your room?" the Queen asked.

"I can help you minimize this matter."

The Queen said nothing. She was staring at her own reflection, into her own eyes.

"His Majesty must be told," Mari said.

"Go back to your room at once."

317

"Roberta is also an insurgent. He can't punish you for something of which he himself is just as guilty!"

The Queen whirled around. "*Of course he can! He's the King!*" She took a few teetering steps and collapsed like a tent, her skirt puffing up hugely and slowly deflating. She hung her head and wept. Tears welled in Mari's eyes. The sight of the Queen in a quaking heap on the floor was too much for her heart to bear.

"I can get you through this unscathed," Mari said, though her voice cracked with fear and uncertainty. "I can issue a prophecy to protect you."

The Queen paused her crying and snatched Mari's wrist, hard. "No! You must leave. You know way too much, and they'll torture you for every last bit of it. You have to get out of Spain. Go back to Germany. Everardo will give you some silver. You must leave tonight. That's an order! If you stay here, you'll die with me."

It broke Mari's heart that the Queen could even consider Mari's leaving a possibility, that she had no idea she was worth dying for, the last best thing Mari had left to live for. Mari had spent her entire adult life in the service of another: Dwarfess. Companion. Humble servant. Laboratory assistant. Prophet. Sage. Lucky charm. Jester. Flatterer. Card player. Warm body in the room. Listener. Secret keeper. Marriage counselor. Political strategist. Occasional spy. All anyone had ever asked of her was to be loyal. "I'm not leaving you." Friend. Protector. The one who stayed. The one who did not betray. The one who mattered most, when it mattered most. This court had devoured everything but her loyalty. It had tried and failed. Her loyalty was the only thing left of the real her and was apparently incorruptible, which in a place like this made her as rare a specimen as Nicolasito.

Through a varnish of tears, she stared unflinchingly at the Queen. The royal eyes stared back. This was the moment Mari had wished for but never got with the dying Countess—that look of mutual gratitude, trust, loyalty, years' worth of unspoken *I love yous*, that singular sort of love between dwarfess and lady: deep, vast, silent, uncomplicated, frosty, *wie Alpenschnee*. Like Alpine snow, *ich liebe dich*.

And like flowers, lies didn't survive here.

"I'm not really a prophet."

"I figured."

With this Mari's affection for the Queen swelled exponentially and ferociously. The Queen had figured it out and kept her anyway. Housed and fed and cared for her anyway. Valued and protected and loved her anyway, for no reason, because they were long past the point of needing any kind of reason. For all the time Mari had spent agonizing over her own loyalty, it had never once occurred to her that the Queen of Spain was all the while reciprocating—that Mari, too, was worthy of being the receptacle.

The Queen looked up at her. How odd, seeing Her Majesty from this angle. So childlike, she looked, with her tear-stained cheeks and frightened eyes, Mari pried the royal fingers from her suffering wrist. The Queen snatched a fistful of her coat instead. "They'll have me killed," she said in a tiny voice, tears flashing in the firelight.

Mari grabbed the royal face, giving it a little shake. In her dwarf's breast—*now show me your heart*—a ferocious beast stirred from a life-long slumber; it stretched its claws and gnashed its teeth. "I won't let them," it said in a guttural growl that put a flicker of horror in the Queen's eyes. Mari would die for the Queen. Kill for the Queen. Nobody was going to touch the Queen. Finally, the opportunity to redeem her worth. A four-man chest of silver bought *this*.

The Queen nodded, desperate and obedient. Mari nodded back, firm and unemotional, a German banker. She helped Her Majesty into a chair.

ຄຄ

Mari lay awake with fireworks and musket shots reverberating in her chest and the din of revelers roiling and whooping outside her windows. It was after midnight. Her hearth blazed. Her chamber had been freshened. She had gotten a chicken dinner. At Mari's behest, the Queen had relaxed security and ordered staff to resume duties. Nonessential personnel could join the Juan José frenzy if they wished. Everardo was preparing to travel to Austria to negotiate political asylum for the Queen if it should come to that, though Mari had overheard her tell him she'd sooner die than leave her children.

Juan José was in the Alcázar, supping privately with his father, they'd been told. All Mari could do was pray for their safety. She couldn't sound the alarm on Roberta yet, no matter how serious the threat. She would sooner gamble the King's life—the Empire itself—in order to protect the Queen. And actually, the General's timing could not have been more fortuitous. Security would be all but impenetrable, and the King and Haro would be fully distracted in the coming days.

Mari's thoughts turned to the Marquis, whose habits and peculiarities took on new meaning when examined through the unclouded eyeglass of his treachery. The way he had always laughed a bit too loudly when the Queen spoke nastily of the Catalans. His unwavering conviction that the Retiro plot had been the work of a rogue assassin; that had always irritated the Queen to no end. That time he got weirdly quiet when she referred to Roberta as the King's prized sow and vanished in disgust for several months after she had spoken ill of Roberta's baby. Mari would also bet a thousand ducats that his mother was still alive.

Rebels had infiltrated the Alcázar at its weakest point: the royal marriage. The perverse, loveless union of Philip and Mariana was indeed the Crown's greatest vulnerability, but rebels never could have known it without the aid of a court insider. The informer had to have been a royal confidante who knew both Their Majesties well, their desires and weaknesses, and, as such, had likely served in both Torre Dorada and Torre de la Reina. To Mari's knowledge, there was only one person at this court who had ever had it both ways.

Nicolas and his murky games. Nicolas's secret dinners in houses with seven chimneys, with people who had fresh and interesting perspectives on things, people with dangerous new ideas. He was doubling down on his security, he had told Mari. Anything can happen at any time. The master of having it both ways had known a coup was coming and was making sure he had a tiny glittering foot in the door of the new regime. All those political rants Mari had suffered during their fake friendship now swirled in her mind: his ruthless complaints about the Crown; his frequent tirades about Spain's economic and moral failings under Philip; his scathing criticisms of His Majesty and his weakness as a ruler; the shocking disrespect for the man who kept him, over-salaried him, spoiled him with riches, and cared for him like a son. Then there was his moonlit rendezvous with Roberta, probably less a lovers' frisk than two conspirators meeting under the cover of night, burrowing into the maze to speak unheard. Mari had always had a hard time believing someone like Roberta could desire him romantically, though in her dwarf's heart she'd been overeager to believe it possible.

The Juan José feast would take place two nights from now. Mari had less than forty-eight hours to save the Crown. She would have to act in haste, knowing a miscalculation could cost the Queen her life, while failure to act quickly could cost the King his.

She lay awake all night, devising a plan, examining every angle, weighing every dreadful possibility. She was reasonably certain none of the King's ministers was involved. They had it too good under this regime—they were the regime. Haro knew about the Queen's association with the Marquis, but not, to Mari's knowledge, the Marquis's rebel ties. The only chance of preventing this scandal from exploding was to eliminate the one person who knew every sordid angle of it, and, as always, that person was Nicolas.

By time she noticed again, the plazas had fallen silent. Even the most ardent revelers had staggered off to bed. With Reina's morning staff already racketing in the stairwell, Mari drifted into a thin, troubled sleep.

She woke not an hour later, knowing and dreading what she must do. Meanwhile, over in Torre Dorada, Nicolas Pertusato was watching the sun rise over Spain from his lavish corner apartment for the last time. Before it set tonight, he would be gone. His damning knowledge posed a mortal danger to the Queen, and his faithless heart had nearly toppled the Crown. Spain's little prince must be exiled, banished to the real world, and even Mari's smoldering dislike for him wasn't going to make this any easier.

❦

Chapter 32

THE COURTESAN

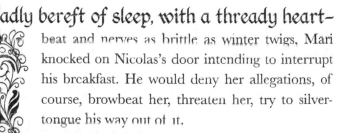adly bereft of sleep, with a thready heart-beat and nerves as brittle as winter twigs, Mari knocked on Nicolas's door intending to interrupt his breakfast. He would deny her allegations, of course, browbeat her, threaten her, try to silver-tongue his way out of it.

She knocked again, harder.

She was being merciful, she would tell him, giving him and Roberta a head start. A full day's travel before the King deployed his huntsmen.

Boots clopped up behind her. "Nicolasito's not here." It was Horacio, the handsome young Dorada page. "He's across the river, training his dogs. He left at sunup."

"Take me to *la Señorita* Roberta," Maribarbola said.

The youth hesitated—the Queen's dwarfess demanding to speak with the King's mistress was a slippery matter—but he thought the better of it as Maribarbola's crazed, sleeplorn stare fell upon his tender groin. "This way," he said.

He took her below the earth to the King's secret tunnel network, those dank bowels where Haro lurked with his glittering mirrors and wolf bones. Mari's dread mounted with every step deeper into the maze, its corridors darkening and narrowing with every sharp turn. At one point she heard muffled voices overhead, a hearty crowd. They were beneath the King's Plaza, already swarmed with Juan José revelers at this early hour. This must be what it felt like to be buried alive, a fate she and the Queen could be facing if Mari failed to contain this matter.

"We're almost there," Horacio said, sensing her unease. The good lad chattered in a misguided attempt to calm her. "That tunnel leads to the del Campo hunting lodge," he said of a horrifically long, flame-licked passageway—Satan's gullet—"and the menagerie is just up ahead. Sometimes you can hear the beasts roar."

Mari had no wish to hear the beasts roar. These warrens were the slender fingers of hell, she decided, tickling the underbelly of the earth, allowing the King to go secretly in sin to his mistress, the Devil's temptress who plotted against him.

At last she heard people up ahead, the jesting and laughter of idle guardsmen.

"*La Profeta Maribarbola para la Señorita Roberta*," Horacio said to the guards. They opened the doors.

They trudged up a winding stair. Through the small, high windows Mari could see Torre de Carlos against the winter sky, red silks rippling from its windows like serpent tongues. They were no longer in the Alcázar proper. At least the King had the decency to keep his courtesan in a dependent building and not under the Queen's own roof.

Horacio knocked on an apartment door. A maidservant answered. "*La Profeta Maribarbola para la Señorita Roberta*," Horacio said.

Mari focused her stare a thousand yards yon and dismissed Horacio with a priest-like hand gesture. She would take the river path back.

324

As Maribarbola, she entered the apartment.

The reception room was nearly as well-appointed as the Queen's. Maidservants busied about. A nursemaid fussed over the bastardly José Roberto in his cradle. Roberta read a newssheet near the hearth, her golden hair snaking down her arms, firelight playing on her wide silver skirt.

"*La Profeta Maribarbola,*" the maidservant announced in a fraught voice. Everyone in the room looked up.

"Leave us," Maribarbola said, staring at the Manzanares River. Roberta had a fine view of it. The servants scrambled from the chamber as if the Queen herself had spoken.

Maribarbola floated forth. Roberta regarded her curiously, kindly even. She was younger than Mari remembered and not as pretty by daylight. "I know your allegiance," Maribarbola said. "My spies have been watching you." Roberta feigned confusion, but her frightened eyes betrayed her. "Tonight I'll be sharing my prophecy with the King, whereupon he will issue your death warrant."

Roberta mustered up some shaky defiance. "Nicolas says you're not really a prophet."

"His Majesty has decreed it so." She sauntered across the carpet. Roberta's panicked eyes followed her. "He has placed his trust in me, and tonight I'm going to leverage it against you."

"The Queen is prepared to sacrifice herself? We know all about her affair with Cristofer. Don't think we'll keep quiet about it."

"The Queen fled on horseback during the night. She's probably lost in Ibérico by now, cloaked in rags. Eventually she'll turn up in Austria, where Emperor Leopold will negotiate her clemency and safe return. She'll be back by the King's side in a few months. The Monarchy will go on, while you lie in your grave a forgotten martyr. Your son will be raised by simple, godly folk. He'll never know his parentage. He'll never speak your name."

Roberta's face blanched at the mention of the child. Mari was getting through.

"But I come in the name of mercy," Maribarbola said. "I invite you and Nicolas to leave court before I speak with the King tonight. Flee today with your lives, or stay here and suffer the wrath of a king who will soon learn that he's been sharing his bed with a traitress and keeping another enemy as close as a son."

Roberta glared at her.

"I trust you'll act wisely," Maribarbola said. She turned to leave.

"He's devastated these lands!" Roberta said in a desperate voice that stopped Mari cold. "Children in Catalonia are eating acorns to survive!"

Mari turned. Roberta's eyes shimmered and pled. The two women stared at one another, allied in helplessness, bonded by truth. He *had* devastated these lands.

"Woe betide you if you stay here past nightfall," Maribarbola said.

ဢဢ

Mari dozed fitfully in her chair that afternoon, mired in dreams of siege and slaughter that mingled with the whooping din of the crowd outside and the urgent chatter of the handmaidens and seamstresses downstairs readying the Queen for tomorrow's pageant feast.

Someone pounded on the door, jolting her awake. Hoping she had dreamt it, she waited. Binnie's voice sliced through the floor at full volume: "That sky looks calamitous."

They pounded again, hard. *Dear God. Don't let it be Nicolas.*

Mari crept to the door. "*¿Quién es?*"

"Padre."

She took an overdue breath and opened the door. Everardo looked like a carnival buffoon with his winter-burned nose and cheeks. He'd been posted atop Torre de Carlos since this morning, at Mari's behest.

"They're gone," he said, handing her her optic tube. It was like ice. "They traveled north and left the city."

တ်

At dusk, Mari neatened herself for the King and went to Torre Dorada.

She went to Nicolas's apartment first. "Is Nicolasito taking calls?" she asked innocently when a page nearly caught her sneaking into the apartment.

"He's staying at the Buen Retiro tonight," the young man said. "He couldn't stand the noise, so he packed up and left. He'll be back tomorrow night for the feast."

Mari waited for his footfalls to fade and slipped into Nicolas's apartment.

She had been in here once before to deliver forty ducats the Queen's treasury owed him in arrears. The delivery had been part of a broader spy mission, back in those halcyon days when the Queen's gravest concern was the King's infidelity. Mari remembered Nicolas's magnificent corner views; only the King had near as good. To the south, Madrid lay winkling in the twilight, promising a third consecutive night of unbridled revelry. To the west lay the Manzanares River, its torchlit pontoons creeping through the fog and the Segovia Bridge glowing with braziers and coach lanterns.

Mari went deep into the reception room, stepping silently on the plush carpet. Nicolas's furniture was tiny and French-looking, all florid gold edges and tortoiseshell veneers. Candles lay strewn on tables; some had rolled onto the floor. He had taken the holders. He had also pulled some canvases from their frames, though dozens remained, too enormous to take—bullfight and battle scenes and many a bare-shouldered young noble lady gazing hintingly at the viewer. Apparently Nicolasito preferred blondes.

With mischief quickening her heart, she went down the hall to his bedchamber. It was richly appointed but mannishly uncluttered. He had a full-sized bed, the better to accommodate full-sized women, Mari presumed with a cringe. On the night table lay a very fine lambskin Bible with gold pages, bookmarked to Proverbs.

She wandered into a dressing area, where scores of rich little suits hung on hooks—crisp, brilliant fabrics in saturated colors, splendidly embellished, expertly stitched. An alcove glittered floor-to-ceiling with slippers. His jewel box lay overturned on a console table, emptied.

Nicolasito was gone.

Mari returned to the reception room. Outside, the crowd whooped and howled, unaware they had lost another prince. And this one would hurt the most. Already Mari felt it: his acute absence, the vast irredeemable emptiness, and she had every reason to be glad to see the back of him. This could kill the King.

She stared out the windows, sickened by what she was about to do. It wasn't enough to banish them from the Alcázar; she had to banish them from the King's heart, and that she could only do by shattering it.

She went downstairs.

The King's apartment bustled lightly with late-day business. Several ministers convened in the reception room, falling silent as Maribarbola floated by, some smirking the way they always did whenever Maribarbola appeared in Torre Dorada, presumably with some nagging request from the Queen.

She went to the King's study. Octavio Barón was just leaving. He hopped aside and held the door for her. Maribarbola glided through as if on a track, trancelike, ignoring him.

The King sat alone behind a deluge of paperwork. The chamber was hot and flashing with firelight. It smelled of the men who'd been coming in and out all day: oiled leather, brazier smoke, mule dung, dirty hair.

Maribarbola stepped into the King's peripheral vision.

He looked up, acknowledging her with a nod.

She gave him her prophecy.

⟨❧❀❧⟩

Chapter 33

THE PROPHECY

ari stood at the Queen's hip, watching the
Salón Grande doors tremor with cheer. She'd
been made to look like a dwarf version of Her
Majesty, bearing a scarlet gown, swanskin shoulder cape, red puppety cheeks, and a colossal wig.
To their left, the King, resplendent in his military
uniform of black brocade and leather armor and
two gold chains crisscrossing his chest, as if his
heart hadn't already been ripped out. *Is that all?*
he had said last night, expressionless, when she
told him Roberta had tried to blow up the Retiro
with him in it.

No, Maribarbola had said. *That is not all.*

The galería chittered with scores of handmaidens teetering on cork heels, some in dresses
as wide as a horse is long, and as many liegemen
to the King, squeaking and jingling in leather and
gold, jeweled rings pinging against sword hilts.

329

Meanwhile, the Queen's guardsmen were all outside tonight, with orders to kill the Marquis of Villamirada on sight.

Gossip fluttered through the galería: already Juan José had made enemies in the King's cabinet and was swaggering around the Alcázar as if he were the legitimate Heir of Spain. Also, amid the commotion of the past few days, thieves had stolen the Indian ruby and great round pearl from the Room of Riches. "Where is Nicolasito?" someone asked.

The clarions sounded. The Salón Grande hushed. The doors swung open. The immense crowd collapsed in reverence. Their Majesties joined hands and went inside.

The air was mellow with perfumed body heat and the beeswax vapors of thousands of lights. Red silks billowed from the great ribbed ceiling vaults, making Mari feel like she was inside an enormous whale. The royal table was festooned with silks and laurels and heaped with roses, pomegranates, and red grapes. A wall of soldiers three men deep guarded the royal stage.

Mari suffered through the seating ceremony, the blessing, and some precursory comedy sketches (a buffoon riddle tourney, a dwarf ballet) meant to jollify the audience and, ever vainly, cheer up the King. She scanned the crowd. Every man was a potential traitor, every woman possibly hiding explosives beneath her giant skirt. Mari was prepared to lay down her life tonight if it should come to that, shield the King with her very body.

The clarions heralded tonight's honored guests, and the Salón exploded in cheer. Crosses of Burgundy floated down on chain pulleys and hovered in the ceiling vaults, fearsome and godlike. The crowd drummed cups on tables and shook the earth with their feet. Women were dabbing their eyes.

As the noise crescendoed to scary heights, the throng of soldiers invaded like a cloud of bats—dark, wolfish, leather-caped men who made the King's ministers seem as menacing as dwarfs and buffoons. They gave Mari gooseflesh and caused a woman in the crowd to faint. Hatless before the King, bedraggled hair lifting in the wind of their stride, and every bodily inch of them imbued with the glories and horrors of battle, they charged forth. Mari knew immediately which man was the General: the haughtiness, the swagger, the peculiar combination of princely bearing and bastardly recklessness. He was unmistakable.

The clarion call for silence was swallowed by the thunder, leaving the General to ascend the stage and kiss his father's hand amid whooping, howling applause, an unprecedented breach of protocol that could not have pleased the King.

He then stalked down the table to where the Queen sat.

The raging cheer evaporated in an instant. There were a couple of bold whistles, a riffle of uneasy laughter. It was well-known that the Queen bore no love for her stepson, who was five years older than she and the single greatest threat to her children's future sovereignty. And threat he was, Mari could clearly see. But the Queen was right—he wasn't as handsome as his picture.

The Queen nodded coolly, proffered her hand.

With great chivalry and passion—and a tinge of mockery, Mari thought—the General crumpled to his knee and pressed his forehead to her hand. The crowd heaved a sentimental moan, followed by laughter then a joyous ovation. The future mortal enemies would pretend, for now.

His pomposity returned the moment he righted himself. He took his seat beside the King, with his men down in front, already tearing into the grapes. There were more prayers and blessings, followed by a mock battle scene with Bosco playing the General and Chico the Idiot playing the Duke of Braganza, the false King of Portugal. To the delight of all, the real Juan José was a good-humored sort who sneered and shook his fist jestingly, raised his cup in self-surrender, and howled with laughter at all the right moments.

They started the feast, an endless cavalcade of colorful, flavorful dishes, and the main course: partridge meat in chocolate sauce for the ladies, and for the men, *huevos de toro*—bull's eggs. Mari picked at a Cross of Burgundy spice bun, having no appetite. Nor did the Queen, apparently, who sipped her búcaro and stared nervously into the crowd. Every slim man with dark shiny hair looked like the Marquis from behind.

After dinner Mudo the Mime stepped forth to raucous applause and stared the crowd into giddy silence. Rumors had been swirling for weeks: this pageant would be the most spectacular any mortal had ever seen. With a teasing hand he tickled the air, timed to a prickling of guitar notes from the musicians' balcony. The crowd howled.

A drumbeat shook the hall, frighteningly baritone; it rumbled Mari's chest. Mudo mimed surprise, fear. There was another beat, and another—an angry giant, marching uphill to crush the Alcázar. Mudo mimed panic, ran in circles, skittered up on stage and hid behind the Queen. The crowd whooped. Juan José chuckled extremely loudly.

The beast paused outside the Salón Grande, teasing the crowd with a spell of silence. Mari took a nervous sip of wine. Men with torches swarmed the entrance. The doors opened. There were gasps and screams. The horns entered first.

The head filled the doorway, a plaster bull with lantern-lit eyes, coming to avenge its testicles. It glided into the hall, legs scissoring to the drumbeat. The crowd whistled, jeered, pelted pomegranates at it. With smoke piping from its nostrils, it rolled forth to the King. His Majesty sat corpselike as usual, but here it looked like he was staring down the bull, which the crowd found hilarious. Dread crept into Mari's chest. There were men inside moving the parts, possible assassins with possible explosives, possibly one of the cleverest, bloodiest coups in history.

A cacophony of screams jolted Mari's heart. The music crested triumphant, and from the arcade sailed a splendid chariot, pulled by Goliat and carrying Spain's six most famous bullfighters, smiling and waving in their magnificent gold-broidered suits. The Salón exploded in a shower of applause and roses. Even the King clapped.

The bullfighters hopped off the chariot and danced for the King, a dazzling athletic caper practiced to the peak of perfection and delivered with the intensity and passion of which only Spanish men are capable. There were flips.

To crescendoing music and roaring applause, César Barrio ("*El Carnicero*," they called him—the butcher) brandished a diamond-sprinkled sword. With a theatrical blow he struck the bull's neck, and the head crashed to the floor. The crowd frothed with glee.

Mari watched the neck hole uneasily. With jolly flair, César Barrio knelt before it and held out his hand.

Bosco popped his head out of the bull, playacting confusion. The Salón rumbled with laughter. To a jaunty little pipe tune and using César Barrio's knee as a step, he climbed out, followed by Churro, Manuelito, Inocencia, Trini, Jacobo—a dozen Carlos dwarfs, all dressed as mini matadors, even the women. With great passion and a physical intensity never before seen in dwarfs, they danced for the King—a patriotic jig that included Cross of Burgundy and crucifix formations and much rheumatic suffering, judging by their faces.

They toddled off in a shower of applause and roses, wheeling the bull with them.

A heart-shaking gunshot drew a gasp from the crowd, and hundreds of soldiers filed in to deafening applause: musketeers shooting gold glitter, banner men with their blazonry, and armored infantry in metal skins that jingled sinisterly as they marched, their horses also fully plated—huge, scary, mechanical beasts. Every gunshot joggled Mari's nerves and shocked her heart. Beside her, the Queen brushed gold flakes from her lips, annoyed. Her wig sparkled densely. She was bearing the brunt of the glitter, perhaps by design.

Three colossal white objects bumbled over the Salón threshold and floated up over the crowd: giant plaster heads with hideous, marionette-like faces—Frenchmen, evidently, with their periwigs, flaming rouged cheeks, and black beauty dots. People jeered and pelted pomegranates, cups, a cake of flan that spattered disgustingly.

To the crowd's rabid delight, Juan José's men hacked one up with their swords. The thing bled straw.

The heads floated by the royal table, smiling dumbly. One of the beauty dots was shaped like a fly. The Salón doors swung open for the next invasion. Braced for another nerve-raking military spectacle, Mari was relieved when Bosco and Chico, reprising their roles as Juan José and the Duke of Braganza, rolled in on a small boat to riotous laughter, paddling the air, looking lost.

The crowd gasped with delight as a massive whale nosed through the Salón doors with but a fingerbreadth's clearance on every side. The fifty-foot beast rolled up the aisle, spraying the crowd through its blowhole. Mari tensed as it neared the royal table. There could be forty rebels inside, easily …

It shot a spray at the Queen and disappeared into the arcade.

Another hulking object nosed through the Salón doorway: the hull of a miniature galleon ship. Its cannon shot a spectacular blast of gold glitter into the room, blanketing half the court. Dwarfs Manuelito and Jacobo raised the masts; Churro clambered up one of them like a fat little animal scrabbling awkwardly up a tree. Inocencia and Trini, dressed as pearl-blistered mermaids, flanked a massive chest overheaped by a twinkling mound of treasure.

The galleon rocked up the aisle, sending the dwarfs teetering across the deck. Dolphin-headed dancers frolicked beside it, leaping and capering to the music. Jacobo straddled the cannon while Manuelito blasted the audience with glitter. Inocencia and Trini flung tin chains and glass jewels into the crowd. Half-naked male dancers ran in like hellfire, gymnasticking down the aisle with violent intensity: New World savages. Mari allowed herself an untroubled breath and a drink of wine. This had to be the finale.

Having dispensed with the treasure, Inocencia and Trini peered into the chest, looking baffled. The other dwarfs convened around the chest. The crowd drummed the tables as the suspense mounted. Jacobo and Manuelito reached inside.

There was a massive groan of disappointment as Jacobo and Manuelito lowered the object onto the deck, followed by taunts and jeers. A pomegranate crashed against the oak hull with deadly force.

It was another chest.

The crowd fumed with mock outrage as the dwarfs huddled over the second chest. Mari wondered if they would keep pulling out smaller and smaller chests. Then it came to her: the Indian ruby and great round pearl were inside, not stolen after all. After all this drama and teasing, whatever was in there had better be dazzl—

"Oh God," Mari said, placing her hand over her dying heart. Oh God.

Jacobo broke the lock with his sword.

The lid burst open with explosive force, as if by demonic volition. The dwarfs flew back. Mari's stomach dropped and nearly slipped out with her bowels. The audience raged so mightily she felt it in her teeth. A gleaming sword rose from the chest and waved teasingly at the crowd. He was still here. Roberta had left him here to die.

Nicolasito sat up in the chest, smirking. The Salón shook like the end of the world. Mari's consciousness cleaved atwo: half of her watched in horror as Nicolas climbed out of the trunk dressed as a mini conquistador in golden spurs and leather armor, while her other half stood in the King's study, last night, watching Maribarbola murder a man with her tongue. *No, that is not all,* Maribarbola said to the King. *There is also the matter of Nicolasito.*

Nicolas stalked the deck, sneering playfully at the adoring crowd, the inevitable Feroce by his side. Roses rained upon the ship. *Begone his evil craft and company,* Maribarbola said. *He was bent upon your ruin.* She reminded the King of that night at the Buen Retiro, when she told him an enemy was near. *He was everywhile beside you.*

The ship rocked wildly, but the surefooted Nicolasito pranced with ease. He tucked a rose behind his ear, and the ladies of the court gushed audibly. *Un traidor. Judas. A false servant. A false Christian.*

Only now did Mari consider—as he swaggered before his would-be executioners, smiling, taunting them with his sword—that she'd been gravely wrong about his motives; that his association with the traitress Roberta might have been innocent; that, like the Queen, he'd been guiled by a skilled romancer. Now Roberta had left him to bear the King's wrath alone, plundered his apartment, and left him for dead. Oh God, the couplets!

> *Bewitched by birth a lad eternal,*
> *An instrument of powers infernal.*

They had rolled off Maribarbola's tongue like devil-speak, easy as sin.

> *Author of evil, Prince of Lies,*
> *Purveyor of ills of the gravest wise.*

Through a tiny filthy window in her rotting dying soul, Mari glanced down the table. The King and Queen looked like twin corpses. Juan José had already vacated his chair. Clearly his father had told him everything. The ship neared the stage with Nicolas standing triumphantly on the beakhead, oblivious to the guards gathering below him, unsheathing their swords.

> *He will never grow old. He may never die.*
> *He who defies nature—*

Maribarbola had said—

> *Defies God.*

But even that hadn't been the worst of it. This was:

> *He lured Roberta into the maze, and therein palled his pleasures*
> *with her.*

Good God, the King's face when she had said that!

The ship stopped. Nicolas disappeared below deck. Under the table, the Queen's nails dug into Mari's palm. He would be arrested, interrogated, tortured. He would tell the Inquisition everything he knew, which was everything about everyone. He would burn alive on the Plaza Mayor and take many others with him, the Queen chief among them, probably Mari as well. There was no telling how far-reaching or deadly the King's wrath would be.

A door dropped open in the hull, making a ramp, with Juan José and his men at the bottom, battle-faced. The crowd rumbled the earth with their feet, summoning Nicolasito to reappear.

Nicolas shot out of the hull, riding Feroce like a horse to rapturous applause. People threw roses, laurels, handkerchiefs, a woman's stocking. The mastiff ran headlong into the soldiers. Juan José plucked Nicolas off the dog's back with one hand, by the cape collar. Thinking it was part of the act, the crowd erupted in laughter. Mari watched, sickened, as many more men than was necessary seized the child-sized body and twisted his little arms behind his back. Worst of all was Nicolas's laughter because he thought it was a jest, and the terror in his eyes the moment he realized it wasn't.

❦

Chapter 34

THE INQUISITION

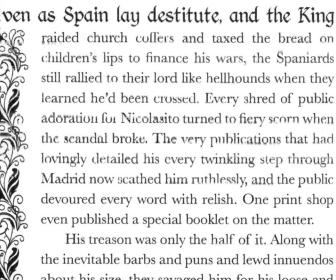

ven as Spain lay destitute, and the King raided church coffers and taxed the bread on children's lips to finance his wars, the Spaniards still rallied to their lord like hellhounds when they learned he'd been crossed. Every shred of public adoration for Nicolasito turned to fiery scorn when the scandal broke. The very publications that had lovingly detailed his every twinkling step through Madrid now scathed him ruthlessly, and the public devoured every word with relish. One print shop even published a special booklet on the matter.

His treason was only the half of it. Along with the inevitable barbs and puns and lewd innuendos about his size, they savaged him for his loose and lavish living. One pamphleteer gained access to palace archives and published a shocking exposé detailing the thousands of ducats Nicolas had collected during his tenure as the King's favorite, in the form of clothing, jewels, artwork, furniture, coaches, horses, salaries, and lifelong pensions for a man frozen in childhood. The author claimed Pertusato's dogs ate better than the average Spaniard, and the amount of wheat consumed starching Nicolasito's ruffs could feed a dozen orphans for a year. No other courtier enjoyed so large an income, he wrote, or lived in such princely magnificence and yet paid not a Devil's maravedi in taxes—and he wasn't even a Spaniard! There were erroneous reports of solid gold chamber pots, pet lions in jeweled muzzles, and a ring bearing a bloodied splinter of Christ's cross. Others alleged Nicolasito's suits were stitched by child slaves living in wretched conditions, and his many so-called charity engagements had in fact been paid appearances. There was an explosive interview with a mountain witch, who set forth in chilling detail the demonic forces required to supplant God's natural laws and keep a man forever in his youth. Women came forward with tales of seduction and abandonment, even allegations of a Moorish lovechild, while countless others offered accounts of their own vulgar dealings with him: merchants he had swindled, peasants he had snubbed, children he had frightened. A complete list of his sins, one writer concluded, would darken a hundred pages.

Still, only one opinion mattered, and to that the King's justice was swift and severe. For his treachery, heresy, and deviltry, Nicolas would pay with his life. His execution would take place the following Friday on the Plaza Mayor.

He hadn't been seen or heard of since his arrest, nor had Inquisitors raided Torre de la Reina, which meant that either Nicolas had been spared the torture chamber, or he happened to be the most ironhearted man on earth. The Queen begged for lenience on his behalf—he was still her property and pensioned through her treasury—though her plea was less likely born from the goodness of her heart than her rational fear of joining him at the stake. There was also the question of whether or not even the most depraved Inquisitors could exact their methods on a child-sized body.

As Nicolas awaited his death, Mari, by now convinced she had fingered an innocent man, prayed for the hastening of her own. She hadn't eaten since the feast and had slept in only twenty-minute snatches. She hadn't left her apartment, though she couldn't have anyway; there was a guard on her floor, ostensibly for her protection, but in truth the Queen was probably scared to death—rightly so— that Mari's conscience would get the better of her and cause her to confess everything to the King. So Mari sat in her frigid, fireless chamber, praying every frosty breath would be her last. She refused all calls, even water and waste service. She couldn't bear to look at anyone, least of all herself. Days ago, when she had still been mobile, she had covered every reflective surface in her apartment.

The longer she sat sequestered with her thoughts, the sicker she became with herself. There had never been any solid evidence of Nicolas's involvement with or even knowledge of a rebel coup, only Mari's half-baked suspicions and feeble-minded assumptions. That judicious, laboratory-trained thinker she'd once been was long dead. In her place was this feckless, foolish, *dangerous* half-wit—and a coward to boot. She fixated on her idiocy because the only other explanation for what she'd done was so unconscionable, so evil, she couldn't allow herself to acknowledge it. But still it hovered, just beyond the edge of her consciousness, threatening to obliterate her very last shred of humanity: she had wanted to banish him. Needed to. Needed to send him out into the cruel, abusive world. It was the only way to get him back in the cage. And she needed him back in the cage, because looking at him through the bars was just too infuriating, too painful. She had wanted to make him suffer, the way a proper dwarf should suffer.

She managed complete isolation until the Thursday that would be Nicolas's last full day on earth, when she developed the overwhelming fatal urge to see him. She needed to face him, look into the eyes of the man she had murdered, torture herself properly, explain her vicious, depraved actions, beg forgiveness, and perhaps find the courage to do the unthinkable: tell the King the truth and condemn the Queen to the flames instead.

Knowing the guard wouldn't dare intercept a letter to His Majesty, she petitioned the King for permission to visit Nicolas, claiming there were "unearthly matters" that still needed to be discussed. She summoned a page, wrangled with the guard over the delivery, and within an hour received His Majesty's reply: *Permiso concedido. Yo, el Rey.*

ʚ૨ʚ

A squire drove her to the Grand Inquisitor's office. Bearing written permission from the King, Mari gained swift entry and was escorted, hospitably even, to the underground dungeons.

She followed the guard through a dank, ill-lit corridor lined with cavernous cells. As her eyes adjusted she made out forms in the dark: men hugging their knees like children, rocking and shivering; others slumped in lifeless mounds on the floor. She heard whimpering, or maybe it was giggling, and a loud, steady drip coming from somewhere—wastewater from the street, judging by the horrid stench.

The guard stopped at a cell and lowered his torch. Behind the iron grid sat Nicolasito on a wall bench, his knees pulled up to his chin, wrapped in a blanket. His gaze landed on Mari, though he registered no response.

"Leave us," Mari said to the guard.

She waited while his footsteps receded down the corridor. Nicolas stared at her, weirdly expressionless, his baby face besmirched by a patchy beard that would have been hilarious under any other circumstances. "I didn't think you were capable of such lies," he said in a flat, despondent voice she had never heard before.

"I believed what I was telling him at the time."

"An instrument of the Devil?"

"Please, I'm sorry!" She lowered her face and wept, hard. Nicolas watched icily. Minutes passed before she could speak again. "Who were those people you wanted me to feast with last fall?"

"Italian bankers."

"*Italian bankers?*"

"They broker my investments," he said wearily. "I've been putting money into New World trade. Furs, sugar, tobacco. Philip would be devastated if he knew I was investing in French and English enterprises. And then he'd tax me to pauperdom, because that's what Philip does."

"And your relationship with Roberta?"

This was met with humiliated silence. Mari didn't press. She knew. Roberta had used him for his proximity to the King, beguiled and seduced him, teased and flattered him, dangled the irresistible possibility low before him: that someone like him could be loved by someone like her, a beautiful woman who lay with kings.

"It seems you overestimated my cunning," he said, "and I clearly underestimated yours. But I always knew you weren't a prophet. I knew it your first night here, when you delivered a prophecy that didn't even remotely resemble a prophecy." Mari didn't defend herself. She deserved this. "Your storm prophecy was more impressive, but Churro can feel the rain in his knees, too, and he doesn't walk around claiming to be a prophet. You got lucky with Prospero and Ferdinand; that was a fifty-fifty chance—and I prayed hard for your success, by the way. I still don't know how you saw that red moon coming."

"Why didn't you tell him? He made policy decisions based on my word."

Nicolas thought for a moment. "Because there was a light in his eyes I'd never seen before. Because I saw him laugh twice in one month, whereas that usually only happens about once a year. Besides, he was so desperate for a miracle, he wouldn't have believed me anyway."

This only shamed her more, knowing she had played the King's heart like a lute. "The Queen has intervened to spare you an interrogation," she said.

"Good of her," Nicolas said, spiced with sarcasm. "Although you needn't pander to me now. The last thing I should do is endanger the one person who has any chance in hell of getting me out of this."

Mari nodded eagerly. "Of course. I'll speak to her right away. Maybe she can convince him to—"

"I wasn't talking about her. She has no influence over him. That's always been the root of all our problems, if you think about it. I was talking about you. If anyone can change his mind, it's you. You're the only one from Reina he'll listen to. He respects you."

The only way to reverse the sentence was to tell the King the truth and sacrifice many lives in exchange for Nicolas's—not just the Queen's and her own, but anyone who had known about the Queen's affair and looked the other way: Everardo, Binnie, Josefina, the guards who had regularly seen the Marquis ride off at four in the morning, Reina staff who had relished every morsel of gossip while keeping tightlipped as priests. Any one of them could find themselves ensnared in scandal and engulfed in flames.

"I know you'll do what's right," Nicolas said. "You're a good woman who got in over your head is all, overplayed your hand. What power does to everyone, it's done to you as well. I've seen how this court changes people, how greedy and ambitious they become, how cunning and callous they learn to be. I've seen humble servants backstab their way into senior chamberlain positions. I've seen fourteen-year-olds become ruthless politicians by age sixteen. You're interesting though. I knew right away you were a fraud, but I watched you closely, even tested you myself a few times. I kept waiting for that look to appear in your eyes, that calculating stare we all have, but you never quite got it. Even as the lies rolled from your tongue, you still maintained a shred of decency. Which is why you've come here today. You can't bear to see me punished unjustly. In condemning me, you've condemned yourself. If I die tomorrow, you'll never know peace again as long as you live. Not a moment will pass that you won't feel the flames licking your own body, hear me screaming in agony, smell my burning flesh, taste it in your throat. In the end, this will have killed us both."

Mari closed her eyes and held up a shaking hand, imploring him to stop. He stopped. She gripped the cold iron bars and willed herself not to be sick.

"For the love of God, get me out of here," said the man in the well, his voice cracking with fear. Mari forced herself to look at him. His eyes shimmered with terror, a frightened, bearded child. "Please, Mari."

She wanted so badly to promise him, but she didn't know if she was brave enough. She could only promise to try.

"I'll speak to him as soon as I get back."

Chapter 35

THE SEER

is Majesty sat at his desk with several men standing around him—Haro, for one, and some military officers Mari didn't recognize. The King was the first to notice her. One by one the others turned. Mari's grave face silenced the room.

The King lifted his hand, and the men filed out in an air of awkward curiosity.

Mari stepped forth. She had that remote feeling, as if viewing the King through an optic tube. "I was wrong about Nicolas," she heard herself say from far away. "He's not an enemy of the Crown or an enemy of the Cross. He's not Satan's little marionette." Maribarbola had said that, too. "He's just a mortal man, with the same desires and weaknesses all men have, imprisoned in a child's body."

The King stared at her blankly, that long, despairing face. Mari continued: "He didn't seduce Roberta. It was she who tempted him to

347

strengthen her position at the court and thicken her ties to you. Nicolas's only crime is having been a fool.

"You've seen what just a taste of wine can do to his tiny body," she said, referring to the now-famous 1658 New Year's Jubilee incident involving Nicolas and a mere thimbleful of Bordeaux. That had been one of only three recorded times the King had ever laughed in public. "Imagine what just a taste of womanly affection can do to his tiny heart." In matters of the heart dwarfs were easily persuaded. Mari remembered how she herself had been decimated by Udo's last look. That look she had so eagerly misread as *I could love you* had really just meant *Goodbye*, and *I'm sorry*. And yet she had lain awake until dawn that night, delirious with possibilities. Drunk with just a taste.

"He is a truehearted servant," Mari said, "a loyal son of Spain." This was a stretch. "But to you he has been far more." The King's eye twitched. "You are well-acquainted with the sorrow of being a king without an heir," she said carefully, "but you know less the sorrow of being a man without a son, so long as Nicolasito has been in your life." Their relationship hadn't been pageantry. It was real. Mari had been so blinded by her jealousy of Nicolas, she couldn't see anything about him as genuine. But in all this pain she had caused by tearing them apart, she finally saw what he was to the King: a surrogate son, one who would stay with him forever, never grow up, never leave, never die, the way the others always did. Mari finally got it. She finally understood the strange, tiny miracle that was Nicolasito. "There is no other man like him on earth," she said, "and yet God willed him here, because no man on earth needed a son more than you did."

She thought she saw a flicker of sadness in the King's eyes. Encouraged, she continued: "Now presents the opportunity for you to exercise your boundless mercy and forgiveness and hold yourself up to all as a true and proper Catholic." He had to have liked that. Mari raised an admonishing finger. "In death, Nicolas will plague you in ways unforeseen. The public shares your anger now, but time will soften their hearts. Fondness always blooms for the dead, even the wickedest men. People will resent you for having had Nicolasito slaughtered when you could have just as easily forgiven him. They'll whisper on the street that you are a false Christian."

The King's eyes blazed at the very thought. She was getting through.

"His worth to you alive is incalculable. He will be deeply in your debt and eager to prove his loyalty. If you cannot accept him back into your grace, gift him to an enemy. A more charming, cunning man than Nicolasito there never was. He will slip easily into enemy ranks, sneak into their offices, eavesdrop on their conversations, and relay every word back to Haro. So stealth a weapon can hardly be imagined. Nicolas alone is worth an army of men. If you use him cleverly, victory will be inevitable."

"Is this your prophecy?" said the King, startling her. She had tickled the hungry lion with her talk of war and victory.

"Not a prophecy. A strategy."

Thinking it best to leave him with visions of conquest percolating in his mind, Mari bent her neck and made to leave. Halfway to the door she stopped and turned. "Your heart will not bear the weight of his loss," she said, slipping back into her Maribarbola voice, despite having sworn off Maribarbola forever. "In destroying him, you will destroy yourself also." She made to leave again but paused at the door. "That was a prophecy."

ᛤ

Chapter 36

THE CONFLAGRATION

awn began her quiet assault on Madrid,
her creeping pewter light, then the full ambush of
morning—the winter fog, the church bells, plum-
ing bakehouse chimneys, toy-sized wagons and
toy-sized people already clotting around the Plaza
Mayor, where hours from now they would behold
the King's fiery justice.

No pardon had come during the night.

Mari had always known this day would come,
this day of zero options, the day she'd be forced to
do the unthinkable. There was no more stalling,
no more hedging, no time left to buy with her cowardly schemes. Nicolas had hours to live. The only
thing left to do now was tell the King the truth:
she was not a prophet, or a purveyor of fortune, or
even a wise old sage. She was nothing but a fraud.

Still she couldn't bring herself to move and
spent her last moments of freedom paralyzed with

fear, not for herself—she deserved every torment that lay in wait—but for those she'd be taking down with her. She could hear them downstairs, bustling through the Queen's morning routine, unaware Torre de la Reina was about to be cleansed, the Inquisition's torture chamber the furthermost thing from their minds.

She stared out the window for a long time, willing herself to move. When the vendor fires blazed up around the Plaza Mayor, to fry the chestnuts and fritters for Nicolas's execution, Mari rose from her chair.

That guard was still posted outside her apartment. "Where are you going?" he asked.

"Torre Dorada."

"You'll need permission from the Queen."

"I have urgent business with His Majesty. You'd be unwise to meddle in the King's affairs."

"The King's not here. He's praying in San Lorenzo. He left this morning before sunup."

Mari stared through his abdomen. "He left?"

The guard nodded. This was the day of zero options.

Mari kept staring through him, swaying slightly. "Are you unwell?" he said, muted by the roar of flames in her ears.

Blank and stupefied, she turned to the stairs. The only way out of hell was up.

"It's cold up there," the guard called after her.

Mari climbed to the fifth floor. Already the flames were licking her ankles. Already she could taste his smoke.

She stepped into the frigid round chamber. A legion of crows flapped violently in the ceiling vault, squawking horridly. Mari floated to the unglazed windows, already a ghost, already dead. She had known the very first time she looked up and saw the Alcázar looming against the twilit sky that this would end badly, though she never dreamed it would end like this.

She looked down at Plaza Mayor, now teeming with black-hatted people, swarming vermin. Her hollow gaze swept the palace grounds—the dead gardens, the murky cherub pool, the maze, and the dependent buildings, where Lalo lay near death, besieged by infection from his wounds, another of Maribarbola's victims.

Spain sprawled before her, colorless and barren, a godforsaken land. She was leaving it far worse than she had found it. With Maribarbola in the Alcázar, Spain had only plunged deeper into despair. She was not only a liar and fraud but a purveyor of misfortune, false hopes, ruin, and dead babies. The promise of the red moon would be laughable now had it not been so cruel. And Maribarbola's destruction would continue long after her death and end at nothing short of the complete demise of Spain. See, it was she who had advised the King to sign the treaty with France; she who caused him to travel, desperate and penniless, to the Franco-Spanish border and deliver his daughter to the French. Mari had later learned (from an infuriated Queen) that Teresa's forfeiture of all rights of succession to the Spanish throne were contingent upon a half-million-escudo dowry, of which Philip had not yet paid a single peso, which meant the only thing standing between French ambitions and the Spanish Crown was the wretched Baby Charles, who had yet to lift his head, and if he lived would be an idiot, doctors were saying. Also as part of the treaty, the French had agreed to withdraw support from Portugal, hence Juan José's imminent incursion, which would only bring more carnage, more killing, more dead fifteen-year olds, more fresh wet blood for Maribarbola's hands.

All she had wanted was a place to live. A place to belong and be loved. A place to die. Mari hoisted herself onto the stone sill.

She looked down at the cobbled street where she would soon lie dead. Two men stood in her way, palace officials, chatting with the guards. Mari perched in the window, coatless and shivering, waiting for them to move. She wasn't about to take them with her. The point was to kill Maribarbola before she could kill another. Kill the witch within.

Finally they left. Mari stood up on the window ledge, bracing herself against the sides. She closed her eyes and prayed for her soul.

A mounted knight came galloping across the courtyard. Mari could hear his breast chains jingling all the way up here. "Don't," she said quietly as he trotted toward the tower.

He parked his horse by the entrance, right in her spot. He dismounted and went inside.

Mari rolled her eyes. She needed to do this before she lost her nerve. She looked down and wondered if she had it in her to kill a horse. No. She did not.

She climbed down, went to the east windows, and poked her head out. Reina East was even busier, with knights and equerries scattered around the entrance. She considered relocating, doing this elsewhere. Traffic around Torre Dorada would only be worse, and she could think of nothing less dignified than jumping from Torre de Carlos, from the very spot where the buffoons held their pissing contests.

No. She was the Queen's dwarf. She must die in the shadow of Reina.

She peered over the sill again. Guards were talking and laughing in small frosty clouds of breath. One of them glanced up at her but registered not an iota of concern. She should go downstairs and get her coat. She could be waiting up here a long time. It was always extra busy around here when the Queen was—

"Regent," Mari said, staring out at the easterly plains.

She whirled around. "*She's regent!*" she shrieked, clearing every crow from the tower. She lunged for the door and burst into the stairwell. "She's regent! She's regent!" She filled the tower with her screams as she raced downstairs to find the Queen.

ꙮ

Mari clung to her squire's back as he steered his horse through the jam of coaches and mule wagons on Calle Mayor. Thousands had come to bear witness: gapers and gossips, idlers and swaggerers, rich and poor, young and old. Today their bloodlust would go unquenched. Wedged in Mari's coat breast was a scroll bearing the order to halt Nicolas's execution, signed by Her Majesty, who right now wielded supreme authority over the land.

Nicolas had always drawn the biggest crowds of any courtier, including the King, but today he topped even himself. People packed shoulder to shoulder onto the Plaza Mayor, while thousands more thronged the streets, hoping to glimpse Nicolasito's fiery departure from this earth. Vendor grills sizzled, spewing savory smoke into the cold air. Corner musicians piped out inappropriately festive melodies. Balconies overlooking the plaza were crowded with doll-like people: nobles and courtiers in wide wigs and lavish coats, the very plum and chocolate hues Nicolas had ushered into fashion earlier this fall.

A plume of black smoke snaked up over the plaza—not a cooking fire. "*Hurry!*" Mari screamed. They had come to a full stop. The street was impassable. She drove her heels into the horse's flanks. The squire shouted at people to move, making wide shooing gestures with his arms. The throng didn't budge.

Mari struggled to turn herself sideways, kneeing her horseman in the back. "What are you—" he said as she slid off the horse's rump and hurtled to the ground.

She landed prone on the street, hard.

Dazed from the impact but too cold to feel her injuries, Mari staggered to her feet and plunged into the crowd. "Move!" she screamed, punching skirts and ramming legs. "Let me through!"

The black plume towered and billowed as executioners stoked the blaze. The Inquisition liked to drive up the flames and suspend sinners high above the crowd, to heighten the spectacle and maximize the horror. "Stop them! I have an order from the Queen!" The pain was starting now. She had bent her ankle when she landed and possibly broken a finger.

Something drew a delighted gasp from the crowd and a shower of sparks from the fire. Mari plowed forth evermore ruthlessly, leaving a swath of furious, foulmouthed peasants in her wake. Children she shoved aside like a heartless bully, spilling their chestnuts and sweet drinks. Most were crying before they hit the ground.

The crowd whooped again. Mari looked up to see a tiny gilded chair arc through the air and crash onto the inferno in a cascade of sparks. A matching table followed. They were fueling the fire with Nicolas's own riches, no doubt to pacify the penniless, sunken-cheeked masses, who'd been made bitterly aware of his appalling extravagance during his recent savaging in the press. "Let me through!" Mari yelled, choking on smoke. The heat was becoming unbearable. Ashes alighted like snowflakes on people's coats.

A skirmish opened a chasm in the crowd and a view of the inferno. Furniture and chattels burned red-hot among the fagots and billets: elegant little chairs and benches, chests of drawers, enormous picture frames, a harp. Behind a quivering veil of heat, a mound of jeweled slippers burned freshly, some still glittering, others blackening and curling in the flames. Two peasant women fought viciously over one that had tumbled from the heap intact.

The executioners stood yards away in their pointy black hoods, unloading Nicolas's belongings from a wagon and flinging them onto the blaze. Mari shoved toward them, pulling the scroll from her coat and raising it like a sword. "Stop!" she yelled. "Queen's orders!"

A rack of brilliant little suits crashed onto the pile and burned on contact. Smoldering patches of delicate fabric caught an updraft and leapt out over the crowd. People shrieked and shoved as a swatch of Flemish lace drifted, red-hot and glimmering, down toward their heads. Mari got caught in the crush of panic. She screamed in terror as her feet lost contact with the ground. The crowd crunched ever tighter, with Mari corked in down below, eye-level with groins and belt daggers and crushing hipbones.

The mass of bodies careened sideways, making a ghastly whooping sound. Mari couldn't see her hand, but she felt the moment the scroll got knocked out of it.

The crowd reeled back the other way, overcorrecting, spitting Mari out onto the ground. A man pulled her up by her armpits, probably mistaking her for a stout child from behind. Dazed from near suffocation, Mari turned toward the fire to see Inquisitors sliding a ladder from a wagon bed … five rungs … six rungs … tiny slippered feet, red gems winking and laughing like Satan … little stockinged legs bound at the ankles. They had dressed Nicolasito up for this.

"*No!*" she cried, a guttural scream that shook her heart and brain. She charged through the smoke-thinned crowd, toppling a few more people. "He's innocent!"

The executioners raised the ladder. The crowd gasped with delighted horror.

Mari lunged at the nearest black-hooded figure. "Stop!" she screamed, attacking his thigh, pawing and clawing his hard flesh. "Burn me in his place! I'm the wicked one! I'm the wicked one! I'm Maribarbola! *I'm a false prophet a criminal a liar and a fraud!*"

The pulley chains tinkled on their spool, and the crowd whooped and howled as the ladder swung up over the flames, bearing Nicolas's childly silhouette, shrouded in smoke, his hands bound in prayer.

Mari crumpled to her knees. "No … no … no … no," she moaned, staggering on all fours like a drunken hound. She dry heaved. Behind her, the crowd frothed with cheer. There was laughter and whistling. Mari let the hot black smoke fill her lungs and begged God to take her.

Through the haze of suffocation, a faraway chant: "*¡Misericordia!*" Mercy.

"*¡Nicolasito vive!*"

A blunt slap on her cheek opened her eyes. The Inquisitor crouched before her, the one she'd attacked. "*¿Qué?*" he said.

Her confession had slipped through his legs, unheard.

Mari snatched the breast of his habit. A tear slid from her eye and dried instantly in the blistering air. "Nicolas is innocent," she said, fighting to stay conscious. "I had a pardon from the Queen."

"He's at the Alcázar," the man said, prying her crazed, desperate hands from his tunic. "The King ordered him back during the night."

Mari couldn't comprehend his words. The smoke and heat were simmering her brain.

Gruffly, he pulled her up and swiveled her toward the fire.

The ladder swung over the flames, high above the jubilant crowd. The dapper little figure burned, feet and legs blackened, flames licking off the cherry-plum silk suit as if it were jam, spun-sugar ruff caramelizing beneath a featureless straw face.

Nicolasito burned in effigy.

Chapter 37

THE GIFT

hurro kept apologizing for the mess, but in truth Torre de Carlos was about as clean as Reina. All those times the Queen had half-jestingly threatened to banish Mari here, where the walls were spattered with piss and custard, according to the Queen, and the buffoons shrieked and babbled in the corridors at all hours. But it was actually pleasant here. This tower was a century older than Reina, narrower and darker, cozy, and quiet because there was no Binnie. It smelled nice too, like beeswax and cloves. Some corridors were garnished with Yule boughs and wax fruits and paper flowers; one had a bowling lane painted on the floor; in another the dwarfs had lined up by height and traced their silhouettes on the wall with chalk.

It looked like children lived here, and in a way they did—God's children, and by proxy the King's. Every unfit soul in the land found his or her way to the court: every lumbering giant and crippled dwarf, every cretin and loon, men and women with the wits and ways of children. Be they feebleminded, mad, grotesque, or just plain novel—like Sombra, the tall skinny African, always consigned to play a dwarf's shadow in Torre de Carlos comedies—all were invited to live under the grace and protection of His Most Benevolent Majesty in exchange for entertaining and coloring the court.

Although Mari had been successful in sparing Nicolas's life, her efforts had done little to raise the King's opinion of him, and he was being held under house arrest in an apartment here in Carlos—a grave (and clearly deliberate) insult to a man who never counted himself among the ordinary dwarfs and seemed scarcely aware he was even a dwarf.

"He's sending me to Teresa as a Christmas gift," Nicolas said, prying open a spice bun with his thumbs. Mari had interrupted his breakfast. "I guess she's lonely and miserable in France." His apartment was small and boxy and minimally appointed with children's furniture. They sat at a sturdy little wooden table with a play-worn top. The Inquisition had burned every last stick of his furniture, Nicolas had told her. "Of course the real reason he's sending me up there is to keep an eye on Louis. How he expects me to get close enough to the King of France to spy on him, and then relay that information back to Haro without being beheaded, I've no idea."

Mari wasn't worried. Nicolasito's talents were nonpareil. She watched him arrange his ham and fruit slivers like a busy lad at play, a wholesome shepherd boy in that wool smock they put him in. He had a childlike resilience, too, she noticed: just two days ago he'd been in an Inquisition dungeon awaiting death by fire, and now here he sat, perfectly untroubled. It was as if his emotions only ran as deep as his chest, which itself was slimmer than most books.

"I need you to look after Philip," he said. "When I'm gone he'll have no one."

"He still has Haro."

"Haro's looking out for Haro."

"The King has his staunchest ally in the Queen. If only he'd open his eyes and see it."

Nicolas's response was thick, provocative silence.

"What?" Mari said.

He sat back in his chair. "I never told you this before, but one night—this was shortly after Charles was born—I was in Roberta's apartment, entertaining her at Philip's behest, when out of nowhere in walks the Queen, completely unescorted and unannounced." Mari stared at him. She had no idea where this was going. "As Roberta and her servants were diving to the floor to prostrate themselves, I was able to step behind a sofa without being seen.

"Mariana went straight to José Roberto's crib. She picked up the child from a sound sleep, lifted his dress to check his sex, and then coddled him for a moment before putting him back in his cradle. As she was leaving she made some shrewish remark about how pleased she was to see the King finally treating Roberta better, and that was it. She walked out."

"That's it?" Mari was at once disappointed and relieved. "So?"

He relished her puzzlement. "Did you ever actually see Roberta's baby?"

Mari had to think. "No. I don't think I ever did."

"You'd remember. See, José Roberto is a handsome lad. In fact, he's a devastatingly handsome lad. Lush black hair, dark Spanish eyes"—his eyes locked Mari's—"cute little nub of a chin." Mari stared at him, helpless as usual against his onslaught of unwanted information. "Everyone but Philip could see he wasn't Philip's. Surely Mariana saw it too. What's interesting though, I expected her to go shouting it from every tower and have Roberta banished from the Alcázar that very night, but she looked the other way, even as Philip moved to legitimize the boy."

"What are you suggesting?"

"That she always knew much more than she was letting on."

"By which I'm to conclude what? That she knew about the plot against the King and said nothing?" This conversation was reminding Mari why she had severed ties with him to begin with—these powder kegs he liked to lob into people's laps, the insinuations and provocations; there wasn't a pot on earth Nicolas didn't want to stir. "What reason could she have for wanting her husband assassinated?"

Nicolas looked at her incredulously. "Mother of an idiot infant king? She'd rule as regent for decades. She and Everardo would be two of the most powerful people in the world. She has the most compelling reason of anyone for wanting him gone."

"It should come to that anyway someday. He's thirty years older than she is."

"Not if his ministers manage to get rid of her first."

Mari reminded herself that this was Nicolas's idea of sport. He'd been trying to drive a wedge between her and the Queen since her earliest days here. Prison hadn't changed him; it had only given him uninterrupted time to muse and scheme. Nevertheless, her thoughts raced. All those times she'd watched the Marquis saunter down the footpath at dawn carrying a jewel or fat purse of silver for his "charity." No question the Queen had been financing rebel initiatives. The question was, had she known it?

ΩΩ

That evening saw Mari alone with the Queen for a quiet night of cards. Nicolas had again gotten the better of her; his allegations, even if baseless, had troubled her all afternoon. She'd intended to never again speak of the matter, least of all to the Queen, but she was on her third cup of sherry and felt tiddly and daring. She hazarded to test the Queen.

"Did you ever see Roberta's baby?"

The Queen glanced up icily but chose to play. "Once," she said. "Shortly after Charles was born. I was at the height of my paranoia. One night it occurred to me that I'd never actually seen the King's wench pregnant, and I started to wonder if there really was any such baby or if it was just some ruse Haro had cooked up to try to provoke me. So I paid her a visit. You should have seen her face when I barged into her apartment unannounced. I even made it a point to wake her baby."

They enjoyed a chuckle at Roberta's expense. "What did he look like?"

The Queen shrugged. "He looked like a baby. Don't they all sort of look the same?"

Baby Charles's witchy face flashed in Mari's mind. "I suppose." She paused. "Why didn't you just send me to investigate?"

The Queen hesitated. "As I said, this was at the height of my paranoia."

Mari nodded. She was hurt, but she understood. Nobody fully trusted anyone around here.

They picked quietly at their cards. Encouraged by the Queen's candor and before she could think the better of it, Mari asked, "What happened between you and Nicolas?" She had never been satisfied with Everardo's theory of a quiet parting of ways. No two people were less capable. Binnie, a far more reliable source of gossip, had spoken of an unspeakable betrayal. "How did he betray you?"

The Queen took a long, slow sip of sherry and planted her cup down softly. "He didn't. I betrayed him."

Mari hid her shock. She let the Queen continue.

"We'd been in Spain but a year or two. We were children, basically, taken from our homes—our countries—and forced to sink or swim in this place. We had much to learn, I especially. Despite my schooling, I hadn't the faintest idea what being the Queen of Spain entailed, what pressures and decisions I would face."

After another drink, she continued. "I had a handmaiden at the time. Olivia was her name, a banker's daughter. Lovely girl. A blue-eyed blonde." That last bit goosed Mari's heart. She had a vague sense of where this was going. "Nicolas was smitten with her and spared no charm or expense in courting her. I was only mildly surprised when she reciprocated his affection.

"There was talk of marriage. We were only fifteen or sixteen at the time, but Nicolas was ready. You know how he gets when he sets on something." Mari nodded. She knew. "Despite his celebrity, the gossip sheets never caught wind of Nicolasito's romance. He fiercely protected the girl's honor.

"Olivia's father found out though, and soon he was paying me court, imploring me to put an end to the perversion—his word—and sanction a more suitable match for his daughter. I explained that Nicolas came from a wealthy merchant family, but of course his pedigree was never the problem."

"Of course not," Mari said bitterly. Dwarfs weren't real people. That was the problem.

"Catalonia was in revolt at the time. Juan José was planning his final incursion to take back Barcelona. The Crown needed a massive loan to finance the invasion, and the banker threatened to renege if I didn't help him with his Nicolas problem. I literally had to choose between shattering Nicolas's heart and losing Barcelona, possibly forever. All my life my father told me"—she shook a finger—"'Whatever you do, don't ire the bankers. They are the shadow kings. Our true masters.'"

She paused for a drink, giving Mari time to think. Funny thing, power. Even the kings and queens and emperors thought they were being controlled by someone else. "Who rules the bankers?" Mari thought aloud.

"Not even God," said the Queen, stamping down her cup. "I matched Olivia with the heir to the Duke of Loya. Today she lives in Toledo and has three children. Nicolas left my company and didn't speak to me for several years. He only started to acknowledge me again around the time you came."

Mari was stunned. All this time she had vilified Nicolas in her mind, but it was he who'd been betrayed, his heart brutalized. This went a long way in explaining his lack of loyalty, his self-serving attitude. Mari could also see why he rejected his dwarfism; it had robbed him of his power, his heart's desire, given others license to shatter him. No one would have dared tread on him if he'd been a proper-sized man.

The Queen flicked down a card. "Of course as he was leaving, he accused me of being in love with him." A question must have played on Mari's face because the Queen snapped, "I wasn't."

Mari started giggling and couldn't stop. It must have been the sherry, and the nervous energy from testing the Queen's candor, and the vanity and brazenness of Nicolasito. The Queen indulged her, slapping a card down with a stony glare.

"If I could live my life over again," Mari said, "I think I'd want to be Nicolasito."

The Queen said she would be a shepherdess in the Austrian Alps.

ตณ

He was meant to leave quietly on a Tuesday morning, but when word of Nicolasito's departure leaked, breakfast tables were deserted, duties neglected, posts abandoned, and a great thunderclap could be heard coming from the royal chapel as hundreds of Bibles slapped shut. Courtiers gathered on the plaza in numbers and ranks that could not have pleased the King: clergymen and noblemen, ladies, cavaliers and squires, chamberlains and handmaidens, scribes, painters, musicians, dwarfs and fools, even Inquisitors and Torre Dorada ministers, including Haro, standing but an arm's length away from the Queen.

All hushed as Nicolas emerged from the Alcázar flanked by guards, dressed for travel in a little leather cape and boots, Feroce close behind. He broke his stride when he saw the crowd and smiled sweetly. There were whistles, a smattering of applause. Women were dabbing their eyes. Even some of the Inquisitors looked misty.

He worked his way through the crowd, dispensing the last of his dewdrop kisses to weeping women, cheering them with his Nicolasito charms, while men gave him hearty backslaps and fatherly pats on the cheek.

His face was checkered with greasepaint kisses when he finally reached the Queen, his jacket blooming with roses. The crowd held its breath as he stood before her. With supreme chivalry and a sincerity and humility never before seen in Nicolas, he sank to his knee and bowed deeply, reducing himself to a small mound at her feet. The crowd heaved a sentimental moan, followed by applause and whistles. The Queen removed her glove, proffered her hand. Nicolas kissed it tenderly. There wasn't a dry eye on the plaza when the Queen, her own eyes glazed with tears, touched the royal hand to Nicolas's cheek and looked upon him for the last time. They had come to this court together, a child bride and her playmate, he in her arms, according to legend. They became famous together, became Spanish together, learned how to survive this snake pit together—two fourteen-year-olds becoming ruthless politicians by age sixteen, together. He could have condemned her to save himself. He could have made a deal, told the Inquisition everything, but he hadn't. For all the disappointments and betrayals between them, for all the rivalry and grudges, in the end Nicolas was loyal to Mariana. When it really counted, he had been willing to burn alive.

Everardo blessed him ahead of his journey and handed him a purse of silver the Queen's treasury owed him in arrears. Haro crouched down and imparted some last-minute spy instructions.

Nicolas hugged Mari with nearly the strength of a full-sized man. "Don't cry," he said. "Remember the bad times." Mari laughed. They'd had their share.

She walked him to his coach so they could have a few final words, down below, dwarf to dwarf. "Be sure to look after Philip while I'm gone," he said. Mari promised she would, though she had no idea how she'd manage this without ruffling the Queen. "Inocencia's taking bets as to how soon he'll send for me. If you decide to play, put your money on months, not years."

He was being overly optimistic, Mari knew. He had a long, complicated mission ahead of him. It could take him years to penetrate Louis's inner circle, if ever.

He bucked his chin at something high in the distance. "Look. Already he wants me back." Mari followed his gaze up to the third floor of Torre Dorada, where a lonely black figure stood in the window, watching. His Majesty, the King.

Nicolas gave the crowd a jaunty salute, and he and Feroce bounded up the stairs into the coach, a lad and his dog, chasing adventure. There was a snap of reins, the rhythm of horse hooves, a tiny hand in the window, waving goodbye.

Nicolasito's coach trundled toward France.

✦✦✦

Chapter 38

THE QUEEN'S JUSTICE

fter Nicolas left, the winds changed dramatically in the Queen's favor. Haro fell ill and died, and with him much of the spite that had long plagued relations between the Queen and the King's cabinet. It was like pulling a boiling kettle from a fire; the Queen's mood evened, her paranoia abated, and Dorada and Reina settled into a state of mutual indifference that almost felt like trust, or at least grudging acceptance. Moreover, the King still hadn't appointed a new *valido* despite many cutthroat contenders. Rather, he had found an unlikely favorite in a mountain nun he had met on retreat, with whom he'd been keeping an avid correspondence and through whom he supposedly spoke directly to God. The holy sister was half-jestingly said to be running the Spanish Empire from her cloister in Ibérico, advising the King on everything from warfare (she was a militant defender of the faith) to—another boon for the Queen— the company he was allowed to keep. His theater outings became fewer and were usually followed by a week's penance at the Escorial in San Lorenzo.

Baby Charles grew fussy and ravenous—strong as a bull, the Queen boasted to the newssheets. People began regarding him unreservedly as the future King, and Mari decided there was no fitter ruler for Spain than he. He was the very incarnation of the land he would inherit: feeble, sickly, hexed, the victim of selfish, shortsighted forebears, his leanness and wretchedness belied by a costume of jewels and silks. And yet, he was surviving. The Queen and Everardo spent a lot of time talking about the future. Mari could hear them downstairs, speaking German in that calm, measured tone of ruthless ambition, planning for the day when they would be two of the most powerful people on earth.

Already Mariana's influence was sharply on the rise. With the King's nun pulling him ever deeper into the spiritual realm, and Haro gone, the chore of governance defaulted to the Queen, who grudgingly obliged. Her regency was met with hope and rejoicing countrywide. Spain had continued her slide toward ruin. Entire industries had been taxed into oblivion to pay for Philip's wars, farmlands lay bare, and the populace dwindled as every young person with an iota of ambition sought to move to France or the New World. Penury had even touched the Alcázar. Feasts were leaner, portions slimmer. Bruised fruits and stale breads decked even the King's table. Sherbets and jams were but sweet memories. Dresses and wigs trended narrower to save on materials, though fashion in general deteriorated in Nicolas's absence. The Queen was forced to sell some of her jewels to keep her household running at full staff. Even then, Mari hadn't seen a payday in months and was owed nearly fifty ducats in arrears.

As Spain plunged deeper into despair, so did the King. He went little seen as he spent his days steeped in melancholy—this latest bout compounded by a religious fanaticism that had even some priests worried—scratching out thrice-daily letters to his nun. He was not long for this world as it were, and many feared that his losing Nicolasito and Haro would shorten his days. He had plenty else to be depressed about, too. Juan José was faring poorly in the west. The King's forlorn hope of reuniting the peninsula was slipping away. By now everyone but Philip knew that Portugal was lost forever, and Catalonia would be next—it was only a matter of when. Mari hadn't looked in on him as she'd promised she would. He seemed to have forgotten she existed, and she didn't feel like reminding him.

She spent most of her days idle and untroubled, reading the newssheets, walking in the gardens, enjoying the occasional comedy or machine play at the Buen Retiro. The Queen rarely socialized anymore, and whenever Mari did see her, all she talked about was council meetings, throne duty, roads and buildings, and of course wastewater and mule dung.

With boredom threatening her sanity, Mari petitioned His Majesty for a small office in one of the dependent buildings to furnish as a laboratory. It was denied. The nun wouldn't tolerate sorcery, and the Crown couldn't afford it anyway. Mari even considered charting horoscopes for recreation and pocket money, but from there it was just a short slide back to Maribarbola, just a short slide back to the lying and pretending, the pawn-play and puppet strings, the summonses in the night. She hadn't issued a prophecy since the one that nearly killed Nicolas, except for the standard health-and-happiness tidings she had flung out from the stage at the New Year's Jubilee. The Queen already knew she wasn't a prophet (though she still sometimes called Mari her lucky charm), and the King's opinion mattered little; he had never been easier to avoid than he was now. So Maribarbola stayed banished to whenceever dark place she came—probably the scheming coils of Mari's brain, or those depths of her heart where God's light didn't reach and evil sometimes festered. There she stayed more or less safely locked away, like a ghost in a trunk, waiting to be summoned. Every now and then she jiggled the latch.

Mari thought a lot about Nicolas. She regretted having been the one to drive him from the court, robbing the King of a joy he couldn't afford to lose and Spain of one of her few remaining treasures. With Nicolasito's absence looming hugely over the nation and most acutely over the Alcázar, Mari finally understood his utter irreplaceability, his incalculable worth—that of a thousand rooms of riches. Like the Maestro's painting of a painting that beheld the beholder, Nicolas was a priceless curio, a doll that owned the owner, played with the player, and could be anything his master or mistress required: companion, confidante, co-conspirator, dazzler, diplomat. A spy. A son. Mari missed him, his tiny charms, but more than anything she missed the game, the intrigue, his powder kegs, moves and counter-moves. Now trapped like a pageant-person in her clockwork world of waking and eating and loafing and eating, cards and dice, feasts and jubilees, she often found herself wishing Nicolasito would return, to play some more.

Watching the Carlos dwarfs line up and whirl like tops one night—the King's toys—Mari could see why Nicolas loathed these dances—the way the dwarfs toddled, merrily, in their prisons of unearthly cuteness. It wasn't dwarfhood Nicolas rejected; it was the implicit lack of personhood that came with it. The never fully counting, always being half, always being at the mercy of this cruel world, in a body that screamed look at me, laugh at me, mock me, abuse me, delight in me, adore me, own me, sell me, betray me. I'm an object, a most curious combination of adult and child, servant and pet, playmate and toy. All her life Mari had more or less accepted this—or maybe she just hid from it—until she came here and met a man who didn't.

Besides, she couldn't judge Nicolas for pretending to be someone else when she was just as guilty. Everyone had survival strategies. Everyone was clawing out an existence, snatching what crumbs of power were left of the apparently finite supply on earth after the monarchs and moneymen took their share, and in the game of power dwarfs were already starting so far in the hole. Mari had tasted it, splashed around in it, got a little drunk off it, but now her overriding ambition was to recover that long-buried part of herself that hadn't known or needed power—live humbly and merrily, like a Carlos dwarf without the dancing, and enjoy the quiet power that came from not wanting power.

Inside every martyr, Nicolas once said during one of his political rants, beats the heart of a tyrant. Mari had long convinced herself that Maribarbola's lies and frauds had been survival strategies, that she had been protecting herself by gaming for the Queen, that the Queen's interests were Mari's interests, the Queen being her last chance on earth at any life worth living. But every time Maribarbola jiggled the latch, Mari had to wonder how much of it had been self-preservation and how much had been for her love of the game, the thrill of deception, of victory, of not letting the Queen's enemies win, these men who had been winning for centuries. "What was your prior capacity again?" the Queen once asked her, meaning her old life in Germany. "Because you're frightfully cunning," said the Queen, "such a little fox." What power does to everyone it had done to Mari with ease. And here all this time she thought she had lost herself in Spain, at this court. She had found herself.

ཙཙ

Mari sat with the Queen in the Salón Grande one afternoon, watching rehearsals for Torre de la Reina's first-ever pageant comedy. It had been Mari's idea, a tiddly suggestion she would soon regret. As the only dwarf in Reina, the lion's share of buffoonery had fallen to her.

They were politely suffering through the junior pages' Moorish-inspired dance when a rumble of boot heels charged down the corridor. Seconds later, a column of knights stormed the Salón, with Lalo in front, looking hearty and hale and mightily pleased. With machine-like unison, they sank before the Queen. "This better be good," she said.

Lalo drew his sword with a chilling metallic scrape and held it under the Queen's nose. The tip gleamed crimson; the blood groove was dark.

"Where was he?" the Queen asked.

"In a bodega in the theater district," Lalo said. "Hiding in plain sight."

"Is he dead?"

"Not quite. We thought you might like a word with him."

"I don't," said the Queen. "Put him out of his misery at once. Take the corpse to the Buen Retiro."

Lalo hesitated, confused.

"You heard me correctly."

ಬಬ

The slow macabre music quickened and intensified. The audience held its breath as the cloth was folded back, revealing the body, a newly executed criminal, looking serene and lovely surrounded by tapers. With the incisor's knife winking in the torchlight, the lector spread his arms and invited the packed audience to witness the glory of God in the human entrails. "He's a handsome sort," he jested to the ladies in the stew pan. "Let's hope he looks as good inwardly as he does out!" A froth of jolly laughter filled the theater.

So began a most fruitful and scholarly excavation of the human form—hours of slicing, sawing, snipping, showing, and copious lecturing. They opened the body from gullet to groin, slashed the stomach to reveal the sinner's last meal (a salad), and, to a bizarre musical interlude complete with magic lantern effects, unraveled the bowels and stretched them across the stage. So fine a corpse, the lector kept noting, such pearly tissues and lean, succulent parts—and a curious specimen at that, a mustacheless man.

From there he segued into an extremely long-winded discussion of the bodily humors. From her dark perch in the royal balcony, Mari dozed.

The cresting music and hail of applause wrenched her from sleep. She woke in time to see the incisor walk to the edge of the stage and step into the wild, dancing torchlight. The music waxed triumphant; the audience thundered with cheer.

With both hands, he raised the heart to the royal box.

The Queen nodded coolly.

ひひ

Nicolas had been gone nearly two months when the filthy, emaciated dog limped across the Alcázar's main plaza at five o'clock one morning. Thinking it was a starving wolf, a guard nearly shot it before he noticed the tail wag and then the black butterfly marking on the snout.

Feroce.

An urgent dispatch to Teresa in France confirmed Nicolas never arrived. Searchers eventually found his coach abandoned in the Sierra de Guara, plundered by highwaymen and bearing no sign of Nicolasito or his two escorts. The inconsolable King deployed a small army to the region and ordered all of Madrid to pray for his return.

As soon as the news broke, Mari doubled down with Inocencia—months not years—and began watching the horizon from her windows, fingering her beads. Often she sensed a glimmer of movement behind a sofa, the whisper of slippers, Feroce's nails clicking on marble, a teasing whiff of maybe-*vinagrillo*. Wherever he was, whomever he was with, he would find his way back—of that she was certain. So rare a jewel would not stay out of exalted company for long. Just as tiny Mercury hugs the sun, Nicolasito had a narrow orbit that revolved only around majesty. His place was in the grace of kings—perched in his little chair, charming beauties and diplomats, delighting masses, disarming enemies, collecting pensions and secrets, luxuriating in beauty and finery, in love and adoration, caught in a lifelong hail of blessings. Yet no sum of wealth could ever furnish him fairly, nor any treasure fully equal him—not the softest, purest gold or fieriest stone or even the greatest painting of all time. So rare a man there never was, and probably shouldn't be. Too dazzling an accident was he, too proud and precious, a living gem. Prince of dwarfs, treasure of men.

AUTHOR'S NOTE

Thank you for reading *The Queen's Prophet*. Here's the part where I confess my sins against the historical record and explain why they felt necessary in writing this story. For brevity's sake, this disclosure will only focus on my more serious infractions.

Philip IV is relatively obscure to non-historians and has basically gone down in history as a footnote in the biography of his legendary court painter, Diego Velázquez. English-language literature on the king is limited but includes at least one seminal text published in 1907 by British historian Martin Hume. Though Hume may have been a reputable scholar in his day, his book, *The Court of Philip IV: Spain in Decadence*, employs hilarious levels of conjecture and melodrama, offering tale upon tale of political intrigue, an emotionally tortured king who seduces actresses and nuns alike, gun powder beneath the stage at the Buen Retiro, and a Spanish empire in spectacular decline. Not until the 1980s did anglophone scholars reexamine Philip, this time producing fairer, soberer analyses (R.A. Stradling's *Philip IV and the Government of Spain, 1621–1665* is a notable text from this era). It should come as no surprise that, as I undertook to write what I hoped would be a juicy page-turner, Hume was my guy.

Historians understandably focus on the earlier part of Philip's reign, the 1620s and 1630s, a period of intense intrigue, disastrous domestic and foreign policies, and war raging in Europe. During this time, Philip acted under the heavy influence of his chief minister, the Count-Duke of Olivares, an archetypal cunning, domineering royal favorite who purportedly isolated and distracted the young king while he, Olivares, ruled unchecked. Rife with conflict, the Olivares years would have made for great storytelling; my problem was, the dwarfs Maribarbola and Nicolas did not join the court until years after Olivares's ouster and death.

The Queen's Prophet takes place in the vastly quieter 1650s. Older and wiser, Philip kept his new favorite, Luis de Haro (Olivares's nephew, and not nearly the tyrant his uncle was) at an arm's length while keeping a second advisor, via correspondence, in María de Ágreda, a mystical nun. Using the Olivares era as a model for dramatic conflict, I nevertheless fashioned Haro—unfairly and erroneously—as a nebulous villain and political threat to Mariana, though there is no historical evidence of friction between the two.

In 1649, a widowed forty-four-year-old Philip reluctantly married his fourteen-year-old niece, Mariana, to strengthen ties between the Spanish and Austrian branches of the Habsburg dynasty. The marriage seems to have been cordial, if passionless and perfunctory. Regardless, their union was a solid political treaty and, to my knowledge, never in any danger of being dissolved.

Hume describes Mariana as a girl of "frank, unabashed gaiety," though "selfish and hardhearted" and "Austrian to her fingertips," which inclined her to put Austria's interests before Spain's. She became quite the power player after Philip's 1665 death, ruling Spain as regent for her disabled son, Charles, for years. In the 1670s she locked horns viciously with General Juan José (Philips's illegitimate son with an actress) in a political showdown that forced Mariana into exile for two years. As regent she found her own controversial favorite—and rumored paramour—in a handsome, socially ambitious marquis. The Marquis of Villamirada in my novel, however, is a completely fabricated character.

At least one dramatic element of *The Queen's Prophet* is based in reality: the morbidity of Philip and Mariana's children, likely due to generations of inbreeding. Prospero and Ferdinand, however, were not twins (and I never called them "twins"). They were born in the late 1650s thirteen months apart. Prospero lived three years, Ferdinand ten months. In writing this story, I wanted to create an illusion of events unfolding quickly, but the queen's pregnancies each padded my narrative by nine months. So I decided to couple the boys as implied twins. Philip and Mariana's third son, Charles, really was known as *Carlos el Hechizado* (Charles the Hexed) due to congenital abnormalities. I did, however, greatly exaggerate his facial deformities.

Scholarship on the historical Maribarbola is thin and easily traceable. In 1724, Velázquez biographer Antonio Palomino reliably identified her in *Las Meninas*. Two centuries later she reappears in the literature in José Moreno Villa's 1939 book, *Locos, enanos, negros y niños palaciegos*, which catalogs the many dwarfs, buffoons, and other "entertainers" employed by the Spanish court in the sixteenth and seventeenth centuries. Maribarbola "Asquín" (likely a corruption of "Haunsin") and Nicolas Pertusato both appear in Moreno Villa's 1939 catalog.

In 2009, scholar Luisa Rubini Messerli published an essay, "The Death of the Royal Dwarf: Mari-Barbóla in Velázquez's *Las Meninas*." In her article, Dr. Rubini Messerli describes three 1662 letters she unearthed in the Upper Austrian State Archives in Linz pertaining to the execution of the last will and testament of "To Her Royal Majesty of Hispania, her former dwarfess, Maria Barbara Haunsin." Significantly, Juan Everardo Nithard, Father Confessor and right-hand man to Queen Mariana of Spain, played a hand in executing the will (which confers 120 thaler to a toll collector relative in Vienna). That so high an official would involve himself in a dwarf's will, Rubini Messerli argues, suggests that the deceased enjoyed a close relationship with the queen.

Although Maribarbola first appears on the palace books in 1651, for narrative purposes I shifted her arrival in Spain to 1656. My rationale was: apart from the queen's miscarriages, I found little drama to exploit in the early 1650s. The latter part of that decade, however, sees the painting of *Las Meninas* (1656), the births and deaths of the princes, and the Treaty of the Pyrenees (the treaty with France mentioned in this story), which signals the end of Spain's Golden Age and a new era of French dominance in Europe.

Nicolas Pertusato, originally from Alessandria, Italy, likely came to Madrid in the company of the newly queened Mariana, whose wedding convoy would have passed through northern Italy in autumn of 1649. His date of birth is unknown, but he died an elderly man circa 1710, so he might have been in his teens or even early twenties when Velázquez painted him in *Las Meninas*. From 1650–1660, he is on the palace books as "Nicolasito," a dwarf. In the mid-1660s, however, palace scribes begin referring to him as "*don* Nicolas*" as he rises in rank and salary and is eventually appointed chamberlain by the king. Despite my characterization of him as faithless and self-serving, the real Nicolas Pertusato was apparently a loyal and valued member of royal household and enjoyed Mariana's favor until her 1696 death.

I routinely compromised historical accuracy for the sake of readability. For example, I greatly simplified the political situation in 17th-century Spain, which was actually several autonomous kingdoms united under Philip, each with its own constitution and government. And I barely scratched the surface in conveying the weirdness and decadence of Philip's court, a people enslaved by ritual and decorum, with the monarch's every move tediously choreographed and attended by servants. The queen probably never would have been just hanging out in her apartment alone, as I often have her doing. Also, these people were intensely religious—a realistic rendering of their lives would have them performing devotional activities daily and expressing their faith passionately and frequently. Despite the Inquisition's reputation for swift and severe punishment, Nicolas would have had a trial, and his "execution" would have been a solemn religious ceremony preceded by hours of prayer and sermons (and even then, public executions were rare). I was also imprecise in my use of the word "science" to describe the Countess's activities, as science as an institution or methodology was still several generations away. What we today consider scientific thought and activity would have, back then, fallen under the umbrella of "philosophy."

I took none of these decisions lightly. Like many writers of historical fiction, I set out with the best intentions but quickly realized that good intentions were standing in the way of a good story, and that flouting the facts was, given the limits of my imagination, the best conceivable way forward. I also hoped that the relative obscurity of these historical figures would allow me to take creative liberties without ruffling the average reader. To anyone looking for an airtight history lesson in this tale, I apologize for the deception.

ACKNOWLEDGMENT

My sincerest thanks to:

Donna Patitucci, my sister and first reader, for supporting and encouraging me from the beginning.

Jenny, for your very significant contributions to this story. Thank you.

My literary agent, Mark Gottlieb, for your impeccable professionalism and for having enough confidence in this project for the both of us. Thanks also to the dedicated people of Trident Media Group.

The talented and committed professionals at or affiliated with Turner Publishing: Stephanie Beard, for taking a chance on me and Mari; Jon O'Neal, for your expert guidance and reassurance; Kara Furlong, for your careful and considerate copyedits; Maddie Cothren, for your beautiful, *Las Meninas*-worthy cover design; book designer Tim Holtz, for giving me a German storybook motif without my even having to ask; Caroline Herd and Leslie Hinson, for your much-appreciated marketing efforts; and Todd Bottorff, whose leadership and vision resulted in this wonderful team.

Fellow historical novelists Nina Romano and Barbara Wood, and author/historian Deborah Davis, for graciously reading and offering your opinions.

The academicians and language consultants who unreservedly offered their time and expertise. Any historical inaccuracies, foreign language mistakes, and other faults in this book are entirely my own, but without the following people, such blunders would have been much, much worse: Dr. Craig Koslofsky, for welcoming me to your campus and answering my questions about daily life in early modern Europe; Dr. Albaina, for your meticulous translation work; and my brilliant German teacher, Terry Smejkal, for the patience and generosity you've shown me over the years.

My always supportive friends and family: Sandy Allpow; my parents, Robert and Gloria Patitucci; Kim Kucharski, Marlene Walko, Dr. Kristine Christensen, Donna Mazalin, Marilyn Strauch Palm; my brother-in-law, Dr. Michael Angarone, and my nephews, Ben and Luca.

My colleagues and students at Moraine Valley Community College.

And finally, Francesca Vrattos, whose enthusiasm and encouragement in my younger days sustained me on my twenty-year journey to publication. This book would not exist without you, Francesca. Thank you.

CPSIA information can be obtained
at www.ICGtesting.com
Printed in the USA
BVOW06*0359200917
495334BV00004BA/16/P